BULL GOD

ROBERTA GELLIS

BULL GOD

A Baen Books Original

Baen Publishing Enterprises
P.O. Box 1403
Riverdale, NY 10471

ISBN: 0-671-57868-5

Cover art by Stephen Hickman

First printing, May 2000

Distributed by Simon & Schuster
1230 Avenue of the Americas
New York, NY 10020

Production by Windhaven Press, Auburn, NH
Printed in the United States of America

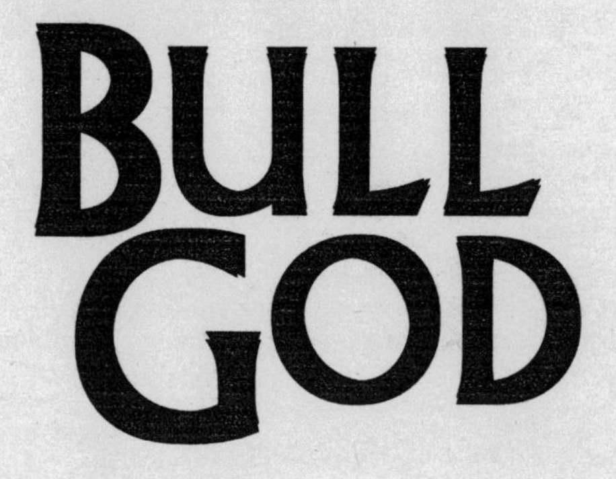
BULL
GOD

PART ONE:

THE BULL FROM THE SEA

CHAPTER 1

Ariadne stared at the face in the polished oval of brass and could not believe it was hers. The full lips were dyed a shocking dark red, as if stained with wine—or blood—the dark lines of kohl that outlined her large, black eyes made them look deep and knowing, and the way her shining black hair was dressed, in an elaboration of loops and braids and falling ringlets plus the two thick locks curling in front of her ears, made her look ten years older. Until this morning she had worn it in two thick plaits like any other child.

"Yes, yes," a sharp voice said. "You are very beautiful—as am I—but that's no reason to spend the day staring at yourself. We must be at the shrine when the sun rises. Stand up so you can be dressed."

Silently Ariadne laid down the brass mirror and turned to face her mother. It was true that Pasiphae was beautiful—and not only in flickering torchlight. Even in bright sun light, no one would believe that Ariadne was Pasiphae's seventh child or that there was an eighth, Phaidra. Both Pasiphae's face and her body seemed unmarked by the sons and daughters she had provided her lord, King Minos. Perhaps, Ariadne thought sadly, it was because she hardly noticed the children she had borne . . . except when they could be useful.

Like today, when her daughter would be consecrated as high priestess of Dionysus so that Pasiphae herself, queen and high priestess of Potnia, the Snake Goddess, wouldn't need to be bothered conducting the rites of a minor godling whose shrine had been built to satisfy common vine growers and winemakers. Ariadne swallowed hard as she allowed a servant to slip off the loose gown in which she had been combed and painted and wrap around her the white, many-tiered bell skirt, embroidered elaborately in the same wine red her lips had been dyed. When it was fastened with the rich gold girdle wound twice around her waist and tied so the ends fell to about midthigh, Ariadne thrust her arms through the sleeves of the bodice and stood while the servant laced it up below her bare breasts. Even the tightest lacing and the firmest boning could do little for them. Barely swelling, they were a child's breasts.

The servant *tskd*. Pasiphae frowned and said, "Can you do nothing to make her look like a woman?"

"But I'm not a woman," Ariadne said. "No lacing or padding will make me more than a child."

It was a reproach, but it glanced off Pasiphae's perfect armor of self-interest. She said, "Well, it is unfortunate that your grandmother died sooner than expected, but your moon times have come upon you so you do qualify. It's most unlikely that you will need to prove yourself a woman."

That, Ariadne had to admit, probably was true. The god of the vine was supposed to mate ritually with his high priestess at the equinoxes and solstices, but Dionysus had not actually appeared in the shrine in two or three generations. It was enough for the ritual, apparently, that the priestess be there, on the altar, ready to accommodate him.

If he had never appeared, Ariadne would have been rather pleased with her appointment. A seventh child, third daughter, had little enough importance even in a king's household. It would be very nice to have duties to perform and a special place and purpose that was all her own. But there were records that the god had appeared—quite often when her great-great-aunt was priestess—and Ariadne wasn't really ready to offer her body in public as a symbol of the earth to be ploughed and set with seed so that the grapes on the hill sides would flourish.

Not that she had any choice. The high priestess must be either the queen herself or a royal virgin dedicated and married to the god. Since her two older sisters were married and Phaidra was almost two years younger than she, once her mother refused the office there was no one else. That meant that Ariadne would have no human husband, but that had its good side as well as its bad. Her older sisters had had the best of the men of sufficient status and wealth. She would have had to take a man of lesser family or an older man. And even among the best, one sister at least had been bitterly disappointed in her marriage. The god would make few demands, if he ever made any, and she would have a household of her own in the shrine. . . .

Buried in her thoughts, Ariadne hadn't been aware of the final touches made to her toilette until her mother turned her toward the door and gave her a push. Obedient to her duty, she went forward down the long corridor to the colonnaded chamber that opened on the wide, formal stairway. As she started down, voices rose in a hymn from the youths and maidens gathered in the open court below. They would never leap the bulls for her, Ariadne thought; that was for the Snake Goddess, not for a godling of the vine growers.

The voices rose to a crescendo as she reached the foot of the stair and the singers, her eldest brother Androgeos in the forefront, parted before her and then fell in behind as she started across. It was not all bad to be deprived of presiding over the bull dancing either, Ariadne thought. Oh, it was a high honor, a symbol of power, to be seated before the great golden horns while the bull dancers performed, but it was horrible when one slipped and was gored or trampled and the evil omen had to be explained. She would have no more to do than to lie on an altar four times a year to provide the hope of a good crop of grapes.

Greatly cheered by that thought, Ariadne walked the last painted corridor and went out the northwestern entrance of the palace. Torchbearers had been waiting at the doorway and now they marched to either side, torches held high. More torches flanked the ranks of singers who followed her. In fact the torches weren't altogether necessary; every window in every house on the Royal Road was open, torchlit, and full of watchers and the sky was already paling.

Not that Ariadne had need of torches or sunlight to find her way. The Royal Road was as familiar as the corridor between the toilet and her bedchamber. She even knew exactly how far it was to the great highway. Before she had quite completed the two hundred paces, Ariadne's confident stride faltered. Ahead were more torches, some of these waving so that the flames guttered and roared, and voices, louder, coarser voices, also singing. A hand flat on her back prodded her.

"Go on," Pasiphae's voice urged. "Those are your worshipers. Don't disappoint them."

To save herself from falling under the pressure on her back, Ariadne stepped forward and then stepped forward again. Her mouth was dry. Don't disappoint them! But what if she did? Would they tear her apart as worshipers of Dionysus were known to do? And then she chided herself for being so silly. Certainly they wouldn't harm her now, before she was even consecrated. And very few, if any, would be able to get into the shrine grounds, so they would know only what her mother and father chose to tell them. And they had never harmed her grandmother, even though the god never came to her call and sometimes the wine was bad or the harvest failed.

She turned into the great road and, despite all her reasoning, shuddered slightly. She had just remembered that her grandmother had been queen as well as priestess, doubly protected. As far as she could see, all the way up Gypsades Hill, there were torches. This "godling" that her mother scorned was either loved or feared by many more worshipers than ever attended the rites of the Snake Goddess. Of course, these were common folk and of no great account. . . . And then she heard her mother's voice again, low and sharp.

"I had no idea—"

So, common as they were, these folk *were* of account, Ariadne thought, at least in sufficient numbers. That was important to remember, but she became aware of the quickened pace of the singing around her. She was being urged to hurry, and realized that the torches were paling to nothing; the sky was much lighter. Fortunately she didn't need to be at the shrine until the sun topped Gypsades Hill itself and that would be some time after it cleared the lowest horizon.

Still, it was a near thing. The light was actually glinting off the gilded vine leaves of Dionysus' crown when Ariadne reached the altar and swung around to face those who followed her, seeing with some relief, that it was indeed mostly those of Knossos who filled the small courtyard. Her father had joined her mother at the foot of the stairs in the palace and had walked with them. Now he came forward and the singers burst out again into an invocation. When the voices died, King Minos kissed Ariadne's forehead, and prayed aloud, formally renouncing into the hands of the god Dionysus his rights as king and father over her as a daughter. Again the chorus rose, and during the singing, from out of a door to the left of the large painting behind the altar, came two rather elderly priests and two priestesses.

A new hymn rose in the air. Ariadne joined in this one, which praised the god and begged him to show his favor and bless his priestess and her land with his virility. The priestesses carried a brightly polished scrying bowl; the priests a large rhyton. Her father now backed away. The priestess held out the scrying bowl; Ariadne took it and, speaking the arcane words she had been taught, turned to the one of the priests, who poured a dark red wine into the bowl. When it was full to within a fingerwidth of the top, Ariadne knelt down—with considerable care not to spill the wine—and set the bowl into a hollow at the foot of the altar.

The sun was now well up into the sky and its light struck the highly polished rim and the dark surface of the wine, rippled by the slight unsteadiness of Ariadne's grip when she set down the bowl. Glare and glitter flashed back into Ariadne's eyes. The chorus was quiet now and Ariadne alone raised her voice.

A very great distance away, across a sea and a range of mountains, in a gleaming marble city called Olympus, Dionysus lifted his head from his pillow and cocked it. Someone was Calling him. He sat up and looked around. The large room was empty and silent, but the Call came again, clear and sweet, inside his head. Smiling, for he was one of the youngest among the great mages and he still took a mildly amused pleasure in having worshipers who believed him a god, he hopped out of bed and padded into the next chamber. Here a carved stone table held a flagon of wine and a cup. Dionysus dreamed mad dreams often and wakened with a dry mouth. He poured the wine into the cup and, as the Call came a third time, looked in.

Dionysus' breath drew in sharply. Instead of his own image, an enchanting female face looked up out of the wine's dark surface. The girl's eyes widened with surprise and he could see her draw breath as sharply as he had. He smiled.

"Come, godly Dionysus, come to me," she called.

His smile broadened. "I come," he said and gestured. The surface of the wine became empty. Still watching the cup, Dionysus asked, "Where?"

An image formed. Dionysus frowned. Knossos. He had not been Called from Knossos for . . . he could not remember how long, but very long. He stood a moment, the lips of his wide, generous mouth turned down, remembering pain. The priestess had been lover and friend and then, for no reason he could tell, had turned away from him, stopped Calling. He had missed talking to her for she was very wise and could often make sense of the Visions that tormented him. Once he had gone to the shrine without being Called, to ask the priestess why she was angry with him, but there had been a strange woman there who said she was queen and priestess and shrieked and threatened him. He should have torn her apart, but he hadn't been in the throes of frenzy, only startled, and he had "leapt" home to Olympus.

Later he had realized that his priestess no longer presided in the shrine. He had thought of returning, of demanding that his own priestess be brought back, but then he had become embroiled with Pentheus who was persecuting his followers and by the time he had seen to Pentheus' punishment, it had occurred to him that natives had far, far shorter lives than Olympians, that his priestess had not been young when she first Called him; she must be dead. His throat tightened. He still missed her.

He turned away from the cup, eyes staring blindly, sorry he had answered the Call. Mingling with natives . . . He had been warned against that, warned that they were always trouble—and it had been true. Dionysus turned his head fretfully, and his full lips thinned. But he had said he would come. He hesitated, knowing that the other Olympians did not regard a promise to the native folk very seriously. Perhaps, he thought, but *he* did not lie, not even to natives. And then a slow smile curved his lips, which parted to say the words that initiated the spell to translocate him to his shrine at Knossos. The woman's face had been very beautiful, very different from the beauty of the Olympians. They were all bright gold, she a dark mystery with her shining black hair and the bottomless black pools that were her eyes. If she were the new priestess . . .

For some time after the face disappeared from the scrying bowl, Ariadne remained on her knees staring into the blank surface of the wine. Had she really seen that strange face, so different from any she had ever seen before? On the still surface of the wine she painted the face again. His skin was pale, almost as white as polished limestone, and his hair a mass of golden curls tumbling down to touch darker golden brows. Below those his eyes, too large, too brilliant, glinted a blue paler than the ocean. Between those startling eyes a fine, straight nose, and below it the generous mouth with beautifully shaped lips that had parted a little with surprise when the eyes focused on her and then smiled sweetly. When she had seen that smile, she had Called with all her heart, "Come, godly Dionysus, come to me." And she had heard him reply. Surely she hadn't imagined that—but then the face was gone.

A hand touched Ariadne's shoulder and she blinked, realizing she had been staring into the scrying bowl for a long time. Slowly she rose to her feet, lifted the bowl and handed it to one of the priestesses, who poured from it into a cup, which she offered Ariadne. Automatically, still wondering if she had seen or imagined that face in the bowl, and how she could have imagined something she had never seen before, Ariadne sipped the wine. When she had drunk a little from the cup, she held it out and the priest who still held the rhyton took it from her. The other took the scrying bowl from the priestess and both walked back to the door behind the altar.

The worshipers began to sing again and the priestesses advanced on Ariadne. At first, she didn't understand their purpose, all she saw was their serene and indifferent expressions and her chest suddenly felt hollow. They hadn't seen anything in the scrying bowl and they hadn't heard the voice answering her. Her head drooped and tears stung her eyes. For a moment she had thought she had touched the god, that he would answer her Call. And then she felt the hands on the laces of her bodice, on the tie of her belt. They were going to undress her, lay her naked on the altar to wait for a god who would never come!

Ariadne's eyes flashed over the heads of the priestesses to the witnesses below: her mother, half smiling with satisfaction because it was not she who would be exposed to no purpose; her father, serious, perhaps hopeful but ready to accept the lack of response; Androgeos, eyes lowered, head turned slightly away, sympathetic enough to desire not to see her shame but helpless; the courtiers, already whispering, mildly contemptuous. Well, she would not be shamed. Her hands rose and pushed the priestesses away.

"The ritual is for me to perform," she cried.

She saw the shock in their faces, heard gasps and cries from the people ranged below the dais, saw the glance each priestess gave the other to judge whether they should seize her and force her. Then a strong voice came from behind.

"I have come."

The crowd cried out with one voice and Ariadne spun on her heel to look across the altar at the painting of the god. It still glowed on the wall, the right hand of the god holding a vine from which depended a cluster of ripe grapes and the left resting lightly on the shoulder of a young satyr, who nuzzled his horned head against one of the god's thighs while one cleft hoof rubbed shyly the back of a goatlike hairy leg. Now before it stood a living being—living, but not a man, Ariadne thought. She had never seen a man so tall or so strong, with the skin exposed by his scant tunic the color of milk and hair seemingly of coiled gold wires.

"Dionysus," she whispered, stretching her hands toward him over the altar.

He stared at her, his too-large eyes open wider than she had seen them in the scrying bowl, but his face bore no more expression than that of the painting behind him. Ariadne heard two soft thumps. The priestesses had fallen to the floor, either in obeisance or in a faint. She wondered whether Dionysus was waiting for her to flatten herself and press her face to the floor and felt bitterly disappointed. The sweet smile that had drawn that last Calling from her had held nothing of that kind of pride.

From the waiting crowd came gasps and whimpers, rustles, as robes stiff with jewels and metal-thread embroidery creased and crumpled while their wearers sank to the floor, but Ariadne didn't, couldn't, move. And then the god did. He whispered a word she didn't understand and made a gesture, and the sounds from behind her were cut off as if a door had closed.

"*You* Called me?" he asked.

"Yes, Lord Dionysus," she whispered, tears in her trembling voice. "It is the ritual. It is done at each change of season."

"I heard no Call last solstice nor for many, many years before that."

"That was while the old priestess, my father's mother, served your shrine. I don't know what she did wrong that you didn't hear her. She died and I was chosen to take her place." She swallowed. She couldn't say that she had wanted him to come. A god might be able to read her heart; if he learned she was lying . . . "I performed the ritual very exactly."

"But you are only a little girl, a child. How dare they offer me so unripe a fruit."

His eyes passed over her to stare at the kneeling worshipers beyond. Although his face still showed little, Ariadne heard the fury in his voice and terror caught at her. She had no idea what would be done to her if he rejected her. That had never happened in all the time the shrine had existed. He had come in the distant past, and the wines of Crete had been prized and praised in every land. Then the priestess died and some past queen had wanted the glory of being Dionysus' priestess as well as queen. In that she failed, for the god hadn't come to her Calling nor to the following queen/priestesses, but he had never *rejected* a priestess.

If her father did not sacrifice her there at the altar, Ariadne thought, the people would tear her to bits. She drew her hands back from their reach toward the god and clasped them desperately under her barely swelling breasts. Tears began to course down her cheeks, smearing the kohl that lined her eyes. She hadn't felt ready for mating, but surely that would be better than to be turned away.

"I'm *not* unripe," she sobbed. "My moon times have come. I'm ready for marriage. Oh, don't turn me away, my lord. The people will tear me to bits for displeasing you."

"Tear you to bits . . ."

Something flickered behind his eyes—knowledge of such frenzies? Horror? Ariadne began to tremble as she remembered the stories about the winter worship, not that in the shrine but out on the hills and in the forests when it was said the followers of Dionysus went mad and tore beasts and men apart with teeth and nails. When he hadn't come to the shrine, had he led those worshipers? The breath caught in her throat as he suddenly strode forward, stepped onto the altar, and pulled her up beside him.

"Don't weep, child," he said, putting an arm gently around her shoulders and drawing her close. "I won't harm you. *You* don't displease me. But those who chose so unfit a sacrifice—"

Relief made her bold enough to glance up at him. He was again looking out at the crowd of people. His eyes were clear blue, very pale, bright and hard as polished gems—mad and merciless. And in them Ariadne Saw, but not with her eyes, father and mother, brother and courtiers, all gone mad, striking and tearing at each other, covered with blood.

She couldn't bear to look and couldn't look away. Fear made her sick. Her stomach churned; her heart pounded so hard she felt a tearing pain around it—pain so great she sagged against Dionysus' side. He looked down and the Vision of chaos faded. Instead she Saw a covering around her heart unfold, like the petals of a strange flower. They held the beating heart at their center, and as that flower pulsed, a mist of gently swaying silver strands flowed out toward Dionysus. When they touched him, she breathed in deeply as feeling and knowledge flowed back along the strands to her.

Had less happened to her that day, had she not seen a *god* appear and heard him speak to her, she wouldn't have believed what she felt and saw inside her head. Awe made her receptive. She knew she had received a Gift, given when she was consecrated to make her a true priestess. Through that Gift she could read her god's will and she knew that he felt belittled and abused, and that his Power was to make those who scorned him punish themselves through holy frenzy. But it was understanding that had come to her through those tenuous silver strands, not fear. Her weakness had distracted him. The people were still safe.

"My lord," she cried softly, gripping his arm with one hand and winding the other in his tunic, "there was no one else. I am the eldest virgin daughter of the king. You were offered the best my father and mother had to give."

"The eldest virgin daughter," he repeated, now looking down at her, his voice puzzled rather than angry. "Is that the custom?"

"A royal virgin," Ariadne said, smiling up at him tremulously. "Is that not your demand? If it isn't, I will make clear what you do desire to my father and have it written in the records of the shrine so there is no mistake in the future. But I hope you won't turn me away. Please? I wish to serve you. I am ready. Truly I am."

He laughed suddenly, made a gesture as if he were drawing a line around them, and said, "*Epikaloumai melanotes.*"

Ariadne's sight seemed to dim, not as if ill had befallen her eyes, but as if someone had drawn a very thin gray silk curtain between her and the others. The priestesses had backed to the very edge of the dais and were still down on their faces, but her father and brother and some of the others were now standing and saluting the god. She saw that their mouths were moving, speaking or praying, but she couldn't hear them, and she realized that she had been seeing that for some time without "noticing" it.

"What is it?" she asked, clinging tighter to Dionysus. "What have you done to them?"

"Nothing at all," he said. "I didn't wish them to hear what I said to you—it's no business of the common folk to hear what a god says to his priestess—so I put a wall of silence around us. And then I added a wall of darkness. Do they think we of Olympus are animals that we couple in public?"

She could feel the blood rush into her face as excitement and anxiety twisted together quickened her heartbeat. "Then you will take me?"

He laughed again, softly, and that smile of infinite

sweetness changed his eyes so that, still bright, they did not glare or look hard. "As my priestess, yes, and gladly, but I cannot couple with a little maid who should be playing with toys in the nursery."

Tears filled her eyes again. "They will not understand. They expect to see the god sowing the land in the person of his priestess."

"I never did!" he said indignantly, stepping down off the altar and lifting Ariadne down as if being on it might trap him into an action he rejected. "Even with my chosen priestess, whom I dearly loved, and she was a woman in her middle years. I never coupled with her in the sight of all."

Ariadne shrugged, surprised that she should feel so disappointed by his refusal to take her after all her earlier fears. "I don't know where they came by the notion, but they believe that the fertility of the land is bound to the coupling of the god and the priestess."

His eyes narrowed. "And they will punish you if I do not perform like a rutting beast?"

"I will have failed my purpose," she said very softly. "There will be no assurance of a rich crop of sweet grapes, of wine that is sweet and potent with no bite and sourness of acid—"

"We don't need to couple for that. You are a priestess who can Call me. When you do so, I will come and run along the hillsides and dance among the casks."

"Will you?"

He smiled down at her. "Your eyes are like dark stars. They are black as obsidian and yet so bright! Yes, I will bless the vines and the wine." Then his lips thinned. "But I will *not* copulate with you before their eyes for their lascivious entertainment."

She knew it wasn't safe to press him further and yet it might be equally dangerous to let him leave without some proof of what he had promised. She glanced out toward the people, most still kneeling and all in attitudes of prayer. They couldn't hear what she and Dionysus said, he had told her—and then she noticed that gray film and remembered that he had said they couldn't see either.

"My lord," she whispered, "I can see your worshippers, but you said they couldn't see or hear us."

"They cannot."

She joined her hands prayerfully before her small breasts again. "Then they cannot know what we have been doing, can they? Oh, my lord, would it outrage you just to be seen naked with me?"

He looked at her, eyes half lidded and kind again. "You're a clever little minx. If that will satisfy them and confirm you as my priestess, I'm willing. Let the fools believe what they will."

His hands went to the heavy gold brooch that held his tunic at the shoulder and pulled it loose. The cloth dropped down exposing his broad chest, not bare as Cretan men's chests were—either by nature or by plucking—but with an inverted triangle of golden curls stretching between and a little above his nipples. The point was at the end of his breastbone, and from it grew a narrow band of sleek blond hair that reached down toward his navel. Ariadne had started to undo the laces of her bodice, but her fingers lay idle as she watched him untie his belt. He caught the tunic as it slid down his body and tossed it on the foot of the altar.

When he turned back to her, she was still staring at him and he said, "Are you afraid? I promise I won't hurt you."

"You are beautiful," she said. "I don't fear you. I am your priestess. You are my god. You won't harm me."

She didn't know what he read in her face, but he

looked pleased, and what she said was true. It was the right thing to say, too, at least to this god, because he came close, smiling.

"Let me help you," he offered.

"Is it right for a god to wait upon his handmaiden?" she asked anxiously.

He only laughed in response, but she dropped her hands submissively and let him undo the laces of her bodice and then the ties of her belt and skirt. The heavy garment fell into a heap and she stepped over it, wriggling out of the bodice, which she dropped unceremoniously atop the skirt. It didn't occur to her as she took his hand and drew him back upon the altar that she didn't feel the smallest flicker of discomfort.

"Shall we lie down?" she asked.

"Why not?" he said, grinning, and then, "You atop me. I would mash you like trampled grapes if I lay on you."

She giggled. "Oh no. Jests are made of men who allow their wives to take that role, and the god must plow the earth." He looked rebellious, and she flung her arms around his neck and kissed his cheek. "I'll come to no harm. You can support yourself on your arms, and we can rise at once as you remove the blackness."

He nodded brusquely and Ariadne lay down on the cold stone. He knelt beside her, then straddled her, and she thought how terrified she would have been if he had simply taken her. Now the brief moment that he covered her with his body was a warm joy and she would have held him to her if she hadn't been afraid to anger him. She did grip him for an instant as a roar of sound suddenly smote her, but she let her arms fall away as Dionysus pulled free and rose, realizing that he had dismissed the wall of silence as well as that of darkness and the crowd was screaming with joy and enthusiasm. Then he reached down and helped her up.

With a hand on her shoulder, he turned to face those before the dais and the two priestesses, who still knelt at the edge. "This is my Chosen, my priestess," he said. "Let her be honored among you. Let her word be as mine, and when it passes her lips, let it be obeyed."

"Yes, lord," Minos cried, his fist to his forehead.

Behind him a strong voice began a song of thanksgiving. Ariadne was pleased by the satisfaction she saw in her father's face and a little amused by the astonishment on that of her brother. Her mother looked stunned, and she kept casting quick glances around her as if to assess the sincerity of the worshipers. Ariadne thought it was real enough. After all, they had seen Dionysus appear from thin air, they had seen him cast a pall of darkness between himself and them. Two miracles were not to be lightly dismissed. And there was his appearance, too. Ready to burst with joy, she laid her hand over his and squeezed it gently. He looked down at her.

As the song died, Dionysus raised his hand. "I accept your worship and am well pleased with my priestess. Now you may leave so I may commune with her in private."

The two priestesses scrambled to their feet and sidled around the edge of the dais toward the door to the left of the painting, but from the very front of the crowd there was a sound of protest that drew Ariadne's eyes. Her own widened as she saw Pasiphae pulling free of her father's hand on her arm, lifting her own hand toward Dionysus, and smiling her most seductive smile.

"Lord God," she murmured, "I—"

"Go," Dionysus broke in. "I wish to be alone with my priestess."

"But I should be—"

Dionysus lifted his hand. Suddenly Ariadne was again aware of those silvery strands that reached from her to Dionysus and they transmitted a strange feeling. A tingling? A gathering of weight that was without weight? Ariadne remembered she had felt that—that Power—when Dionysus cast the spell of darkness. She felt danger too, and knew he was about to be rid of what, to him, was a minor nuisance. She drew breath hastily to cry for mercy, but Minos had turned back and now pulled his wife roughly away toward the gates that closed off the grounds of the shrine.

Ariadne saw that Pasiphae didn't go willingly. She dragged back and kept looking over her shoulder, her eyes flicking from Ariadne to Dionysus. Ariadne felt chilled and pressed herself against Dionysus' side. That look bode no good for her. She shivered as Pasiphae went through the gate, the very last to leave, still looking back. Then she felt Dionysus gesture, and the gates swung shut.

CHAPTER 2

"You had better put some clothing on," Dionysus said.

Ariadne looked up at him, startled, because her shivering had all to do with her mother and nothing to do with the cold, but now that he had reminded her she realized that the early morning air was chilly. Obediently, if a little reluctantly, she detached herself from his side, wrapped her skirt around her and pulled on her bodice. Then she knelt down and raised her hands.

"I'm ready to hear your commands and obey, Lord Dionysus."

He had taken up his tunic, fastened the shoulder with the brooch, and pulled it on. As he belted it, he turned to look at her and laughed aloud. "When everyone else fell on their faces, you stood looking at me as if you smelled bad fish. Now you're on your knees ready to obey any command."

Ariadne grinned. The expression might not be respectful, but she knew a teasing tone when she heard it. Her brother Androgeos was an unmerciful tease. "That was because you looked so kind when you smiled at me in the scrying bowl and when you came you seemed proud and cold. I didn't wish to be priestess to a cold, proud god. I was disappointed—but I know I didn't look at you as if I smelled bad fish. For one thing, you smell wonderful, sharp and sweet, like certain lilies in the sun; for another—" she looked up at him through her long, black lashes "—I was too frightened even to fall to the floor. It's not every day that a god appears in front of his altar."

"Maybe not, but don't kneel to me now. I have no orders to give you, only a mild complaint to make."

Ariadne stood up at once and hung her head. "My Lord God," she whispered, "I am very, very sorry you don't think me fit to make sacrifice to you and fulfill you." Then she looked up and clasped her hands prayerfully. "I beg you not to desert me. I swear I will grow up as fast as ever I can so I can truly be your priestess. Let me serve you. I—I love you."

Dionysus, who seemed to be about to wave away her prayer, looked startled at her final words. Then he frowned a little and shook his head. "You mistake me," he said. "I wasn't going to complain about your youth. That doesn't matter any more. I am well content with you as my priestess. But do you *have* to have these ceremonies so early in the morning?"

His expression was now pained, his voice plaintive. "The sun was barely up when you Called me. I was still in bed, and I didn't even get to wash my face or comb my hair—or have any breakfast—before I had to come here."

"Oh, don't go yet!" Ariadne cried. "I'll bring you washing water and a comb and brush and a fine brass mirror. And—if gods can eat mortal food—I can bring you bread and cheese and olives and eggs and cold meat and—"

"Enough," Dionysus said, starting to laugh. "I am a m— god, not a bottomless pit. The bread, cheese, and olives with wine to wash them down will do to assuage my hunger. But do we have to stay here? Is there nowhere more comfortable? Do I not remember—"

He stopped suddenly, remembering all too clearly the visits he had made to this shrine in the distant past. His priestess had always taken him into the hillside behind the painting to her chambers, and they had sat and talked, yes, and eaten and drunk wine. And she had explained to him the Visions that tormented him so that they became real things that he could understand or sometimes even act upon.

"Of course, Lord Dionysus," Ariadne's voice cut into the memory, and she went toward the door he remembered so well.

But *she* wouldn't be there. Tears misted his eyes. He didn't even remember her name . . . Dionysus stared resentfully at the child who was holding open the door for him; his lips parted to say the spell words that would carry him back to Olympus—and suddenly he did remember. Her name had also been Ariadne, and she, too, had been very small, very dark, and looked . . . why, she looked as this child would look when she was growing old. His soul lifted toward the Mother. *Have you given her back to me, Mother?* he asked. But there was no answer, no Vision, no touch of warmth.

"My lord?" Ariadne asked softly, plainly puzzled about why he was standing and staring.

He didn't answer, merely strode forward toward the door she was holding for him. It wasn't fitting that natives know that their "gods" prayed to a far more powerful divinity, especially when the "god" couldn't even tell whether his prayer had been answered. Dionysus shuddered as he passed from the sunny courtyard shrine to the dim, cool passage cut into the hillside. It was lit with lamps filled with scented oil. He remembered that, too, now, and steeled himself to face the familiar room empty of the presence that had comforted him, steadied him, in a world where he did not always know what was real and what was Vision.

The door was opened for him. Jaws tight, he stepped past the child who held it and into . . . nothing he had ever seen before. Shocked, he turned back and snarled, "Where is the priestess's chamber?"

"This is it, my lord," the girl replied, her voice quavering in response to his anger.

"It isn't what I remember," he snapped, more angry at himself for frightening her than at her, but as always unable to control his rage or express it.

She blinked as if her vision had clouded, stretched a hand toward him but without touching him, and then smiled slightly. "No, of course not." The quaver was gone from her voice. She seemed older. Although her body was still that of a too-thin child, her face was calm, gently amused. "Each priestess furnishes anew, and you never came in my father's mother's time, so you wouldn't recognize the chamber as it is now."

Ariadne was utterly bewildered by her own calm words. She felt like two different people locked into one skin, a young girl torn between terror and adoration of a powerful and unpredictable god and a woman, guided by a mist of silvery threads that brought to her a tale of pain and doubt and a need for comfort. The woman had spoken to the god. The girl looked around the room and blinked again.

She had been brought to see the shrine and the priestess's chambers within it a few days before her consecration, but her mind had been filled with a mingling of fear and resentment—and hope, too—so that she hadn't taken in what she had seen. And when she opened the door for Dionysus, his expression of hurt and anger had struck her like a blow. The shock had again torn open that flower shape, which seemed to surround her heart, and called forth those silvery tendrils that let her understand his distress. His emotion and her response had so absorbed her that she saw nothing. Now the astonishment and distaste on his face fixed her attention outward, on her surroundings.

Girl and woman came together and she had to bite her lips to keep from laughing. To put it in plain language, her father's mother had been a greedy old bitch, and it seemed as if every gilded gewgaw, every piece of overcarved furniture, every garishly painted chest she had been able to collect was crammed into the room. There was space enough to walk . . . barely, if one was careful.

Ariadne's eyes skipped from piece to piece. Together they were garish and overdone, but each piece alone . . . Oh, yes, every single one, Ariadne thought, eyes narrowing with calculation, was costly. It was clear enough where the revenues of the shrine went. No wonder the priests and priestesses looked a bit threadbare—and little wonder that Dionysus didn't bother to visit Knossos. Doubtless the sacrifices to him were cheap and scant.

Even as she thought it, she knew that wasn't the reason. If he had noticed the high priestess was cheating him—Ariadne felt a sudden chill—there would have been nothing left in the shrine but blood-stained rags. Her Gift told her that she had seen the beginning of that kind of rage when he looked out at the worshipers after he said she was unripe. Terror flicked her and then departed. She had stopped the rage before it blossomed then and again when he saw the room.

The room. "It is a bit . . . a bit too much, isn't it?" she asked uncertainly, realizing that she walked the honed edge of a sword blade with this god. She mustn't offend him and she didn't know how gods lived.

"A bit?" Dionysus replied, staring around. "I have never seen so much ugly clutter in my life. One can hardly breathe in here."

"I'm glad you think so," Ariadne said in tones of heartfelt relief. "I will have it all cleared out."

I'll sell it, she thought, sell it quickly, before mother or father can lay hands on it. I'll attend to the needs of the priests and priestesses so they will look to me as mistress and provider. I'll save the best pieces and offer them to *him* as sacrifice. And I'll buy . . . she looked up at Dionysus.

"If you will tell me what you remember and what you would like," she added, "I will make sure that the chamber is refurnished so that you are content when you come again."

He shook his head and her heart clenched with fear that he would tell her he wouldn't come again, but all he said was, "It was very long ago. I don't really remember, only that it was . . . comfortable, a place two people could talk."

A tremor of excitement ran through Ariadne. Far from warning that this would be his only visit, what he said implied that he wished and expected to talk to his priestess and that he did so often enough to desire comfort. Chill followed the warmth of excitement. Did she want him to come, this god in whom rage rose so swiftly, so unpredictably? Through that strange flower within her, Ariadne was now certain that the tales were true, that this god could become a frenzied beast. She glanced sidelong at him, so beautiful, so strong. She couldn't give him up, she couldn't! What could she do to tame and control this wild god?

Comfort—he had told her he desired comfort. "This place offers no comfort," she sighed. "However, we can make do for this once. Come, the bathing chamber is through this door. Shall I get water for you, or shall I tell the priests to bring hot water? That will take a few minutes."

His lips quirked. "I can get the water and heat it too. What I need is food. I'm starving."

"At once, my lord."

Rather than retracing her steps, out the door and through the corridor to the priests' and priestesses' quarters, Ariadne went into the bedchamber. A glance told her that it wasn't much better than the reception room, but what she sought was beside the gilded and ornate bed—a twisted cord that hung down from the ceiling. She pulled it and heard, just beyond the wall at the head of the bed, a bell ring. The door in the corner of the room opened almost at once and one of the elderly priestesses, still gray with pallor, looked at her with wide eyes.

"Lord Dionysus is washing," Ariadne said softly. "He's hungry. Bring bread and cheese, olives, wine, honey cakes if there are any."

"For a god?" the priestess whispered, trembling. "What we have is coarse, common food."

Ariadne remembered Dionysus' laughter when she

offered what was common to breaking the fast in her father's house. He didn't seem surprised or disgusted with her suggestions, only amused. And he was a *big* man, with solid muscles. She felt a spasm of doubt about the tales of nectar and ambrosia and a little more sure of cheese and olives.

"Hunger is the best spice," she said. "Bring the very best you have and I'll explain to him, if the quality is less than he expects, that we were unprepared."

The priestess got even wider eyed at the calm with which Ariadne said she would explain to a god, but she bowed and hurried away. Ariadne seized two pillows from the huge bed and ran back into the reception room. A quick survey showed a corner minimally less cluttered than the rest of the room. Left of that corner, a horizontal shaft had been cut to make a large window. Near it was a chair with a footstool and a small table beside it. Ariadne wove her way through the clutter, dropped the pillows beside the chair and began to carry and push away other tables and chairs to make a space.

She was struggling with a high-backed, armed, double bench when from the doorway Dionysus said, "That's too heavy for you. Where do you want it to go?" And came and took it from her.

"Is it fitting for gods to move furniture?" she asked doubtfully.

Dionysus, hair damp, eyes calm, grinned. "The nice thing about being a god is that anything we wish to do is fitting, so you can stop asking me that. Where do you want me to put this?"

"Oh, I don't care. I was just trying to make a little space around that chair so you would not feel so crowded. I don't want anything to disturb you, my lord. The more content you are, the longer you will stay."

He looked at her and a slight frown creased his brow, but Ariadne stood still, face raised to his steady gaze, until he sighed and put the bench down with its back to the chair she had prepared for him. She had already moved three chairs and two small, gilt tables and the space near the window was now open and well lit but without glare. Gently, Dionysus touched her hair; then he went and settled into the chair.

The light from the shaft well was soft, despite a sky of aching blue without a cloud, because the direct light of the sun was blocked by the deep inset. Dionysus looked out over the terraced vines that climbed Gypsades Hill. He knew he couldn't read hearts like Aphrodite, but he had no doubt that Ariadne truly desired him to stay. That eagerness to be with him made him uneasy. Few, even among the Olympians, sought his company; rather they looked at him sidelong, asked what he wanted, gave it to him, and waited for him to go. And natives were only trouble, he knew that—even his own dear priestess, who had died.

What would this priestess ask for, he wondered cynically. Natives prayed and sacrificed, but they expected a return. She had already asked him to bless the vines and the wine. He shifted in the chair as if he would rise, but he remembered that his dear priestess had asked that of him too, and, indeed, it was little trouble, actually a joy, to make the grapes full and sweet and the wine rich and potent.

A small tinkling drew his eyes to the doorway and he saw Ariadne go quickly and take a tray from a kneeling priestess so she could serve him herself. He remembered suddenly how she had said, "I—I love you," and an odd sense of peace came over him, until it was tinged with pain because *his* priestess would never again come and sit beside him. But Ariadne was very young, he told himself. There was little danger of losing her for many years—only . . . could she bring him the peace that his old priestess provided?

He watched Ariadne's coming with the tray. She set it down on the table beside him and sat on the pillows near his chair. He reached for the wine, tasted it, and winced.

"Please forgive us for the coarseness of the provisions," Ariadne said. "You have been too long away from Knossos, Lord Dionysus. The wine is not what it once was."

"I was angry," he replied softly, took a bite of cheese, an olive, and some bread. When he had swallowed, he said, "I thought my priestess had turned away from me because she no longer Called. I didn't realize she had died. . . ."

"And you didn't hear the new priestess?" Ariadne shook her head and looked troubled. "Something must have been forgotten in the ritual."

"No, I don't think it was the ritual," Dionysus said. "I think it was the priestess herself. Some don't have the power to Call, some do. You do." He ate in silence for a while, then noticed her watching him. "Are you hungry, too?" he asked.

She smiled. "I was offered food and I was too frightened to take any. But you've been so kind, and I'm not afraid any more. Yes, I am hungry."

He laughed. "Then bring your pillows around to the other side of the table and eat. There is surely enough here for two . . . or three or four."

"Thank you."

Ariadne obeyed him promptly and took some cheese and olives, but there was only one cup. She looked around and soon noticed a small decorative bowl. Setting down her food, she took that and, after wiping it, filled it for herself and sipped from it. The wine was terrible. That was wrong. The best should be offered to the shrine of the god of wine. And she would see that it was—if Dionysus kept his promise and the vines blossomed well. She looked up at him.

"You won't forget, Lord Dionysus? You will come to bless the vines?" she asked anxiously.

"If you remember to Call, how can I forget?"

"Is it true that I can Call you?"

"You did this morning, but if you doubt it, why don't you try again?"

"But you're here beside me."

He shrugged. "Go to the end of the room and Call me, silently, with your mind only. I'll close my eyes so I can't see from the expression on your face when you Call. Let's see if I hear you."

He had said it wasn't the ritual, but Ariadne filled her bowl with wine and carried it to the far end of the room. There she looked into the bowl and in her mind Called, "Lord Dionysus, hear me."

Dionysus started and winced. "Stop. I hear you."

Ariadne almost dropped the bowl because his face had appeared in it and his voice seemed to come from it. "Oh," she breathed. "I saw you in the wine. And I heard you speak from the bowl. I do—I must have the power to Call you."

He watched her come back toward him. She walked more lightly, more gracefully than his old priestess, but oddly the spirit in her seemed to have more weight. He thought she had more power. That "hear me" had rung like a blast of brass horns in his head. And she was very young. He wondered what more she could do than Call to him.

When she was settled on the pillows beside him and had eaten some cheese and bread and a few olives, he said lightly, as if it were of no importance, "I've had the strangest dream. I've Seen a white bull, huge and very beautiful, walk up out of the sea and come, all of its own will to a man in a lordly gown, wearing a crown. It walked with him into the land and went, without being led, to a great shrine. There it knelt at the altar, ready to be sacrificed, but he who wore the crown did not pick up the double axe laid ready. Instead he urged the bull away, leading it some distance to a green field upon which grazed a herd of lovely cows."

He paused a moment when he heard Ariadne gasp, but she had bowed her head so that her face was hidden. He waited expectantly for her to speak, but she didn't, and he was bitterly disappointed. He was wrong, he thought, she wasn't Mother-sent; but a kind of desperation seized him, a need not to give up, and he went on, "And the bull ran out to the cows and coupled with them, but it was as if what should have made him content cast an evil spell. A man's head appeared under the bull's horns and he turned on the cows and gored them, and then he trampled the herdsmen who came to drive him away. Finally he ran into the countryside and wrought more destruction, tearing up gardens, overthrowing houses, and killing those within . . . whom he tore apart and ate. Day by day he grew larger and stronger and more vicious. . . ."

Dionysus' voice drifted away and he shook his head, beaten by her silence. "It doesn't sound like anything." His voice was no longer light and he shivered hard, once. "I cannot say why, but there is a sense of horror about it, like a doom drawing closer and closer . . ." He shook his head again and he sounded angry and resentful when he said, "I hate it! It's awful because it doesn't make any sense, and yet I have dreamed it over and over for nearly a year."

Torn by conflicting loyalties, Ariadne had at first been afraid to speak, but Dionysus' need was too powerful for her to resist. She lifted her head. "I know what it means," she whispered. "Well, not all of it, but—"

He had turned away after his painful confession and had been staring out of the window. When she spoke, he twisted his head sharply to look at her. "You've gone all pale," he said.

"The bull from the sea, it was here on Crete that it came ashore."

"A real bull? Out of the ocean?"

"Yes, a real bull, all white, as you said, came out of the ocean. I saw it myself."

"How? Why?"

Ariadne caught a glimpse of the intensity of his look; she thought that if he could have eaten her with his eyes, he would have done so. However, she felt no fear; her attention was distracted to a whole mist of silvery threads that played about her, rising and falling, touching her, touching him.

"The bull came to my father. He was the eldest son but his brothers Radamanthys and Sarpedon wouldn't agree that he should be king of all. They wished to divide Crete. My father knew that although he and his brothers would manage well, in the future that division would cause great harm. Still he didn't wish to fight his brothers, nor, to tell the truth, did they wish to fight him, so my father went to the shrine of Poseidon and prayed to the god to send him a sign that he, and he alone, was meant to be king."

"Poseidon!" Dionysus exclaimed.

Ariadne clasped her hands tightly, but her voice was steady as she went on. "And from a trance, the priest of Poseidon told my father that his sign would be a white bull that would rise from the sea and go with him. And that bull was to be sacrificed to Poseidon."

"One is better off not meddling with Poseidon," Dionysus said thoughtfully. "But he sent the bull?"

"Yes. Just as you Saw it in your dream. The bull came from the sea. Half of Crete saw it rise from the waves, and Radamanthys and Sarpedon bowed down to my father and accepted him as king."

"But if the bull was sacrificed—"

"It was not," Ariadne said. She started to look away, but Dionysus caught her chin and held her face so that her eyes met his. "My father was seduced by its beauty. He couldn't bear to put the axe to its neck. He sacrificed three fine bulls at the altar of Poseidon's shrine, but not that bull."

Dionysus stared into Ariadne's eyes a moment longer, his face now blank as a marble mask, and then looked away out the window. Ariadne licked her lips and waited. He didn't look angry, she thought, although he might be after her confession that her father had cheated the god who had consented to help him. Would that not connect in his mind with the priestess who used what came to the shrine to enrich herself instead of offering it to her god? But the silver threads had subsided, although she could feel that the flowerlike place where they usually nested was open wide. Her tongue flicked out to wet her lips again as they dried with the thought that he might be disgusted with her for betraying her father to him. Her lips were forming her defense when he turned toward her.

"Ah," Dionysus said; his eyes were bright and clear—and completely sane. "Now I understand why I have been dreaming of the bull coupling with the cows and then changing to a monster and destroying everything. And the man's head—" he frowned "—but the face was not Poseidon's."

Ariadne shook her head. "I don't understand that, my lord. It's as if something is missing from the dream." But she was hardly paying attention to what she said. Her attention was still fixed on her own anxiety so that she went on quickly, "I hope you don't think it wrong to have spoken of my father's sin to you, my lord. When I was consecrated priestess this morning, he told me that I was no longer his but yours. Ahead of his right as king, as father, as blood of my blood, my first loyalty, my first responsibility, is to you. Is that not right?"

The slight look of puzzlement he had been wearing shifted to a clear expression of satisfaction when she spoke of her father relinquishing all right to her, and she remembered the rage that had roused in him when he thought she wasn't the best her father and mother had to offer. There was kindness and gentleness in him—he had shown enough of them to her—but to belittle or overlook him was to rouse a monster. This was indeed a jealous god, but she wasn't afraid of that. He *was* first for her. She had no need to pretend or to worry about that pretense showing. Praise and admiration was what she felt, and praise and admiration would keep Dionysus calm.

"You are mine and *only* mine," he said sharply, confirming her thoughts. "*No one* has any claim to you but me. Your father can be no more than any other man to you."

"He isn't," Ariadne affirmed steadily. "You are all men and all women, too, to me. You are all in all. My god."

Dionysus nodded. "That is how it must be. How else could you serve me and speak of my Visions? For they must be told to free me of them. You must warn your father, as my Mouth, that the bull from the sea must die on Poseidon's altar or great evil will follow."

Ariadne swallowed hard. "I must speak of this Vision to my father?" she said faintly.

"He must be warned."

"He has been warned. Poseidon's priest has told him over and over that the bull must be sacrificed. He won't listen. He says he must have cattle bred from that animal."

Dionysus caught her chin again. "You don't wish to be my Mouth, to speak to your father of my Vision?"

"I do wish to be your Mouth, my lord, but I am also afraid to speak of *this* Vision."

"Why? You are mine, under my protection. Of what are you afraid?"

Ariadne took a deep breath. "My father spoke the words of renunciation that are part of the ritual of consecration, but I know that to him those were only words. I have been thirteen years his daughter; he expects silence and obedience from me. *I* have felt your presence; your touch is on my soul. His awe at seeing you, will be short-lived, I fear."

"You mean he will punish you if you say I told you that the bull must die?" Dionysus' voice was dangerously gentle. "He won't do it more than once."

Minos touch his priestess? Dionysus smiled. He could almost See his human hounds coursing on Minos' trail, hear the king's screams as his flesh was torn. Then, because he still held her chin, he felt Ariadne shiver convulsively; he looked and saw her eyes close. Tears ran from under her lids. She raised them and looked at him without trying to wipe the drops away.

"You are my god," she said. "You are first in my mind and in my heart, and I will do as you bid me regardless of punishment or any other ill. But, Lord God, Minos is my father. Whatever you do is right, and yet, I cannot bear that he should be hurt because of me. He's not an evil man. In most things he is noble, just, even generous. It's only this accursed bull that has seduced him from the proper path. I will be your Mouth and speak your warning, but I beg you, Lord Dionysus, if he will not hear and obey, admonish him gently."

For the third or fourth time that morning the red frenzy that had begun to flicker behind his eyes faded to nothing. Dionysus cast a rather bemused glance at the lovely face—a little marred with tear streaks and smudges of kohl—that was raised pleadingly to his. Most often when he felt Called to mingle with the natives, the Call ended in trouble—an orgy or a murder—but that had not been true when his priestess had Called him in the past, and it was not true with this priestess either. He ran a knuckle down her tear-wet cheek. She was so very young, so very beautiful. What did it matter if she didn't speak the Vision that had come to him?

He was shocked by the thought. What did it matter? If she didn't speak he might go on dreaming of or Seeing that man-headed bull until proper warning was given. He frowned. But warning *had* been given. The priests of Poseidon had told Minos that evil would come of the bull if Minos didn't sacrifice it. He hadn't known of that warning, but he knew of it now. Surely that would be sufficient. He felt remarkably relieved. If that warning was sufficient, Ariadne wouldn't have to confront her father, Minos wouldn't be tempted to punish her, and he wouldn't be required to chastise Minos for treating his priestess with a lack of respect.

He smiled down at Ariadne and patted her shoulder. "All's well. If Minos has been warned already, there's no need for you to speak to him about the matter—at least, not now. If the Vision recurs, you may have to relate it to Minos, but for now . . . Poseidon is very well able to deal with those who disobey him. Probably he wouldn't even thank me for my interference."

His hand still lay on her shoulder; she bent her head and kissed it. "You are merciful and indulgent, my lord."

It was heartfelt praise, but Dionysus realized it was also too true. He was too comfortable, too happy, sitting with her beside him, nibbling olives. He had already made her need his purpose. He suspected if she asked for anything else, he would be sorely tempted to give that to her also. Discomfort warred with ease and satisfaction, warning that the pleasure she gave him made him vulnerable. Suspicion pricked him, making him so uneasy that he began to feel disappointment was better than doubt. Smiling, to hide his disgust—at her? at himself?—he made an offer that would taint his happiness and comfort and armor him against her.

"I'm now indulgent," he said. "You would be wise, since my mood is so good, to ask for what you desire from me."

"What *I* desire?" She shook her head. "But I have asked for that already, my lord. You said you would come and bless the vines and the wine. You will, won't you?"

"Yes, I'll do that as I promised." He stood up. "But I meant you should ask something for yourself."

"For myself?" She rose too, her hand clinging to his as it began to drop from her shoulder. Her face flushed slightly and her eyes were magnified by tears. "You're making ready to leave. I know I mustn't beg you to stay. You are a god and have interests and duties far more important than me. For myself? Oh, if you would give me a gift for myself, come again, my lord. Come again soon. Come often. That's the greatest gift, the finest gift, you could ever give to me."

She wanted him, only him? Was she then Mother-sent? His priestess come again? Dionysus remembered the pain when her Call no longer came, the renewed pain when he realized she was dead and would never Call again. Was that future misery worth his present joy? It didn't matter; at this moment, he couldn't ignore the fear, the pleading, in this priestess's face, the tears in her eyes.

"I will," he promised. "I'll come to you whenever you Call." And then doubt shook him again, but he no longer could bear the notion of disappointment and he warned, "But that promise will hold only so long as you do not misuse it." And before he yielded even more, he loosened Ariadne's hand from his, whispered "*Dei me exelthein Olympus*," and "leapt" home.

CHAPTER 3

Ariadne stared unbelievingly at the spot where Dionysus had stood, then whirled around to look for him in the room, although she knew perfectly well he wasn't there. He had disappeared right before her eyes; she had seen it happen. She knew he had come the same way, but she hadn't seen that; he'd been behind her. She swallowed hard and sank down on the floor, her knees suddenly refusing to support her. He was a *god*. She'd spent the entire morning with a *god*, feeding him coarse bread and cheese and olives and bad wine, letting him get his own washing water and carry furniture.

She felt weak and dizzy and breathed in gasps, almost expecting to be smitten with lightning for her behavior. But nothing happened, and after a while the panic receded. Her eyes had been resting unseeingly on the table bearing the dishes of food, and slowly she made sense of what she was looking at. Little remained. God he was, but Dionysus had eaten very heartily of the coarse food and even drunk most of the terrible wine. Ariadne shuddered at the thought of offering such wine to the wine god and then giggled weakly as she remembered his ready laughter, the kindness with which he invited her to share his meal, the way he'd grinned like a mischievous boy and said that the nice thing about being a god was that anything he chose to do was fitting.

The memory of his gentleness tempered the awe that had overcome her and let her climb to her feet and sink into the chair he'd used. His scent was still on it, spicy sweet; it evoked a new cascade of memories, the first of which was far less comforting. He had been gentle to her, but he wasn't a gentle god. Ariadne saw again those pale eyes turned on his worshipers, later turned on her mother, eyes hard as gems and quite mad with quick, senseless rage—rage he seemed unable or unwilling to control.

Ariadne slowly shook her head. Why had she not fainted with terror? screamed and run from him? How had she known what to say? She remembered the flower around her heart, the silvery, misty threads that carried to her an understanding of what drove him to fury because *he* didn't understand it, but now that he was gone she didn't really believe in them.

If she had imagined that, could she have imagined Dionysus also? Anxiety rose and was instantly dispelled. No, the priestesses and priests, her father and mother, and all the other worshipers had seen him. A small smile curved her lips. She, Ariadne, seventh child and of no importance at all, had summoned a god, had talked with him, eaten with him, had received his promise to bless the vines and the wine and that he would come again at her Call. She let pleasure wash over her, but it lasted no longer than the panic had.

Gods, she remembered her father saying somewhat bitterly, had a tendency to make known their desires and then disappear and leave humans to struggle with fulfilling them. Not that Dionysus had asked for much, just to have the room made comfortable. Then Ariadne's lower lip crept between her teeth: even without making demands, Dionysus had left behind more trouble than he knew. She'd seen her mother's face, both when he first appeared and when he bid everyone leave. Ariadne shivered and hugged her arms around herself.

Would her mother try to usurp her place because she'd seen the god appear? Ariadne bit down on her lip, recalling how Pasiphae had held out her hand to him and smiled. She'd been about to say that she should have been the priestess. Ariadne let her lip go and ground her teeth, tears rising in her eyes. Pasiphae was so beautiful, and *she* was not unripe fruit. Then Ariadne sniffed, reminding herself that Dionysus had looked right at her mother and not only gestured her to go away but when she persisted and spoke again, had been angered enough to do her harm. *I* am his priestess, Ariadne thought; *I* was consecrated to him, he accepted *me*, and *no one* can take my place.

Her sense of satisfaction was liberally tinged with apprehension. Pasiphae wasn't going to be pleased and she could make life remarkably unpleasant for anyone who prevented her from having her own way. Ariadne shivered and gritted her teeth again, then jumped to her feet. She wouldn't think about that now. Her first duty was to Dionysus and his stated wish to have her rooms made comfortable.

She summoned the priests and priestesses; it was very soothing to have them respond immediately and then salute her as worshipers. But, she reminded herself, they were old and they were accustomed to the old queen's ways. Perhaps they even thought the high priestess's chamber needed to look like an overcrowded shop. She'd better give her orders, Ariadne thought, while Dionysus' aura still touched her and before they remembered she was only thirteen years old.

"The god," she said, "bade me clear away what was unjustly accumulated by the old priestess. He wasn't pleased by her behavior and showed it by turning his back on us, although no one seemed to understand. But having come to my Call, he'll no longer overlook being robbed of his just due. The best in this chamber and the bedchamber is to be put aside for him and offered on his altar when he demands it. The rest is to be sold and I'm to use the money to repair the shrine and to furnish proper clothing and decent food for his attendants. It's time, also, that novices and acolytes be found."

One of the priests dropped his fist from his forehead and met her eyes. "No one wished to serve before," he said, "because the god never came nor vouchsafed a sending and the grapes rotted and the wine soured. Now . . ." He took a deep breath and his face almost glowed. "Now we'll need to turn away those who wish to serve, the vines will need to be propped to support the weight of the grapes, and the wine will be as rich and sweet as ambrosia."

But what if it doesn't happen, Ariadne thought,

more accustomed to having her hopes dashed than fulfilled. "The god Dionysus appeared before his painting on the altar," she said. "He accepted me as his priestess. He promised to come if I Called to him and that he would bless the grapes and the wine. He said nothing about ambrosia."

The four old attendants drew together, perhaps reminded by her repressive tone that Dionysus wasn't the easiest god to serve. "How will we know what the god Dionysus feels is best?" a priestess asked in a rather quavering voice.

"I will know," Ariadne replied. "I will choose for him. And on my head will it be if I am wrong. I'll also choose pieces that are to be left in the room and arranged for the comfort of eye and body." She met their eyes boldly. No one contradicted her and she nodded. "We can begin now."

One priest bowed and went to get the shrine slaves. Ariadne walked slowly through the clutter, choosing a few pieces here and there and marking the furniture she wished to keep in the chamber with bits of ribbon one of the priestesses brought her. She kept the bowl she had drunk out of and in which she had seen Dionysus' face for herself. From its weight, she thought it might be pure gold. Aside from a few other vessels of precious metal, some studded with jewels, and two exquisite ivory tables that she ordered put aside to be offered to the god, most of the contents of the chamber went into the storeroom behind the altar.

The chests were last. Several were filled with cloth. That she bade the priestesses use to have new robes made for themselves and the priests and even for the shrine slaves, depending on the quality. She did warn them, however, that if they found anything very valuable, cloth set with gems or woven with gold, to put that aside as an offering to the god also. Other chests contained scrolls and wooden bound sheets of parchment and papyrus. Two she looked in and hastily closed: one seemed to be filled with jewelry, the other with gold and silver. Those, like the chests full of writings, Ariadne said were to stay just where they were. The god himself must decide what to do with the contents. She hoped no one had seen the hoard, but she felt that even the slaves would hesitate to steal from a deity who'd been manifest so recently.

After that, there was really nothing more for Ariadne to do. She would have to go home, she thought, stiffened against a shiver, and looked around a little desperately. With a sense of relief she saw that the sun was almost at its zenith; she could put off going to the palace by eating her meal with the priests and priestesses. Then, still delaying the evil moment, she spent a little more time giving directions about the bedchamber. However, she couldn't deceive herself any longer; she knew she couldn't avoid facing her mother and refusing to give up her god.

The priests and priestesses escorted her from the shrine down the hill. One comfort, which also increased her anxiety, was the way all others on the road made way for her and the profound obeisance offered by those working in the fields and vineyards. If her mother heard of this, she'd be even more furious, but surely she wouldn't dare *do* anything to the acknowledged high priestess of Dionysus.

As they walked toward the Royal Road, Ariadne briefly considered whether she should keep her escort with her. It didn't take her long to decide that four old and threadbare attendants wouldn't impress her mother or affect her actions in any way. Also it was better not to allow her priests and priestesses to see her scolded and punished.

Perhaps if she went by the west porch she would be able to sneak up the stairs and get to her chamber.

Ariadne grimaced; that would be useless. Sooner or later she'd have to confront Pasiphae, and it would be best to do it sooner and know the worst. Yes, she would enter as was fitting for a god-touched high priestess by the formal north entrance.

At the foot of the ramp that led to the north portico, she thanked her attendants, told them she would return to the shrine soon, and dismissed them. Turning, she was amazed to see both the guards at the porch entry, weapons grounded, standing stiffly with right arms in the fist-to-forehead salute of a worshiper. For a moment Ariadne was tempted to look behind to see if Dionysus was there, but she knew he wasn't; she would have felt his presence.

The formality jolted her into a realization of being all alone. She should have kept her attendants. Rightly there should be a procession. Even the bulls being led to the bull-dancing court had a procession, Ariadne thought with a touch of resentment, and then swallowed hard. The bulls were sacrificed after their moment of glory. She wished she hadn't thought of that. Then she reminded herself firmly that there could be no procession because Dionysus himself had ordered his worshipers to disperse. Remembering his promise to protect her, Ariadne drew a deep if somewhat tremulous breath and went forward up the ramp.

When she reached the saluting guards at the top, she said softly, "I see you," the response of priest or priestess to a worshiper's appeal.

The guards dropped their arms. One smiled, and the other, also smiling, told her her father was waiting for her in the king's chamber.

The fear that had touched her dissipated. Her father would be pleased with her, she was sure, and she went light-footed through the hall of the pillars, down the corridor, and across the bull-dancing court. On the landing of the great staircase, she paused, realizing that her mother would be with her father, but she started down nonetheless and was further reassured when she heard the sound of voices as she came into the corridor. Minos and Pasiphae weren't alone and Minos wouldn't let Pasiphae humiliate or hurt her before the courtiers. Some of them had seen Dionysus and heard him accept her.

She paused in the doorway and saw that both suppositions were correct. The light-well to her right held a shaft of sunlight that made the wine-red pillars glow and enhanced the brilliant skirts of the women and the flashing armlets and necklets of the men. Across the room, below the rich mural of a crowned male walking with his hands on the manes of two lions, Pasiphae was seated beside Minos on a small chair by his great one on the dais.

Actually Ariadne couldn't see much of the mural because the room was full of people, fuller than she'd expected. Surprise drew a low exclamation from her. One head turned, then another. Next she heard her name flowing like a wave across the chamber. And with that wave, every right arm went up, left fist to forehead. Ariadne cast one quick glance at her mother. Pasiphae sat rigid, her full lips pressed into a thin line. The courtiers waited, all facing Ariadne, rigid in the posture of worship.

Ariadne held her breath, afraid to acknowledge the homage done her and also afraid not to. Dionysus wouldn't be pleased if she didn't accept the reverence as his due, and her mother would think she was accepting it for herself and be even more enraged if she responded. But Dionysus was more important to her than Pasiphae.

"I see you," Ariadne said clearly, then bowed her head in grave acknowledgment and walked forward.

The courtiers dropped their arms, but they drew respectfully aside to leave an open aisle and each turned to face her as she moved. When she reached her parents, however, she herself bowed gracefully, hoping Dionysus either wouldn't know or would accept that even a high priestess must bow to a king and queen.

Pasiphae's lips parted, but Minos tightened his grip on her arm until his fingers whitened and she didn't speak.

"Where have you been all this time?" he asked gently.

"Mostly with my god," Ariadne replied, "and then obeying his demands."

"What demands?" Minos asked, more sharply this time.

"He didn't like what had been done with the priestess's chambers and he wasn't too pleased to see that valuable sacrifices hadn't been offered to him but kept by the high priestess."

"They had been placed on the altar," Minos said quickly. "The god didn't choose to take them, so my mother kept them safe for him."

He didn't meet Ariadne's eyes, however, and she suspected that the god would have had to snatch them very fast to get them before they were removed to the old queen's keeping. But her father had had little control over his mother's actions and Ariadne couldn't blame him for her behavior.

"Perhaps he didn't hear her Call," she said mildly, and then, wanting to be sure that her father wouldn't simply appropriate what was in the shrine, reminded him, "Lord Dionysus does hear me. He has seen what was kept from him. Now he will take what is his."

That didn't seem to trouble Minos and Ariadne wondered if she had suspected him unjustly. She never would have, she thought, before he kept that accursed bull. Perhaps she should tell him of Dionysus' Vision. Perhaps if a second god confirmed what Poseidon's priest had said, Minos would listen. But Minos spoke before she could quite gather her courage.

"And what else did the god demand?"

"Nothing," Ariadne said.

"He took all that time to ask for nothing?" Pasiphae said spitefully.

"No." Ariadne again felt an urge to deliver Dionysus' warning. "He described a Vision to me, of a white bull that came from the sea and that—"

"Brought us all good fortune," Pasiphae finished, cutting Ariadne off and diverting attention from Minos, who had paled and drawn in a sharp breath. "I am sure he wished to keep what he said of his Vision private, since he veiled you and himself in a black cloud of silence. You mustn't repeat to us what the god concealed."

Ariadne could have said—the truth—that Dionysus had bidden her speak and only retracted the command to save her from possibly being punished. In the face of her mother's flat prohibition and the stony set of her father's expression she wasn't quite brave enough.

"We are blessed, indeed, in this land that two gods have made manifest their favor to us," Pasiphae continued, smoothly. "But your skirt is all draggled, child, and your laces very poorly done. I will come with you to your chamber and help you repair the damage to your face and dress."

Ariadne cast a single look of appeal at her father, but he was staring past her above his courtiers' heads at the four double doors that separated his inner from his outer chamber. One set of doors was open to admit light and air, pushed back into the hollow of the pillar made to receive it. Ariadne knew another set of doors of the four that closed off the outer chamber from the south and east porches must be open, but what her father sought out there she couldn't guess. The flower around her heart was closed; it opened only for Dionysus, she was sure. And Pasiphae had risen to her feet. Ariadne could only bend her head in acknowledgment of what her mother had said and turn toward the doorway.

"Wait!" Pasiphae commanded, catching her arm, her voice too low to carry to the courtiers but as intense as a scream. "You haven't yet risen so high that you may precede me."

Without a sound, Ariadne stepped aside and let her mother pass. They walked by bowing courtiers, Ariadne grateful that there was no way to tell to whom the bows were addressed, and out into the corridor. Ariadne took a deep breath and braced herself, but her mother didn't stop or turn toward her until they had passed around the corner to the queen's chamber and climbed the small private wooden stair beside it. This left them only a few steps from the rooms Ariadne shared with her younger sister Phaidra.

Pasiphae sailed into the room, turning about so quickly that she almost slammed the door in Ariadne's face. She jerked it fully open again, yanked Ariadne inside, and then slammed it.

"What did you do?" she snarled, shaking her daughter.

"I did exactly what Daidalos taught me," Ariadne cried. "He said he found the words and the ritual in some old scroll, and told me the words to say and showed me what to do. I did *exactly* what he taught me. You *saw* what I did. You heard me."

"So why did the god come to you when he never came to Queen Europa?"

"How would I know?" Ariadne snapped. Pasiphae's grip had relaxed a trifle and Ariadne wrenched herself free and moved away. Her mother stared at her but didn't follow. Feeling safer at a distance, Ariadne added, "Perhaps grandmother didn't follow the ritual exactly, but Dionysus said that some priestesses can Call and some cannot."

Pasiphae sniffed contemptuously and shrugged. "I am sure he would hear me."

"Mother—" Ariadne's voice emerged high pitched and quavering.

Pasiphae laughed. "Oh, don't be afraid. I don't want your little godling."

Ariadne shook her head, but didn't try to correct her mother's misapprehension. Although fear had stabbed her when Pasiphae said she was sure Dionysus would hear her, it was no longer fear that he would prefer her mother. He had made his choice. Ariadne now knew that to ignore his will or imply a decision he had made was wrong was dangerous. Pasiphae believed herself inviolable and in most circumstances that was true, but Ariadne recalled Dionysus' hard stare, the flickers of madness behind his eyes—a madness fatally contagious to others—when Pasiphae had persisted in trying to draw his attention despite his dismissal. It was an odd feeling to be afraid for her mother instead of being afraid of her.

"Yes, you can keep your little godling," Pasiphae continued, looking down her nose. "When *I* Call, it will be a being that rules over more than vines and wine."

Although she still said nothing and dropped her lids over her eyes to hide what she thought, Ariadne had some difficulty in swallowing laughter. If Dionysus came as he had promised and blessed the vines and the wine—if he brought back the sweet, smooth, potent beverage that Crete had once produced—it would be as if gold was fermented in the great pithoi. Not only the farmers and the vintners but the high nobles on whose estates they labored would bless her name. She would have no need to envy any priestess, no matter how powerful her god or goddess. Indifferent to her mother's jibe, Ariadne began to turn away.

"Where are you going?" Pasiphae snapped. "Take off that skirt. It looks as if you were rolling around the floor in it."

That shaft flew right by Ariadne also. She did not recognize it as a sexual jibe because her skirt had been soiled while the priestess's chamber was being cleared; in fact, the remark brought back the pleasant memory of how submissive the priests and priestesses had been when she ordered them to store and move the old priestess's possessions. But when Ariadne had untied the skirt and laid it across her bed, Pasiphae burst out laughing.

"Why, he didn't even make a woman of you!" she exclaimed.

Ariadne stiffened. She had forgotten that the blood that should have marked her maiden sacrifice did not stain her thighs, and Pasiphae had noticed she was clean.

"Have you never heard of washing, mother?" Ariadne turned away sharply and began to look for a clean skirt as if she were embarrassed and trying to cover it with boldness.

On the one hand, she didn't like to lie; on the other, if Pasiphae believed that she hadn't consummated her role as high priestess, her mother might begin to think again of usurping that role. Dionysus would kill her, Ariadne thought, and tried to cover her shudder with the act of tying her skirt. She mustn't let that happen. She might not love her mother, but she couldn't bear that Dionysus should have Pasiphae's blood on his hands. There would be a blood debt between them that could never be paid. Something squeezed her heart, and she was sure it was those flower petals, and that if Dionysus killed her mother they would never be able to open again.

"I have heard of washing," Pasiphae said, and Ariadne heard the smiling contempt in her voice, "but I don't think that's why your thighs are clean. However, I have a larger fish, a *much* larger fish that I hope to catch. That is why I want to know what you did—*exactly* what you did."

Mixed with Ariadne's relief was a new anxiety. *If the god Pasiphae calls doesn't come*, she thought, *she'll blame me for it.* "I'll tell you and show you, mother," she said slowly, "but don't you think you should learn the words and the ritual as I did from the scroll Daidalos found? What if I've slightly changed a gesture or slurred a word and when you learn them from me you exaggerate my fault until the chant or ritual is spoiled? Dionysus may be willing to overlook what a greater god will not."

Pasiphae eyed her coldly. "Perhaps, and perhaps it is your small mistakes that have perfected a chant and ritual that haven't summoned even your little godling since long before you were born. Show me."

Having made her excuse beforehand, Ariadne did as her mother commanded, repeating the words and the gestures she had been taught and listening while Pasiphae learned the chant and ritual. She had no bowl and no wine, of course, and when she came to that part she said, "Then you say the name of the god you wish to Call upon and you try to see his or her face inside your head—perhaps looking at the painting in the shrine will help—and then you say 'Come to me' and wish for the god to come. But remember, Dionysus said that not all priestesses can Call, and—"

Pasiphae's lips pursed and a gesture cut off the rest of what Ariadne intended to say. "If you can Call," Pasiphae said, "it is not possible that I cannot." She started toward the door, opened it but did not step out, and turned back. "Another thing. I hope you know that I still expect you to dance the Mother's ritual on Her day."

"But, mother—"

"No buts. There is no one else fitting to dance, and it doesn't require a virgin. Since I must sit on the throne, I cannot dance; your eldest sister, Euryale, has her own dancing floor to fill; Prokris is heavy with child; and Phaidra is too young and too clumsy. So you must dance."

"Mother, I love to dance—"

"Of course you do." Pasiphae interrupted her with a sneer. "Is it not said by all that in Knossos the dancing place was wrought by Daidalos for Ariadne of the lovely tresses—as if no one else ever danced there." And she stepped out and slammed the door behind her.

Ariadne stood looking at the painted wood, feeling as if she were caught between the upper and nether millstones. The upper millstone was the real pleasure she felt in dancing for the Mother. Not, as Pasiphae said, because it brought her praise . . . Well, Ariadne thought, sensitive now to the fact that what she truly felt might be perceived by a too-real deity, her love of dancing wasn't *entirely* because of the admiration. She liked that, she confessed to herself with a little prick of shame, but even more she liked the warmth that enveloped her, the feeling that an enormous but gentle hand lifted her hair and made it fly gracefully about her and with that flight her steps became light as feathers and her gestures fluid as air. And she loved the Mother, who was always to her associated with that gentle, enveloping warmth, a warmth she had never felt from her own mother.

She wanted to dance, but the lower millstone might rise against the upper and crush her. Would Dionysus permit her to worship another god? Most people did, of course, worship many gods, sacrificing to Poseidon for good fortune in fishing, to Aphrodite for a successful love affair, and to others for other purposes, but they were just people. She was Dionysus' high priestess, and he was a jealous god, easy to anger.

Within herself the petals of the flower were closed around her heart. Apparently when he wasn't with her, they couldn't help her touch Dionysus' feelings. But couldn't she ask him directly? She could go to the shrine and fill her gold cup with wine and Call him. Her lips curved and the lids dropped over her eyes. He said he would answer if she Called . . . and then the smile became tremulous and disappeared. He had said he would come, but he had also warned her not to Call for selfish purposes.

Was her desire to dance for the Mother selfish? Would Dionysus consider her mother's command trivial? Well, it might be to him, but how could *she* refuse? It wasn't only her mother who expected the praise-dance to be performed; the dance was part of a whole ritual that couldn't be completed without it.

Ariadne stood frowning in doubt, so close to the door that it almost hit her when it popped open. She stepped back sharply, drawing a breath and then let it out in a long sigh when her sister, Phaidra, came in.

"Are you all right?" Phaidra asked, wide-eyed. "I heard everyone talking about you. That the god really came? Is it true? What did he say? What did he do to you?"

"I am very well," Ariadne said, smiling. "Yes, the god really came. He did me no harm. He was kind and promised to come and bless the vines and the wine." She looked her sister up and down. "Did mother return to the court?"

"Yes. I ran up when I saw her come in." She

hesitated and then said, "Why are you looking at me so strangely?"

"I am thinking that you do not look so different from the way I did two years ago, and that was when mother had Prokris teach me the praise-dance for the Mother."

"Oh no!" Phaidra cried, backing away and reaching for the door behind her. "The dance is a quarter moon from now. You had moons and moons to learn it."

Ariadne grabbed her before she could get out of the door. "I am not saying that you must dance this time, but if my god learns of my worshiping the Mother and forbids me to dance again, then you will have to do it. Come, I will teach you."

"I have not even begun my courses yet," Phaidra protested. "I am not a woman. How can I dance for the Mother?"

"You're over eleven years old and your moon-times may come any day. Mine did before I was fully twelve. And as you said, it takes some time to learn the dance, so it will do no harm to begin early."

"I don't want to learn," Phaidra said, turning her head away. "If mother makes me a subpriestess—and what other place is there for me?—I will never get away from here. I will live and die at Knossos, under her hand."

CHAPTER 4

Ariadne woke in the morning with her problem unresolved. Should she Call Dionysus and ask if she would be permitted to dance for the Mother? Should she just dance and beg mercy if he disapproved? Oddly she didn't feel particularly frightened and her lack of fear gave her some reassurance that her god might not be jealous of the Mother. She would dance. But that brought a new problem to mind—Phaidra.

Despite her sister's protests, she had taught her the key movements of the dance, promising not to tell their mother that she had done so. Phaidra was stiff and about as graceful as a jointed wooden toy, but Ariadne suspected that was more because she was unwilling than because she was naturally ungraceful or the gestures were new or difficult. Still, she would make sure her sister practiced until she could create a praise-dance. It was unthinkable that there should be no lady of royal blood to dance for the Mother.

While Queen Europa was alive, although she didn't usually attend the ceremonies, it didn't matter. In an emergency, she could always have sat on the throne before the sacral horns and Pasiphae could have danced if Ariadne couldn't. Now there was no one. Prokris would be leaving Knossos as soon as her child was delivered and, like Ariadne's other sister, would have her own dancing floor.

Ariadne looked toward her sleeping sister and sighed. Phaidra seemed unable to accept Pasiphae's dominance. Ariadne herself had never minded that. If her mother had been loving to her, she would gladly have been her subpriestess, gladly taken to herself those duties that Pasiphae found dull or distasteful. She sighed again. Of course, Pasiphae was no more loving to Phaidra than to herself, but that didn't seem to be what troubled Phaidra. Too much like Pasiphae, Phaidra wanted to be first—not necessarily to rule Knossos, which she recognized was impossible for now and for the future, but to be a queen in her own right. Ariadne shook her head and slid out of bed. She could do nothing about that.

Pulling on a loose gown, she padded down the corridor to the toilet, emptying the jar of water into the drain to flush away the soil when she had relieved herself. When the rains came, one didn't have to bother, since the cisterns on the roof allowed a constant stream of water to flush the drains. The bathing room was across the corridor. Ariadne only used the bowl for washing her hands and face. She had taken a bath the day before and it wasn't yet hot enough to need to bathe every day or twice a day.

She returned to her room and sat down at the shelf of polished gypsum that protruded from the wall at table height. One end held Phaidra's toilet articles, the other her own, her comb and brush and, since yesterday's preparations, pots of kohl, lip salve and rouge, charcoal sticks, and a small bronze mirror. She didn't touch that, combing her hair by touch, until suddenly she paused and frowned. Then she lifted the bronze mirror, and looked in it uncertainly.

Should she just braid her hair as she always used to do . . . as if nothing had happened yesterday? No, that would be wrong. But Ariadne knew she could never achieve the convoluted style that her mother's hairdresser had produced. She shook her head. That didn't matter; such a style wouldn't be proper for an ordinary day. Pursing her lips, she pulled two thick locks forward of her ears and turned them round her finger, smoothing them with the brush until the hair lay in a smooth, shining coil. From each side of her forehead, she took much thicker strands and wove them into two braids. These she coiled atop her head and fixed in place with a few colored slivers of polished wood left over from yesterday's hairdressing. The remainder of her hair she allowed to flow freely down her back.

Dress. Lower lip between her teeth, Ariadne examined the contents of her chest and shook her head. She would need new clothing. Most of what she had was the short kilt that all children wore. That was no longer suitable. Now she would never train to be a bull dancer. She smiled. She no longer regretted that. She was a priestess. And that was part of the answer. There was cloth enough at the shrine, some of it very fine. She would look through the chests she had offered the priestesses, or . . . since she would never marry now, perhaps her father would offer her the clothes of a woman. Yes, she would try that first.

Meanwhile she chose the skirt she wore to practice dancing. It was as full and flounced as the dancing skirt, so that she would be accustomed to the weight and movement and not trip or stumble in the praise-dance, just not as rich in cloth or decoration. It would do very well for ordinary wear. She reached for a bodice, then hesitated and looked down, wrinkling her nose in dissatisfaction as she saw no more than the slight swelling around the nipples that had been there the day before. Leaving the bodices where they were, she just drew a shawl over her shoulders to ward off the morning chill and went out and along the corridor to the Southeastern Hall where the royal family ate.

On a shelf like that which held her toiletries near the door, there was porridge, rich with cream and sweetened with honey, plenty of dried fruit, bread and cheese and, of course, olives. Ariadne smiled fondly at the big bowl, more aware since she'd truly seen a god, of connections she'd always known existed but hardly thought about before. What would they do without the gifts of the sacred tree? That was a god manifest all the time, providing food and oil with so many purposes that she could hardly name them, and few appreciated it.

"Good morning . . . sister. May I still call you sister?"

Ariadne turned startled eyes to Androgeos, who had risen from his seat at the central table and come toward her, but he wasn't teasing. His expression was perfectly serious. Her instinct had been to laugh and say "Don't be ridiculous. I *am* your sister, so you may call me sister." But suddenly she remembered that

Androgeos, although much more loving than her mother, had always casually commanded her service as if that were her purpose in life. That, she realized, must end, He could no longer tell her to fetch and carry for him, to wash him, to bring food to him whenever he wanted. Often in the past he'd asked her to serve him and his friends when she had another task she wished to complete. He'd expected that she would always put his desire ahead of any other, and she'd done so, but now, if she had a duty at Dionysus' shrine, she could no longer do that.

"In love I'm still your sister," she replied. "Of my own will, I'd gladly serve you, but my own will isn't paramount. The god comes first."

"Why not?" Glaukos asked with a laugh. "It will save you a great deal of work."

"Be still, Glaukos," Androgeos ordered his younger brother sharply. "You weren't at the shrine. You didn't see Dionysus appear—just appear!—before his own painting. You didn't see silence enclose Ariadne and him at his gesture—we could see them speak but not hear a sound—and then a wall of black appear. . . . No, I'm glad, god-touched, she'll still call me brother."

"I'm not proud for myself, Glaukos," she said, after stepping forward and kissing Androgeos on the cheek. "I'll even bring you more breakfast if you desire it."

"Good. You can—"

"Lady Ariadne?"

The thin, timid voice made Ariadne turn and look at the doorway. In it stood a young page, his eyes so round the irises looked like ripe olives about to fall out of a white cup.

"Yes?" Ariadne asked.

"A priest has come, lady. You are needed at the shrine of Dionysus. He's waiting for you on the south porch."

"I'm coming," Ariadne said, a chill down her back.

Had Dionysus felt her decision to dance for the Mother and decided to forbid her? She turned and started out of the room.

"Holla, where do you go? You said you'd get me my breakfast," Glaukos cried.

Ariadne continued on her way without even the smallest hesitation in her stride. Glaukos rose, frowning, but Androgeos put a hand on his shoulder and kept him from following her.

"Don't be a fool," Androgeos said. "I tell you she is his, entirely. You mustn't touch her, command her, or deny her—ever. Don't you remember what happened to Pentheus, who sought to interfere with the worshipers of Dionysus?"

Glaukos shrugged. "You believe he was torn to bits by his own mother and her women? Surely that's a tale concocted by the man who usurped his throne or, perhaps, by the priests to bring more sacrifices to their shrines and keep any king from collecting his share of the spoils."

"Now I'll believe any tale of Dionysus," Androgeos said, and shuddered. "When he looked at us, after he had first seen how young Ariadne was, I felt a rage rise in me, a burning lust for blood. . . ." He swallowed. "What she did or said, I don't know—he'd already drawn a wall of silence around them—but he looked at her, and that need to kill suddenly left me. Glaukos, that mad rage was nothing of mine. I had no reason, no cause, for anger. That rage was *his*. Another hundred or two of heartbeats and I would've leapt at our father to tear out his throat."

"It was real, then?" Glaukos asked softly. "I had thought that our father and mother had played some trick. No one plays games with the Mother, but a little godling who's dear to the common people . . . I thought they'd set up a play to make the farmers and vintners more docile."

"That was no play," Androgeos said.

He walked to the open window from which he could see the end of the long sets of steps, built on two right angled turns, that climbed from the river to the south portico of the palace. There was a road from the bottom of the steps that made a curve and joined the main road, which went over the viaduct, passed the caravanserai, and then went on south, putting out a branch that went up Gypsades Hill. That was the shortest way to the shrine of Dionysus, but not used for formal processions because the south portico led to the domestic quarters and workshops of the palace, rather than the great reception chambers and religious shrines.

"She's hurrying up the hill," Androgeos said. "I hope he hasn't come again. In the end, I can't believe that any good can come of gods made manifest. Men should live their own small lives their own way. Divine help breeds more trouble than . . ."

"Oh, don't start on that bull again. Would you rather our father fought a war against our uncles?"

"Of course not, but I'd rather our father had cut that beautiful white neck with the sacrificial double axe and freed us from—"

"From what?" Glaukos asked with a shrug. "Even the priest of Poseidon has fallen silent. Let's see what kind of calves the cows drop. Then will be soon enough to speak again of sacrificing the bull from the sea."

When Ariadne reached the south porch, she stopped to draw a breath. The old priest looked rather dazed, but not frightened or horrified.

"Has Dionysus come again?" she asked quickly.

"No, Priestess," the old man said, "but I think everyone else in a day's walk of Knossos has, and every one of them has brought an offering. We have cows and bulls and goats and sheep, and grain and olives and wine—much better wine than we had before. But there's no room—"

"Hush," she said urgently, looking over her shoulder at the guards, but they didn't seem to be paying attention. Turning the priest toward the stairs and urging him to start down them, she spoke more loudly than necessary for ears so close. "I'll ask the god what to do. The offerings aren't ours. They belong to Dionysus. He must know that showing himself would bring forth a flood of sacrifices and he'll expect those sacrifices to be rendered up to him."

The priest, who had been very excited, nodded with a somewhat deflated air. Ariadne smiled at him. "I believe that Dionysus will allow us to keep a share," she said more softly. "But I prefer that only we know what's given to the shrine. Since it's our purpose to serve and protect the god's shrine, we'd be blamed if others thought we were growing too rich and seized what was offered."

"Then why did the god not come and take what he desired," the priest muttered. "We prayed and laid the sacrifices on the altar. The old priestess did no more."

"Yes, and the grapes rotted on the vine and the wine soured in the pithoi," Ariadne snapped. "Do you think a god has no more to do than pay attention to one shrine? He has hundreds, perhaps thousands of shrines, and in this season many must offer sacrifices, many priests and priestesses pray. And perhaps he didn't hear you. Dionysus told me that not all can Call him."

"Well, I suppose that's true, but what are we to do? The shrine is small. We have chickens in our eating chamber, rabbits and doves in the kitchen, goats and cows and bulls staked out in a gully. And we are two old women and two old men. How can we protect the god's offerings? Perhaps gods have no troubles with keeping things; perhaps they gesture and a new room appears."

"I'll Call and see if he will answer me."

It was all Ariadne had to offer, but she was shocked herself when she entered the small courtyard, which now contained six sheep, four pigs, a dozen geese, and casks and amphorae and bales containing indeterminate contents. She paused for a moment, staring around, thinking that Dionysus might not have realized, since he saw only the altar and courtyard and the high priestess's chambers, that the shrine was small. She wove a way through the goods and protesting animals and hurried to her own room.

Here she paused again, savoring for a moment the quiet and elegance. The room was lit softly by its deep window shaft. Dionysus' chair, footstool, and table sat nearest the light with the golden bowl Ariadne had used glowing softly on the table. A little distance away was a padded stool for her to sit on in the god's presence, and beyond that, near the other end of the room, a double bench red-cushioned with back and arms lacquered a deep crimson and painted over the lacquer with golden lilies. Low chairs of the same finish, with golden silken cushions, flanked the bench, and before it was a space now occupied by a knee-high table which could be replaced by a large brazier to give warmth in the winter. Around the walls, the carved and decorated chests, mostly done in sea scenes of blue and green and aqua, now lent contrast and interest instead of heightening the confusion. The floors had been polished to a high shine. The chamber breathed of peace and comfort.

Ariadne looked back through the open door and said to the priest, "Bring me a rhyton of the best wine."

She saluted the empty chair, remembering with a

blush that she had never shown Dionysus himself that mark of worship, then took the golden bowl and allowed the priest to fill it. Taking a deep breath, she looked down into the dark surface of the wine and Called, "Lord Dionysus, hear me."

Almost at once, his startled face appeared, the eyes too large and staring wildly. "Who? Who?" he cried.

"It is Ariadne, your high priestess of the shrine at Gypsades Hill, Knossos," she said to the wine.

"I have no scrying bowl," he said. "I can't see you. Didn't I warn you not to Call me for amusement? What do you want?"

His tone was sharp, but his eyes were half lidded again, and she saw they were heavy with sleep. A god needed a scrying bowl too? And if he did, couldn't he summon one to his hand? Then she wondered where he was, and to her amazement, his face became smaller and she could see his shoulders rising from the wildly tumbled bedclothes of a bed, carved and gilded . . . and half buried in the bedclothes behind him, a mass of long, blonde hair. She jerked eyes and mind away.

"Lord God," she breathed, "the people, having seen you, welcomed your return to Knossos, to Crete, with many offerings. This is a very small shrine. We are overrun by the devotion of your followers and we have no room to store the offerings. Can you come and choose and take what you want and give us leave to dispose of the rest?"

She saw him frown, start to make a gesture of negation, and then give a heavy sigh. "Do you of Crete do nothing in the afternoon?" he asked. "This is the second time you have waked me." And before she could think of an answer, he added, "Yes, I'll come and look. Where are you? I can't see."

"In the high priestess's chamber," Ariadne replied. "Wait for me by the altar."

He lifted his hand and Ariadne knew he was about to end her vision of him. "My lord," she said hastily, "we have better food and better wine to offer, if you wish to break your fast here."

The frown and uncertainty disappeared from his face and he laughed. "Yes," he said, and gestured, and the wine went dark and blank.

Ariadne drank the wine in the bowl, then turned to the priest, who was staring at her with dilated eyes. She suppressed both a sigh of relief and a desire to say "so there" to him. Plainly the old man had been recovering from whatever awe the priestesses, who had actually seen Dionysus, had woken in him. She didn't know whether he had seen or heard the god in the scrying bowl, but he had heard her answer Dionysus' questions and was now afraid she *could* Call the god. Until he was sure, doubtless he would be obedient.

"Seek through the offerings of the past and of yesterday. Find some fine platters. Place on those the very best-eating pieces of hard cheese and thin sliced bread spread with the soft cheese, olives both ripe and oil-cured—and a second platter with honey cakes. You had better find a large platter or heap a smaller one high. He ate all the honey cakes last time and could have eaten more, I think. And the best wine. Bring it here and set it on the table where the golden bowl stood. That is his chair." She handed the priest the bowl. "Wash this and put it on the low table. Seek out the best. The best of everything we have."

He saluted and went out and she on his heels. He went quickly down the corridor to the lesser priests' and priestesses' quarters, she went to stand beside the altar. She didn't know how long Dionysus would take, but she suspected only a few moments because he said he would break his fast at the shrine. She took the time she had to tuck her shawl more firmly into the tight belt of her skirt. Her waist was starting to narrow, giving a hint of feminine curvature to her hips. If she hid her chest with its nonexistent breasts . . . And then she remembered the blonde hair, which must have belonged to a woman in his bed. Her lips tightened, but before she could form any definite thoughts, Dionysus was there.

He was simply there, where he hadn't been a heartbeat before, standing before the painting. Ariadne heard a muffled gasp and a kind of whimper. She assumed it must be the priests or priestesses peeking through their door, but her eyes were fixed on Dionysus. This time his face wasn't expressionless; it wore a look of utter befuddlement as he stared around the littered courtyard and at the cackling geese, the bleating sheep, the squealing pigs. The expression, completely ungodlike, was so comical that Ariadne again forgot to salute him and found her awe at his sudden appearance less overwhelming than at his disappearance the previous day. The woman in his bed vanished completely from her mind. Slowly, without pain, the flower around her heart opened to welcome him.

"But why?" he asked. "This never happened when I came to my old priestess's Call. Only on a special festival were so many offerings made."

The mist of tendrils touched him, brought back to her puzzlement and a hint of satisfaction. She smiled. "Because you have been long absent," the "woman" Ariadne said. "Be cause the grapes and the wine have lost the legendary perfection they had in the past. Because they know I'll ask you to bless the grapes and the wine and each is afraid that, if he doesn't sacrifice, you'll skip over his vines or his fermenting casks and storage pithoi."

"They think I know each and every one of them?"

That betrayed that he didn't but Ariadne wouldn't

hurt her dear god by showing her knowledge of that weakness. It didn't matter to her that he was not all-powerful and all-knowing as other gods claimed to be. He was hers, and—she recalled that contagious madness—quite powerful enough.

"They *fear* you know every one of them."

He brought his eyes from the courtyard and looked at her and smiled. "You are just as pretty without all that paint on your face," he said. Then he looked back at the courtyard.

"There are cattle and goats too, my lord," Ariadne said. "They are tethered outside the shrine. I also need to know whether you want any of the furniture that was in the high priestesses' chamber. I set aside the most precious things, some goblets of well-bejeweled gold and two ivory tables."

He shook his head. "I am half asleep and half deafened by the noise. I cannot think."

"Come then to my chamber, my lord. Food and drink for breaking your fast will be there, and you can sit in your chair and decide."

In the doorway he paused, and she felt his satisfaction again even before he turned and smiled approval at her. Then he walked across to the chair, sat down, and lifted the cup of wine standing ready. He sipped the wine and shrugged, gestured at the cup and the flagon that stood on the table, and drank more freely. Ariadne guessed he had changed the quality of the drink.

"It is the best Crete can produce since we somehow offended you," she said. "The offerings, they are meant to appease that hurt."

He looked past her around the room that now presented quiet comfort, reached out absently for the food. As he bit into the bread and cheese, chewed an olive, he shrugged again. "That was unfair, perhaps. The little folk did nothing to hurt me. I had thought my priestess rejected me, but even after I learned it was no fault of hers, that she had died, I wouldn't come to Knossos. I suppose the 'blessing' eroded from the soil in the years of my neglect."

"But you will restore it, my lord?"

"Yes. I've already promised and you—little thorn in my flesh—I'm sure won't allow me to forget."

"I don't mean to be a thorn in your flesh, my lord."

He laughed merrily around a mouthful of honey cake. "No? Then don't call me so early in the morning."

That reminded Ariadne of the woman in his bed, but she didn't dare say that if he hadn't been disporting himself all night he wouldn't have found her call early. Instead she said meekly, "I'm very sorry. I thought it unwise to have so many offerings in the open. And we have no feed for the animals nor anyone to care for them. The priests and priestesses are old."

He didn't answer at once, going on with his breakfast, mostly honey cakes and wine now, with a thoughtful frown. At last he said, "Get rid of the furniture you have in the storage room. Sell it and get another storage room cut into the hill. That should be place enough for the new offerings. The animals will have to be slaughtered and butchered. You may keep what you like and what you think you can use, either alive or butchered parts."

"Do you want the flesh salted down?"

"No, I'm not fond of salt meat."

Ariadne blinked. "But there are cows and bulls, goats and sheep and pigs, not to mention the fowl. I'll place it all on the altar if you desire, but it will have to be taken by tomorrow or the next day at the latest. It's growing warm and the flesh will rot."

"You must bespell it to stasis."

"Stasis? What's that? And I know no spells, Lord Dionysus. I dance for the Mother, but I'm no witch."

"Stasis is like freezing, but not cold. Everything stops. If you bespell a haunch of meat to stasis, the blood does not ooze from it and it won't rot so long as the spell lasts."

"But I don't know the spell," she said, her voice beginning to tremble, "and I have never cast a spell in my life."

"I can give you the spell," he said. "We'll see if you can take it and then cast it."

Ariadne stared at him, her breath fluttering between her parted lips. Spells! If it hadn't been for the misty tendrils, which brought from him such a sense of pleasant indifference, as if what he proposed was the most ordinary thing in the world, she might have collapsed, weeping. Ordinary for gods, her mind said, but not for me. Only she remembered that she wouldn't be alone. Some priests and priestesses had powers of healing or could see the future. And Daidalos could do things that seemed impossible. Maybe she would be able to do such things also.

"Watch my mouth," Dionysus said, and allowed his lips to part slightly.

Between them Ariadne saw a silvery shadow. It was different from her tendrils, harder and brighter looking, but not rigid. It oozed from between his lips and began to form a bubble, as babies sometimes formed bubbles of their own spit, but this grew larger and held its shape firmly until it was a ball as large as she could cup in her hand. He gestured her to him and she went, reluctantly, knowing that he desired her to sip that ball out of his mouth although he hadn't told her. Eyes wide, shaking her head slightly and hoping he would change his mind, she knelt before him. He leaned forward and took her head in his hands. Her lips parted to cry a protest, but he lowered his head too quickly and the silver bubble touched her mouth.

It was nothing like what she had imagined, not cold or wet or slimy. It was warm and tingled very faintly, and it didn't fill her mouth or choke her. Indeed, it didn't seem to have any tangible substance and seemed to dissipate as it slipped through her lips so that her mouth met his. She felt him smile when their lips touched, and his tasted only of honey cake and wine. Forgetting the silver ball, she would gladly have held him to her, mouth to mouth, but he lifted his head promptly.

"Inside you there is a place that's different—"

"The flower around my heart? How did you know of that?"

He laughed. "Gods know." Then he sobered and shook his head. "Not everything, and even what we know we sometimes don't understand. But leave that aside for now. All those who have Power have some place, see or feel it in some way."

"See it? The mist of tendrils. Is that Power?"

"That's the way you see it. Now look at the special place within you from which the mist comes. There should be a bright spot—"

"A little bud!" Her voice came out rather high with surprise and delight. It was such a pretty thing, nestled close to her heart just where two of the petals of the heartflower met.

"You are a very quick learner, Ariadne," Dionysus said.

He seemed pleased and Ariadne banned all the reluctance she had initially felt about becoming a witch. Daidalos had once offered to teach her magic, but he was a frightening person. Dionysus, who, she realized, should have been even more frightening, was to her a most seductive teacher.

"You make the lessons easy," she replied.

"You have the art. There's almost no need for lessons. However, it's dangerous to play with what you don't understand, so I'll teach you and hope you don't begin to try to create new spells—"

Ariadne shook her head. "You needn't worry about that. My Power, if I have any, is bound to you. The heartflower only opens when you're near me." She frowned. "I didn't think of that. It may be that I won't be able to cast any spell if you aren't near."

"We'll see," he said. "Now look at your little bud. Will it to grow larger."

She did as he said, surprised to see the mist nearest the bud float toward it and enwrap it. The bud grew swiftly and when Dionysus told her to break it off, she did so.

"Now, quick," he said, "before the place seals over, desire a new bud to grow but leave that one small."

That was harder. The mist was already thin, and Ariadne felt as if her chest were all hollow and ice coated that emptiness. Her heartbeat slowed. She was about to cry that she could not, when Dionysus laid his hand upon her breast. A touch of warmth flowed from his hand; it didn't fill the hollow, but she no longer felt as if she were falling in upon herself. She looked up and his eyes caught hers and held them. His will caught hers, bound it, bent it. And then, there was another bud, tiny but perfect, where the first had grown . . . and Ariadne knew how to grow as many more as she would ever need. She wasn't given time to consider that.

"Where's the large bud?" Dionysus asked. His eyes were gem-bright, his voice hard as flint.

So weak and trembling that she would have sunk down, except that the hand on her breast seemed to hold her upright on her knees, gaze still locked with her god's, Ariadne "looked" within her, without moving her eyes, and found the ball of light.

"Place your hand beneath your breast. Will the spell to flow out into your hand."

She uttered a tiny whimper, expecting the ball of light to rip through bone and flesh and skin and leave a gaping, bleeding wound, but she couldn't tear her eyes from his, couldn't thrust away his demand. And his will grasped hers, shaped it, pointed it. Trembling and crying, eyes unmoving, Ariadne "saw" the ball of light touch her chest, just between her barely swelling breasts, and with only the faintest sensation of chill, slip out into her hand.

Dionysus pulled his hand away and Ariadne was able to move her eyes. Unbelieving, she looked down, and there on her hand lay a silver ball of light. Of course she knew she would see it just as clearly if her eyes were closed or if she were still looking at her god's face, but that she could see it there, trembling a little as her hand shook, gave her an odd joy.

"Cut it in half," Dionysus ordered, "and then in half again."

With a knife? she wondered. How did one cut in half a ball of light that wasn't really there? And suddenly she knew it didn't matter. She could create a knife in her mind, or she could imagine ghostly fingers pinching the spell in half or she could just "will" the division. Because she thought it more elegant, she "made" a little knife and sliced the spell apart, and as it started to join together, she told it firmly to remain in two parts. Two smaller balls of light lay on her hand and she cut each of those in half with the knife also.

"Drop one part of the spell on what remains of the cheese, the bread, and the honey cakes, and say with each, '*Anagkazo teleia stigme stasis*.' Then take the last piece back within you. You can just close your hand on it and will it back into your well of power."

The food on the table was out of her reach, and she had no idea how to will the spell there so she tried to get to her feet. She couldn't; she was cold and sweating and her legs had no more strength than the jelly around cooked fish. She gasped and tried again. This time Dionysus caught her free hand and lifted her up. Oddly, there was no pull on her arm; the feeling as she rose had much in common with the way she grew light when the Mother lifted her hair.

That reminded her that she must tell Dionysus about her need to dance on the Mother's day, but she didn't dare divert her thoughts from the words she needed to say so she first went to the table and pushed a little ball of light onto the plate of cheese. "*Anagkazo teleia stigme stasis*," she said, and repeated the words twice more. With each repetition she grew colder and weaker, but she thought she had cast the spell successfully because each portion of food became surrounded by the faintest shimmering. Still, she would have fallen had not Dionysus supported her.

"Take back the last part," he reminded her.

Ariadne closed her hand slowly and was fascinated by the "taking back" of what remained of the spell, watching, first with her eyes and then with her eyes closed, as the last portion shrank between her fingers until it was gone. She felt a little warmer, a little less hollow as the silver light disappeared, and when Dionysus urged her toward the stool she was able to walk there, but she sat down rather heavily.

"It will grow easier with practice," Dionysus said. "The use of Power is like any other sport or labor. Practice improves performance."

That was true, Ariadne thought, with a sense of relief. She had thought she would die of exhaustion when she had begun to learn to dance for the Mother, but . . . "Oh," she cried, "I am yours first and wholly, but I have long done the praise-dance for the Mother on Her days. Lord God, may I continue to dance for

Her?" He stared at her, frowning, and she hurried on. "There is no one else. My mother must sit between the sacral horns as Her image, my older sisters—" He lifted his hand, and she stopped, biting her lip.

"You dance for the Mother?" he asked.

"Yes, lord," she whispered.

He seemed uncertain, looking at her and then out of the window shaft. Ariadne couldn't see what caught his eye, but he turned back to her abruptly and said, "Worship of the Mother is always permitted. You may also ask Her to fill your well with Power. When do you dance?"

"In six . . . no, five days. Oh, thank you, for your kindness and understanding, my lord. It would be dreadful if there were no one of the royal blood to dance for Her."

He didn't respond to that, saying instead, "When the offerings are prepared and laid upon the altar, Call me." Then he smiled at her. "But *not* in the early morning."

And he was gone.

CHAPTER 5

The next five days Ariadne was so busy with her duties at Dionysus' shrine and so exhausted that she returned to Knossos only to tumble into bed and sleep. She had discovered that she could use the spell Dionysus had given her even though the flower around her heart was closed. The bright bud clung to the outer part of the petals and she could make it grow and renew itself.

She also managed to find the power to place the spell of stasis on the slaughtered offerings, but the toll on her was terrible. By the end of each day she was chilled and shaking. The day before she was to dance, she Called Dionysus— just before sunset—and he said she must clear the shrine of all but the offerings, staying in her chambers and forbidding the priests and priestesses and the new novices, three boys and three girls offered by their parents, to leave the chambers assigned to them.

In the morning, a round-eyed little boy had come to her bedchamber to tell her that everything had disappeared, the meat, the gutted fowls, the ivory tables and jeweled cups, the casks of cheese and the pithoi of wine and oil. Ariadne sent him back with her approval and with the message that she would not come to the shrine that day. Then she pulled the blanket over her head and tried to go back to sleep, wondering how she would find the strength to dance.

She had the whole day because the praise-dance would begin when the long rays of evening sunlight lay across the dancing floor. She would dance into the dusk and then again as the full moon rose—if she could. Her doubts increased through the day; even a second blanket and a footwarmer couldn't drive out the chill inside her. She was too tired to get out of bed and too weak to eat much, even when Phaidra brought the food to her.

Midafternoon she rose at last, heavy-eyed and unwilling, because she knew how long it would take to dress. Having her hair coiled and combed was torture and she had to cling to the wall and brace her trembling knees when the dancing skirt, its thirty dark red flounces all embroidered in gold and black, was fastened around her waist. The bodice didn't add much weight, but the gold thread apron pulling at her, bowing her forward, almost seemed the last straw.

They let her sit to paint her face. The bronze mirror showed her features so drawn that she didn't need the paint the maids were applying to make her look older. She felt a single prick of surprise that no one remarked on her dull silence. She had always been eager and excited to dance for the Mother. That thought was overridden by the fact that Pasiphae would have a fit, but Ariadne was too tired to care even about that, and when Pasiphae came she said nothing at all beyond, "Are you ready?"

She hardly seemed to see Ariadne. In a way that was nothing new, Pasiphae had never cared what Ariadne felt or thought, but in the past she had always been alert to anything that might spoil an act of worship in which she played the role of the goddess. Now Pasiphae seemed indifferent to Ariadne and her performance but not dull or ill. She looked excited, even feverish, however the intensity was all turned inward toward some purpose of her own.

"It's time, let us go," Pasiphae added.

Ariadne levered herself to her feet, wondering dully whether Dionysus had known this would happen, had wanted her to be unfit for the praise-dance so she would disgrace herself and become unwelcome to the Mother. Tears dimmed her eyes as she followed Pasiphae to the grand stair where Minos and the noble boys and girls of the dance chorus were waiting. She took her place just behind her mother and father, foremost of the dancers. When she looked down the stairs, a wave of dizziness swept over her and she swayed. A hand caught her arm and steadied her.

I love Dionysus, she thought, but I love the Mother too. May I not show that love? A little spurt of anger, a little thrill of resentment, because she could never follow her own heart gave her some strength, and she started down the stair. I will not give in, she thought. I will show that my heart is large enough to hold both. And upheld by a stubborn will to have done her duty to Dionysus and still praise the Mother, she walked steadily behind Pasiphae across the bull court, through the passage, down the ramp, and the few hundred paces to the steps down to the dancing floor.

The steps themselves and the rising ground around the dancing floor were crowded with people, except for the aisle beside the sacral platform which she and the dancers would take down to the dancing floor. The watchers rose to their feet and saluted as the procession of "god" and "goddess" and performers came into sight. Ariadne hesitated, imagining the surprise and scorn on all those now-respectful faces when she staggered and stumbled. If she could have, she would have turned away, but the other dancers were a solid wall behind her. Eyes fixed on nothing, blind with shame and fear, she stepped and stepped again.

The sun was just gilding the tops of the trees to the west. Dionysus shook his head and gestured irritably as a slave proffered a bowl of fruit. The boy drew it back at once and left the room hastily. Dionysus looked down at the polished table. He was mad, and he made everyone near him mad also. When the rage came, he couldn't . . . But before despair could grip him and rage follow despair, he remembered that Ariadne could divert him. Only it was because of Ariadne that he was angry now.

The word made him pause and think and gave him a sense of relief. Yes, he was angry, but not mad. He had no impulse to rend and tear and would not transmit that impulse to any other. He was angry over a real thing, because he wanted to see Ariadne dance, and knew he shouldn't want it.

Why couldn't he just think of her as he thought of the others, if he thought of them at all, as a good priestess, willingly passing all the sacrifices to him? The meat and other offerings Hermes had collected from the shrine had permitted him to pay back a lot of favors. Not that he ever lacked trading points. All the mages liked wine, and that he had from many shrines, but this bounty, not marked with the stamp of his Gift, he had given freely as presents.

Well, he thought, grinning suddenly, perhaps not totally free. A jeweled cup had brought Aphrodite to his bed. Not that he had expected or even hoped that would happen when he gave her the cup. It was meant as a "thank you" for her many kindnesses. Of all the great mages, Aphrodite alone didn't fear him, didn't ask what he wanted as soon as he arrived so she could be rid of him the sooner. Perhaps because there was no violence in her that he could rouse, perhaps because she understood what he did—if not why he did it. She, after all, also used what was within a person to punish and manipulate.

He sighed gently. No, not even Aphrodite, so like him in her ability to use emotion as a weapon or a reward, was able to understand why. Only Ariadne felt what he felt and could soothe him. Aphrodite . . . Ariadne . . . No, Ariadne was only a child. But Aphrodite looked little more than a child herself. He smiled, doubts and fears forgotten for the moment.

That coupling had been a revelation, a warm and laughing joy, as different from the orgiastic rutting of his worshipers with him and each other as beasts were from men. And yet he didn't desire to renew his pleasuring with Aphrodite. Even when he laughed with her and loved her he was a little repulsed. He was a jealous creature; he needed a lover who was his only, and Aphrodite, wonderful as she was, couldn't even comprehend the idea. She was perfectly promiscuous . . . and she couldn't drive Ariadne from his mind. He could dwell on coupling with Aphrodite, but he still wanted to see Ariadne dance.

Why shouldn't he? Dionysus thought. He would harm no one . . . except possibly himself. But that was his own affair. He would do better this time. He wouldn't roam the fields and woods and cities drawing men and women into wild excess to assuage his grief. He knew now the bacchanals couldn't help. And it would be many, many years before this Ariadne died.

He stood abruptly and walked out of the dining chamber of his house into the megaron and then out onto the gleaming marble portico. Here he paused, looking down the street of close-fitted stone to the open square dominated by his father's house, grander than all the others. Why not? He laughed and strode out.

He thought back to his coming to Olympus as he walked. Hekate had brought him there and presented him to Zeus. How she had known or guessed that he was Zeus' son, Dionysus had no idea. He suspected his mother, Semele, had told her when she found herself with child. If she had sought Hekate's protection, either it had failed or Hekate had refused her help. Semele had been buried in a heap of gold only days after Dionysus had been born and had been sacrificed to Hades, god of the Underworld.

Whether Hekate had felt guilt over Semele's fate or was simply curious, Dionysus knew she had kept an eye on him—and Dionysus was very grateful for it. When he reached puberty and the Visions began, he would have gone mad without her steadying assurances and explanations. She could not interpret those dreams and visions or free him from them, as Ariadne could, but she had been able to assure him that he was not mad and make clear what was dream and what was real. Then she had fled her father's malice and Dionysus had been left to struggle with his growing power alone, until one day Hekate was there again, holding out her hand and saying she had found his father, who would welcome him to a new home.

Dionysus grinned as he reached the great hammered bronze doors of Zeus' palace. Doubtless Zeus sadly regretted sending that welcome to Olympus with Hekate—more the fool he for being so eager to spite his wife that he did not more carefully examine what kind of a son he had fathered—but it was too late now.

The double doors were open, as they most often were during the day, and Dionysus walked in. A servant scurried to his side and asked how he could help him.

"I want to see my father," he said.

"Of course," the servant said. "Come with me."

That was what everyone said to him. "Of course," they said, and gave him what he asked for, and waited for him to go. Dionysus felt a flash of heat. The servant cringed.

"Tell him where I am," Dionysus said, and went into the nearest empty chamber.

Zeus came in moments. "What is the matter, Dionysus?" he asked.

"Nothing is the matter," Dionysus said. "I want to be a Cretan for a few hours."

"A transformation?" Zeus asked, the tenseness in his arms and shoulders relaxing. "Just for this once or will you want to use the form again?"

Dionysus looked away. "I shouldn't use it again, but likely I will."

Zeus laughed, relief in the sound. "A woman," he said, and smiled with knowing and pleasure. He went to the door and called out, "Bring me a scrying bowl," and when the servant came with it, he handed it to Dionysus. "Show me what you want to look like," he said, "and give the form a name."

At the sacral platform the procession halted. The crowd raised their voices, invoking the presence of the deities inside the bodies of their avatars. Minos and Pasiphae faced the celebrants and sang the ritual responses. Waiting beyond her father and mother, Ariadne swayed, tried to brace her knees and, feeling them tremble, at last yielded to her weakness. She tried to call out, to say she was unfit to dance, but a burst of ritual chant from the celebrants drowned out her breathless voice. In that moment, the dancers turned and pressed her forward again.

And then, deliverance! As soon as Ariadne's bare feet touched the smooth stones of the sacred place, warmth rose in her, steadying her legs, firming the muscles of her thighs, tightening her belly, pulling breath into her chest, and making her arms strong and lithe. Shock and joy uplifted her; she felt dizzy with reprieve, ready to leap down the steps and begin to whirl about and laugh, but that would have been as shocking to those who came to worship the Mother as to have her stumble and stagger. She had to grit her teeth and bite her lips against a fit of giggling.

Habit held her to the ritual. She stopped at the bottom of the stair and faced the sacral platform, the other dancers behind her. Raising fist to forehead, she saluted, waiting for Pasiphae with Minos at her side to take their places on the seats before the great horns, symbolic both of the horns of the growing moon, which promised the Mother's care and, in the horns of the bull, the virility of the male god.

King and queen, "god" and "goddess," they seated themselves in the full light of the westering sun. From the four corners of the dancing floor, first one priestess and then another raised her sistrum, black flounced skirts embroidered in red and gold, breasts jutting proudly, hair bound high in gold headdresses. Utter silence fell as the bell-toned rattles sounded, coming together into a rhythm that caught the breath and made the heart pound in time. Between the corners of the dancing floor stood the priests. Each raised his flute to his lips, and a lilting melody soon wove in and between the sound of the sistra.

Smiling now, Ariadne dropped her arm from its salute. Slowly she paced to the center of the dancing floor, struggling against the need to march in time with the music and keep to the sliding glide of the votary. Not yet, she told herself, not yet. At the center of the floor she stopped and waited for the other dancers to weave a pattern around her, right and left. When they were placed, she turned, foremost among them again, to face the sacral platform, and slowly raised her arms, palms upward, toward the "god" and "goddess."

In a heartbeat she felt as if her hands were full of feather-light ribbons. She had always felt that, but today she could "see" them, gossamer bands of golden light. She threw them up and stepped forward into the cascade. Now she let the music engulf her. The Goddess caught her hair. She whirled and leapt in the joyous greeting of recognition, the ribbons winding and weaving around her body. Having greeted, she paused, the dancing chorus moving around her in decorous steps of submission and pleading. Returned to their places, the dancers were still, leaving the praise to music alone; then Ariadne began the dance of life. In the rich afternoon light, she bent and swayed, gestured and leapt, miming birth and growth, work and rest.

As the light faded into evening the beat of the sistra slackened, the flute song grew fainter. Ariadne's steps slowed and the ribbons fell more softly but glowed all the brighter as she portrayed also love and death, all that the Mother provides, sinking, as darkness fell, to lie curled on the ground.

The ribbons encased her as a shroud, but their golden touch was warm and soft, not binding. Ariadne did not struggle against the Mother's caress; she simply lay, waiting for the moon to rise. Around her, singers formed a crescent moon, one horn male, the other female, and raised their voices. The men chanted the first plea of the ritual. Pasiphae answered. Then the women sang. Minos, playing the role of the young god, replied to them, turned to the "goddess" and wooed her. She responded. The chorus sang the old, old tale of the slow yearly seasons, of the quicker cycles of death and rebirth of the moon.

Ariadne in her golden shroud smiled. Waiting in joy for when she would dance the welcome to the Mother as the new day began with the moonrise, she felt the golden bands become part of her. The flower around her heart opened, and each petal was edged in golden light. Dionysus? she thought. And back to her, but very faintly, like a murmur meant not to disturb, came his whisper; this was the Mother's time and Ariadne must think of Her. Joy added to joy. Although she didn't move, she felt as if, if she desired, she could will herself to float off the ground and into the sky.

When the moon cast a brilliant, silvery light into the hollow of the dancing place, she unfolded herself from her fetal curl, swayed on her knees, letting her arms and fingers speak of the wonder of hope, of the endless renewal. She danced the welcome, danced in joy, light-footed, light-hearted, for once free of all doubt and fear. And when the ritual was complete, and she stood at the center of the floor again, saluting the figures on the sacral platform, she dared to look for Dionysus.

She couldn't find him. All the celebrants were Cretans, dark, handsome perhaps, but not one burned with the golden brilliance of the sun. She was hardly disappointed. The warning that this was the Mother's time implied that he would not show himself. It was a generosity she hadn't expected and made her glad, even though she was denied his presence. But he had been there; he had seen her dance and approved; she was sure of that.

At the top of the steps, Ariadne saluted the "god" and "goddess" again and she was free. Most of the dancers were swallowed into the crowd as relatives greeted them and praised their performance. Ariadne gladly slipped away. She had no desire to join the celebration that followed. She had celebrated with her whole heart and was replete. She went back to her chamber enwrapped in warmth, secure in the power the Mother had given to her, sated with delight.

The next morning Ariadne woke very early but, knowing her duties at the shrine were few and light, didn't get out of bed and drifted off to sleep again full of contentment. It was her stomach, clapping against her backbone and groaning dismally of her neglect, that finally induced her to rise. Her clothes chest produced only a sigh. The practice skirt was draggled, even stained with blood from some of the offerings on which she had not imposed stasis quickly enough. She would lay it across the chest for one of the slaves to collect and clean. The consecration skirt had been cleaned and stored, but it was crazy to wear so elaborate a white skirt for a common day's work.

Prodded by hunger, Ariadne shrugged and put on a kilt. It might not be dignified enough for her new station in life, but she had nothing else. Good. Today she would have time to tell that to her father and ask for her woman's dowry. She would never have a husband so the dowry could outfit the priestess. Considering whether she should just ask outright or make a more calculated approach and if so what kind, Ariadne went to the toilet, washed, combed her hair, and made her way to the eating hall, which was almost empty.

However, to her surprise, Phaidra was there. Usually their mother had duties for her daughters—like overseeing the household slaves or carrying messages to the craftsmen in the workrooms—when they were not engaged by their tutors in lessons. Ariadne had expected that Phaidra would be twice as busy because of her own work at Dionysus' shrine. She hadn't had a chance to urge her sister to practice the praise-dance, and perhaps it wasn't necessary now, but life was uncertain. What if she fell or was taken ill? If Phaidra had free time, she would go over the movements with her.

Ariadne took her breakfast and went to sit beside her sister. As she approached, however, she realized how dejected Phaidra's posture was and saw that her eyes were red and her lips downturned. Guilt stabbed Ariadne. She hadn't been idling over the last week, but her labor, no matter how exhausting, had been full of a rich satisfaction. Phaidra had been doing double duty for a thankless and ungrateful taskmistress.

"Oh, sister," Ariadne sighed, sinking down beside Phaidra. "I'm sorry to have left you with all the work of the palace. I swear, I hadn't a moment to spare from the god's service. But now the work of the shrine is mostly finished and I can help you."

"I have nothing to do," Phaidra said dully.

Ariadne, prepared to hear a long list of woes, choked on the bite of cheese she had taken. "Nothing?" she gasped, when she had controlled her coughing. "Then why are you weeping? I thought you were overworn."

"I'm afraid," Phaidra whispered.

"Afraid!" Ariadne repeated, also in a whisper, although there was no one close enough to hear. "What's happened?"

"Nothing has happened," Phaidra replied, keeping her voice very low, and shuddering convulsively, "but something will, soon . . . something terrible."

"Oh, Phaidra," Ariadne sighed, shaking her head with exasperation, "you're frightening yourself with boggles again. Why do you take such pleasure in doom and gloom? You nearly frightened me to death. Why do you think something terrible will happen?"

"Because Daidalos is so angry, I think he's ready to bring down the palace. Because mother, who hates Daidalos, has spent all ten-day in his workroom urging him on to some task he is unwilling to perform. Because Daidalos went to father and told him he must curb mother, but though he looks as if his guts are being torn out, father still ordered Daidalos to create what mother demanded. No one is allowed in the workroom but mother and Daidalos—even Icarus has been cast out."

Ariadne shrugged over Phaidra's first sentence and went on eating calmly. Daidalos was always angry. He had come to father's protection because of a blood feud in his own land, one he said was unjust. Minos had agreed to protect him, but at a price—that he would create, by craft and by magic, any artifact Minos desired. Possibly Daidalos had thought he would be treated as a royal exile with nothing to do but live off his host's fat and enjoy himself. Instead, he found his place little above any of the other palace craftsmen, and he resented Minos' demands. In fact, the only task Ariadne remembered him doing with good will was the creation of the dancing floor.

Phaidra's second sentence moved Ariadne little more than the first. She made an indistinct sound of comfort around the olive meats she was chewing and took a swallow of wine. Pasiphae and Daidalos didn't like each other, but both knew on which side of the bread the cheese had been spread. They would work together if necessary. When Phaidra spoke of Minos' behavior, however, Ariadne put down the cheese into which she was preparing to bite and frowned. And what Phaidra said of Icarus drew an exclamation of concern from her. Icarus was Daidalos' son, a fine artificer in his own right, and an eager student of any new craft or magic that Daidalos used.

"I tell you mother is going to do something terrible and father isn't going to stop her." Phaidra shuddered again and sobbed. "When I asked her who was required to pay his duty before seed corn was issued to him, she laughed and said 'Give it to all of them. Soon I'll have a stronger rod to make them obey me than issuing corn.' And her face . . ."

"Oh, dear gods," Ariadne whispered. "I think perhaps she tried to Call a god—one of the great ones, like Zeus or Hera or, maybe the Mother Herself—she told me she intended to do that. I think the god would not reply, and now she's making Daidalos do something that she thinks will force the god to answer her." She took Phaidra's hands in hers and sat hold ing them, thinking. Then she said, "But what could Daidalos do to compel a *god*? If he had that power, surely father would have demanded that he compel Dionysus to come when some years the vines started to die and the wine would not ferment sweet."

"I don't know," Phaidra breathed. "But I'm afraid."

"Where are Androgeos and Glaukos? Perhaps if they spoke to father—"

"He sent them away. Two days ago, he sent them to the west to catch a bull."

"A *bull*! Oh, this must be to do with that accursed white bull." Ariadne bit her lip. "Father never let mother do anything really bad or dangerous, and he was as just and honest as Hades himself . . . before that bull came to shore." Now she shuddered. "I remember when I came back from the shrine and tried to tell them that Dionysus had warned me that the bull must die, mother stopped me and turned my warning into a sign of the god's favor. And anything to do with the bull means Poseidon. Oh, dear, Dionysus said that one was better off not meddling with Poseidon."

"Can I hide in the shrine with you?" Phaidra asked.

That surprised Ariadne so much that she uttered a choke of laughter. "Silly," she said, "how can the shrine protect us?" Then the sense of her own words came to her and she shivered. "If Poseidon grows angry at mother and decides to shake the earth, perhaps the shrine wouldn't collapse. It's carved of solid rock . . . No, Phaidra, think of all the people that would be hurt and killed or lose all their livelihood. We must try to find out what mother is doing, and—"

"And what?" Phaidra asked bitterly. "If father won't interfere, how can we?" She began to cry again. "Won't your god protect you?"

"I don't think so," Ariadne admitted. "He warned me already not to Call him for my personal troubles and said specially not to meddle with Poseidon. But Daidalos likes me."

"What good is that?" Phaidra's voice grated. "He likes Icarus better and wouldn't tell him what he's doing."

"Yes, but if he feels what he's doing may call down a god's anger, he might send Icarus away to protect him. He wouldn't care that much about me. He might want to complain to me about our mother. I'll try. The worst that can happen is that he'll send me away."

Since her appetite had been killed by the little she had eaten and the anxiety her conversation with Phaidra had generated, Ariadne rose without ado and went down the nearest stair. Passing the veranda that provided the artisans with a place to sit in the shade during their rest times, she went along a short corridor to another set of steps, which led to the lowest level of the palace.

It was cool there, and dark. Few light wells penetrated so deep and what light they gave was muted. The doors nearest the outer wall were Daidalos' and Icarus' private rooms, and Ariadne did not touch either door. She went on and soon the last scrap of light from the stairwell faded; only a few lamps lit the passage to a pair of doors that flanked the end of the corridor. Softly but firmly, she opened the door on the right, then closed it swiftly, taking care not to let the latch click. The room had been dark and silent; it wasn't empty, but no one was working there. Swallowing hard, Ariadne turned to the door on the left.

She opened this door boldly, without the caution she had used on the other, wanting to seem assured, and stepped forward into the room. This was brilliantly lit, mostly by lamps suspended on chains from the ceiling; they glowed with a strange white light, brighter by far than the usual golden flame of burning oil, and without smoking. But Ariadne had seen those before and she spared them no more than a quick glance, sweeping her eyes over the large, cluttered room. Her first reaction was relief; her mother wasn't there. Then her eye was caught by movement. At the far extreme of the chamber in the leftmost corner, Daidalos was turning quickly to face her from behind a large table.

Behind him, Ariadne caught a single glimpse of a shining white hide as he roared, "What are you doing here? Get out!"

"But Daidalos—" Ariadne began.

The hide was gone, as if it had fallen from the strange framework that had supported it. That framework seemed familiar, but it disappeared as swiftly as the white hide—had it also fallen silently to the floor?—and Ariadne had seen it too briefly to identify it firmly. In its place, rising as if she had been bent down behind the table, was Pasiphae.

"Out!" Daidalos bellowed, rounding the table with every sign that he intended to throw Ariadne out physically if she didn't go.

"And don't come back here," Pasiphae added. Her lips were drawn back from her teeth in what might have been a threat or a grimace of pain. Her eyes were red-rimmed but open so wide that white showed all around the dark iris. Her hair was a rat's nest, and in the brilliant light Ariadne saw lines on her face that she had never seen before. "I swear," Pasiphae hissed, "that if you try to interfere with me, I'll destroy you, destroy your precious shrine, drive the worship of your puny godling out of Crete altogether."

"Out!"

Ariadne backed out of the doorway and pulled the door shut. Breathing in panting gasps, although not for fear of the threats against her, she leaned against the rough-worked stone between the doors. Pasiphae was mad. She pressed both hands against her lips and closed her eyes. Phaidra was right. Her mother was planning something terrible and desperate . . . but what?

When she had steadied herself, she started back along the passage to the stairwell. She climbed very slowly, still shaky from her reaction to the scene in Daidalos' workshop, thinking about what she had seen. The white hide, the framework—wood? metal? Suddenly Ariadne realized why that framework looked familiar. It was like the skeleton of a horse or a cow or . . . a bull? White hide and a bull's skeleton . . .

Having reached the artisans' veranda, Ariadne sank down on one of the benches protruding from the wall to think. A false bull? Daidalos was constructing a false white bull? But for what purpose? Could Pasiphae intend to substitute it for Poseidon's real bull which she would then sacrifice as the god had demanded and thus draw his attention to her? If that were her purpose, Ariadne would certainly not interfere; there was no need of threats to ensure her cooperation. She agreed heartily that the bull from the sea had to die, no matter how angry that made Minos.

Her mind checked on that thought, however, as she realized that sacrifice of Poseidon's bull could not be her mother's purpose. Minos had been told what Daidalos was doing and had agreed he must continue. Well, Phaidra said he looked as if his guts were being torn out, so perhaps . . . Nonsense. If he had been brought to agree to the death of the bull from the sea, he would sacrifice it himself, not leave the credit to Pasiphae, and there would be no need of the false bull as a substitute.

A substitute? Oh, sweet fields of death, could they intend to sacrifice the *false* bull to Poseidon? But three white bulls had already been given to the god and he was not appeased. A false bull, a thing of wickerwork and tanned hide, certainly could not fool him. Unless . . . Daidalos could do magic. Could he take some hair from the bull, some saliva, sweat, a nick of flesh, and bespell it so that the aura of the false bull and the real bull were the same, then sacrifice the false bull? No, that was nonsense too. Why build a bull when there were plenty of live ones to which Daidalos might attach the aura of the bull from the sea? Or did the aura of the real bull interfere with that bespelled onto it? She cocked her head to the side. Was that why Glaukos and Androgeos had been sent to catch a bull, so no taint of the palace herds should besmirch it?

Ariadne stared out toward Gypsades Hill, but she

didn't really see it and found no comfort there. Her last thought made no more sense than those that came before. The main sticking point was Pasiphae's mad intensity on her purpose. Whether it was the sacrifice of the bull from the sea or one of the simulacra Ariadne had imagined, Ariadne could see no reward large enough to make Pasiphae so desperate nor any reason for Daidalos to be nearly as mad as Pasiphae to keep the secret. Worse still, somehow from the flower around her heart came a sense of sickness in that room, of wrongness, which Ariadne, who had visited Daidalos from time to time for various reasons, had never felt before.

There was one more thing Ariadne could do. She could use her need to talk about clothing as an excuse to visit her father. She went to the end of the artisans' veranda and through an open pillared hall. At the end, which opened onto the south-facing veranda of Minos' chambers, the guard smiled recognition and let her pass. She saw why at once. The veranda was empty. Often Minos sat there to break his fast and even to attend to some business. It was a beautiful spot, pleasant and sheltered. And the doors were closed. Ariadne's heart sank. On a fine day like this, the doors to the outer room should be open.

She entered the corridor that ran along the outer room and opened into the inner chamber. That door was open, but the room was empty, except for a guard. Ariadne asked if he would enquire whether her father was busy. She needed to ask about obtaining garments suitable for her position. The guard—she knew he was a high nobleman's son, but could not call his name to mind—shook his head.

"He will see no one," he said. "I have turned away men on serious business. Those are my orders. No one to be admitted for any purpose, until further orders are given."

"Is my father ill?" Ariadne asked.

"I have not seen the physicians come," the guard said. "Nor do I have permission to admit them if any did."

Realizing she could accomplish no more, Ariadne thanked him and turned away. She walked slowly through the maze of rooms and corridors until she came to the portico that faced on the bull court. There she sat on the balustrade and went over the facts in her mind, but nothing new occurred to her. Eventually she gave up, and went to find Phaidra. She told her sister what she had seen, what she had guessed, mentioned how unlikely it all seemed, and asked Phaidra what she thought of it.

To her surprise Phaidra looked relieved. To sacrifice a false bull or a wild one instead of Poseidon's own bull was certainly dangerous because the god could take offense, she pointed out, but it was unlikely he would take such terrible offense over one bull as to shake the whole island into the sea.

Seeing her sister somewhat happier, Ariadne didn't try to explain the sense of horror she had felt in Daidalos' workshop. Truly, she had no foreboding that their danger was from any massive retaliation Poseidon might visit on them. The horror was personal, something their mother would bring down upon them as a family rather than on Crete as a whole. That was some comfort, and Ariadne left Phaidra to her household chores and went to the shrine. She would have loved to Call Dionysus and ask his advice and for the comfort of his arm around her, but she knew that was forbidden. He had been annoyed when she Called to tell him of the offerings, as if it was her responsibility to solve such problems on her own.

Still, there were little things to do. A few more sacrifices to put in stasis, a more careful examination of some of the old offerings that were piled in the storage room, questions to the priests and priestesses about the progress of the novices. She did what was necessary, ate a meal in lonely splendor in her chamber, and eventually went back to the palace. Nothing had changed there; no disaster had befallen them. Nor did any occur on the next day or the next. Ariadne began to worry about Androgeos and Glaukos, but they came home safe on the fourth day, bringing with them a fine, wide-horned, bellowing prisoner, angry but unharmed, to be penned beyond the house where the bull-dancers in training lived.

The fifth day passed. Androgeos and Glaukos spent most of their time gentling the new bull—not taming it but making it sufficiently accustomed to the presence of humans not to run mad. Phaidra was still anxious, but she always was, and Ariadne found the horror that had gripped her dulling, slipping away. One cannot live on a high pitch for long, be it joy or fear. She might have begun to wonder why she had reacted so strongly to what she had seen in Daidalos' workroom . . . except that her father still remained locked in his chamber and her mother seemed to have disappeared entirely.

CHAPTER 6

"Ariadne!"

The bellow of mingled rage and fear erupted in her mind with such force that Ariadne was jolted wide awake. She jerked upright, thrusting aside the gauze bed hangings so fiercely that a pole was torn loose and clattered to the floor as she leapt from the bed. The polished gypsum floor chilled her feet and she reached back blindly to seize her coverlet and draw it around her even as she took her first steps toward the door.

"Ariadne!"

This time despair filled the mental voice. Ariadne flew down the corridor, down the stairs, past her mother's chamber, and through the crooked corridor into the king's inner room. A guard at the closed doors of the outer chamber, where Minos slept in the heat of summer, called out to her but she made no answer, flying out into the corridor that led to the south portico and thence to the steps and the viaduct. A blackness had seized her spirit, a blackness that wasn't hers, that wasn't yet broken with the red lightnings of rage but soon would be.

She careened down the stairs, gasping with fright as she nearly missed a sharp turn and plunged into the slippery, curving water course that kept the torrential spring and autumn rains from wearing away the steps. There was the road. Red flickers of madness lit the edges of the blackness in her mind, but something held them back, making the blackness thicker, so thick that Ariadne could hardly breathe. The flower around her heart was fully open. The silvery mist of threads reached outward but thinned and dissipated into nothing. Her goal was too far away. She had to be nearer.

She ran like an angry blast off the ocean, but her breath was beginning to rattle in her throat and pain was lancing her side.

"Mother!" she prayed. "Help him. Help me."

The blackness in her pressed on her, made her feet leaden, but all at once she felt her hair lifted, as it lifted when she danced. Warmth and strength infused her. She felt the heavy blackness, but it no longer weighed her down. She ran faster, faster, blind in the dark but never stumbling, up the road, up Gypsades Hill, and burst into the courtyard of the shrine.

"Dionysus," she gasped.

He was sitting on the altar, naked—not at all godlike, sick and shivering, his head in his hands. She rushed to him, pulling the coverlet from her shoulders and wrapping it around him.

"Dionysus."

He looked up, blinking, grasped her wrist in a grip that made her whimper. "Not you!" he snarled. "Not you!"

Red lightning flashed through the darkness that filled her mind. "No," she cried. "You are my lord, my god. I will never do what you disapprove."

"I am your only lord, your only god!"

"My only lord. My only god," she agreed, kneeling before him and looking without fear into his staring eyes. "I love you."

The silver mist that flowed from her heartflower played over him. After a moment the grip on her wrist eased and he released her to pull the blanket tighter around his shoulders. The red streaks had faded from the black and only pain and despair echoed back from the silver threads.

"Where were you when I Called?" he asked.

"In bed. Asleep."

"Liar!" he bellowed, rising suddenly. "I looked in the bedchamber. No one slept in that bed tonight."

"No, no," Ariadne cried, rising with him and gripping his arms. "In the palace. You know I sleep in the palace, not in the shrine. I have a sister, she is only eleven and very fearful. We share a bedchamber. I told you."

"But I Saw . . . I Saw . . ." His eyes fixed over her head and his hands released the coverlet, which fell to the floor.

"What, my lord?" the woman-Ariadne asked. "Come within, where there is no wind and tell me what you Saw."

He shuddered but followed her docilely. Ariadne was greatly relieved to find that the lamps that lit the corridor had been left alight to burn through the night as she'd ordered. There was no light in the high priestess's chamber or in the bedchamber, but it took only a moment to set a wooden sliver ablaze in the lamp in the corridor and light those in the chambers.

When she released the hand by which she had led him, Dionysus stood still, staring into nothing. However, when she tried to get him into the bed, he resisted. She promptly took the blankets and offered them to him, suggesting that he sit in his chair instead. He made no reply, and it was Ariadne who wrapped the blankets around him, and, when he didn't move, led the way again. However, when he saw his chair, with its small table and glowing golden bowl beside it, he sat. She knelt before him, seeking one of his hands in the cocoon of blankets and drawing it out so she could hold it.

"You Saw?" she murmured.

He didn't look at her and his voice was hushed with horror. "A field and in the distance the Palace of Knossos. The sky was dark and there was no moon, like tonight. From the direction of the palace came a man and a woman heavily cloaked and with a hood drawn forward so I couldn't see her face—but she was small, like you."

"It was not I, my lord."

His head bent toward her when she spoke, but she didn't think he saw her. "Not tonight," he said. "There's no time in my Seeing."

He might not see her, his sight being still fixed on his Vision, but he had answered. And his voice still held horror, but there was nothing dreadful in what he described. From her previous reading of his Seeing, Ariadne knew he must spit out the whole Vision or it would return again and again and torment him into wreaking havoc.

"The man? Did you know him?" she asked.

"No, but he was not Cretan. His skin was too pale

and his hair was too light. Also it was straight and cut short. He was heavier boned than a Cretan, too, with bulky shoulders as if he did much hard labor. A Greek, I think."

"Daidalos."

"You know him?"

There was a sharpness, an angry suspicion in the question that puzzled Ariadne, but she answered it with the truth because she still wasn't sure Dionysus wouldn't know if she lied. "He's my father's artificer-mage. He built the dancing floor for me. In that sense, my lord, I know him."

Now the bright blue eyes focused on her and the hand she held tightened on hers, until she drew a sharp breath in anticipation of pain. "Don't go with him! No matter what reason he gives, don't go with him."

"I will not, my lord, my god. I love only you."

The grip of his hand eased and he almost smiled, but then his eyes shifted from her face and the staring look returned. "He was carrying something," Dionysus said, "some framework I thought, draped in a cloth, and when he and the woman reached the middle of the field, he set his burden down." He hesitated and swallowed. "I don't understand," he said, piteously. "The horror of it freezes my soul, and yet there was nothing horrible in what I Saw. That was just silly, like a foolish dream."

"You Saw?" Ariadne urged softly, knowing there was no way for her to escape even if she tried to shirk her duty and refused to lift the burden of his Seeing from him.

"The woman then went under the cloth. I think she cried out faintly as if she had been hurt, but then the man pulled off the cloth and there was no woman nor was what he had carried a framework—instead the cloth covered a white cow. Is that not ridiculous?"

But his question held a note of uncertainty because Ariadne had gasped as soon as he mentioned the white cow. He paused and looked down at her. Calm spread from her small hand clasped in his. Not that she was calm. He sensed that she was frightened and horrified by what he'd said, but, oddly, that eased his own oppression. Whatever that mad Vision meant, she understood and she would explain it to him and he wouldn't be tormented by sorrow and horror any longer.

"Was that all you Saw?" she asked. She heard the thread of eagerness in her voice; she couldn't help hoping he would agree, but she wasn't surprised when he shook his head.

"No." Despite the ease she had brought him and the warmth of the blanket, he shivered. "The worst is yet to come," he admitted. "The man then disappeared and the cow began to low. Soon a magnificent white bull came running across the field, and the closer he drew the clearer I could see that it was a man's face under the horns, not a bull's. It was Poseidon's face."

"Oh, Merciful Mother, preserve us," Ariadne breathed.

"Not you!" Dionysus bellowed, pushing off the blankets and seizing Ariadne by the shoulders. "The Poseidon-bull coupled with that cow, she groaning and lowing with pleasure. Not you! I let you dance for the Mother because even we gods honor Her, but you will *not* be Poseidon's meat. You are *my* priestess. You will play no cow to that bull's lust."

"No, no," Ariadne cried. "Not me! It wasn't I! It will never be me."

"Then why is your face gray with terror?"

She closed her eyes. "Not terror, shame," she whispered. "The woman is or was my mother—and my father knows."

There was a long moment's silence. Then Dionysus said, "You know what all this means, don't you? It's all to do with Knossos and the bull from the sea, all tangled up with that first Vision that nearly drove me mad." Then, suddenly, he drew her up on his lap and pulled the blankets around them both. "You are shivering, child. I'm sorry I didn't notice you were as naked as I. Now, tell me what I have been Seeing."

The heartflower was open wide; the mist of silver threads encompassed them both and seemed to reach outward, bringing in and weaving together prophesy, knowledge, and memory. Ariadne was again aware of being two: on the surface she seemed a child who had known little love and was now almost bursting with joy because of the warm embrace, the kindness of her god; but in her deepest core she was a woman, wise with years, who could take in what the silver threads brought and had listened many times and many times soothed this most restless and dangerous being.

"You know of my father's sin in not sacrificing the bull from the sea to Poseidon," she said. "This, I believe, is his punishment for that sin."

"But why? It is almost a year since that happening. Why now?"

Ariadne sighed and snuggled closer. "Of that I'm not sure. Perhaps the bull is such a small matter to Poseidon that it went from his mind, or perhaps he thought my father was waiting for a certain time of the year when a great celebration of bull dancing is held and then he forgot about his bull. I think . . . I think something happened that reminded him of Knossos and the bull."

"That makes sense, but what fool prodded Poseidon?"

"My mother, I fear."

Dionysus drew back a little so he could look down and see her face. "Your mother?"

"When you accepted me as your priestess, the people all acclaimed me, saluted me with honor for your sake. My mother hadn't thought you would appear, had thought my consecration at your shrine would be an empty ritual. She . . . she likes praise and adulation. She envied me the salutes and the bows. She tried to call your attention to herself, but you denied her."

"So I did. I remember that. She was the woman who wouldn't leave when I said I wished to be alone with you. But what has this to do with Poseidon?"

"She wanted a god to acknowledge her also, and for the people to honor her more than they honored me, so she went to Poseidon's temple and tried to Call him—"

Dionysus burst out laughing. "I hope she chose a more reasonable time than you did. I suspect that Poseidon is even less fond of being wakened at the crack of dawn than I—after all, sometimes I am still awake at that time, not having got to bed at all."

Ariadne, all child for the moment, grinned up at him. "Oh, is that why you object to dawn ceremonies? Perhaps if you didn't dance and drink all night . . ."

He began to grin in response, but suddenly her smile disappeared and her voice faded. "What is it?" he asked. "Surely you can't object to the god of wine drinking a cup or two?"

"No, it was . . . When I Called you about all the sacrifices, I saw the woman in your bed—"

"That's enough!" he snapped. "Priestess and Mouth you may be, but you have no right—"

"No, no, my lord. I didn't mean any criticism on that subject. It just reminded me of why my father kept the bull. He wished to breed from it, for it was finer than any bull in his herd, his or any other, and a horrible notion came into my mind."

Puzzled, Dionysus frowned. Then his mouth dropped open, and a moment later he was roaring with laughter. "I didn't think Poseidon had so much sense of humor," he gasped when he could speak. "What a punishment! Minos kept Poseidon's bull to breed to his cows, so Poseidon would breed to Minos' cow."

"But it isn't funny, Lord God," Ariadne cried. "Have you forgotten the first Vision you spoke of to me? Have you forgotten the bull with a man's face, not Poseidon's face, who turned on the cows and tore them with his horns and his teeth, who killed the herdsmen who tried to save the cows and then ravaged the whole countryside?" She shuddered convulsively. "What good could come of the fruit of Poseidon's rage and my mother's ambition?"

Dionysus held her tight, comfortingly. "Ah, yes, you are a true Mouth. You've woven together the two Visions and have spoken the truth, I fear. Poseidon doesn't have any sense of humor. He'll try to make sure that his seed sets firm and that the fruit of that seed would be no blessing to Minos." He put her off his lap gently and stood her upright before him. "Now, we must set a lesser evil against a greater. I know you fear to be punished if you speak out against the will of your parents, who are also king and queen of this realm, but I'll watch and protect you if real hurt threatens you for it. You may Call me if you need me, and I will come. This time you must be my Mouth and speak this Vision aloud."

"I will," Ariadne breathed, although she was cold with fear. "I will."

Ariadne had been ready to go right then, but Dionysus had insisted she spend what remained of the night in the priestess's bedchamber and return to the palace in the morning. If his Vision had been of what would happen that night, he pointed out, it had happened already. Even if it hadn't, there was no way that she could interfere with Poseidon, and for him to meddle might bring worse upon them. If he enraged Poseidon, the Earth Shaker might bury Crete in the sea.

She had paled when he said that. Crete was not infrequently shaken by Poseidon's warnings and once had been nearly destroyed by the heaving of the earth. To comfort her, he reminded her that if his Vision was of the future, morning would be early enough to warn her mother of the evil that would follow the coupling she desired and certainly early enough to warn her to clean out her womb if she had yielded already. Ariadne accepted that with some relief. The confrontation would be bad enough in daylight; at night it would be terrible.

Having calmed her and seen her fall asleep, Dionysus took himself to Olympus where he went back to his own bed—and found he could not sleep. He wondered irritably if he was a fool. Knossos's troubles were of their own making and wouldn't shake the world at large or be noticed in Olympus, and he knew with an inner certainty that the Visions that had troubled him were ended. He no longer needed the young priestess's counsel. But with that resentful thought came an image of her sweet face with those eyes like luminous black pools full of trust. Besides, he had given his word that he would protect her, and unlike others of Olympus, he kept his word. And even the most careless Olympian protected his or her Mouth. He sighed and stopped arguing with himself. In the morning he would seek out Hermes.

He found the hazel-eyed young god, who was only a little older than he, looking over a necklet of such fantastic workmanship that it could only have been made by Hades himself. Dionysus clucked with concern and Hermes looked up at him, laughing.

"From whom did you have that?" Dionysus asked.

"I . . . er . . . from Ares, who planned to give it to Aphrodite, I suppose." He snickered, lifting the necklet so Dionysus could see it better. "I only took it to save him from a grave mistake. Can you imagine anything that would fit her less? This is for a full-bosomed, dark-eyed beauty, not for Aphrodite's fragile perfection. That man not only has iron in his thews but in his head also. Will you tell?"

"Have I ever?"

Now Hermes clicked his tongue against his upper palate. "That was very foolish," he said, his eyes dancing with mischief. "You should have said, 'I won't tell if you will do for me what I desire.' Then you wouldn't need to offer me wine or any other token in exchange."

Dionysus wrinkled his nose. "I have plenty of wine, and you, no more than I, would use a threat to gain a favor from a friend. All you want is to make our elders uneasy." Then he laughed but without much amusement. "I make them uneasy enough just by being, so I don't need to prick and prod them. But some day, Hermes, you'll go too far."

Although Hermes didn't fear Dionysus because he could remove himself from that maddening presence quickly enough to save himself from frenzy or from being harmed by those in whom Dionysus had induced frenzy, he didn't like to set off his fellow mage's wild rage. Someone, even if not himself, often got hurt and Dionysus would then be sorry and ashamed. Far from fearing him, Hermes pitied Dionysus for his lack of control.

"I know this is not yours—" Hermes gestured to the necklet, which he had laid down "—so you can't be angry about that." He searched his conscience, but could find nothing and finally asked, "Have I trod on your toes somehow?"

"No, not at all." Dionysus shook his head. "Nor have I Seen anything concerning you. Only that sometimes I fear for you." His lips twisted. "There aren't so many who are willing to talk to me that I can afford to lose one. But I didn't come for idle talk. I want to know whether a translocation spell can be set upon a person."

"Certainly, if that person has power enough to invoke it," Hermes said.

"I have never lacked for power," Dionysus replied.

"You. Of course not. But you said a person." He raised his brows inquiringly. "Have you started Seeing yourself as separate people?"

Dionysus laughed. "I said that wrong. I want a translocation spell that will take me to a particular person no matter where that person happens to be."

Hermes cocked his head as if he were listening to something Dionysus had left unsaid. "A native woman, no doubt."

"The high priestess of my shrine at Knossos," Dionysus replied with a half-smile, acknowledging and denying what Hermes had implied. Then, relenting, he explained. "She's a true Mouth, both to me and to the people."

"And in danger? Your priestess? After Pentheus?"

"My hands are somewhat tied in this matter," Dionysus said. "Those to whom she will bring unwelcome news are her own father and mother, who also happen to be the king and queen of Knossos."

Hermes pushed aside the necklet with an impatient gesture and his brows knitted. "Wasn't there some trouble in Knossos some time ago? A contested kingship? I remember that Zeus decided not to meddle in it because the issue was not clear. Yes, yes.

Minos was eldest but Rhadamanthys and Sarpedon were equally worthy. And eldest doesn't count much with Zeus, who was the youngest of Kronos' sons and still took the throne. Zeus was about to give his blessing to the division of Crete because he could see that the brothers would rule well together, but Hera stopped him. She said she Saw that after them chaos would follow."

"Ah, my priestess didn't know the reason but she knew of the prophecy of chaos after a divided rule. But, since Zeus wouldn't answer, Minos appealed to Poseidon."

He told Hermes the whole tale of the result of that plea. When he was done, the young god of thieves nodded. "And now Poseidon is taking his revenge. Well, he isn't the kind to put aside an affront. But why are you being bothered with the troubles of Knossos?"

"Because I have Visions of them." Dionysus shrugged. "And if I See those troubles, isn't that a sign to me from the Mother that I must do something?"

"What?" Hermes asked. "Can your Mouth tell you?"

"No. Perhaps the Mother knows, but She hasn't even given me the skill to understand what I See, and She certainly hasn't informed me of Her purpose. Only . . . She, too, loves my priestess who dances the Welcome for Her."

"Scry her for me," Hermes said then, abandoning further argument.

A gesture brought a servant who ran for a scrying bowl and dark wine. Into it Dionysus brought the image of Ariadne, not as he had first seen her, all painted and dyed and in magnificent garments, but as she'd appeared to him before the altar of the shrine, with her huge black eyes wide with concern and her flowing wealth of hair her only garment. Hermes glanced sidelong at Dionysus but said nothing, only rising and going toward the back of the house where his work chamber was.

Ariadne had wakened even earlier than Dionysus and the burden of what she must do fell upon her as soon as she opened her eyes. For a few moments, she felt that the weight was so great she wouldn't be able to get out of bed, and to add to her troubles she remembered that she had run naked from her bed in answer to Dionysus' Call. Was she to return to the palace wrapped in a bed cover? And confront her mother with a dire warning from a god in a child's kilt?

The answer to the second problem came first. If she was acting as her god's Mouth, then she could wear the dress in which she had been consecrated to him. And then the answer to the first problem came easily. There was cloth enough in the chests. A kilt and shawl could be easily devised.

Somehow finding solutions to the little problems made the real burden lighter. Ariadne rose and rang the bell that would bring the priestesses. The younger of the two appeared with a look of indignation on her face, which melted into apprehension as she bowed.

"I thought it was one of the children, priestess," she stammered. "When did you come? How . . . ?"

"The god Called me and I came," Ariadne answered, then momentarily forgetting the reason for the summons, laughed. "I came straight from my bed and without bothering to dress. I must find suitable garments to wear to return to the palace. And I would like breakfast, too."

When the food came, however, she found it hard to swallow. Only the wine, bad as it was, went down easily because it reminded her of how Dionysus had held her and warmed her. Eventually she chose, somewhat at random, one of the lengths of cloth that the elder priestess had been displaying to her while she tried to eat. A kilt was cobbled from it. Ariadne braided her hair and told the priestess that a small lamp must be left alight in the sitting room and bedchamber in the future.

"Lord Dionysus comes at his own will, it seems, and not only when he is Called," she said. "The shrine and my apartment must always be ready for him."

She left then, knowing that if she didn't go at once she would find reason after reason for not going at all, but she had learned from what had happened when she wakened. She fixed her mind on the next step. She must arrange her hair and paint her face so that she would not look like a pathetic child. Then she must dress and, yes, because it was still early and cool, she could wear a shawl over her bodice that would hide her flat chest.

A far greater problem, which she had kept pushing to the back of her mind because she had no solution, was how she would get past her mother's guards and into her presence. That, however, proved to be no problem at all. When the guard saw her with her hair dressed high, with the locks of dedication in long curls before her ears, with her eyes and lips painted, and wearing the many-flounced bell skirt in which the god had responded to her Call, his arm shot up in salute and he stepped aside.

"I see you," Ariadne responded automatically, and walked past him into her mother's antechamber. That was empty, but Ariadne could see movement in the bedchamber beyond and she walked through the drawn-back sliding doors.

"Queen Pasiphae," Ariadne said.

Her voice was not loud or shrill, which she had feared, but the two maids who were attending her mother, one dressing her hair and another drawing a line of kohl around her eye, and the third, who was holding the gown her mother would wear, all gasped and then all saluted. Pasiphae, still heavy-eyed and full-lipped, shot to her feet.

"You weren't summoned here or invited," she shrieked. "Get out!"

For the first time, Ariadne didn't flinch before her mother's rage. "The Mouth of a god needs no invitation," she replied calmly.

"Mouth of a god, indeed!" Pasiphae laughed harshly. "A babe swelled up with importance by the notice of a petty godling more like. You are nothing. You will be less than nothing soon." Her hand went to her abdomen. "I carry here a new god. One who will wipe little Dionysus from the hearts of the people, high lord and low peasant alike."

Ariadne felt the color leach from her cheeks. It was too late! She almost turned and fled, but deep within her an older, wiser woman stirred. No matter that the seed was set. A Mouth must speak her god's warning. Perhaps disaster could yet be averted.

"I am a *true* god's Mouth and I must speak his Vision. What you carry is no god but a curse set on Knossos by the Lord Poseidon to punish King Minos for violating his oath. The bull from the sea must be sacrificed and you must clean out your womb or great evil will come to Knossos."

"Lies!" Pasiphae screamed. "You're envious because I have received a far greater god than you. You wish to deprive me of my honor, my worship, as the mother of a god."

"The Mouth of a god cannot lie," Ariadne said. But a moment later tears sprang to her eyes, and the cold voice in which she had spoken, the voice from within, broke on a childish sob. "Mother, I beg you, don't bring this curse upon us."

Pasiphae sprang forward and slapped Ariadne so hard she staggered back. "It's not a lie! I'll bear a god! I will! I will!"

CHAPTER 7

Ariadne's first instinct upon being struck was to Call for Dionysus. Not that her mother had never slapped her before, but that she should dare strike her when in full regalia as high priestess was terrible. As swiftly as her anger flared, it died in cold terror. If she Called Dionysus he would come—and her mother would die, likely at the hands of her own maids. She shuddered. Could she ever again nestle trustingly in Dionysus' arms when her mother's blood dyed them?

She righted herself. "I will not Call my lord, who would shed your blood. You were my mother, and kin-blood stains deep. But the blessing on grape and wine will be withheld from this house alone of all on Crete until you come to my lord's shrine, where I will now live, to make sacrifice and restitution. Remember that, Queen Pasiphae."

On the words she swept out of the apartment, barely acknowledging the salute of the guard. She had intended to go back to the chamber she shared with Phaidra, but her feet did not carry her to the stair just outside her mother's bedchamber door, which would have taken her up there. Instead she went directly out through the southern portico, across the grassy area at the back to the road, which took her to Gypsades Hill and her temple. There was nothing she had left behind that she cared about—except Phaidra.

Ariadne bit her lip, remembering that she was abandoning her poor sister to bear her mother's ill will and to pick up all the tasks that had been hers. But there was no going back. She would have to explain what had happened to Phaidra and, if necessary, offer her a sanctuary in the shrine.

When she reached the temple, she sent one of the boy to the palace to seek out her sister and bring her to the shrine. Although the child didn't return with Phaidra until near dusk, the interview wasn't as painful as Ariadne expected.

"I didn't dare come sooner," Phaidra said, after kissing her sister. "What happened? Mother told me you were dead! If your little acolyte hadn't caught me on my way to answer her summons and told me you were here waiting for me, I would've died of fright myself. Whatever did you say to her?"

"I told her a truth she didn't want to hear." Ariadne hesitated and then continued, "Do you remember, Phaidra how frightened you were last ten-day? Do you remember telling me that something dreadful was about to happen?"

"But nothing did happen." Phaidra smiled. "You were right when you scolded me for frightening myself with boggles and loving doom and gloom."

Ariadne took a deep breath. "Something dreadful has happened. The thing mother and Daidalos were doing together was turning mother into a cow so that the bull from the sea would couple with her."

"No," Phaidra said, revulsion clear in face and voice. "That's impossible. I've seen a bull coupling with a cow. No woman could . . ."

"It wasn't the bull," Ariadne said. "It was Poseidon. Lord Dionysus Saw that in a Vision. He knows Poseidon. He said it was Poseidon's revenge, that as father had kept his bull to couple with our cows, he would couple with father's cow."

"Oh!" Phaidra now looked delighted. "If it was the god, then all's well. It's not as if mother took another man to her bed and shamed father. A god . . ."

Ariadne's lips parted, then closed. She'd spoken her warning to Pasiphae and been rejected. In a moon or two, she would speak the same warning to her father—after Dionysus had blessed the budding vines and Minos could see that his were scanty and weak compared with those on the rest of Crete. Perhaps Minos would finally sacrifice the bull and convince Pasiphae she had made a mistake. But there was no sense in frightening Phaidra. There was nothing the child could do, so why make her miserable?

"Father didn't like it," Ariadne then said mildly, "but he and mother must work that out for themselves. It's you I'm worried about. As you know, mother took ill what I said to her and I can't come back to the palace, which means, my love, that all the chores and all mother's demands will fall upon you. What I wanted to tell you was that you can come here and live with me if mother makes you unhappy."

"Oh no." Phaidra smiled and her eyes were bright.

"She's been very kind to me, saying I'm now her only daughter and her only support."

"Very well," Ariadne agreed, surprised at her feeling of relief and only then realizing that she didn't want Phaidra there when Dionysus came. Ashamed of herself, she added, "If you're content, then I am also. Just remember that you may come to me for help if you need it."

When she made that offer, Ariadne had no idea that her promise would deeply involve her in the disaster she had fled. For a few ten-days she did worry about receiving an hysterical Phaidra and then having to outface her mother to protect her sister, but that didn't happen. Phaidra did make several visits to Dionysus' shrine, but she came only to giggle and gossip, to report that their mother was so busy with some plans of her own that Phaidra could do much as she pleased, and to assure Ariadne that she wasn't at all missed at the palace.

Had Ariadne not herself been busier and happier than ever before in her life, Phaidra's remarks might have been cruel. As it was, they added another layer of gladness to a life that seemed all delight. The pleasures had begun simply enough the morning after Phaidra's visit when Ariadne got out of bed and realized she had nothing to wear except the far too elaborate consecration gown and that she could no longer hope her father would supply her with a new wardrobe. That drove her first to questioning the priestess who brought her a fast-breaking meal about the possibility of having clothing made from the cloth in the chests and thence to the discovery that all the old priestess's clothing was stored with the extra furniture.

Examination of this treasure trove proved fruitful. At the end of her life, the old priestess had shrunken so that most of the newer clothing was a reasonably good fit for Ariadne. Moreover, in the last months of her life, she had found the heavy flounced formal skirts too much of a burden and that the bodices, which exposed breasts flabby and flapping with age, were no longer flattering. She had had made several straight gowns, elaborately embroidered and of beautiful cloth—and then had taken to her bed and never left it so the gowns had never been worn.

Ariadne immediately adopted all of those, directing that they be well shaken and hung in the fresh air. Much of the remainder of the clothing was too rich for Ariadne's taste, but when she considered that she might have to receive those who wished to worship at Dionysus' shrine and make sacrifice, she reexamined the chest contents. There were two garments she selected to be refreshed with the gowns she planned to use for common wear. One had a straight gold underskirt with at least twenty rows of black flounces trimmed and embroidered in gold; the bodice was also black but up the sides and around the breasts it was densely embroidered with vines. The second was the deep red of wine. This skirt wasn't flounced but stiffened into a firm bell shape with bands of gold—real, beaten gold—engraved with bunches of grapes. The bodice looked at first to be solid gold too, but when Ariadne lifted it she realized it was thin leather, embossed with grapes and lightly gilded.

"She never wore the black one," the priestess attending Ariadne said. "After she ordered it made, she said the color made her sad. And she wore the red one only once. It was too heavy for her. She was very frail in the end."

"She lived a long life," Ariadne said without much sympathy, thinking of the threadbare robes of the attendants and the wizened grapes and sour wine. As she spoke she had lifted out a skirt that was not only dirty but torn. "What is this?" she asked.

The priestess shrugged. "She never threw away anything or—" she hesitated and then went on somewhat uncertainly "—or allowed us to use what she no longer wanted."

A hint? Ariadne hesitated. Her first impulse was always to give, but young as she was, she had already discovered that generosity, far from breeding gratitude, usually only induced greed and resentment. Nonetheless, this seemed reasonable enough and might also serve as a test.

"That's not sensible," she said. "What good are torn, dirty gowns in the bottom of a chest? But I have no more time to spend on this. You may look through all the chests of clothing. Remove what is dirty and torn. Unless it's set with precious stones or gold, you may use what you think will be useful. Lord Dionysus told me to sell the furniture that's been piled in the storeroom and to use that money to have one or more new storerooms carved into the hill. I'm sure that means the more valuable garments that won't befit me must also be sold. He'll come soon to bless the vines and again in the summer to bless the grapes. I suspect that there will be more offerings after each blessing, so we'd better be ready."

"Yes, indeed," the priestess breathed, eyes glowing with fervor, and then, nearly whispering, "When *he* comes, may we see him?"

Ariadne smiled. "I don't know when he'll come. I'm only his priestess, and he says no more to me than 'I will come to bless the vines.' But if you wish and you think the other priestess and priests would wish, I can ask Lord Dionysus if I might present you to him." She hesitated, then added, "Don't be troubled if it isn't this time. He can be a very angry god, and I'll wait until he's calm and pleased before I ask."

"Oh, yes!"

There was no doubt in Ariadne's mind about the sincerity of the priestess's reply. Ariadne suspected that she, her sister priestess and the priests might have been barely touched by an overflow of Dionysus' rage when he thought he had been offered an unfit sacrifice. But she said nothing about that nor made the smallest attempt to reduce the awe the priestess felt. She was sure it was only by virtue of that awe that she was minutely and instantly obeyed. Instead she turned the subject and asked whether among them the priests and priestesses knew who would be likely to buy what the temple had to sell or who could carve the new storerooms into the hill.

She learned that in the past traders came regularly to the temple to buy those offerings that the old priestess didn't wish to keep for herself. They had come after news of Dionysus' appearance had spread, but the priests had sent them away because Ariadne had said all would be offered to the god and this time the god would accept the sacrifices.

"Well," she said, "Lord Dionysus has taken what he wanted and bade me sell the rest, so the traders may be told to come again. Tell me how the old priestess managed her dealings with such men and women."

Although Ariadne had no fondness and little respect for the avaricious grandmother who had lost the favor of the god, she wasn't such a fool as to reject her devices for getting a good bargain. She had even an extra lever with which to pry out a good price. Gowned in lavender embroidered in green vines on which were suspended amethyst grapes, she shook her elaborately coiffed head at the ridiculous offers the first traders made to one they thought a gullible child.

"It's by Lord Dionysus' order that these things are offered for sale. He desires to do good by giving employment to the poor—" she offered a cold smile

"—perhaps so that they can afford to buy more wine, in carving out new storerooms in the hillside. Consider then that what you offer for the god's goods must include a sacrifice to him as well as a fair price."

Two of the men paled. They'd been in the crowd and seen Dionysus appear, had been touched by the god-induced fury that could have destroyed them all, and had witnessed how the god cut off sound and then sight from them. To cheat a child was one thing; to cheat such a god another. Prices were hurriedly revised upward until Ariadne nodded graciously, accepting what she felt was fair. She was a little nervous, not wanting to use the traders' fear of Dionysus to gouge them, but was satisfied when she saw pleasure and relief on several faces.

She spent a happy ten-day at this employment, in choosing and having made an entire wardrobe, and in selecting a work gang. Having discussed with the overseer of the gang where she wanted the storerooms and how she wanted them protected from damp and collapse, she had begun to wonder what next to do when she was wakened from sleep by Dionysus' Call.

"I'll come after midday," the voice in her head informed her, and then, with a touch of coldness, "I thought you'd Call me."

"My lord, I was afraid—"

"Never mind. Be waiting at the altar for me."

And he was gone from her consciousness, but the coldness in his voice had brought back to her her dismal failure as a Mouth. She'd managed to put Pasiphae's rejection of her warning out of her mind while she was successfully performing other duties her god had demanded, but now she'd have to confess.

Fortunately it wasn't long until dawn because she slept no more that night nor could she eat what the servants brought her in the morning. When they arrived, she sent the workmen away from the shrine and, after the priestesses had helped her to dress her hair and arrange her black gown, she ordered them to keep strictly to their quarters and make sure the novices and priests did also.

"The Lord Dionysus isn't pleased," she told them. "I have failed as his Mouth. I spoke as he bade me, but I wasn't able to accomplish his purpose."

"We'll keep to our quarters," the older priestess assured her and then, with tears in her eyes, whispered, "Surely he won't punish you for failing. You're so young and of such good heart—"

"Enough!" Ariadne said. "Lord Dionysus is my lord and my god. What he does is right and good to me."

She was kneeling on the altar when he came, facing the painting before which he always appeared. She jumped when he spoke, for she had been kneeling there for some time and had closed her tired eyes.

"Holy Mother," he said. "For what are you dressed?"

"For confession. I have failed you, my lord."

The overlarge blue eyes became even larger and brighter. "Failed me how?"

Ariadne swallowed. "I spoke as you bade me, but it was too late. As you Saw, my mother had already coupled with the bull that was Poseidon and she said she had conceived. I told her that what she carried was a curse, Poseidon's revenge, and she should be rid of it, but she wouldn't heed me. I have failed as your Mouth."

"Oh, that." Dionysus shrugged. "That's no failure. So long as you gave the warning, if she wouldn't listen the consequences will be on her head. The Vision no longer troubles me, so I'm satisfied." He smiled suddenly. "Was that why you didn't Call me, because you were afraid I would blame you for not being able to force the queen of Crete to your will?"

"That and because you told me not to Call you for

my own pleasure. It's very hard, my lord, to know when I'm using a duty only to have you near and give me pleasure."

He laughed at that and said, "I promised to bless the vines and I don't like to fail in a promise. I also have a terrible memory and could easily have forgotten you, so you should have Called. If that duty is a pleasure, so much the better for us both."

She smiled in response. "I won't fail again—" and then she frowned. "At least, not in Calling you—and I won't Call at daybreak, I promise."

"No, because . . ." He hesitated, stared into her eyes for a moment, and then looked away. "For now we will bless the vines on a moonless night when there are none to see us." He reached out and took her chin in his hand. "You are too young now to celebrate the blessing as many priestesses do." He laughed again when he saw her worried expression. "And you needn't fear. The vines and the wine will not suffer."

"Oh, thank you my lord. Thank you. You must be the kindest god in the world."

He looked away from her and a slight shiver passed over him. "Not always."

She knew that, had felt his rage, but she touched his hand. "You are kind to me . . . without failing."

He cocked his head as if listening to something she hadn't said aloud, then shook it. "Come down off that stone, child, and tell me why a shadow comes over your face each time you speak of failing."

She tried to rise, but found her legs were numb and he shook his head again and scolded her gently for kneeling for so long. Then he picked her up as if she had no weight at all and carried her into her chamber. By the time he set her down, she could stand, but he wouldn't let her kneel again when he sat in his chair and she fetched cushions to sit beside him. Before she sat down, however, she asked if he had eaten and he said he hadn't.

"I enjoy company when I eat," he said, "and at home I have none."

"I'll very gladly eat with you," Ariadne replied, grinning, "if it pleases you, my lord. To speak the truth, I'm starving, for I feared you'd be very angry with me and had no stomach for my bread and cheese this morning."

"You are responsible for telling my Visions. You aren't responsible for the acts of those whom the Visions concern unless they concern you or this shrine." He blinked, then frowned. "I don't even know if it's possible to act in such a way as to change my Visions." His frown grew blacker. "I don't know why the Visions are sent to me . . ."

Ariadne bent forward and took his hands. "You'll worry less about Visions when your belly is full," she said. "Give me leave to send for the priestesses . . ." She hesitated, saw that he was smiling at her, and added, "They've begged me to allow them to see you. Are you willing for me to present them to you today?"

"So long as they bring a good meal with them," he said.

She didn't reply but went to ring the bell that brought the priestesses to her and instructed the women to bring the platter she had had prepared at the beginning of the ten-day and had put into stasis. When she took the large platter to carry it to Dionysus, she told the priestess to be sure that she and the priests be dressed in their best. After Lord Dionysus had eaten, he had agreed that they should be presented to him.

As she carried the tray in, she dissolved the spell of stasis. Immediately wisps of steam rose from the tureen of soup and from several platters. Dionysus turned his head toward the enticing odors.

"How did you do that?" he asked. "Was a meal ready that you snatched out of the mouths of your household?"

Ariadne laughed merrily. "I'm not so improvident as to feed my household on dishes like these," she said. "We eat well, but these are dainties prepared for a grand state dinner. One of the palace cooks has a soft spot in his heart for me. He heard I was living here instead of in the palace and wasn't invited, so he sent word that he'd save a selection for me. You may be sure I went with the servant and put a stasis on the tray. And here it is."

"You saved it all for me?" Dionysus asked softly.

"Except for a few pieces of meat and stuffed grape leaves," Ariadne replied. "I had to make sure the stasis would work on the hot food, so I put a bit aside and had it for dinner two days after. It was still hot then, so I hoped it would keep until you came, and it seems to have done so."

He looked at her; his lips parted as if to speak, but he said nothing and looked away to pick up a skewer with which he chose a small sizzling roll of hashed stuffing in a pastry shell. Having burnt his tongue and breathed out heavily to cool it, he remarked that the little roll was delicious, skewered another, and told Ariadne to join him. Before she sat, she ladled some soup from the tureen to a bowl. There were several of those and she served herself also. They both ate in appreciative silence for a little while.

"I have a poor memory," Dionysus said suddenly, "but not so bad that I have forgotten your worry over the word 'failure.' Were you hoping to distract me with this meal?"

Ariadne caught the slight sharpness in the question

and didn't convey to her mouth the slice of sauced meat she had folded into a bite-sized piece with her skewer. "Oh, no, my lord," she said. "Although I do hope that I did what you will think is right, I need your advice on how to proceed further."

"Yes?" Impatience in the tone and flick of the eyes.

"When I told Queen Pasiphae of your Vision, she was very rude. I know that you might have had her torn apart for her lack of respect, but she *was* my mother, my lord."

Dionysus made a dissatisfied but accepting grunt, then sighed and nodded.

"So I told her that the blessing of vine and wine would be withheld from Knossos alone of all places on Crete until apology and restitution were made."

He was silent, thinking while he chewed slowly, then nodded and said. "I do approve. Although my punishment *would* have been harsher, a priestess shouldn't shed kin-blood. But if you've pronounced sentence already, about what do you need my advice?"

"My lord," Ariadne said, downcast eyes fixed on her folded hands, "I know what will happen and I am torn two ways. Pasiphae will make no apology nor restitution of any kind, but King Minos will come and plead with me to forgive them both and will offer sacrifice and his own apology." She looked up, her big black eyes pleading. "Please, my lord, I know the queen deserves punishment, but must I ruin Minos and those who were my brothers because she is unmanageable?"

"You mean King Minos will sacrifice and beg pardon but he can't force his wife to do so?"

"That's true, my lord. The queen is the avatar of the Snake Goddess . . . and she is, truly. She always knows who will leap the bulls safely and what the pattern of the bull dances means. By that pattern is the planting done. She knows, too, when the land will shake. The people wouldn't permit her to be scorned or harmed. King Minos really cannot force her."

Dionysus looked away from her, out the window onto the hillside where the long shadows of late afternoon were beginning to fade into a generalized dusk. Ariadne studied his face and saw in it uneasiness mingled with irritation and then, following a sidelong glance at her, resignation.

"Queen Pasiphae emerges then free of any flick of punishment or shadow of blame while everyone else pays for her sins?"

Ariadne sighed. "That's how it often is."

Dionysus uttered a sharp bark of laughter without any mirth in it. "Not this time," he said, and then patted Ariadne, who had drawn in her breath and paled. "No, she won't meet her doom through me. I'll hold my hand. Her death would be a reward to those who let her run amuck and though your heart is soft for love of them, they must suffer too. No, no. I need do nothing. If Queen Pasiphae bears what she carries . . ." He shrugged. "You may make whatever arrangement you think best with King Minos—so long as he knows for whose guilt he is paying. But do you know the bounds of the land that's Minos' own?"

"I know his lands around Knossos," Ariadne said. "He does have other lands in other places on Crete. I don't know those. But the lands around Knossos are the greatest."

"I suppose that will have to . . ." Dionysus' voice faded as an idea came to him. Then he smiled beatifically. "No, we'll withhold my blessing from all his lands. Tonight we will bless the lands near this shrine, ignoring Minos' vines. In the next ten-day you'll travel to each of my other shrines on Crete. You are my chosen high priestess, my Mouth, and all the other priests and priestesses must acknowledge you. I'll come to you at each shrine, and we'll bless those lands, but the priestesses of each shrine will know which are the king's lands, and we'll avoid them."

"Yes," Ariadne sighed, "that will make the lesson sharper."

"You aren't happy. Are you afraid King Minos will try to punish you when he sees his vines alone do not prosper?"

She was surprised at his sensitivity to her feeling, but before she could explain that in this case it was not fear, only sadness because those she loved must suffer, he had put down the skewer he was still holding and looked down into his empty hands.

"Don't fear," he added, as a silvery ball formed between his fingers. "Come here."

She rose without hesitation, even as he spoke, to walk around the little table and kneel at his feet. He looked down at her, staring into her fearless, trustful eyes.

"This is a spell that will bring me to your side whenever you need me. Call and I'll come if any ever threaten you—but don't abuse that power."

He touched the silvery globe to the top of her head while he spoke. Ariadne could feel it flowing over her, slipping under her clothing, tingling slightly and chilling her as it covered her skin. For just a moment she saw the silver mist drift over her small breasts and down her arms to flicker and die around her clasped fingers.

She said, "No, no. I'll be careful. I'll Call only when it's time for blessing the grapes to bring them to full ripeness or for pressing them into wine . . . or in dire need." Then she lowered her head, bit her lip, and at last looked up, holding out her hands. "But . . . but may I *never* Call to you just for love?

Just for the joy you wake in me by being with me? Never?"

He looked at the outstretched, pleading hands; she was reaching toward his but not so bold as to touch them. His lips twisted, almost as if he were in pain, but a moment later he laughed. "Purely for love and joy . . . well, that's no bad thing, that my priestess should love me and joy in me. So you may Call. But not each day or even monthly. Twice or thrice a year—say on your birth day or name day—you may scry me and ask if it's convenient for me to come to you. If nothing holds me . . . perhaps I'll come."

"Oh, thank you. Thank you."

He flicked her nose with a finger, pointed back at the cushions on which she'd been sitting, and began to tell her how they would go about blessing the vines, beginning with the fact that she would have to put on clothing that wasn't covered with flounces, which would catch in every twig. She showed him what she had and he settled on a straight gown of soft, white wool and a pair of sturdy sandals. Then he told her what they would do. By the time he had finished explaining, there was little on the tray or in the flagon, dusk had darkened into true night, and Dionysus had lit the nearest lamp with a flick of his fingers.

The priests and priestesses who came in answer to Ariadne's bell, carried tapers with which, after asking permission, they lit more lamps. Ariadne saw they were dressed in their new best, good cloth, clean and unworn with only simple embroidered patterns of vines and grapes. She remembered then that she had asked permission to present them, and she gestured them all forward to stand before their god. All came stiffly to salute, catching and holding deep breaths.

"Say to them 'I see you,'" Ariadne whispered in Dionysus' ear.

"I see you," he said, and then with his erratic perceptiveness seemed to know that wasn't enough. In her mind, as if he were scrying her, Ariadne heard him ask for their names and she answered, without effort, in the same manner.

"Dido, I see you," he said to the elder priestess and to the younger, "I see you, Hagne." Upon which he turned to the priests and said "I see you, Kadmos. I see you, Leiandros."

Breath sighed out of all of them in a trembling gust.

"The Lord Dionysus is a merciful god. As you asked, so you have been acknowledged," Ariadne said before any could speak. "Now you may take the tray and the dishes."

When they were gone, Dionysus turned to Ariadne and asked, "What does that mean? I see you. Of course I saw them. How should I not? They were standing right in front of me."

Ariadne looked startled, then cocked her head in thought. "It's a royal greeting," she said, grinning suddenly. "It's very clever, really. It permits a powerful person to acknowledge recognition of a suitor or a courtier without making any promises."

Dionysus looked back at her with widened eyes, then also grinned. "Well, well, well," he murmured, "that *is* clever, and I know who'll be most grateful to me for suggesting such a device." He stood up then and caught Ariadne to him in a hug. With an arm still around her, he led her out of the inner chambers to the outer shrine.

The stars were very bright, but still Ariadne hesitated on the threshold, wondering how she would see when she was out in the fields. Dionysus seemed to understand and went back inside, where he took from the wall a hooked staff used for cutting bunches of grapes from high arbors or trees into which they had climbed. A touch set it glowing. Another touch, this on Ariadne's breast, left a glowing patch which, without needing explanation, she somehow sucked inside herself and attached to a leaf of her heartflower. Then Dionysus took her hand—and vanished.

He was there. She could feel his strong grip and the warmth of his body not far from hers, but she couldn't see him. "It's a gift of Hekate's," he said. "She made the spell for Eros, but then she gave it to me also. It takes a *lot* of power, but I never lacked for that."

"But why don't you wish to be seen, my dear lord? The people *love* you. They would—"

"They would want to follow me and play games for which, little priestess, you are too young. When you're older . . . I'll see. For now, if people see you walking alone through the vineyard, they'll accept a solemn blessing. And when the vines grow strong and the grapes rich, that will increase your power and, through you, mine. For now, that will be enough."

They went together, his hand in hers, and, though her eyes couldn't make out his form, the silver mist that flowed from her and back into her made him out clearly and "showed" her and "told" her what to do. Soon Dionysus blessed only the right of the lane through which they passed and Ariadne blessed the left with wide swings of her glowing staff. She felt the power flow from her as she felt it flow when she set stasis on any object; but here in the fields, blessing the vines, she didn't feel cold or empty. Warmth flowed into her as fast, faster, than she could cast it over the vines she passed. Her steps quickened, until she was running lightly, surely, along the rows of vines, Dionysus' hand still locked firmly in hers.

Ariadne would've sworn that no one could run all night, not even she who danced for the Mother. Then she had her periods of rest. Whether she'd ever stopped all night long, she didn't know; all she was sure of was that she had passed through every vineyard in the land ruled directly from the Palace of Knossos—except those that belonged to Minos.

In the courtyard of the temple, Dionysus reappeared to her sight, laughing, his eyes alight, for once not with rage but with pure delight.

"How?" she asked him, also laughing with pleasure, "how could I run for stadia and stadia and not feel breathless or tired at all? When I use power to make a stasis, I'm exhausted, cold and weak. Now I'm warm and stronger than before I started. And you aren't tired either."

"That's because when you make a stasis, you're using a spell that is no part of you. The ability to make vines strong is my Gift—and seemingly yours also. A Gift is as much a part of you or me as the beating of our hearts. That doesn't make us tired. Nor does the use of a Gift natural to us."

"But I felt the power flow out of me, as when I make stasis. Only it flowed back in even faster."

He smiled. "The Mother gives us our Gifts. I suppose She provides the power for them when we use them according to Her will."

Ariadne glanced quickly at him and away. Did gods need Gifts from the Mother? Hadn't they all the power— She put the thought aside quickly as Dionysus cocked his head at her and said, "I wish She'd provided a filling for my stomach too. I'm very hungry."

She laughed and said she'd fetch food, no dainty dishes this time but olives and cheese and bread, but as she went to get the meal, conscious of the emptiness of her own belly after so much exercise, she wondered again about the need of a god for the same food that common humans ate. No slaughtered kine were offered to the Mother. Braziers of incense were lit, sweet music of drum, pipe, and sistrum was offered, and the beauty of the dance. The Mother did not eat, and yet Ariadne was very aware of the power of the Mother. What else sustained her to dance and dance or to run all night long as she had just done?

Still, as the days passed, she couldn't doubt the power of Dionysus either, even if he did eat cheese and olives. On five succeeding nights he came to fetch her. On each night, she would be standing in his embrace before the altar of the shrine one moment; in the next, she would be standing with his hands on her shoulders before an utterly strange shrine. Often there was shock and consternation among the priests and priestesses; sometimes Ariadne read anger and envy in the face of the local priestess.

Dionysus gave no one time to incite his wrath, however. He announced who Ariadne was—his chosen high priestess—and he touched the servants of each shrine with a single wave of rage and terror so violent that they fell groveling to the ground. While they lay, he led Ariadne out into the moonless dark and they blessed the fields. The last night, there was a hair-thin crescent of moon. That night, which was almost warm, Ariadne brought the renewing meal out and they ate sitting on the altar. When he was finished, Dionysus touched her face with slightly greasy fingers.

"I won't see you again for a time," he said. "There are other fields and vines to bless than those of Crete. I may make merrier over them, but remember—if you hear lewd tales of me—that I've had greater pleasure with you than in all those bacchanals."

He was gone before she could reply and for a tenday or two she had little to do and felt very sad, but then the people began to come up Gypsades Hill. The priests and priestesses told her that all through the vineyard leaves were bursting from bud almost with violence; the vines seemed to pulse with the force of their growing. And early and strong there were flowerlets that promised thick bunches of grapes. Only in the vineyard that belonged to the king were there reluctant, blighted leaves, thin growth, and no sign of coming grapes.

The road up Gypsades Hill could be seen from the south side of the Place of Knossos, in fact from the porch that sheltered the king's own apartment. Perhaps Minos himself saw the constant stream of people driving and carrying sacrifices up the road or perhaps those who tended the vines on his lands complained of their sad condition. Whichever was the spark, one moon to the day that Ariadne and Dionysus had blessed the vineyard, her younger brother Glaukos, followed by a glittering retinue, stalked into the shrine.

He demanded Ariadne's own presence from Dido and Kadmos, who had been accepting and recording offerings, and Hagne went to fetch her. Summoned, Ariadne twitched with the impulse to spring to her feet and hurry to perform whatever service her brother demanded. She reminded herself of who and what she was now, and took the time to dress and make sure her hair was properly combed.

Although she kept her face without expression, Ariadne was delighted to see Glaukos' haughty demeanor wilt a trifle when she came from the inner chambers and took her place directly before the painting of Dionysus. She knew that it almost seemed that the hands of the god, thrust forward a little in the painting, rested on her shoulders. Her wine red dress, banded in beaten gold, dazzled her brother's eyes, and he blinked and looked away from her high-dressed hair, wound with gold chains of winking gems, which set off the long curled locks of consecration that fell before her ears down on her budding breasts.

She saw him swallow and his lips thin—doubtless as he reminded himself she was only his little sister, but she said nothing, only waited, staring at him.

At length he cleared his throat. "Third daughter of Minos," he snapped. "Your father summons you to appear before him."

"I am no daughter of Minos'," Ariadne replied evenly and coldly. "In the dawn of the turn of the year, before this very altar, Minos yielded me into the hand of Dionysus, who deigned to accept me. I am the high priestess of Dionysus, his Mouth, with power to bless the vineyards of Crete."

"You haven't blessed them on King Minos' land," Glaukos retorted angrily.

"No, indeed. On Minos' land, the god withheld his blessing."

"But you're Minos' daughter. You were *his* sacrifice to the god, who you say, deigned to accept you. His vines should be specially favored."

"The house of King Minos *has* been specially favored through my pleas and intercession. Remember what befell King Pentheus, who offended the god Dionysus and was torn apart by his own people, his mother first among them. Be glad that no worse has befallen Knossos beyond the failure of its vineyard."

Although Glaukos hadn't himself attended the consecration of Ariadne, his elder brother's shaken recounting of what had occurred and Androgeos' new respect for his sister had made an impression. And Glaukos did remember what had happened to King Pentheus. The king and his household all dead, the whole country ravaged by ravening hordes, who killed and tore for no apparent reason, all totally mad. Fifty years had passed, but that poor bloodstained realm was still a shambles avoided by all.

"What are you talking about?" Glaukos asked, burying fear in bluster.

"I am the Mouth of Dionysus. When I came to speak my god's warning, as I am bound to do, I was insulted and assaulted, driven out. You know what Dionysus does to those who reject him. Only by my tears and pleading did I withhold his hand from you all. Accept the cursing of the vines and be grateful. Praise Dionysus, who can be merciful."

Glaukos stared at her for a long moment, then turned and left the shrine, his men following. Ariadne bit her lip, wondering whether she had convinced him and what he would say to her father. She had an answer quickly enough. The very next day, a messenger came from the palace requesting an audience before Dionysus' priestess for King Minos himself.

Ariadne wore black to receive him, and to her relief he came forward alone and saluted her with fist to forehead.

"I see you, King Minos," Ariadne murmured.

His lips twisted at the formal greeting and his hand came down with some force, showing how little he'd expected it. "Are we cursed forever?" he asked angrily. "Are we damned to be ground between the upper millstone of Poseidon's will and the lower one of Dionysus' rage? Don't you see that the failure of the king's vines, and only the king's vines, will make nobles and commons alike look askance at me and shake my rule. You spoke of sacrifice and restitution. What sacrifice? The bull from the sea is already gone. In the morning after Pasiphae . . . did whatever she did, the bull was gone. What restitution? I would make my peace with you but I cannot force Pasiphae to give up what she bears."

"You need make no peace with me. It is Lord Dionysus you have offended."

"Lord Dionysus?" Minos' voice was now uncertain.

"He came to bless the vines, as he promised. And he learned how his Mouth had been received. It is only through my pleas that all of Knossos is not a bloody shambles. Lord Dionysus is not a patient god."

Minos licked his lips. "You know your mother. What could I do? What can I do?"

Nothing, Ariadne thought. But the first sin had been his in keeping the bull from the sea. If it was Poseidon's will that Pasiphae bear what she carried, to thwart the Earth-Shaker might bring much worse upon Crete than a family tragedy. Poseidon might tear the island apart, bury it in the sea. Beyond that she remembered her father's bitter question about whether they must be ground between Poseidon's will and Dionysus' rage. Poseidon's will seemed fixed, but Dionysus was no longer angry, and it was the duty of a Mouth to speak the truth.

She shook her head. "The punishment that befell you has nothing to do with Lord Dionysus' Vision. His warning was given to you in mercy, to save you from a disaster if it was possible. If you don't heed his warning, doubtless you'll suffer, but not by Lord Dionysus' act or will. Lord Dionysus didn't withhold the blessing on the vineyard of Knossos because your wife wishes to carry the curse of Poseidon to fruition or because you wouldn't sacrifice the bull from the sea. Your vineyards were overpassed because Queen Pasiphae insulted his Vision and threatened harm to the Mouth that spoke it."

Minos' eyes had narrowed as Ariadne spoke. She assumed he was angry and she was sorry for him, knowing how hard it must be to swallow reprimand from his own child—a mere daughter and very young at that. Her sympathy didn't last long; Ariadne was appalled when her father's brow lifted and a sneer bent his lips.

"So Dionysus won't contest with Poseidon for power."

For one moment Ariadne was struck dumb with

shock. She could never have guessed how Minos would interpret her attempt to soothe him. Then the woman inside her stirred.

"Contest about a curse laid upon a foolish native?" She laughed; the voice was not hers. "Because you were my father before I was consecrated to him Dionysus wished to warn you, but I doubt if he really cares if a double curse falls on you."

Doubt flickered on Minos' face as he remembered his blighted vines in the midst of burgeoning growth. He wasn't so sure Pasiphae's burden was a curse—beyond the fact that the god had cuckolded him—but since Dionysus apparently no longer demanded Pasiphae abort the child, a little humbling was a cheap price to pay if that would restore his vines.

So, when Ariadne began to turn away, he cried, "Wait," and raised his fist to his brow in salute again. "From this time forward," he said, "the Mouth of Dionysus will be welcome and respected in the Place of Knossos and I will double the offerings that are traditional. And I sue humbly for the curse to be removed from my vines so that the peace of the realm may not be troubled."

His voice was smooth, his face expressionless. Ariadne's heart sank. She'd seen that face and heard that voice whenever her father negotiated for advantages with the paraoh of Egypt or the kings of Greece. Behind that blandness was calculation. She'd made matters worse. She'd failed to convince Minos that the fruit of Pasiphae's womb was a curse. She might even have made Poseidon's get desirable—something her father hoped to use as a weapon to keep his people meek and quiet despite Dionysus' displeasure.

Was this matter serious enough to Call to Dionysus? In the privacy of her own chamber, Ariadne stared at the god's chair and shuddered. Must she betray what she feared were her father's intentions?

And what if Dionysus, to show his power the greater, killed what was in Pasiphae's womb? Would Poseidon accept that tamely? Would he match power with Dionysus, daring the madness Dionysus could cast upon him? Or would he take the easier path, assume the people of Crete were guilty and break their island apart as he'd done in the past?

PART TWO:

ASTERION

CHAPTER 8

No one likes to admit a serious blunder or set loose a catastrophe. Ariadne didn't want to tell Dionysus that his Vision had been rejected by her parents, that her mother insisted on bearing what Poseidon had set into her and that her father agreed. She put off Calling him while she sought reasons for him not to punish her family further, but she sought in vain and in the end he appeared beside her bed early one morning without being Called.

He looked terrible, so ashen pale that his skin had

a faint greenish tinge, mouth swollen, eyes heavy-lidded and ringed with bruised-looking mauve-colored skin. She'd have been frightened, if she hadn't seen the look before, on her brothers when they'd been making too merry among the wine pots and the women of pleasure. But could a god get wine-sick and drained out by lust?

Pushing that thought into the back of her mind, she sat up and held out her hand. "How can I serve you, my lord?"

He took the hand she had offered in so tight a grip that Ariadne had to bite her lip to keep from crying out. When he saw that, he eased his hold.

"I just wanted to make sure you were here, that I hadn't dreamed of how the vineyards of Crete were blessed." He took a deep breath and forced a small smile. "I'll go now that I've seen you."

"Oh, don't go so soon, my lord." She scrambled out of bed, her eyes widening as she came closer and saw that his clothing and his body, where it was not covered, looked as overworn as his face. "You are soiled and exhausted. Let me draw a bath for you and—" she hesitated, wondering if she dared mention that he was marked with nicks and scratches and trickles of blood. Could gods be injured and bleed like common mortals?

"And?" He was smiling more naturally.

"And find some salve for your hurts?" she finished timidly.

He hesitated, staring at her, and then said, "Yes."

"Lie down then, my lord," she said, steering him toward the bed, "while I make all ready."

She was surprised by an initial stiffening, as if he would resist, but she was already turning away, reaching for the robe that lay over a chair. Before she could face him again and ask what was wrong, he released her hand and lay down with a long sigh. His eyes were closed before she was out of the door, so she didn't hurry, rousing the servants to heat and carry water and telling the priestesses to be sure there was more than enough and of the best quality for breaking the fast.

When they were busy about their tasks, she went quietly to where the medicines were kept and took a pot of the unguent used for wounds. This she hid in the folds of her robe while she returned to the bedchamber. Whatever her own doubts about gods who needed to eat bread and cheese and who could be scratched by brambles and scraped by stones, she didn't want to arouse similar doubts in others.

As she had hoped, Dionysus was soundly asleep, his body huddled in on itself as if he were cold . . . or trying to ward off some ill. She put the unguent pot at the back of a shelf, where it wouldn't be easily seen, and then drew her coverlet over him. He was so beautiful, even sapped out and filthy, that she could have stood staring forever, but a faint movement of his head, as if he were trying to turn away, warned her and she left the room and closed the door.

After standing for a moment, she went to tell the servants to fill the bath with cold water only and keep the hot water on the hob until it was needed. Then, remembering the little frown between Dionysus' brows and the greenish tinge of his skin, she ran as quickly as she could to the kitchens of the palace, where she asked the cook for that remedy he made for her brothers when they had been carousing.

Although he scolded her for running errands—a high priestess, he said, should send servants to do her will—he prepared the draught right there. This time, Ariadne paid close attention so that in the future she could make up the drink herself.

She was breathless, more with anxiety than with the effort of running, when she returned, but all was quiet, and she took the potion to her chamber and set it beside the unguent. She frowned at that. It would do no good to have hidden the salve if Dionysus' body was exposed for any to see, but he was far too large for her to borrow a priest's tunic. Ariadne spent more time contriving a garment from the cloth she kept for herself, but even when that task was accomplished, he slept. Eventually she broke her fast alone and told Hagne, who carried away most of the meal, that a special midday meal should be prepared. She had begun to think that, too, would have to be set aside when Dionysus finally called from the bedchamber.

At first—at least after the cook's remedy had taken effect—Dionysus found Ariadne's preparations, which included fetching the hot water herself so the servants shouldn't see him and anointing his cuts and bruises after the bath, very funny. For a time he seemed utterly contemptuous of what the servants and priests and priestesses saw. Then he began to cast odd glances at her, and by the time he had finished eating and leaned back in his chair with a cup of wine in his hand, he was staring at Ariadne with such intensity that she began to tremble. Seeing that, he crooked a finger at her and she came and knelt at his feet.

"So you're wondering what I am, are you?" he asked.

"You are my lord, my god," Ariadne answered, head bowed.

"No matter whether I am a god or not? Isn't that what you mean?"

"You are my lord, my god," Ariadne repeated stubbornly.

"Because you're afraid of what I will do if you doubt my divinity?"

She lifted her head and met his eyes. "Because I love you. Because you've been kinder to me than any other person in the world has been. Because . . ." her voice slowed and faded, but then she went on more firmly, "bcause you *are* a person." She dropped her head again. "The Mother is kind to me also. I feel Her warmth. She gives me strength. But . . . but She . . . She's so much beyond my understanding, my reach." She looked up. "You are my god, Dionysus, my own precious god."

She knew he was no god, that was clear enough. Dionysus looked into his wine cup instead of at the fragile, kneeling girl. He knew what Zeus would say, or Athena, or Apollo, that he should kill her before she . . . Before she what? Told anyone? Ridiculous. Hadn't he just been laughing because she had gone to such lengths to be sure that even the consecrated priests and priestesses of his temple shouldn't know he was wine-sick, that he could be wounded?

She was more careful not to cast any doubt on his divinity than he was. And she was aware of his power. She could feel it even when she was spared its effects; she'd begged for mercy for those in the shrine on the day of her consecration. So, for their own sakes, she wouldn't allow anyone to think he could be challenged.

The other side of the coin was even more dangerous. If she knew he was no god, wouldn't she soon guess the other Olympian mages were not divine? They would be less merciful.

"So I'm your god out of love, but what of those you don't love? What of Poseidon?"

Ariadne shuddered. "One doesn't question what the Earth-Shaker is when one lives on Crete. Nor is it safe or sane to ask questions about any of the others. If they aren't like the Mother, they're still able to rule us through Her Gifts and their power."

"That's very wise. It would be wise also not to talk of this to anyone."

Now Ariadne smiled. "To whom do I have to talk? The priestesses are too awed and, to tell the truth, too old to be interested in the things I am; the novices newly sworn to the temple are too young."

"You have a father, a mother, a sister, brothers . . ." His voice faded as he watched her face. He could see that her eyes, no matter they were already downcast, shifted. "So," he said, "your family has been troubling you again, about the vines that were not blessed, no doubt."

"Glaukos came as if he would brazen out a demand, but he yielded quickly. Then my father came." She hesitated. "He has doubled his offerings and swears if I come again to Knossos as your Mouth that I will be listened to respectfully and not threatened. He says that to leave his vines blighted when those of all the rest of Crete are full and rich might shake his rule, the people and nobles thinking that he isn't acceptable to you. He begs humbly that you bless his vines."

Dionysus stared at her for a moment longer, then burst out laughing. "You should've told me this tale when I first came into your bedchamber. Now I'm fed and rested, I hear more than the words. So you've told me the better, now out with the bitter."

Ariadne looked up at him under her long lashes. "If I had told you when you first came to me, you would've roared over to the palace and everyone in it would be dead. That's not what I want, even though I no longer acknowledge parents or siblings. Which takes me back to what you began to say about whom I had as a confidant: remember I have no father and mother; I was consecrated to you. I'll talk to no one but you, of course, about anything we say privately to each other."

"But you will try to protect your family from me—"

"Not from you, my lord. From Poseidon."

He cocked his head. "You want me to stand between your family and Poseidon?"

"No! Mother forfend! I only want you not to do what must offend Poseidon."

"Why should I offend Poseidon? Of all the Olympians, he is the one with whom I have least contact." His lips twisted. "And I don't have much contact with any of them."

Ariadne was silent, head bent. After a moment, Dionysus set his cup on the small table. She looked up. "My father won't part with what Pasiphae carries."

Dionysus shrugged. "He's a fool, but it's nothing to me."

"But I think he plans to use whatever . . . whoever . . . it is to diminish your authority in Crete. Perhaps to drive you out."

The words came out in a rush, after which Ariadne caught her breath. Dionysus burst out laughing. "Who cares? It's the vines of Crete that will suffer and the wines made from them. Perhaps I'm a little sorry for the farmers and the merchants who've suffered my indifference before. Do you think this little island is all my domain? There is Egypt and all the lands of the east and the west. Do you think I care about Crete?" He reached out and took her chin in his hand, lifting her head. "I care for you, Chosen."

She breathed a huge sigh and squirmed forward so she could lay her head on his knee. "Then I don't care either." After a moment, she looked up, her eyes pleading. "Oh, my lord, will you tell me of those other lands?"

He smiled into her eager face. "I'd tell you gladly, but I'm sorry to say there's not much I know." He grinned at her more broadly. "I don't travel for pleasure or to see the sights of the land, after all. All I know is the temples and the vineyards." And then his expression grew thoughtful. "Well, no. Perhaps I've seen more in some places." He stared at her, and then shook his head. "It's only here in Knossos that I stay so close to the temple."

Ariadne grinned in turn. "Because of me?"

"Yes."

"Then I'm doubly glad you go abroad in other places, first because you can tell me about them and second because that means no other priestess is as pleasant for you to be with as I am."

He tapped a finger on her nose. "Don't get above yourself. Perhaps I never thought before of making a friend of a priestess."

Although Ariadne suspected from what he'd said in the past that he had made a friend and lover, too, of the first Ariadne, she had no intention of reminding him of that. She caught at his hand. "Oh, don't, my lord. Don't look for another. I'll not get overproud, I promise. And I'll be whatever you want me to be. You've only to tell me what you desire."

Dionysus shook his head, but when she asked why, he wouldn't answer and asked whether she wanted to hear about foreign lands or not, whereupon she nodded eagerly and settled herself to listen.

Altogether it was a delightful afternoon, most of it spent talking in the chamber but also walking in the temple garden in the early dusk and then—Dionysus invisible again—examining the nearer vineyards. He left when the Hunter hung overhead without even a fare-thee-well; she only knew when his hand released hers. She continued to walk through the rows of grapes, a little sad but vastly content also, somehow knowing that he would come again, and soon.

So he did, sometimes sick as he had been that first time, sometimes raging over something he wouldn't explain, sometimes only weary and hurt. He would appear beside her wherever she happened to be and she would welcome him with delight, her heartflower bursting open and spinning out its silver strands. And whatever his mood, when those enwrapped him, he calmed and smiled.

They never spoke of her family again, except on his second visit, when she told him there was much talk against her father and that she would like to bless what grapes had formed on the vines of Knossos so the curse on him shouldn't seem absolute. To that, utterly indifferent, Dionysus gave permission—and changed the subject. When he came, they lived in their own little world. He taught her magic, to light lamps, torches, and fires with a gesture; to freeze a person where he stood; to fetch articles from other rooms in the temple.

Magic left her tired, although not so drained as it once had, and while she rested, they talked of many things, or rather, Dionysus talked and Ariadne listened. She was fascinated by what he told her and it enlarged her rather narrow view of life. She learned that she was very fortunate to have been born a Cretan. Cretan women were much more free and powerful than women in most other societies. Egypt was next best. But in many places women were accounted for very little, powerless, not permitted to own property or even rights to their own bodies. Ariadne realized that those lands had lost the worship of the Mother, had overlaid her power with that of mostly male deities, and were much given to war.

The city-states of Greece were prime examples. They fought each other constantly, each calling on the patron god of that city, who sometimes helped and sometimes ignored the calls. Ariadne did not need to ask why; that much she knew from her father's dealings with his nobles. To keep them divided among themselves made him stronger. To keep the worshipers in doubt as to the god's favor, induced more generous giving at the temples. Ariadne had some proof of that already. Although the offerings were still adequate, they were not anything near that first outpouring. There would be another outflow, she guessed, when the wine fermented sweet and rich, but if the plenty continued unabated, the offerings would grow fewer, unless they were stimulated in some way.

Sometimes, however, Dionysus spoke of more personal matters. He told her unhappily more than once of the mother who had been seduced by Zeus and then abandoned, except for leaving her covered with a heap of gold. And although Dionysus had never known her, he'd quarreled with Zeus about her and had eventually gone into the Underworld and badgered Hades into allowing him to bring Semele to Olympus. Hades had warned him it was a mistake, but wouldn't say why. And Hades had been right; Semele knew her son no more than he knew her. Like all the others, she was afraid of him. She wouldn't stay with him and had returned to Plutos.

Did he live all alone? Ariadne had asked. That set off another set of tales. He explained about his household in Olympus, describing Bacchus and Silenos who lived with him. Good friends, he called them, but Ariadne realized from what he said that they were given over entirely to the joys of the body and, possibly, weren't too clever. He didn't say it in words, but Ariadne understood that he was lonely.

The tales and explanations were long ones, full of byways, some joy, much anguish, and not to be spun out in an hour. Ten-days passed. At midsummer they ran the vineyards again spreading the Mother's blessing so that the grapes were full and sweet; and in the autumn, they went a third time. That time Dionysus taught Ariadne how to touch a bunch here and there with a certain mold, which would lend a special flavor to the wine. After they had covered the whole island, Ariadne was a trifle anxious, fearing that Dionysus would settle into Olympus for the winter and not come to her, but she was wrong about that.

Since he had become so sure she would welcome him in any and all circumstances and conditions without fear or questions, he was easier and lighter hearted, teasing and joking and clearly taking great joy in the fact that Ariadne also teased him and played childish tricks on him. He abandoned all pretense that he came as a godly duty and began to bring with him games and scrolls full of stories and ancient lore. They played the games but Dionysus found the stories silly and they left the scrolls alone.

On the morning of the winter equinox, the courtyard of the shrine was packed, the people overflowing onto the sides of Gypsades Hill. The wine was already sweet and strong and would be like the nectar of the gods when it had aged. When Ariadne looked into the scrying bowl as the sunlight touched the rim, she thought a wry smile and words that appeared in no ritual: "Sorry, my love, I know it's too early for you, but custom is custom. Will you come?"

Half growling, half laughing, he obediently rose and dressed and came, and the shouts of the people, despite an unusual bitter cold, nearly shivered loose the stones of the shrine. Minos, in the first row, saluted with the others, but his lips didn't part in any hymn of praise. Pasiphae was not present. She was said to be almost too big with child to walk and her delivery was imminent.

It was a shock for Ariadne to remember that, to realize suddenly that if Pasiphae had conceived on the night of Dionysus' Vision, she'd carried the babe more than a month over the normal time. A hope flared in her that her mother had lied, that she hadn't conceived or the god hadn't come and what she carried was Minos'—or some other man's—get.

The hope fled as Dionysus tilted her face up for his kiss. His Visions were always true. Could Pasiphae be carrying her young for the term of a cow's breeding? Ariadne buried that horrible thought and began to wonder whether she would ever be permitted to bear Dionysus' child.

Not that time, in any event. He shrouded them in darkness, but did no more than hug her and explain that he couldn't linger this time. A faint shadow crossed his face but he only said he had been invited to a celebration of the winter equinox that he couldn't fail to attend. Ariadne kissed him again as he dismissed the darkness, and hastened to draw on the robe she'd just removed and to help a shivering Dionysus with his himation. At the god's gesture, the audience departed and they hurried inside, Dionysus shaking his head and wondering aloud who could be so idiotic as to expect god and priestess to couple on a freezing stone altar.

"Surely even a god would have more common sense than that!" he protested indignantly.

Ariadne was still laughing when he disappeared. He would be back as soon as he could come, she was sure.

The next day, however, she was wakened suddenly by the frantic pealing of the bell at the temple gate. Pale light came through the shaft window; it was morning, but much earlier than Ariadne normally left her bed. Still, she sat up at once. The bell pealed again. Although she was no healer nor could she imagine any emergency that a priestess of Dionysus could be expected to amend in the middle of the winter, she rose and hurriedly pulled on a warm gown. There was something in the pealing of that bell that brought her pounding heart right up into her throat.

The voice that called her name was Phaidra's, high and hysterical. Some disaster had struck Knossos. Disaster. Ariadne's mind leapt to her thought of the previous morning, that Pasiphae was due to expel whatever she had carried in her overfull belly. She ran out to meet Phaidra.

"I can't! I can't!" Phaidra wailed, casting herself into Ariadne's arms. "It's too horrible. I can't do it. You must help me."

"Of course I'll help you," Ariadne soothed, "but you have to tell me first what it is you can't do."

"I can't care for it. I can't. Mother had no right to bear a monster and cast its care on me."

Cold washed down Ariadne's back. Through stiff lips, she asked, "The child is born?"

"Child?" Phaidra echoed and shuddered. "I don't know what it is. Come. You must come. She's already very angry with me because it's crying, but I can't touch it. I can't. And the maids fled away. Come. You must come."

There was no "must" about it. Ariadne had warned Pasiphae to clean out her womb; she wasn't responsible for the result of the queen's refusal. She had also forsworn her family and could say with a clear conscience that she was no longer bound to them by blood ties. But it wasn't that simple. The queen had borne what a god had imposed on her. And all Ariadne's life, except these past nine moons, she had cared for Phaidra. Moreover, Phaidra hadn't cast her off. She had come often to the temple to give Ariadne news, to gossip and laugh. If Pasiphae was angry with Phaidra, the child would be made to suffer. Ariadne couldn't abandon Phaidra to her mother's rage.

"Come. You must come," Phaidra insisted.

Ariadne yielded to Phaidra's pull and went with her out of the gate and down the hill. She was so sick with apprehension, that she could feel bile in her throat and she didn't dare ask a question for fear she would spew. Phaidra was silent too, except for one sentence, muttered under her breath, "Oh, why wouldn't it die quietly," which reminded Ariadne that her sister had said "It was crying."

She heard the thin wailing as soon as she came out of the stairwell that led to the second floor, and her heart lurched. The cries were broken, exhausted, as if the child had been unattended for a very long time. Phaidra dropped her hand, but Ariadne knew perfectly well where to go and broke into a run.

She faltered at the doorway. The room stank. Then the cradle lurched and the tired wailing, which had been still for a moment, began again. Ariadne hurried forward, her teeth set, and looked into the cradle. The child was naked and lying on its stomach, and at first sight was not so dreadful, except for the filth. True, a thick mane of black hair grew over the head and halfway down the back, but it had two arms and two legs and the correct number of fingers and toes.

The condition of the cradle was far worse than a little extra hair, and it was far too cold to leave an infant not only wet and soiled but naked. Ariadne snatched up a clean blanket from a pile on a wall shelf, threw it over the child's back and picked it up. As she turned it, a gasping cry was wrung from her, and she had to tighten her arms consciously not to drop the child.

What caught the eye was the black mass that protruded into a broad muzzle and covered almost the whole bottom half of the face. In it were two large holes that quivered as the little creature drew breath; below it a wide slit of a mouth with no lips and almost no chin opened to emit another wail. The eyes were large, bulbous, and set too far apart, but the lids were furnished with long, thick, curling lashes—a travesty of beauty that was almost more horrible than more ugliness would have been. A finger width of brow separated the eyes from the growth of black hair, which continued on down the child's back, and there were two bumps under the hair just above the brow.

Ariadne stared, transfixed, aware that the horror of that little face was not really strange to her, that she had seen it before and not found it horrible at all. And then she remembered where she'd seen it and wavered where she stood, her soul in turmoil. She knew what Poseidon had done, and something inside her screamed and screamed for help while tears of pity and remorse ran down her face.

"Turn it around! Turn it around!" Phaidra cried from the doorway. "How can you bear to look at it?"

Ariadne almost couldn't bear it, but the little creature had stopped screaming now that she held it. At Phaidra's voice, it twitched in her grip and uttered a tiny whimper. Instinctively she rocked it in her arms, and it made a small hiccup. Ariadne drew a fold of the blanket over the child's face.

It was her fault that the poor thing was being shunned, all her fault. She was no seer. She had misunderstood Dionysus' Vision and been too sure that Poseidon's curse would fall on all of Knossos, perhaps all of Crete. She had spoken that conviction aloud for too many to hear. She had set into everyone's mind that what Pasiphae was bearing was a great evil. The babe *was* a curse—a cruel, cruel revenge that Poseidon had taken, but not a great evil, except to itself. Minos would never forget that he had tried to cheat a god. Every time he looked into his youngest son's face, he would see the head of a bull.

Whipped by her own regret, Ariadne turned furiously on Phaidra. "Come in here and take that mess out of the cradle," she snapped. "What's wrong with you? It's not the child's fault that he's so ugly. You are the monsters, not he. How could you be so cruel as to leave a helpless infant unfed, wallowing in his own dirt. Get those foolish maids back in here at once."

"They won't come," Phaidra said sullenly.

"They'll come or I'll have them torn apart." Ariadne's black eyes showed sparks of red, and Phaidra backed up a step. "If you run, I'll come after you and whip you myself, and what your mother will do to you, I don't like to think. Now, do as I say. You may tell the maids they don't yet need to handle the child, but they must provide me with clean padding for the cradle, warm water for washing, and oil for anointing. I want a wet-nurse—"

"That you won't get," Phaidra said, "no matter what you threaten. That thing almost tore the nipple off the woman who tried to suckle him. The next will last no longer than the first. *I* won't try to find another."

About to tell Phaidra not to be ridiculous, that the child must eat, Ariadne paused. She wasn't sure the mouth was made for suckling, except the long teat of a cow.

"Then bring me a long-spouted cruet, a small one, and warmed pots of goat's milk, ewe's milk, and cow's milk, and quickly. And don't be such a fool! It's ugly, poor little thing, but it's only a baby."

"It's a curse upon us!"

"No," Ariadne said, tears starting to her eyes again. "Only on itself, and for the rest of his life, a bitter reminder to King Minos of how he tried to cheat the Lord Poseidon."

Under Phaidra's urging, backed by the threat that she would tell Queen Pasiphae if they wouldn't obey her, the maids crept back into the nursery. Their fears were somewhat reduced when they saw Ariadne holding the child as if it were any other baby, rocking it in her arms and murmuring to it. One, shrinkingly, brought the cruet and the pots of milk forward. Another, when Ariadne asked, said it was believed that ewe's milk was the richest and the easiest for a child to take in lieu of mother's milk. So Ariadne bid her pour ewe's milk into the cruet, laid the child on her knees, and lifting its head so it would not choke, dribbled a few drops of milk into the mouth that opened to wail again.

The wail was cut off abruptly to swallow; the mouth opened again eagerly. The contents of the cruet disappeared in an amazingly short time with only a few mishaps when the eager baby tried to reach the spout more quickly and spilled milk or, once, almost knocked the cruet from Ariadne's hand. When the child had had its fill, and had been dandled on her knee and shoulder until it brought up wind, Ariadne washed it and dried it and wrapped it in swaddling cloths—and stared as the cloths virtually burst open under the thrusts of the babe's arms and legs.

Only then did she really look at the child and realize that it was half again larger than any newborn babe she had ever seen, remember how it had lifted its head off her arm, almost lifted its entire body, in an attempt to reach the milk. She blinked back new tears. It was very strong. Poseidon was taking no chance that his revenge would be cut short by a natural failing. Surely that infant had been Gifted with strength. Swallowing, she tried gently to rewrap it, but it wouldn't bear the confinement and it yelled and struck out, hard enough to hurt her a little.

Stroking the furred head until it calmed, she turned the creature on its stomach, adjusted the head so that the protruding muzzle was not in the way, and covered it. She stroked the head a while longer and the bulbous eyes closed, the black nostrils fluttered with little snorts. It slept.

Ariadne ground her teeth together to keep them

from chattering. All she wanted to do was to run back to the shrine and forget what she had seen. Her guilt stabbed at her. She knew if the maids and Phaidra guessed she wouldn't return, they would also leave. She turned to confront her sister.

"Now you can see it's only a babe, no great evil—"

"Why did you tend it?" Phaidra asked bitterly. "I thought you would silence it. . . ."

"Phaidra!" Ariadne exclaimed. "It is a poor, helpless babe. How could you think I would harm it? And don't you be such a fool either. There can be no doubt this is the Earth-Shaker's child. Can you imagine what he would do to Knossos, to all of Crete, if deliberate harm were inflicted on his son?"

Phaidra came close and whispered in Ariadne's ear, "But if only one person did the harm and that person was protected by another god, perhaps . . ."

"Oh, no," Ariadne snapped, pushing Phaidra away. "This matter is more serious than taking a whipping for your sake as I have done in the past. I don't think the god Poseidon would trouble himself to distinguish between one common native and another. He would blame us all if any did harm to his get. His get . . . Hasn't the child been named?"

"Oh, yes," Phaidra said, her lips down turned. "Mother did that much. Its name is Asterion."

At the mention of her mother, Ariadne cast a glance over her shoulder at the child. The birthing of such a one could not have been easy, even though Pasiphae had borne eight before. "How is the queen?" she asked. "It must have been a hard bearing."

"She will bear no more children," Phaidra said, eyes downcast, "but she will live."

A thin finger of ice ran down Ariadne's spine. Could Phaidra have wished for her mother's death? But when her sister's eyes lifted again, there was no malice in them. Ariadne let out the breath she had unconsciously caught.

Phaidra burst into tears. "It's not fair. If mother were well, she would attend to this 'godling' of hers. I can't!"

"Oh, don't be ridiculous. From all I've heard from our elder sisters, the queen never cared for any of her babes. Until she married, it was Euryale's task to oversee the maids who attended to the new babes, and then Prokris watched over the younger ones. Now I am Dionysus' priestess and it's your turn."

"I can't." Phaidra shivered and clutched her arms around herself.

Ariadne went and gave her a hug. "Now, now. I know your monthly courses have begun. You're a woman now. It's only a very ugly baby. You know it did me no harm. Did he act in any way other than any other babe? Think what Poseidon will do if his son does not survive. Do you wish to take the chance if any harm came to Asterion that he would break Crete in pieces as he has done aforetimes?"

"I'm not a woman, courses or not." Phaidra wept. "I'm only one little girl, and the maids won't obey me. You saw how they ran away."

Ariadne looked around at the cowering women. "If you don't run away, neither will they. If they do you need only tell the queen and she will attend to them. After a few are whipped and broken, the others will be obedient." What she had said was true enough, but some of those maids had served her and her sister, and she really didn't want them to be whipped and broken. She sighed. "I'm willing to help care for Asterion for a few days longer, but I must give instruction to my priests and priestesses about what to do with the midwinter offerings and do some other business at the shrine. I'll return as soon as I can. Meanwhile, let Asterion sleep. If he wakes, feed him as you saw me do and clean him if needful."

She went out quickly, aware of the resentful looks cast at her and the contented snuffling of the child. She hoped that by calling it by name she had made it more of a person. It was horrible to think that Phaidra had run to her in the expectation that she would murder a helpless babe. As she fled down the stair and through the corridors that would take her out of the palace, she reconsidered the matter and by the time she was making her way up Gypsades Hill, she was almost smiling.

What a fool I am, Ariadne thought, walking a little slower now that she was no longer trying to escape her own horror. As Phaidra said, despite the start of her womanly courses, she was little more than a babe herself, mostly because, being youngest, she had never had much responsibility thrust upon her. Asterion was probably no more real to her than a doll.

Back in the days before Ariadne understood she would never sit between the sacral horns and judge the bull dancing, she had played at being priestess of the Snake Goddess. She could remember how she, herself, would impale a doll on a toy bull's horn to reenact the horror and excitement of a failure in the dance. She had not hesitated to "sacrifice" a doll. As Asterion grew up in Phaidra's care, he would grow real to her and she would come to love him.

"No one will 'come' to love him."

Ariadne's head jerked up and she gasped with shock, losing her balance and starting so violently that she banged her shoulder against the door frame as she entered her chamber. Dionysus stood just beyond the doorway in worse case than she had ever seen him. His face was lined and pallid and streaked with flaking brownish stains; his tunic was blotched, in places soaked, with what she realized was dried blood.

More blood covered his hands, blackened his nails, streaked his upper arms and legs.

Deliberately blind, Ariadne cried, "Oh, my lord, have you been waiting long for me? I am so sorry—"

"I haven't been waiting at all," he said. "I've been with you from when you first saw the bull-headed child. You screamed for help. I came."

He was perfectly expressionless, his blue eyes staring at her and at the same time through her. Ariadne braced herself against a shudder. If he saw her fear, he didn't offer comfort; his face might have been carved from rock or painted.

"I screamed for help?" Ariadne whispered, but she remembered the terrible shock, the nearly mindless pleas that had echoed through her and had wiped out all thought for a few moments. "How can you have been there and I not seen you?" she added.

"I can be unseen when I wish. You know that. Why you didn't see me isn't important. You're wrong about the child, Ariadne. He will bring death and bitter grief upon your family, infamy upon your people. You're wrong about Poseidon too. He neither knows nor cares about the child. If it dies, he'll think his spell was not perfect and, likely, having achieved the revenge of cuckolding the king and causing the queen to produce a monster, if no further insult is offered him, forget. If he doesn't forget, the blame will fall upon me."

Until those last words, Ariadne stood silent, staring. "What do you mean, the blame will fall upon you?" she asked, pale with horror.

"The child must die, but you may say it was by my prophecy."

"No!" Ariadne cried, weeping anew. "It's little and helpless. It struggled so hard to live, crying and crying for hours when no one would help it and any other babe would have given up. Why do you say it will bring death and grief? It's strong, but how can a tiny baby do such harm?"

His eyes focused on her. "Chosen, don't be such a fool. A babe doesn't stay a babe. It grows. And this will grow into such a monstrous thing—"

"No, no! It's my fault. I'm not a true seer. I only wished to hold you near me, so I told a tale about the bull with a man's head. This is no bull with a man's head. It's a small baby, a little helpless creature. It's ugly but not harmful."

Dionysus shook his head. "Whether you like it or not, you *are* a true seer. I know because the pain of the Vision departed when you found the meaning for it."

"It's not true. I know what I did. I put upon that poor malformed little boy all the horror I felt when I realized that my mother was going to betray my father, prostitute herself to Poseidon, just because you had come to my Call. I will do no more hurt to poor Asterion than I have already done by making everyone fear him as a curse."

"Will it be more harm to end his life quickly, without pain or fear, than to let him live to know what he is? To see horror and terror in everyone who looks at him? I'll show you how to put your hand on his body and stop its life. The babe will feel nothing. He'll be at peace."

"No! I comforted him. I held him in my arms. I cleaned him and fed him. I? I stop a babe's life? Never!"

"Listen to me. This . . . this thing must die, as the bull from the sea should have died. If you won't do this for the child's sake, you must do it for the good of all the people. He isn't a monster now—only, as you say, ugly—but he will become a monster. King Minos and Queen Pasiphae won't be content to conceal their shame. They'll call him a godling and use him to drive out the worship of those they'll call lesser gods, and they'll bring disaster upon themselves and the people of Crete."

Ariadne's eyes widened and her face paled further to a ghastly gray. "You would make me a murderer of an innocent babe just so that your worship would continue unabated?" She backed away a step, and then another step. "Compared with my brother's death on my soul, I don't care if no offering is ever made to you again. I don't even care if no grape ever ripens on Crete again. How would I live, Dionysus? How would I live, having murdered a helpless babe?"

Dionysus' lips thinned. "Stupid native with your tiny mind! What's a single life here and there among your teeming masses?" He stared at her, then bellowed, "Look at me! I am near drowned in blood from the feeding of the earth at the turning of the year. Have you always lied to yourself about what I am, about how most vineyards are made fertile? The beast must die, sooner or later. I'm only trying to spare you—and Asterion—pain." He made an angry gesture and his face filled with a disgusted contempt. "Oh, never mind. I'll do it myself. What's a little more blood?"

"No!" Ariadne screamed, spreading her arms across the doorway although she knew he could put her aside with one hand. "I will not worship a god who murders babes to enhance his own power! Make me mad! Turn my hand against myself. Call my servants and priests and priestesses. Make them mad so they will tear me apart. That would be better for me than to live knowing my god had betrayed me, that the being I love had taken a helpless, innocent life for his own profit. No, I could never forget my brother's death at your hands. I won't worship or honor a god who sheds kin-blood."

Dionysus stared at her in silence for one long moment, and then he was gone.

CHAPTER 9

Ariadne gasped with horror and ran back to the palace as fast as she could go. But Dionysus hadn't preceded her there to commit murder. She found Asterion just as she had left him, fast asleep, snorting a little with each breath. She collapsed when she saw that the child was safe, sinking to the floor and bowing her head into her hands in a passion of weeping. She knew what she had done. Dionysus was gone and wouldn't return.

Because of her misery, she spent more time caring for Asterion than she had intended. He wasn't a difficult child, aside from demanding frequent and huge feedings. When he was full and clean, however, he slept or lay quietly watching his own hands wave aimlessly about with those bulbous eyes. He was much stronger than any babe any of the maids had ever seen, and he grew at an almost inconceivable rate, but otherwise he was very like an ordinary baby.

Over the moon following his birth, the maids and Phaidra did seem to lose their fear of him and Phaidra even appeared to be growing fond. Pasiphae came once, after the second ten-day, leaning on a maid and still pale from loss of blood. From the shadows to which she had withdrawn, Ariadne watched, but her mother didn't cry out in horror at the bull's head which, free from the compression of birth, was now unmistakable. She was clearly delighted with Asterion's appearance.

She glanced at Ariadne only once, and her lips curved upward in a smile of triumph. "See that no harm comes to the new god," she said, lightly touching the protrusions on the baby's head where, to Ariadne's horror, the sharp points of horns were beginning to show. "Soon I will show how those of Knossos have been honored."

Her heart so heavy it was a burden within her, Ariadne acknowledged what she had pushed from her mind since Dionysus had told her. Her mother intended to display Asterion to the nobles and, possibly, even the commons of Crete and declare him a god. Would that bring upon the island punishment from the other gods? Had she been wrong to save Asterion's life when the price might be so high? Unconsciously, she picked up the child and he rubbed his muzzle confidingly against her shoulder and made a small chuckling noise.

Before the turning of the year to spring, Asterion was so large and so strong that he didn't need to be held to be fed. Nor could he be contented with milk. He cried and reached for whatever Ariadne ate and, seeing he already had teeth, she tried him on little pieces of this and that. Nothing she gave him ever caused him any discomfort, but what he took most eagerly was meat.

Once he could be propped up with cushions and simply handed solid food, Phaidra was willing to feed him and she would even shake a rattle or play at hiding behind her own fingers to see him laugh. Ariadne went back to the shrine. After a ten-day of indecision, on the day before the solstice, she filled her golden bowl with dark wine and Called.

The surface trembled and then Ariadne saw golden hair and blue eyes looking back. She had almost sobbed with relief when she saw the face was not that of Dionysus.

"You are the priestess of Knossos," the man said. "What do you want?"

"By my lord's order, I Call to remind him that tomorrow is the first day of spring when he comes to the altar."

"No god comes to an altar that rejects him."

"But the child lives!" Ariadne cried, tears running down her face. "I don't reject him. And what of his promise to bless the blooming grapes with me?"

"Bless them yourself, as you blessed the vines, you who place conditions on your worship. A god can do no wrong. Once you said that."

Tears splashed into the wine. The image shivered and was gone. Ariadne bent over the bowl, weeping.

On the next day she performed the ritual faultlessly, but though she caught one glimpse of Dionysus in the scrying bowl, the image disappeared almost instantly and no god appeared before his painting behind the altar. Numb with pain and despair, Ariadne removed her clothing and lay down upon the altar.

In a few moments, the priestesses, faces long with disappointment, lifted her and clothed her again. Having saluted the painted image of her lord, Ariadne began the closing ritual. It was only then she noticed that no member of her family stood below the dais, in fact, that there were very few people in attendance.

She felt no great surprise, assuming that Dionysus had sent signs of her fall from favor. She didn't care, except for being alone. There was no one to talk with and laugh with, to demand bread and cheese and olives and wrinkle his nose at the wine. She knelt before his chair, laid her head on the seat, and wept.

After a time there were no more tears and her knees grew so painful that she shifted her body to sit by the chair rather than kneel. Dimly she was aware of a duty that must be done. That sense of responsibility noted how the light brightened as the day drew on toward noon and then slowly faded. When the light was gone, she rose as stiffly as one of the automata that Daidalos was forever constructing and removed her gold embroidered vest and her stiffened, huge belled skirt, which she replaced with a simple gown.

With set face and staring eyes, forcing breath into herself against the pain that stabbed her throat and chest, she took the vine hook from the wall and stepped outside. In the courtyard of the shrine she looked up into the star-filled sky. "Help me," she whispered. "Mother, help me."

A gentle warmth flowed around her; a soft, warm breeze stirred her hair. Ariadne touched the vine hook, willed light, and it glowed. Filled with such wonder that her pain became bearable, she left the grounds of the shrine and began to walk and then run through the vineyards in the same pattern she had followed when Dionysus ran beside her.

Ariadne was aware of the power that flowed into

her and that she spent in blessing the forming grapes. She was humbly grateful to the Mother for Her support, but there was nothing in it of hand clasping hand and laughter ringing in her ear. She was glad that she could still bring fruitfulness to the vineyards of Knossos, but the deep joy, the contentment of sharing, of loving and being loved was gone.

Although the priestesses had left a tray of carefully selected food on the small table near Dionysus' chair, as they had done at the previous equinoxes and at the solstice, and Ariadne couldn't remember when last she had eaten, she only cast a stasis over the tray. It cost her nothing, for she was tingling with power, but it had neither meaning nor purpose for her now. All she wanted was oblivion.

To her surprise, she found that almost as soon as she lay down in her bed, but she didn't keep it long. Too soon she was dragged back to the leaden realization of what she had lost when Phaidra shook her awake.

"Come!" Phaidra cried. "You must come! Asterion has gone mad. He is screaming and bellowing and striking at anyone who comes near him."

The source of her grief. Ariadne was tempted to turn her back on her sister and tell her she had done all she would for Asterion, but she was so surprised by what Phaidra said—Asterion, except in his demands for food, had been a placid child while she cared for him—that she asked what had caused his rage.

"Mother!" Phaidra said succinctly. "She showed him to a great concourse of people, and of course they shouted and cheered and Asterion was frightened out of his wits. Then, instead of bringing him back to his accustomed crib and his accustomed servants, she brought him to a new apartment near her own, with a great, gilded bed in which, big as he is, he was completely lost and noble attendants who had no idea how to calm him or how or what to feed him. And then she just walked away—as she does—leaving him with those fools."

"Oh, poor Asterion," Ariadne sighed, getting out of bed and reaching for a clean gown, which had been left for her. "But why is he still so upset? Don't tell me that mother tried to display him again."

"As far as I know," Phaidra said through stiff lips, "he never stopped crying. The men mother 'honored' with appointments tried to hide that they couldn't calm him. Seemingly they muffled his cries and didn't tell her that Asterion was beyond their management. It was only when they began to fear that he would die that one of them confessed. Then mother had me summoned, but although he didn't strike at me or try to bite me, he wouldn't quiet. So I came for you."

Not until they arrived at the palace did Ariadne realize that when Phaidra had said Asterion was screaming and bellowing, she was speaking the literal truth. The exhausted and frustrated shrieks of a child mingled with an enraged kind of hoarse lowing that made Ariadne's breath catch. She didn't permit herself to think about it, but ran into the room, calling out, "Hush, hush, Asterion. I'm here. I'll make everything better."

On the words she reached out to the thrashing, wailing child, who gulped, reached for her, and let her catch him up in her arms. Ariadne had to brace her knees against the bed because he was almost too heavy for her to lift, but his arms came around her and he clutched her hard, his wailing diminishing as he pressed his muzzle between her shoulder and her neck.

Ariadne had a moment then to look around and her eyes widened in disgusted amazement at her mother's pride and stupidity. The bed, as Phaidra had said, was gilded, which was silly but insignificant compared to the fact it was so large as to allow a child to roll about and grow more and more fearful of falling; the pillows, some of which had been moved to prevent Asterion from falling off the bed, were all brocaded cloth, embroidered with stiff gold thread, beautiful but only for show. The coverlet, which had never been pulled down to expose the sheets, if there were sheets, had also been an embroidered and embellished glory, but was now soaked with urine and spattered with feces. And Asterion's body showed dents and almost healed scratches where the unsuitable bedclothes had gouged him.

"Come, love, come," she crooned, stroking his thick mane, "I'll take you back to your own crib and your own nurses. They'll clean you and feed you, and then—"

"Where are you going with Asterion?" Pasiphae asked from the doorway, the attendant who had fetched her peering over her shoulder.

Ariadne looked at her mother, who was at her haughtiest, but didn't flinch. She stared back, her lips down turned with contempt. "To his accustomed place, madam," she said, walking calmly toward the queen, "where his nurses know how to care for him."

"Put him down in his bed," Pasiphae ordered. "A god must be fittingly housed and have fitting servants—noblemen, not common peasant women."

"Are you mad?" Ariadne cried. "This is no god. This is a three-months-old babe. Has he run or flown through the air, as Hermes is said to have done? Has he spoken divine verse, like Dionysus, or played the lute as Apollo did when he was a ten-day from the womb? Asterion is like any other uncared for babe—covered with filth, which your 'fitting' servants didn't deign to clean; he's starving, because doubtless they presented food in a way he couldn't eat it; he's sick with crying." Asterion was hiccuping against her shoulder.

"Be still!" Pasiphae shouted. "You lie. You don't wish to yield your power to the god born out of my body."

She ran forward and seized the child, yanking him free of Ariadne's arms. In that instant, Asterion turned his head and fastened his sharp little teeth in Pasiphae's upper arm, sucking at the blood he drew and striking out wildly with clawed hands that tore her face when one of them came in contact with her cheek. Pasiphae screamed and tried to thrust him away and drop him, but for a moment she couldn't free her arm from his teeth and Ariadne had a chance to catch him before he fell.

He struggled for a moment, lowing hoarsely and straining toward Pasiphae, jaws snapping, but Ariadne knew how to handle him and she pushed by her mother, ran past the door to her mother's apartment, and then up the stair. Filthy as he was, she placed Asterion among the supporting cushions in the chair that had been made for him with a sort of little table attached to the front and set a large bowl of milk before him. His cries stopped at once, and he thrust his muzzle into the bowl and began to drink.

Breathing hard, Ariadne stood staring down, tears streaking her cheeks as she remembered what she'd lost to preserve this creature. But she remembered, too, how he'd held out his arms to her when he was still screaming with rage and hunger, how he'd clung to her, nuzzled against her for comfort. A sob forced itself from her throat; Asterion lifted his dripping muzzle from the bowl, cocked his head, and blinked his eyes. Those eyes were no longer bulbous; they were the large, soft brown, long-lashed, beautiful eyes—of any cow. Ariadne sighed and reached out to stroke the black mane that began in a peak on his low forehead and grew down over his shoulders to the middle of his back. Asterion lowered his muzzle to his bowl to drink again.

"How dare you!" Pasiphae said from the doorway, but her voice was not so loud or so certain as it had been.

Ariadne turned to face her. Pasiphae's arm had been bandaged and the blood washed from the scratches on her cheek, and there was a kind of horror in her eyes as she saw Asterion bent over the bowl sucking up milk like any other calf.

"I've dared more to save this child already," Ariadne said bitterly. "Because to me he *is* a child. If you want a dead god, I'll leave him in the care of your 'suitable' attendants. I don't know how long they will find him godlike after wiping up his pee and his shit or presenting food to a beast with a muzzle. If you want a live son, you'll leave him in the care of Phaidra and the nurses until he can walk and feed himself."

Pasiphae shifted her gaze from her daughter's face to Asterion and bit her lip uneasily. "I suppose it's because he's half human that he's slow to manifest all his power," she muttered, and then looked back at Ariadne. "But look at his size. Look at his strength." She drew a deep breath and cried aloud. "This is the Bull God made flesh."

Asterion raised his head from his bowl and began to bellow, working his jaws as if he would like to bite again.

"Queen Pasiphae," Ariadne said softly, "wouldn't a god welcome the prayers and cheers of his people? Asterion rejected their salutations. Would a god weep or rage each time you named him? Asterion has done just that, refusing your claim. Have mercy on yourself, on this poor creature, on Crete. Take the warning that he, himself, keeps giving—"

"Enough." Pasiphae raised a hand. "Are you speaking as Mouth or as a jealous priestess? I've listened—

as I swore to do—respectfully. I've uttered no threat against you, nor will I interfere with your worship of your little godling. Don't you interfere in the worship of a greater god." She looked around at the people crowding the corridor behind her. "Meanwhile, since the god has made clear his preference for a familiar place, he may stay here in Phaidra's care."

She cast a challenging glance at Ariadne, but Ariadne had despaired of dissuading her mother from her madness and watched in silence until she swept away. Then Ariadne turned back to Asterion and, seeing he was lapping at the last thin layer of milk in the bowl, brought him a tray that had been prepared when the maids believed he would be brought back to the nursery. The meat on it was somewhat dried but didn't smell spoiled, and Ariadne presented it. She felt someone close behind her and turned, but it was only Phaidra.

"When he's fed full," she said, "the nurses will be able to clean him. He'll sleep after that. Most likely by the time he wakes he'll have forgotten." She gestured Phaidra to follow her out into the corridor, looked up and down, and finally went into the room they had shared. "I think Pasiphae is mad," she said.

"A little, perhaps," Phaidra replied, plumping herself down on her bed. "She really does want to believe that Asterion is a god." She hesitated and then asked, "Are you so sure he's not? How can the head of a bull and the body of a man be mated, except in a god? Aren't all the gods of Egypt like that? And what ordinary three-months child could sit up and eat cubes of meat with full-grown teeth?"

"Perhaps some of his father's qualities have flowed into his blood. I'm not saying that he isn't Poseidon's get or that he may not develop godlike Gifts. All I'm saying is that for now, Asterion, whatever he may become in the future, is a *baby*. He needs to be cuddled, to be loved, to be given toys and helped to enjoy his playthings." She hesitated, her eyes resting on Phaidra and then, understanding her sister's character and that the best treatment for Asterion would be obtained through Phaidra's self-interest, added slowly, "If he should be a god, the best way to be sure you will be favored by him in the future is to make him love you now."

Phaidra shuddered slightly but then nodded. "You're right about that. I'll tell mother, too, but I don't think she'll listen to me any more than she did to you. and Asterion really doesn't like her."

Was there the faintest shadow of a smile on Phaidra's lips? Ariadne blinked her eyes, which were tired from too much weeping and too little sleep, and the expression, if there had been one, was gone. "She may listen to you," she said. "She's taken me in despite ever since I was favored by Dionysus' response to my Calling."

"Oh, well, soon she won't care about that. She has her own god now and can make him do and say whatever she wants. Didn't you know that father had sent out criers throughout the whole kingdom bidding everyone to assemble at the great temple near Knossos to worship the Bull God, born into flesh? Yesterday morning, when they should have been at the shrine to see Dionysus, they were all watching mother hold up Asterion and pretend to interpret his bellows."

Ariadne, who had just been about to come forward to sit on what had been her bed in the past, stopped and clasped her hands together in front of her. So Dionysus had been right. Her parents did plan to claim publicly that Asterion was a god. That would bring trouble; she knew it. Even so, she couldn't go all the way with Dionysus. Was her parents' foolishness, perhaps blasphemy, reason enough to end poor Asterion's life? *He* had done no wrong, poor creature.

She closed her eyes and then reopened them. She had never doubted the truth of what Dionysus said, and doubtless her shrine—no, his shrine—would suffer. That horrible mating of bull and man, which could be displayed at any time, would waken awe and bring offerings. But wouldn't the people tire of sacrificing to a god that had no power?

"I'd better go back to the shrine," she said to Phaidra. "I'm dropping for sleep."

The words reminded her that it wasn't only being wakened unexpectedly and the anxiety of dealing with her mother and Asterion that had exhausted her. She'd been out in the fields nearly all the previous night and she had blessed them so that they would be fruitful. She stopped dead halfway down the long stone stairway that led from the palace to the road up Gypsades Hill.

She had blessed the vines and they would flourish, but the few worshipers who had come to Dionysus' shrine at dawn the previous day—likely younger sons and younger brothers of families that wished to have a presence in both gods' holy precincts—would spread the word far and wide that Dionysus hadn't come. What then would the people think? Wouldn't they believe the fruitfulness of their vines had been bestowed by the Bull God? Ariadne started down the steps again. Now was the time she needed to Call Dionysus. Should she bless the grapes at midsummer? Withhold the blessing? Wither them?

Dionysus had spoken of the death of Asterion in terms of the good of all of Crete. To further that good, she should bless the vines and the grapes no matter to whom the good was accredited. But had he meant that? Would he care for the good of the people of Crete if they no longer brought offerings to his shrines? In the past he'd neglected them even when they had sacrificed, just because he didn't like the priestess. Ariadne began to walk more quickly, hurrying to the shrine so she could stand and look at the painting behind the altar.

The face was beautiful, but it didn't invite confidences. She remembered the rage he had allowed to suffuse him, a rage that could have killed her parents, her dearest brother. She remembered the words "stupid native with your tiny mind" and the curl of his lips when he spoke of "your teeming masses." No, she wasn't sorry she couldn't Call him and ask for advice. She thought she knew what his advice would be. As long as she could help the people of Crete to be well fed and happy through making and selling fine wine, she would do so. If he were angry . . . Well, he couldn't be much more angry than he was already.

One small pinpoint of hope came to light the darkness of Ariadne's mood on the night of the full moon following the spring equinox. She danced for the Mother that night, although Pasiphae had tried to convince Phaidra to do it. Actually, Ariadne had been surprised that Phaidra hadn't seized the opportunity. Phaidra had grown much more assured over the year that had passed, much more sure of her own worth. And Ariadne learned from her sister that she had relinquished the role only reluctantly when she asked why Phaidra didn't wish to dance.

Shrugging, Phaidra said, "Wishing is nothing to do with it. I *can't* do it. I tried. Daidalos showed me the pattern of the dance and read to me how the steps must be taken, but when I stood up and tried to do it, it was as if a heavy weight pressed me down. I tripped and stumbled, my knees knocked together and were weak." She shrugged again. "I may not be the dancer that you are, but I have never been so clumsy or so exhausted." She sighed and glanced sidelong at Ariadne. "To speak the truth, sister, I don't believe I am welcome to the Mother. Perhaps I'm not very wise, but I'm not stupid enough to try to force myself on Her."

"I'll dance, of course, if you wish it," Ariadne said, keeping her face still although she was suffused with a sensation of warmth and lightness that eased the burden which lay on her chest.

The warm expectation remained with her, intensifying in the afternoon of the day preceding the rising of the full moon. As the sun dipped to the west, Hagne began to dress Ariadne's hair with one of the little girl novices to help while Dido sought out the wine-red, gold stiffened skirt and bodice. When she was ready—the sun was low, but not low enough for the rays to gild the dancing floor—Ariadne set out.

Her timing was good. The procession from the palace had also just arrived at the theatrical area, the "god" and "goddess," standing before their chairs on the sacral dais. But at the top of the stair, the dancers were not in good order. They had closed in on each other and appeared confused and disorganized. Ariadne's lips thinned. Apparently neither Pasiphae nor Phaidra had told them who would lead the dance. Well, that was easily amended. As soon as Ariadne's small procession of priests and priestesses and novices came into view, a soft call of relief came from two or three members of the group and several leaned forward and waved welcome.

One step below, at the edge of the aisle left for the dancers to descend, a tall form with broad shoulders caught Ariadne's eye. Her heartflower flicked open and a lance of joy pierced her. *He* had come! In the next moment the silver strands that had risen, wilted; the flower folded, and she saw that she didn't know the face. The hair and eyes were dark. How could she have mistaken him for her lord?

Shocked and bemused she pulled her gaze away only to meet her mother's angry eyes. Her father, however, nodded to her, and she responded with a courteous bow. Having gestured to her attendants to find places for themselves, she went past the dais that held the royal seats and through the aisle opened for her by the waiting people to the top of the stair. Calling herself a fool, she still turned her head to see more clearly the man who had waited a step below the dancers. He was not there.

As Ariadne took her place and the dancers sorted themselves out into their proper formation, the dancing floor glowed golden. Arms raised, step by step, Ariadne descended the long stair. The crowd sang; the "god" and "goddess" gave the ritual responses; Ariadne's bare feet almost caressed the smooth polished stones of the dancing floor as she crossed to stand formally before the dais and salute the "deities" who seated themselves between the sacral horns.

At the sound of the sistra and the flutes, Ariadne dropped her arm from the salute, turned, and glided to the center of the floor in the sliding stride of a votary. As she turned back to face her parents, arms lifted to shoulder height, palms up, while the other dancers wove a complex pattern around her, she saw *him* again, this time just below the dais. But she didn't feel her heartflower respond. It was *not* Dionysus. It was again the dark-haired, dark-eyed person whom she had earlier mistaken for her god. She closed her eyes, but before grief could pierce her as sharply as joy had when she first thought she saw Dionysus, that strange sensation of the touch of feather-light ribbons drew her thoughts to her dance.

She had no time for conscious thought after that as she danced all life from birth to death. When darkness fell and she sank quietly to the floor to wait for the rising of the moon, the image of that broad-shouldered celebrant returned to her. She deliberately called his face to mind, but only became more and more sure that she didn't know it. But how could that be? She knew every member of the court of Knossos and that big body, so arrogantly held, could be no common man, nor could she confuse it with another.

Vaguely she heard the singers chanting the ritual pleas and first her mother, then her father, singing the replies. The "god" began to woo the "goddess." Ariadne told herself the man she had seen must be a visitor, perhaps a foreign visitor. No, he wasn't foreign; that was impossible. His dress, his looks, his manner, were all Cretan and he wore the cincture around his waist, which had to be worn from youth to achieve the traditional narrowness.

If he couldn't be foreign and he couldn't be Cretan . . . The two together made a paradox, but Ariadne was distracted by the memory of a similar shadowy but magnificent figure when she danced the previous year. Then she had assumed it was Dionysus in disguise. A thrill touched her. Why not now? She "looked" within herself and, yes, the heartflower was open. Deliberately she gathered the silver strands and cast them wide about her in a seeking net.

They snapped back with such speed and force that the thin, wirelike threads would have cut her had they any physical reality. And then the heartflower sprang shut. Ariadne didn't know whether to laugh or weep. No one but Dionysus could affect her heartflower; she was certain now that he had come to watch her dance and that filled her with hope and a tremulous joy. She couldn't help being amused, too, by the irritation at being found out betrayed by the behavior of the threads that connected her with her god, like that of a little boy who had been caught peeping.

It was true that Dionysus' irritation wasn't something with which one should trifle, but even so the worst of her burden of grief and loneliness eased. He hadn't turned from her completely. He still cared.

The comfort that thought brought her weakened the shield of self-absorption that had armored her against outside impressions. Now the flaring light of the torches on the dais where the "god" and "goddess" sat exposed the tension of their bodies, the half-turned heads that betrayed conflict. What now? she wondered. This was new. From everything she had seen and heard in the palace since Asterion's birth, her father had come to terms with what Pasiphae had done, even begun to be glad of it. Surely he had done all in his power to support her when she claimed Asterion was the Bull God made flesh.

Ariadne was distressed. To carry enmity to the rites for the Mother was dangerous. She'd always been aware that there were differences between her mother and father, but those had never been allowed to carry over into matters of state or the greater rites. In politics, Pasiphae was a wise counselor and an adamant supporter of her husband; at the rites of the Snake Goddess and the Mother, Minos was a dedicated votary of his priestess-wife.

Eventually the edge of the full moon crept over the horizon and lit the dancing floor. Ariadne rose to dance the awakening. She offered herself, her love, her little bud of hope, and knew from the warmth that enfolded her that her offering was accepted. Nonetheless, a pall hung over her and the other dancers. The Mother wakened, but without joy.

It was true that Dionysus' initiates wasn't something with which one should trifle, but even so the shock of her emotion of grief and loneliness eased. If it hadn't turned [illegible] completely, she still cared.

The comfort that thought brought her weakened the hold of self-absorption that had smothered her against outside impressions. Now the flaring light of the torches on the dais where the "god" and "goddess" sat exposed the tension of their bodies, the half-turned heads that betrayed conflict. What now? she wondered. This was new. From everything she had seen and heard in the palace since Asterion's birth her father had come to terms with what Pasiphae had done, even begun to be glad of it. Surely he had done all in his power to support her when she claimed [illegible] the Bull-God [illegible].

Ariadne was distressed. To carry quarrels to the rites of the Mother was dangerous. She'd always been aware that there were differences between her mother and father, but those had never been allowed to carry over into matters of State or the greater rites. In politics, Pasiphae was a wise counselor and an adamant supporter of her husband; at the rites of the Snake Goddess and the Mother, Minos was a dedicated votary of his priestess wife.

Eventually the edge of the full moon crept over the horizon and lit the dancing floor. Ariadne [illegible] the awakening. She offered herself, her love, her [illegible] of hope, and knew from the warmth [illegible] that her offering was accepted. Nonetheless, a pall hung over her and the other dancers. The Mother watched, but withheld Her [illegible]

CHAPTER 10

The next day Ariadne learned the source of the quarrel that had tarnished the joy of the Mother's awakening. Phaidra trotted up to the shrine to report that there had been a truly royal battle between the king and the queen when they returned to the palace and that it had been settled by Minos giving permission to Pasiphae to build a temple in which to worship the Bull God. That was interesting, but didn't really touch Ariadne.

"But they had quarreled before the rite, hadn't they?" she asked.

"Yes, well that was all part of the same thing. It started when mother decided to dress Asterion in cloth-of-gold." Phaidra shook her head. "Well, you know how he is about being covered. And now that hair is growing over his chest as well as his back, he's even worse." She shrugged. "And, of course, he doesn't like mother. Well, he began to whimper as soon as she came in, and when she told the nurses to dress him and they tried to obey her, he began to roar." Phaidra shuddered delicately. "I hate when he does that. He sounds like a beast, not like a child—and certainly not like a god."

"He's only a baby," Ariadne said. "He just yells when he's annoyed or frightened. He doesn't care how he sounds as long as he gets what he wants."

Phaidra shrugged again. "I tried to tell mother that Asterion didn't like to be dressed, but father came and asked what was wrong. He didn't wait for an answer, though. As soon as he saw that cloth-of-gold tunic, he told mother that she couldn't bring Asterion to the rite."

"She intended to bring Asterion to the Mother's rite? Why?"

"Because, she says, he's the god of Crete and all worship must be to him or through him." Phaidra looked uneasy. "She told father that Asterion must be seated between the sacral horns and their chairs to either side."

"But the rite is for god and goddess to be united by the Mother so the cycle of life may begin. There's no place for a babe or even another god . . . true or false."

"That's what father said, but mother insisted that the Bull God must be first in Crete." Phaidra sighed. "And all this while Asterion was bellowing like the bulls of Baoshan so that father and mother had to scream to be heard. Then mother tried to pick

Asterion up to quiet him and he almost got his teeth into her again. Maybe that convinced her or the fact that father said if she insisted on bringing Asterion he wouldn't attend and that Asterion could sing the responses."

"Which he cannot do . . . and may never be able to do," Ariadne remarked flatly.

"But then in the morning he agreed to build her a temple for Asterion," Phaidra said.

Ariadne nodded. "Father is arranging safeguards. If Asterion is a god, he has shown piety by building him a temple and giving him his place and times of worship. If he is not, his worship won't intrude on that of the true gods."

A place was chosen, at the foot of the palace adjoining the road to the caravanserai. There was plenty of room for a crowd to gather in front of the temple, and the crowd would be clearly visible from the shrine near the top of Gypsades Hill. Ariadne wondered whether that fact had influenced her mother to choose that place. Did she hope to make Dionysus angry, to drive him to abandon Crete by showing how eagerly the people came to work on the Bull God's temple, how they brought offerings even before the temple was finished? Dionysus had said he didn't care about the worshipers or the offerings, that he cared only for his chosen priestess, but as the ten-days passed and nothing came of her belief that he had come to watch her dance, Ariadne began to wonder.

The building of the temple proceeded apace. It wasn't a complex or elaborate structure, merely a large rectangular building with a rear and two side doors, fronted by a deep porch supported by four typical columns, narrower at the base than at the top. Perhaps to compensate for the simplicity of the design, ornamentation was lavish. Centered between the pillars was a large opening to the dark interior surrounded with carved and gilded bulls' horns. To either side, murals of charging bulls confronted each other. Between the murals and framed by the dark opening was a gilded throne, with arms ending in bellowing bulls' heads as well as a tall back carved with charging bulls.

It was on the throne that Pasiphae intended the Bull God to appear in glory, but for a time Ariadne wondered whether her mother could accomplish her purpose. Asterion wasn't cooperative. He screamed and fought against the clothing Pasiphae wanted him to wear. He wouldn't sit on her lap on a pretend throne, striking at her and snapping as if he wished to tear out her throat. But his instinctive rejection of the trappings of majesty seemed to increase rather than quell the queen's determination. She had him seized and bound, then covered the ropes with a golden cape so that she could bring him to the blessing of the temple grounds. His bellows she interpreted as roars of welcome.

From then on he screamed as soon as he saw her, but he was not yet capable of the speed or agility to escape and she forced his presence for several ceremonies. By the time he was six months old, however, he was walking and as large as an ordinary child of two and her original methods of coercion would no longer work. Doubts would certainly be aroused in worshipers about the powers of a "god" who seemed to be permanently immobile, so Asterion could no longer be bound and carried. The fact that Pasiphae overcame his resistance and succeeded in her purpose in the end was the final proof to Ariadne that Asterion wasn't a god but only the poor deformed victim of Poseidon's spite.

Her pity kept her from abandoning the child, even after he had been moved from the nursery to the over-ornamented quarters Pasiphae had originally created for him. He was now served by "suitable" male attendants—strong ones, armed with "rods of office" that could also be used to hold Asterion off or administer a stinging blow—but not one of them seemed to remember how young he really was. His physical development remained phenomenal; at the next winter solstice when he was a year old, he looked five or six.

Perhaps it was Asterion's size and strength, or her own desperate need to believe, that drove Pasiphae to insist he was a god. There was no other sign of godliness about him: he didn't, or couldn't, speak; he still wet and fouled himself; he didn't seem to understand even the simplest commands. Nonetheless he had been trained as one trains a beast by a mixture of bribery (with portions of raw meat, which was his favorite above all other things) and punishment to cease trying to attack Pasiphae and to allow a golden crown to be placed around his now-prominent horns and a golden kilt to be strapped around his waist.

He also learned to sit on the throne, which had been completed long before the building was ready so that it could be used for his training, and to endure a belt of gilded metal mesh to hold him in place. He didn't like that, but could be distracted from the confinement. Ariadne had inadvertently shown her mother how to get him to sit still. Remembering he was only a baby, she brought him toys, brightly colored blocks and sparkling gewgaws that turned in a breeze or moved by pulling a string. When she piled the blocks upon one another and allowed Asterion to knock them down or jiggled the sparkling toys, he would sit quite still to watch in fascination.

Pasiphae, coming upon them playing, didn't, as Ariadne feared, order her away from Asterion. The queen, almost in despair for a way to make the child climb onto the throne and sit, seized upon the idea that Asterion could be induced by amusement and enlarged it.

Priests and priestesses were promptly selected to serve the Bull God by dancing before his altar, and Pasiphae ordered Daidalos to design garments for them that would glitter and move to bind mind and spirit. The votaries in their shining, animated finery would perform all sorts of acrobatic feats, such as climbing into a pyramid, which they would allow to collapse into a heap of sparkling glitter at a wave from Asterion, or they would increase the pace and convolutions of any dance in accord with his gestures.

Ariadne never attended any of the ceremonies, which brought about a sharp clash with her mother on the day before the winter solstice that would mark Asterion's second birthday. Pasiphae confronted her daughter, who had just brought Asterion a box of bright new toys to mark the day. He could speak a few words now, and his happy shriek of "Ridne," which was as much as he could pronounce of her name, had apparently alerted her mother to her presence.

Asterion, who had been rushing forward to embrace his sister, stopped short when Pasiphae appeared in the doorway, his bull-like lips curling back from a predator's teeth, which looked even more menacing in the bovine muzzle. Snarling, he backed away and Ariadne, who had seen the reaction before, put down the box of toys and turned to Pasiphae.

The queen looked at the carved horse and cart, with its bright-painted wheels set with bits of shining metal that would glitter as the wheels turned when the cart was moved, at two whirligigs and several tops, all also bright with sparkling bits. The toys acknowledged that Asterion's agility and manipulative skills were the equal of the ten-year-old he seemed to be. Her eyebrows lifted.

"So you acknowledge the Bull God's power," Pasiphae said, smiling. "What two-year-old could use such toys?" She laughed aloud. "And since you curry favor with the Bull God with such trinkets, you can dance for him on his birth day and join in our worship."

"No," Ariadne replied. "I dance only for the Mother. I worship only Her and Dionysus."

"Dionysus is gone from Crete!" Pasiphae exclaimed. "He abandoned you as soon as the Bull God appeared in the flesh. Don't be a fool. Dance for the Bull God and I'll allow you some portion of the offerings that come to his temple."

Ariadne smiled slowly. "Dionysus isn't gone from Crete. Don't the vines flourish? Aren't the grapes full and sweet? Isn't the wine the equal of the greatest in Crete's past?"

Fury thinned Pasiphae's lips. Not only was what Ariadne said true but Pasiphae had made a few mistakes in the early months of the Bull God's worship. Then, when she felt her most pressing need was to divert worship from Dionysus to Asterion (and when she still believed that Asterion had power she could direct), she had threatened several nobles who continued to send offerings and lesser members of their families to Dionysus' shrine with the blasting of their vines. The threat had been shown to be toothless. When Phaidra reported what Pasiphae had done, Ariadne made sure that those nobles had the richest crop of grapes and the sweetest on the whole island.

Now Pasiphae confined her threats to matters she could control. If she prophesied misfortune for a family, it was the kind of misfortune that could befall at the hands of armed and masked men who wore no house badges and disappeared after the damage was done. And if she prophesied good fortune it was the kind that political or trade favors could produce. She didn't use the device often. Minos wouldn't stand for it and her own political sense constrained her from excesses. But the crown of her glory would be to bring Dionysus' priestess to acknowledge the Bull God.

"That is by the Bull God's will," Pasiphae said loudly. "It is nothing to do with the blessings of a little godling who has abandoned his priestess. I *demand* that you dance at the Bull God's ceremony at dawn."

"At dawn I will be performing the ritual to Call Dionysus to the vineyards," Ariadne said steadily, although her throat was tight with unshed tears.

"Which your petty godling will ignore!" Pasiphae spat. "Which all Cretans will ignore! You'll be alone with your ancient priests and priestesses and six little children who bitterly regret being consecrated to a dead godling and wish fervently to come down the hill to the Bull God's temple."

"Be *that* as it may, Dionysus is not dead, as our wine attests. He's my god and I'll worship only him and the Mother, who is above all, even the gods."

"*I* am your mother and your queen!" Pasiphae shrieked. In the background Asterion bellowed, but she ignored him. "I *command* you to dance for the Bull God. You *must* obey me."

"No," Ariadne said. "Only Dionysus can command my service."

"Dionysus is gone! Dead! I tell you if you don't dance for the Bull God, I'll have your shrine razed to the ground. I will—"

Ariadne laughed in her face. "And I will blast the vines of the king and queen of Knossos so they will never put forth another leaf. Only the vines of the king and queen. All others will flourish as never before."

Pasiphae uttered a scream of rage and ran forward, raising her arm to strike Ariadne. Asterion bellowed again and one of his attendant shouted a wordless warning. There was a crack, as of wood against flesh. Asterion screeched in pain and Ariadne whirled about to see what had happened to him. A thin streak of blood marked his muzzle, a male attendant was on the floor, scrambling to rise, and Asterion, teeth bared, hands clawed, and murder on his bestial face, was charging toward Pasiphae bellowing, "No hurt Ridne!"

"No, no," Ariadne cried, catching her brother by the arm and pulling him around to face her. "No one is going to hurt me, love. You know mother shouts a lot. Never mind her at all. Come, love. Come play with your new toys. Come and make the tops spin. You know I can never do that as well as you can."

He strained against her for a moment, but she put her arms around him and kissed his cheek. His mouth closed and he blinked his beautiful eyes. "No hurt Ridne?"

"No one will hurt Ariadne." She kissed his cheek again.

He looked across his shoulder—and over hers, and Ariadne realized he was almost as tall as she—and a strange noise, not unlike an animal's growl rumbled in his chest when he caught sight of his mother. Ariadne saw one of the attendants sidling along the wall toward where Pasiphae had been. The growling and tension faded from Asterion's body and Ariadne hoped that the attendant had convinced Pasiphae to leave. She pulled again at Asterion's arm.

"Come, sit here on the floor beside me," she suggested, tugging at him gently. She reached into the box of toys. "Look. Look at this golden top. If you spin it, you'll see red lines run up and down it."

He butted his head against her. "Love Ridne," he said, and spun the top so quickly and dextrously that the red lines raced over the toy and sparkles Ariadne hadn't known were there flashed brightly.

"Well, that was very interesting," Bacchus remarked, lifting his head from the bowl in which he'd been scrying.

Wincing, Silenos turned his heavy body to its side on the couch on which he was lying. His face and the untidily draped himation showed him to be thoroughly bruised. Seeing he was attended, Bacchus described the scene he'd just witnessed between Ariadne and Pasiphae.

"I think you must mirror it for him," Silenos said, studying the handsome blond, whose beauty was marred only slightly by too-small, red-rimmed eyes. Then, before Bacchus could produce a stinging retort, he went on hurriedly, "You know I agreed with you when he first entangled himself with her. But now I think differently."

"You certainly did agree," Bacchus snapped. "You spent half of every night whining to me about what we should do to get him to leave her and come back to his usual ways."

"Well, I thought it was for his own good." Silenos groaned as he levered himself upright. "I remembered what happened when the first one he was so fond of died, and I thought soonest over, soonest mended, so when she defied him that way, it seemed reasonable to harp on her disloyalty and disrespect and turn him against her. I thought he might kill her—or get her killed—mourn a little, and then forget her."

"He never really forgot the other one," Bacchus said. "He thinks this is she, reborn, a special gift from the Mother." His lips twisted on the last word.

Silenos nodded. "I think you're right. And he isn't mending, Bacchus, he's getting worse."

"Do you think he will really go completely mad?" Bacchus asked, his voice now uncertain.

"How far is he from that?" Silenos asked. "He let the maenads turn on *me*. On *me*! And he laughed."

There was a long silence while Bacchus looked down into the scrying bowl again. "He didn't let them kill you," he said at last, sounding as if he almost regretted it.

"You'll be next," Silenos hissed with unaccustomed energy. "You think he doesn't know what we did. Well, he does. He's uncaring about most things, not stupid."

Bacchus bit his lip. "But this may be far worse. She makes him care. The little people we use for our games are *her* kind. I think he intends to bring this one here. And she'll watch more closely what we do than he ever did. That's why I worked so hard to wean him away from her."

"Bring her here?" Silenos echoed, staring. "Watch her grow old and wither and die . . . here?"

"He doesn't intend this one to wither and die," Bacchus snarled. "Don't you remember that he 'convinced' Persephone to grant immortality to his mother—oh, very well," he added in response to Silenos' wordless protest, "to intercede with the Mother to grant Semele life as long as an Olympian's?" He rose and paced the room. "But it was Persephone who did whatever was done to Semele. Why is it necessary to him always to say the power came from another?"

"Because it did," Silenos said quietly. "And that's one way in which he's wise. Perhaps he Sees Her . . . If you want to forget that we . . . they—" his eyes glanced toward the part of the house in which Dionysus lived "—are not gods, he doesn't, and I don't. Too many of them are like you. The Mother overlooks much, but one day . . ."

"Oh, be quiet. We have troubles enough of our own, without foreseeing doom for all." Bacchus paced a little longer, then came to stand before Silenos. "He thinks there are the seeds of the needed power in this priestess. Remember that she's blessed the fields for two years without him and the vineyards are as rich as if he'd been with her. No other priestess has ever done that, not even his old favorite."

Silenos' eyes widened. "Is that so?"

"I watched her through the scrying bowl." Bacchus grimaced. "I thought he'd be angry all over again when I showed him what she was doing, but he wasn't. He looked through me—you know how he does when he Sees something he understands—and he *smiled*. Are you *sure* he knows we kept reminding him of her defiance for our own purposes rather than out of indignation for his sake?"

Silenos laughed and lay down again. "Why do you think I am all swollen and black and blue? At first his hurt and rage because she wasn't absolutely, mindlessly, his, because she *could* defy him, didn't let him think, but that's worn away. He has been thinking. You'll be next to be chastised. And one of these times his rage will take him over completely and he'll laugh as we are torn into bloody gobbets and strewn over the vineyards to make them fertile."

"You're saying I must tell him that she's learned her lesson and worships only him and mirror for him her defiance of her mother?" Bacchus' lips turned down into a petulant pout. "But she'll turn him into a model of sweetness and light. They'll run together—" he sneered "—laughing and singing. We won't be invited—and the good times, the drinking and coupling, will roll no more."

"They're ended for me anyway," Silenos said very

softly, closing his eyes. "There's been too much blood, too much killing, for me. Even if I didn't fear I would be the next sacrifice, I'd withdraw from these 'blessings.' When it happened once or twice a year in widely different lands, it was exciting." His jaw set for a moment as a remembered thrill passed through him. "Now I'm only sickened by the pain and blood. I'll crawl away and live as I can without him."

Bacchus stood looking down at him for a little while. He thought Silenos a soft old fool. The pain and blood always added an orgiastic pleasure to the wild coupling for him, but if Dionysus lost himself entirely to the madness that always coiled in him and allowed the maenads to turn from sexual excesses to killing . . . Dionysus had barely managed to save Silenos, and he was truly fond of the old idiot. And if Silenos was right and Dionysus suspected that *he* had interfered in the relationship with this priestess, he might, indeed, be next to be beaten instead of futtered.

Worse, if Dionysus was as far gone as Silenos believed . . . The old fool was right, Bacchus thought, his brow creasing as he tried to recall Dionysus' behavior before he had taken this priestess as his Chosen. Yes, there *had* been a lot of killing in the last two years, and more and more recently. Could he be next? Gnawing at his lip, he glanced toward the door, then he picked up the scrying bowl and carried it carefully with him.

As he moved, he glanced about the apartment he and Silenos shared—two bedchambers and a luxurious bathing room adjoining a large central chamber. The walls were alternately hung with tapestries depicting merry orgies, everyone laughing and coupling in twos, threes, and fours with cups in their hands or flasks spilling wine. He stared for a moment at the lively works; it hadn't been like that for a long time.

Between the tapestries were shelves filled with wine flasks, goblets of precious glass or jewel-set metal, and pretty bibelots—and books, many scrolls and clay tablets. They were dusty; Dionysus hadn't asked to share the merry tales with Silenos . . . for a long time. The furnishings were lush, cushioned couches and chairs, carved tables of precious woods, of ivory, even of silver, set with delicate porcelain or with game boards and pieces of equally precious materials. Those, too, hadn't been used in far too long.

Silenos must be really frightened to leave all this, he thought. Likely none of the other great ones would take him in. What would he do? Not expect Bacchus to provide for him. He wasn't that much a fool. Doubtless he would take a little room above a shop in the Agora and tell stories for food and a few coins, as he'd done before Dionysus had bade him guest with him. Bacchus shuddered.

He started toward the door knowing there was no help for it. He would have to tell Dionysus that his priestess, if not mindlessly his, was utterly faithful and mirror the scene between her and her mother in the scrying bowl. Better too much sweetness than broken or dead. He hesitated as he stepped out the door into the short corridor and turned his back to the extension that led to the servants' rooms. All was not lost. If he could keep Dionysus from bringing the woman to Olympus, there might be a workable compromise.

Smiling now, he went down the corridor to the central atrium, which one would swear was a sunlit forest glade. Pillars of rough brown marble that could have been trees, except for being cold stone instead of bark, seemed to divide into branches that held up a roof in which that strange, clear substance only Hades could produce let in the sun and glimpses of sky and clouds. In that light flowers, shrubs, trellised vines, and even small trees grew, a fountain played, and more vines bedecked the pillars and balustrades.

Bacchus looked around while passing through but saw at once that the benches and sets of chairs and tables in the arbors were empty. His smile disappeared. It was too early for Dionysus to have gone out, so he must be brooding in his own apartment. That wasn't good. When he had nothing to occupy him, he Saw too much and too often. At least while he was with the priestess he had had only one Vision, and that had been related to her.

Another corridor led from the atrium to Dionysus' rooms. Bacchus breathed a sigh of relief when he saw that the door to the antechamber was open. At least he wasn't closing himself away from all contact, as he'd done the first few days.

The antechamber was empty, as always. In Dionysus' case, it was a useless room. The other great ones sometimes received suppliants—not all the inhabitants of Olympus had real power. Most, in fact, were ordinary folk who herded flocks, tilled fields, threw pots, and performed the tasks that let the great ones live in comfort. Those people often had favors to beg, especially from Aphrodite and Athena and Hermes. Sometimes even from Zeus. But not from Dionysus. They were terrified of him. If he asked for something, it was delivered immediately and without charge.

Bacchus wrinkled his nose. He could have done very well out of requests to jewelers, weavers, and suchlike, but Dionysus wouldn't permit it. He would watch men torn apart and laugh, but wouldn't seize any lesser offering like gold and jewels. Unconsciously, he snorted.

"You may enter, Bacchus."

He barely suppressed a start strong enough to slop the wine out of the scrying bowl, set his teeth for a moment, and then entered Dionysus' sitting room. This, Bacchus thought inordinately gloomy. The walls were of dark green malachite, polished to a gloss that didn't hide the natural mottling, which by some artifice gave the appearance of a thick canopy of leaves. Shutters covered the windows, carved into vine patterns through which bright flowers of Hades' translucent artifice peeped. Had the shutters been open, the room might have seemed a soothing, enclosed bower of peace, but of late Dionysus had kept them closed, allowing only the light that came through the flowers and that of lamps to light the room.

Bacchus moved slowly to allow his eyes to become accustomed to the gloom and he soon perceived Dionysus lying on a padded couch. Clearly, since he had spoken directly to him, Dionysus knew he was there, but he hadn't turned his head to look at him. He seemed to be staring across the chamber at the dark opening into his bedchamber, his eyes fixed and protuberant. Silenos was right, Bacchus thought, the madness was closer to the surface than ever.

"I've seen something very interesting in the scrying bowl," Bacchus said, setting the bowl on a table and moving a chair behind it. "I think it's something you should see yourself. If you'd come here, I'll mirror it for you."

"If it's another flood of offerings, just ask Hermes to collect them. Tell him to take what he wants in payment. I don't care."

He finally turned toward Bacchus, coming fully into the light of the lamp beside the couch, and Bacchus saw that one of Dionysus' eyes was blackened and nearly swollen shut and his arms and shoulders were deeply scratched and almost as bruised as Silenos's. He must have had an even more difficult time wresting Silenos from the maenads than Silenos realized, which meant they were more out of control than Dionysus had expected. Bacchus suppressed a shudder.

"They fear you, my lord," he said. "They hope the offerings will appease you."

"And that if they give enough, I will come no more." Dionysus laughed—so ugly a sound that Bacchus swallowed, but before he could find a soothing comment, Dionysus added, "Knossos made offerings to draw me to Crete . . . But they don't want me any more either. They have their priestess and their new god."

He turned his head to stare into the dark again, and Bacchus felt a horrible mingling of rage and despair wash over him. The misery that engulfed him confirmed Silenos's fears. He bit down hard on his lip. The pain freed him enough to be able to speak.

"It's true that the offerings have all but ceased from Knossos and that most of the people go to the temple of the Bull God . . . But not your priestess."

Dionysus sat up, now fixing his gaze on Bacchus. Did the eyes have more sense in them Bacchus wondered? But Dionysus' voice was sharp and bitter when he said, "What? Has she stopped cuddling that misbegotten monster?"

"No. She still visits him often and treats him kindly, bringing him little toys—wagons and tops and suchlike—but I've just learned she doesn't accept him as a god and won't give him her service as priestess. Come, my lord, let me mirror for you her defiance of her mother, who demanded she dance for the Bull God."

Dionysus rose slowly with some care for his bruises. "So she wouldn't dance for the Bull God but still dances for the Mother?" Despite a wince of pain, pleasure hummed in his voice.

Relief urged Bacchus to confirm the news that had

eased Dionysus' mood. "She said she worships only you . . . and the Mother."

"I gave her leave to worship the Mother," Dionysus said quickly, and seated himself before the scrying bowl.

Bacchus drew a deep breath and closed his eyes for a moment. When he opened them, they were fixed on the scrying bowl. Scrying was his gift. He could see what anyone, anywhere, was doing, if he knew some characteristic of the person on which he could fix. That permitted Dionysus—or anyone else for whom he scryed—to know what was happening in distant temples even when the priests and priestesses could not Call their gods.

Unfortunately he was not alone in his talent. Quite a large number of Olympians, who had no greater Gifts, could scry and mirror what they'd seen. Like Silenos, he had been eking out a living, mostly scrying for the least powerful mages and sinking his frustrations in drink and women, when Dionysus had come across him. His wholehearted enjoyment of Dionysus' indulgence in wine and wild fertility rites had made him welcome as a companion. Later his ability to scry and keep Dionysus in touch with his mostly unGifted priests and priestesses brought him an invitation to be a permanent assistant and guest.

Under Bacchus' gaze the surface of the wine clouded, then cleared, to show an image of Ariadne turning to face Pasiphae, who had just stepped inside the doorway. The entire scene unfolded, ending with Asterion spinning his top and carefully butting his head against Ariadne so that the sharp horns wouldn't touch her. "Love Ridne," the misshapen mouth pronounced.

"Hold that," Dionysus said.

Obediently Bacchus froze the image of Ariadne and Asterion together. Dionysus continued to stare down into the bowl, studying first the monstrous bull's head, with its beautiful bovine eyes turned up to Ariadne, and then her face, the huge black eyes shining with tears, the mouth turned down just a little with pity and . . . distaste. Dionysus sighed.

"The poor creature," he muttered, and the brilliant blue of his too-large, too-bright eyes misted to softness with tears. "No one loves him. No one ever will, not even his Ridne." He shook his head. "He's so pitiful—in a way so innocent. I understand now why she must protect him, but the cost . . ." He looked away, this time at the bright flowers that starred the carved shutters, and gestured for Bacchus to cut off the vision.

When Bacchus saw Dionysus' thoughtful expression as his gaze fixed on the bright beauty that Hades had created, his mind leapt to what Hades's wife Persephone had done for Semele. His suspicion that Dionysus was thinking again of giving an Olympian's length of life to a native who would "love" him intensified—and he liked the idea less now than when it first came to him. He did *not* want that woman here, but he could think of no way of approaching the subject that wouldn't spell disaster for him. Dionysus had turned his head back to the scrying bowl and was staring into it, although nothing but a dark mirror showed.

Apparently his mind was still on the bull-headed boy, for he said, "Yet, if he doesn't die soon, he'll stain Crete with blood. I've Seen it. My Mouth has spoken it. I don't know what to do."

"What's a little more blood? You usually water the earth with human blood to feed the vines, so—"

Dionysus looked up at him. No wild emotion followed that gaze, but Bacchus took warning and swallowed what more he'd been about to say. Then Dionysus smiled at him and there was a reminiscent delight in his expression that had nothing to do with him and that Bacchus didn't like.

"You wouldn't understand," Dionysus said, a tinge of contempt coloring smile and voice. "Crete is clean of blood and has been for a long time. There's no human sacrifice there. In the bull dancing, if a dancer should be gored, it is considered a bad omen, a failure of the ritual that must be expiated and explained by the queen/goddess—and the bull is driven away into the mountains as not fit for sacrifice. I remember now. It was my own priestess, the first Ariadne, who changed the old ways. She was queen and had the power."

"Power? Doubtless she drained *you* to bless the vineyards without lust or blood." Bacchus tried to sound indignant.

Dionysus laughed, and his expression now held a softness of joy in it that almost sickened Bacchus. "She gave to me, not I to her," he said. "She went with me as this Ariadne did, running and laughing. She was old, but the Mother gave her strength and she gave it to me. I could feel the power pour out of me and into the vines, and though we shed no blood and incited no lust, Crete had the best wine in the whole world." He drew a deep breath and nodded. "Yes, it was a lesson, but I didn't understand it then. Now I do understand. If I had taken Ariadne with me—"

"Do you think she would be happy here?" Bacchus interrupted quickly. "You remember how the great ones treated Semele. She didn't stay."

"My mother didn't know me. She was afraid of me." Dionysus hesitated and looked toward the dark for a moment; then a faint smile bent his lips and his eyes went back to the bright flowers. "That, as I know too well, will never be Ariadne's problem. And I should have known that my Ariadne wouldn't touch death. She's all life."

Bacchus' heart sank. Clearly the reminder that his mother had demanded to be sent back to the Underworld rather than live in Olympus hadn't turned Dionysus' mind from planning to bring his priestess to Olympus. Trying another gambit, Bacchus asked, "Will she be willing to leave the bull-head?"

Dionysus frowned, but in thought, not hurt or anger. "Not yet. She won't turn her back on him nor on the trouble he'll bring to Knossos. I know that. She has a caring heart—perhaps that's what makes her Mother-blessed."

The evidence that Dionysus was thinking instead of just feeling and acting made Bacchus even more unhappy. He didn't want Dionysus reasonable and acceptable to others; he didn't want Ariadne sharing Dionysus' house and changing the being who had satisfied all his lusts into a singing, laughing idiot. He would almost rather see Dionysus completely mad. It would wear off; he was sure the grief and rage would wear off. So, if Dionysus committed what to this stupid native was an unforgivable sin, she would withdraw herself.

"If the monster died by some 'accident' and she didn't know you were involved . . ." Bacchus ventured.

Dionysus shook his head. "I don't think I could do it now. Before he was a person, I could have stopped his heart to save everyone hurt and pain. Not now. I saw how the poor creature craves love, how hurt it is already . . ." Dionysus sighed. "Besides, she *would* know. There's something within her that touches me."

"Women always pretend—" Bacchus stopped abruptly as Dionysus got to his feet.

He stared at Bacchus and the corners of his mouth tucked back. Bacchus' mouth went dry. He held out a hand in a placating gesture, but he knew that Dionysus *did* know what he'd done, had weighed and measured him and found him worthless. He didn't dare speak and anyway nothing he said would matter, so when Dionysus waved him away, he took up his scrying bowl and fled.

When Bacchus was gone, Dionysus stared at the door he had closed, but he wasn't thinking of Bacchus. As soon as Bacchus' irritating presence was gone, Dionysus had dismissed that self-absorbed animal's existence from his mind. He had a more important problem—how to reestablish contact with Ariadne.

"I don't See anything," he said to the bright flowers Hades had set into his shutters to keep him, Hades had said, from shutting himself off in the dark.

He smiled, thinking of the passionate devotion of Hades and his wife Persephone. So much love flowed between them that it overflowed, bathing those hungry for it in warmth and understanding. Ah, if he could convince Ariadne to come to him, even the dark would be bright. But it would be useless to try before the problem of the bull-head was solved. Why could he never See what he needed to See? he asked himself impatiently.

Had an answer to the problem of the bull-head come in a Vision, Ariadne would have Seen it also and known what to do. He thought back. The Vision had shown the bull-man killing, not being killed. His offer to end its life was a mistake and his Mouth had rightly rejected it. His lips thinned as he remembered how he'd allowed Bacchus to make more trouble between him and Ariadne.

"I won't travel that road again," he said aloud to the empty room. "I'll make my peace with my priestess. I know the bull-head, poor creature, must die. When she Sees it too . . . but not by my hand or hers."

CHAPTER 11

Although Ariadne realized that Pasiphae would probably bar her from visiting Asterion, immediately after her confrontation she had no idea what a large hole the prohibition would make in her life. Nor did the knowledge of how much time she'd spent with Asterion, of how she'd used him to assuage her own loneliness, come to her at once. She hardly recognized that loneliness until the scab was pulled off the unhealed wound of her separation from Dionysus when she had Called him at the ritual and been *actively* rejected.

She had become accustomed to passive rejection. For two years, the scrying bowl had rippled, flashed, and gone dark and Ariadne knew that Dionysus had refused to answer her. She expected no more for this ritual; however this time the bowl cleared and she saw golden hair and white skin. For a moment her heart almost stopped with joy—and then she saw a strange face looking back at her.

The face was male but pretty as a girl's with long, golden hair and full pouting lips. It watched her throughout the completion of the ritual, giving her time to recognize that the prettiness was not *nice*; the eyes were too small and the nose was thin so that a tinge of viciousness marred the expression. And then she realized she knew the face from Dionysus' description.

"I am Lord Dionysus' priestess at Knossos," she said silently, not knowing whether Dionysus had told Bacchus anything about her. "I am instructed to Call the god for the ritual at this time of year. May I speak to Dionysus?"

Bacchus shook his head so that his golden curls danced and he smiled with a kind of glee, showing small, sharp teeth. "No. He doesn't wish to speak to you. He's still angry with you—oh, very angry. You are also to cease from Calling him. You disturb his sleep. I'll know if there are offerings, so there's no need for you to use the scrying bowl at all. Dionysus says you may watch over your precious brother."

The words did something to her heart so that the silver flower that enclosed it tightened painfully. "But I can't—" she cried, about to explain that there was no way for her to avoid using the scrying bowl. Her duty as a priestess demanded she perform the rituals and Calling was part of the ritual—only she wasn't permitted to finish. The scrying bowl went dark.

Half blind with tears, she rose, removed her clothes, and lay down on the icy altar. Only then did she hear the hopeful murmurs of her priestesses, who had understood by the delay as she held the scrying bowl that she was speaking and being answered. Since Dionysus had been the one to answer in the past, they were eagerly watching the painting, expecting Dionysus to appear before it. Ariadne got up at once and dressed. The god wouldn't come. He'd never come. Swallowing sobs, she waved a symbol of blessing at the few people in the shrine and fled to her chamber, knelt in front of his chair, laid her head on the seat, and wept.

By the time she rang for breakfast, she was cried out and in her misery had come to a decision. She would ignore Bacchus' order and Call her god at the times she should. If that made him angrier, perhaps he'd come to make her mad. At least she would see him.

For some reason that defiant decision cheered her up. She ate her breakfast and before her mood could slip into sadness again, Hagne appeared with a servant carrying a small old chest.

"It was right at the back of the old storeroom in the very darkest corner, covered with some boards," Hagne said, "almost as if someone wanted to hide it. So I thought . . . I thought there might be something special in it."

"Let's open it at once," Ariadne said, directing the servant to put it down and fetch tools.

If it were only a precious cache of jewels, she thought, she'd have an excuse to flout Bacchus' order immediately, but when the servant knelt to examine the lock and see what tools he would need, it became apparent that the chest wasn't locked at all. Ariadne and Hagne both sighed with disappointment, but Ariadne signaled for the man to open the box anyway.

Within was a bundle of threadbare silk garments, disintegrated too much even to be used as rags. Ariadne was just about to direct that they be discarded without further examination, when the servant lifted them out to see what was below and suddenly held the bundle toward her.

"Something is within, Lady," he murmured.

Ariadne looked at the bundle of rags and smiled. She was aware of a warmth, a sense of comfort, coming from what the servant held. She rose and came forward to take it from him, unaware that her hand had risen to her forehead in salute and that she had then knelt and held out her arms for the bundle. She gestured for the table that sat beside Dionysus' chair and laid the bundle on that to unwrap.

As the silks fell away, shredding more than unfolding, a gleaming black statuette was exposed. Without a sound Ariadne set it upright, first bowed her head, and then raised it and stared. It was an extremely simple, even stark, image of a woman. One could make out only a tall form, not obviously clothed but yet not naked, slender and yet with abundant breasts and full hips. The face was a mystery of hollows, the head crowned with a circlet of doves.

"Mother," Ariadne whispered, and felt a flicker of warmth, as if a finger had touched her cheek.

She rose then, surprised to see that Hagne and the servant were also kneeling. They got to their feet when she did, looking astonished at finding themselves down on their knees, but Ariadne made no comment, only telling them to take away the chest and the rotting silks. When they had left the room, she carried the statuette into her bedchamber and realized that there was a niche in the wall just opposite the bed. The statuette fit into it perfectly.

The image must have come from there, Ariadne thought. Who'd dared to remove it? And why?

Dionysus? He was a jealous god; he had told her that. But the pang of anxiety she felt didn't last long. Dionysus had given her permission to dance for the Mother and said that everyone honored the Mother. And the comfort that flowed from the dark form was too precious to give up.

A small cup for incense was hollowed into the front of the niche. Ariadne put a ball of the stuff into the cup and pointed a finger to light it. As the smoke curled up, she examined the statuette more closely. It was clearly ancient, in a primitive style only seen in the deep caves used even before the palaces had been built. So old and so strong.

"Thank you for giving me the comfort of your presence, Mother," she murmured, and unable to resist, danced a few steps of the Welcome she would perform more fully only two days later when the moon was full. She could have sworn when she made a last bow that a shadow shifted among the hollows of the face so that it seemed to be smiling.

Returning briskly, completely refreshed, to the main chamber, she summoned both Hagne and Dido, telling the latter to bring the novices. She'd been teaching them simple supporting roles in the praise dance and now reviewed them to be sure they were move perfect. Then with the two older priestesses, she discussed what she and the girls would wear for the awakening ritual. By the time they had settled on the white dress flounced in gold and had the children try on their simpler costumes, it was time to eat.

Ariadne slipped asleep that night smiling, the last image she saw before she snuffed out her light, the dark form back where it belonged. Her chamber was suffused with peace, with hope.

Unfortunately what had been offered to her did not seem to extend over to her parents. After that first quarrel over Asterion's attendance at the Mother's festival when the child was three months old, they had seemed to settle into a kind of unity. If it wasn't as close as it had been before Asterion had been conceived, at least they were not so distant as to cast a pall over the ritual.

Tonight was different, worse, perhaps, than that first quarrel. They nearly spat the words that were supposed to be full of tenderness and exultation at each other. Ariadne felt leaden, oppressed. She was gasping with exhaustion when she sank down to wait for the moon to rise and there were no golden ribbons from which to draw warmth and strength.

"Forgive them. Forgive them," she prayed, but she could think of no reason to offer the Goddess to forgive and no excuse for her parents' behavior.

This night was dedicated to the Mother and all other problems should be set aside. Ariadne had buried her own sorrow and dismay when Dionysus no longer came to watch her dance. Why couldn't her mother and father think of the joy and the hope of renewal at the turning of the year? A warm breeze out of season fanned her hair as she pleaded for mercy without justice and gave her strength enough to finish her dance. *She*, as representative of the people of Crete, was loved and the Mother would let the earth awaken and new life begin, but the Goddess was not happy.

Ariadne expected that Phaidra would be at the shrine soon to discuss what had happened, but she didn't come. Less acutely aware of Phaidra's absence than she should have been because a surprising number of offerings had been delivered—a few stealthily but more quite openly—Ariadne did not inquire further. She wondered instead whether the Bull God's influence was waning. Perhaps that was why her mother was so desperate to force her to acknowledge and dance for him?

For almost a ten-day, Ariadne was quite busy arranging the gifts on the altar and placing any perishable material in stasis. She was vaguely aware that she no longer suffered cold and fatigue when doing magic, even the draining stasis spell, and if she did feel chilled she had only to go look at the black statuette to be warmed. That was a most pleasant surprise; an unpleasant one was when *everything* was taken from the altar. Dionysus had never before been greedy and had usually left behind most of the offerings for the use of the shrine.

It saddened her because she thought it another sign of his continued anger, but the warmth of the Mother that flowed from the dark image saved her from despair. However, once the flurry of activity generated by the offerings was over, Ariadne realized she had nothing to do. She couldn't, as Bacchus had sneeringly suggested, watch over her brother because she was forbidden to enter the palace. She'd tried once and a guard, although his face twisted with anxiety, had turned her away.

Now Ariadne came face-to-face with the results of her defiance of Pasiphae. Idleness began to plague her, and she began to seek occupation. Her first move was to practice the magic that Dionysus had taught her, but it came easily to her now and she was quite proficient enough to awe her priests and priestesses and any worshipers who came to the shrine. She examined the accounts that the priests kept—not that there was much in them anymore. She checked on the lessons that Dido was giving the novices and discovered that one, Sappho, could scry. She exercised her in that ability.

Somehow the days passed and it was time to bless the vines. She did the vineyards around Knossos, aware of shadowy forms watching her pass in her white gown and saluting, fist to forehead, when they saw her glowing staff. No one watched in Minos' vineyard; Ariadne hesitated before she blessed them but in the end she passed through. She wasn't so eager to be with Asterion as to punish her family over Pasiphae's prohibition. Perhaps Asterion would forget her; it would almost be a relief. If she never went near him again, would Dionysus forgive her?

She had no answer for that, but she had duties enough now. As she had, four times each year, she set out to visit the other shrines to Dionysus. These, she discovered, were far more prosperous than the shrine at Knossos. There were one or two temples going up to the Bull God, one near Phaistos and another near Mallia, but Pasiphae had not dared try to bring Asterion to them, so response to the new deity was tepid. The worship of Dionysus was still strong in the outlying places, since the harvests of grapes and the wine pressed from them were marvelous. More people watched her pass; she heard snatches of praise songs.

Still she wasn't sorry to tell her servants to turn her chariot toward home. In each place, although she was treated with honor, she was asked when the god would manifest himself to them again as he did the first time she came. It was Dionysus they wanted to see, not her, even though they knew she carried his blessing. She had no answer for them; her pride wouldn't let her say he was angry with her and would come no more.

When she arrived at the shrine at Knossos, she was relieved to hear from Hagne that her sister had come several times. Phaidra's long absence had been a worry at the back of her mind. Still, she was less than thrilled that as soon as she had washed and eaten, Hagne asked if she could send a messenger to the palace. Phaidra had demanded most anxiously to be told as soon as Ariadne was at home.

Ariadne sighed. She wasn't really in the mood to hear Phaidra complain—or gossip—but said one of the boy novices should bring Phaidra the news. The child was back too fast. He hadn't seen Phaidra, he admitted. The guard hadn't allowed him to seek her. Ariadne shrugged. She would hear her sister's troubles and gossip soon enough.

The idle thought was all too true. Ariadne had just finished her simple evening meal and was wondering what she should do until it was time for bed, when she heard Phaidra's voice.

"You must send for her." Phaidra was sobbing. "Is there no way you can send her a message to come home?"

"I'm here, love," Ariadne said, coming out into the courtyard.

She stopped abruptly and drew breath. Phaidra looked haggard and her eyes were staring wide.

"Oh, thank the Mother!" Phaidra leapt forward and seized her arm. "Come. You must come at once. The Bull God has gone completely mad."

"Oh, poor Asterion!" Ariadne exclaimed, allowing Phaidra to pull her a few steps forward. Then she stopped and shook her head. "They won't let me in."

"They will now," Phaidra cried, tugging at her. "Father has countermanded mother's order—and this time mother won't fight him. I tell you, the Bull God's gone mad."

Ariadne called behind her for someone to bring a cloak. "But why?" she asked as she hurried out with Phaidra, running along the road in response to her sister's demand. "What have they done to him? He was actually getting to like the ceremonies."

"It's because you haven't come to see him. He began to cry for 'Ridne' the day of the praise-dance for the Mother and bellow your name as if he thought you would hear him. Father wanted to send for you, but mother said she'd never allow you to see him again until you acknowledged him as a god and danced worship."

"That's true," Ariadne said, stopping suddenly and jerking Phaidra to a halt beside her. "I'll gladly go to Asterion and soothe him if I can, but I won't call him a god and I won't dance for him. If that's what mother demands—"

"No." Phaidra pulled her forward again. "She must allow you to see him now. You see, she promised that if he went to the temple for the vine-quickening ceremonies she has devised, that you would come to see him again—she sets them for a few days after you've been out blessing the vines . . . as if that will fool anyone. He was angry when you didn't come at once, but mother told him you were visiting Prokris. Then today she wanted him to come to the temple and . . . and he went mad. He said—well, as much as he could—that he'd never go to the temple again until you came. So they tried to force him . . ."

"Fools!" Ariadne exclaimed.

"Oh, yes, they're fools. He nearly killed two of them."

"Oh, poor child—"

"Child!" Phaidra screeched. "You should see him. He's a foot taller than I and growing stronger by the minute."

"He's still a child, Phaidra," Ariadne snapped. "I don't care how tall he is or how strong. He's two years and two months old. It's because you all forget he's nothing but a baby that you have all this trouble with him. All two-year-olds are difficult."

"I tell you two men are nearly dead. One likely maimed for life. Two more are so bruised, they can barely walk—"

"That's because Asterion is strong as a man and has the sense only of a two-year-old. The fools always hit him instead of tempting him to do what they want in a way that will make him like to do it. If they aren't cleverer than a two-year-old . . . Does he ever strike at you, Phaidra?"

"No, but he pushes me away and says I'm not Ridne." Phaidra's voice was redolent of resentment.

Ariadne ignored that, knowing it was because Phaidra would never touch Asterion, never offer him affection even though she fed him and sometimes even played with him. "But he doesn't hurt you," she insisted, concentrating on what was important.

"No . . ." Phaidra drew out the word doubtfully. "Although sometimes," she added, as they entered the palace and threaded their way through the passages, "when he says, 'Where Ridne?' I don't like the look in his eyes."

"He's probably trying—"

Ariadne stopped abruptly after they passed her father's apartments and the sound of Asterion's bellowing reached them. She wondered how Pasiphae, who was much closer could bear it but only began to run, stopping, shocked at the volume of sound coming through his closed door. Closed and *barred.*

"What is the need for this?" she cried.

"He's trying to get out," one attendant said, his voice quavering. He was badly bruised all along one side of his body, as if he'd been thrown against a wall or to the ground with great force.

"You idiot!" Ariadne exclaimed. "How are you going to feed him? How am I going to get in to calm him?"

"I won't open the door. I won't! He'll rush out and kill us before he even sees you. He tried to kill the queen."

What the man said was all too likely. A two-year-old in a tantrum isn't the most reasonable of creatures. It was indeed likely that Asterion might do considerable damage—to her as well as to his attendants—if he got out.

"Asterion!" Ariadne shouted, pressing herself against the door. "Asterion, be quiet. It's Ariadne. If you are quiet, I'll come in and play with you."

The effort, although she repeated it several times, was a waste. Her voice could hardly be heard above Asterion's bellowing even on this side of the door; it must have been completely obliterated on the other. She was at her wits' end, weeping a little as she remembered how Dionysus had come to help her in the past. Fortunately thinking of him recalled to her mind a trick of magic he had taught her to impress those in a large temple or an open shrine. She could make her voice go far from her and sound in a person's ear.

"Asterion," she sent out. "Asterion, Ariadne is here. If you stop yelling and sit down quietly, I'll come in and play with you. But you mustn't be angry any more. I was far away, love. I couldn't come right away. But I'm here now."

About half way through the speech, the bawling began to diminish. By the end, it had stopped.

"Will you sit still while I come in, love?" Ariadne called through the door.

"Sitting," Asterion roared. "Ridne come in. No one else."

Without waiting for help, Ariadne pushed up the bar securing the door, opened it just enough to enter, and ran in. Asterion leapt to his feet and rushed at her, enveloping her in his arms, crying, "Ridne. Ridne."

Swallowing hard, Ariadne returned his embrace. He was now a head taller than she, he smelled like an overworked ox, and his arms were so strong she had to beg him to be gentle. He relaxed his grip at once, bending his head down toward her, but sidelong so the horns would not touch her.

"No hurt Ridne," he said. "Love Ridne."

"Yes, and I love you too, Asterion." She kissed his cheek, tears of pity hanging in her eyes because she didn't really love him, only pitied him.

His bull's mouth tried to imitate a smile. "Ridne stay? Play?"

"Yes, I'll play with you. Go get the toys you want to show me."

He went to the side of the chamber and lifted a whole chest. Her eyes widened; it would have taken two normal men to lift that weight, but Asterion carried it and put it down beside her without apparent effort. Ariadne swallowed and sank to the floor as he opened the chest. He was making happy, chortling noises. She decided that this would be a good time to reprimand him. It was close enough to the time that he'd misbehaved that he would remember, but in his first joy over seeing her he might be more amenable than a two-year-old usually was.

"Asterion, you've been very naughty, hurting your servants."

"Lied! She lies! Promised Ridne."

"But I've come, dear." It was unlikely that Asterion could remember how long it was since Pasiphae made the promise. "I was far away. I didn't know you wanted me. I came home last night and, see, I've come at once to you."

"Went to temple. No Ridne came." He shook his heavy head. "No Ridne. No temple."

"But you like to go to the temple now, Asterion. You like to see the priests and priestesses dance."

"People come after. Too long. Seat hurts."

"If I speak to mother, love, and she promises to make the ceremony of offering shorter, will you go to the temple when she asks?"

He looked at her, looked away. Plainly he didn't wish to answer. Ariadne felt it would be unwise to push him too hard. Asterion took several tops from the chest and began to spin them one after the other so cleverly that they interwove in a complicated pattern. Ariadne watched. Strength and dexterity seemed to be his Gifts, but what good were they? What he needed was understanding to match his growth of body. As the idea came into her mind so did the blasphemous thought that none of the gods seemed to have much in the way of either understanding or wisdom. Only the Mother . . .

How could a god lack wisdom? The question sent a chill down Ariadne's back. She pushed the rebellious thought away and gave her attention to Asterion, clapping her hands and uttering cries of praise as he pulled a snakelike toy with segments that glittered through the path of the whirling tops. Those he kept in action by snatching each as it barely began to wobble and spinning it again. Then he got his wagon and pulled that around the perimeter of the spinning tops to add to the glitter and the noise. After a time, however, he picked up each wobbler and tossed it into the wagon.

Ariadne searched in the chest and brought out several puzzles. Asterion didn't like these so much, but he did put the large pieces where they belonged—if Ariadne chose the piece and showed him the spot. She noted sadly that he still didn't seem to make any sense out of the distinctive shapes. Nor could he send a ball through a simple maze. It wasn't any fault in his ability to make the ball go anywhere he wanted. He just didn't seem able to grasp the clear, if physically convoluted, pattern to bring it home.

Since those games had annoyed him, Ariadne found one she had never been able to master herself. It consisted of a ball and a paddle with a cup at the base. The idea was to start with the ball in the cup, toss it out so that it could be hit with the paddle, and then catch it in the cup and repeat. The paddle could be used to bounce the ball off the floor or the walls. Ariadne could do it a few times; then she either failed to hit it or catch it. Asterion just went on and on, chasing the ball around the room as paddle strokes sent it up, down, and across, sometimes even awry. Unerringly he caught the ball each time.

"Oh, love, you're making me dizzy," Ariadne cried at last. "Aren't you hungry? It's surely time for the midday meal."

"Temple in afternoon," he said, catching the ball one last time and giving the toy to Ariadne.

"You will go, won't you?" she asked. "I can't stay and play longer today anyhow. I have other duties. Won't you let your servants come in and bring your food and dress you?"

"Shorter time?"

"Not this ceremony, love. Just be a little patient until I have a chance to speak to the queen. But I won't tell you lies. If she won't shorten the making of offerings, I'll tell you true."

"Ridne never lies. Come tomorrow? Please?"

"Oh, Asterion—" she put her arms around him and hugged him tight, kissed his cheek "—I don't know. I'll try to come. I will try."

"Ridne come. Bull God go to temple."

Possibly the attendant waiting outside the chamber heard what Asterion had said; his voice was loud and penetrating even when he wasn't deliberately shouting. In any case, there was no problem about her admission to Asterion the next day or at any other time. His attendants, who had been indifferent, sullen, or actively hostile in the past, now welcomed her with smiles and bows. She ventured a few words of advice on Asterion's management. And, although Pasiphae wouldn't speak to her, wouldn't even look at her, Ariadne was able to pass

Asterion's request for shorter offering ceremonies to her through Phaidra.

Whether the processions were curtailed for that reason or because the original fervor of worship was wearing thin, Ariadne didn't know and didn't care. Asterion went to the ceremonies without complaint and seemed content. His condition improved too; his fur gleamed with brushing and his odor decreased. He still greeted her with shrieks of joy, but she felt there was less desperation in his voice. And one attendant even thanked her for reminding them that Asterion was no more than a baby despite his size.

Relative peace descended on palace, temple, and shrine, and the vines that Ariadne had blessed were blossoming with even more than their usual abundance. Two years of bountiful harvests and wines that fermented sweet and rich were bringing prosperity to Crete. Even if no one had dared scant the Bull God—and a few did dare—there was enough to spare for an offering to honor Dionysus. More sacrifices arrived at the shrine every day. As the spring equinox approached, Ariadne began to worry about what would happen at the ritual because Pasiphae had arranged ceremonies at the Bull God's temple on the same day. Ariadne didn't really believe her mother had accepted defeat on the subject of her daughter's service; however, the one disturbance that occurred wasn't caused by Asterion or Pasiphae.

Bacchus' face appeared in Ariadne's scrying bowl again when she Called Dionysus and he snarled that she'd been ordered not to Call the god ever again. Less shocked and unprepared this time, Ariadne snapped back that she had no choice. As high priestess she *must* perform the ritual, and the ritual demanded a Calling of the god.

"Tell Dionysus that if he wishes me to stop Calling

him, he must come and change the ritual himself. I haven't the power to do that."

A look of such frustrated fury, mingled with fear, appeared on Bacchus' face at her words, that Ariadne suddenly began to wonder if Dionysus even knew of Bacchus' order that she stop Calling him. Was it possible for a god not to know what his own servants were doing? She was hardly aware of undressing, lying on the altar, then rising and dressing again.

Then a less frightening notion occurred to her. Was it possible that Dionysus' anger against her had been kept alive by a companion jealous of the god's attention? Hadn't Pasiphae brought the Bull God upon Knossos because she was envious of Ariadne's contact with a god?

Ariadne was enough cheered by the idea that Dionysus' rage was not self-sustaining that she actually looked at the worshipers in the court. She was surprised by how much larger the group was than she expected, and even more surprised to see among them her brother Androgeos. He was the favorite of all her siblings, but it was not an unadulterated joy to see him there because she suspected he had not come to worship.

Just before she gave a blessing to the crowd, he caught her eye and made a small gesture to indicate he wished to wait and speak to her when she had dismissed the others, which confirmed her suspicions. As the gate closed behind the last person, Androgeos came forward and saluted her courteously.

"Won't Queen Pasiphae be furious if she hears you were at my ritual instead of at hers?" Ariadne asked.

"No, because she sent me to see whether the god came and, if he didn't, to try to convince you to join the Bull God's ritual."

"Ritual? That's a blasphemy," Ariadne said coldly. "Asterion is no god, and you know it, and King Minos knows it, and I'm reasonably sure even Queen Pasiphae knows it, no matter how blind an eye she turns."

Androgeos sighed. "The service you would give would have little enough to do with the Bull God. It's no pleasure to me either to prostrate myself before a mindless monster and call it a god, but—"

"He's not mindless," Ariadne protested. "He's only two years old! Do you think you were so wise and perfect when you were two years old?"

"I know he's two years old! Pasiphae makes a great point that he was born out of her body only two years ago. He's as tall as I and stronger . . . and that's the only miracle she can claim for him."

"Well, his size *does* prove he's Poseidon's get and must be cherished. But worshiped? No. At least, not by me."

"There are other reasons," Androgeos said urgently.

Ariadne saw she wouldn't escape argument so easily. She sighed and gestured for Androgeos to follow her down the corridor. Since it was daylight and she knew the way well, no lamps were alight; however, it was dim in the passage and Androgeos, being a stranger, stumbled. Ariadne immediately waved at the lamps, which lit. She opened the door and entered her apartment, stepping back so her brother could come in.

"And those reasons?" she asked, gesturing at the door, which closed.

Androgeos didn't answer at once, looking around at the now sparsely furnished and elegant room. A few sets of marvelously carved chairs were grouped around low, round, matching wood tables. Another set, two chairs and a loveseat, flanked an oblong table of ivory. Toward the back of the room, nearest to the light well was a cushioned single chair with a low stool and a gilded table beside it. On the table was a golden bowl.

"Please sit," she said, pointing at the loveseat and then at a brazier in which the charcoal immediately began to burn.

Androgeos stared, looking from the glowing coals to his sister's face. Doubt showed in his expression, but after a moment his mouth set hard and he sat down. Ariadne sighed and took the chair opposite.

"You're looking very well, Ariadne," Androgeos began. "You've grown quite beautiful, and it seems you've gained some power of your own. Nonetheless, Dionysus hasn't returned for two years. If he'd wished to keep his worshipers and contest the influence of the Bull God, he'd have done it sooner."

"Why should he? Do you think Crete is important to him? Doesn't Egypt grow grapes? Greece? Sicily? Biblos and Babylon? Dionysus has enough to do without caring about Crete. He gave me the power to bless the grapes and he gave his warning when Asterion was born. If Knossos won't listen, the grief will fall on their heads, not his."

"But don't you see that you can prevent any grief from coming to us?"

"It's too late, I fear," Ariadne said. "I don't think that anything can shield Knossos now."

"Yes. You can. The miracle of the grapes is renewed every year. If you danced at the Bull God's temple—"

"No." The answer was flat, uncompromising. "I dance for the Mother. I am priestess for and perform the ritual for the god Dionysus. I will worship no other god."

"Why not?" Androgeos was annoyed. "Everyone brings offerings to many shrines."

"That's quite different. I, too, might bring doves to Aphrodite's shrine to pray for success with a lover, as a private person, as the girl Ariadne. I wouldn't perform any ritual of worship as a priestess."

"This is a matter of trade and politics, not worship," Androgeos pointed out. "Did you know that mother has invited envoys from many nations and city-states to come and see the Bull God made flesh?"

Ariadne shrugged. "Let them look. Asterion is real enough—"

"Real, yes, but no god. He—he has no *presence*. I was here when Dionysus appeared. I—I knew—" He stopped abruptly, then went on as if he were still speaking of Asterion. "The envoys from Egypt already have doubts. They were astounded on first seeing him and prostrated themselves on the ground, intoning hymns . . . which started him bellowing because he wanted his dancers. They were startled and withdrew, fearing they had offended somehow, but the second time they came, although they had come with rich gifts to appease him . . . they weren't quite so impressed. You know their ideas of the *ka* and the *ba*. I heard one say the beast had no *ka*, that it was soulless."

Sighing, Ariadne said sadly, "He's only a baby. If only mother weren't so impatient. As he gets older, he'll learn to behave in a more dignified fashion . . . I think."

"It will be long too late. The Egyptians have great influence. If they say we worship a false god—"

"Why should they? They don't say the gods of the Greeks are false, even though they're far different from their own. Why should they deny Knossos its god?"

"Because it's a travesty of their own, which are also animal-headed? Because they don't wish to share their kind of god with us?" Androgeos shook his head. "It doesn't matter why. We need the respect, even the fear, of Egypt and others to assist in treaty making and trade agreements. Fear of our god—a god made manifest in the flesh and attending to our affairs—

is less expensive and perhaps less dangerous than a large army and a great fleet of fighting ships."

"Well, perhaps . . . But I don't see what this has to do with me."

"A god works miracles, sometimes by his own hand, sometimes through his priests or priestesses. You work miracles. If you are the Bull God's priestess, then perhaps his deficiencies will be less noticed. If his mere priestess can work wonders, they'll believe he must be a true god."

"First, I don't work miracles. The blessing of the grapes—"

"I saw you light the lamps, the brazier, close the door without touching any of them."

Ariadne shook her head. "That's magic, not a god-given Gift. I wouldn't cheapen worship with such tricks."

"All the more then should you be willing to 'conjure' for the good of Crete. You aren't offering true worship so you'll be doing nothing offensive to your god."

"You can only say that because you don't know Dionysus. He certainly *would* take offense—violent offense."

"How will he know if he never comes?" Androgeos asked, almost sneering. Ariadne shuddered and drew back a little into her chair. Misinterpreting her reaction, Androgeos said, "Very well, if you won't dance, then you won't, but if you would simply stand beside the Bull God and, say, light the torches with a gesture—"

Although Androgeos' question had awakened a persistent anxiety strongly enough to send a chill over Ariadne's flesh—shouldn't a god know what his priestess was doing whether or not he was present physically? Yet Ariadne had good evidence—from Dionysus' own lips—that he did not know, that he hadn't even known that his favorite priestess, the first Ariadne, had died. But it didn't matter whether Dionysus ever knew she had supported the worship of the Bull God. The thought made her sick with revulsion.

"No!"

"You spend hours with him every day. Why won't you spend a little more time and do your people a great good? If we can only confirm the Bull God as a true deity, the profit to Knossos would be enormous."

"Profit," Ariadne said flatly. So Minos was involved.

"Yes, profit," Androgeos returned. "Do you think anyone cares for the actual blessing of the grapes? They care for the juice they will press from them, the wine they will ferment and sell for . . . yes . . . profit."

"Don't talk like a fool," Ariadne snapped. "I have no scorn of profit. Nor am I in any doubt about the value of treaties and trade agreements. A rich people is a happy people. But I tell you, there will be no profit in trying to make Asterion appear what he is not."

Androgeos' lips twisted. "You speak as Mouth?"

"No, I speak as a person of common sense who isn't caught up in a crazy dream. What will happen when a treaty or trade agreement is violated? Do you expect poor Asterion to shake the earth or cast lightning?"

"If crops were blighted—"

Androgeos bit his lip. Clearly he hadn't intended to say so much and, indeed, it revealed how Minos and Pasiphae had planned to draw her step by step into becoming a priestess of the Bull God.

Ariadne stood up. "You're mad! I'm not Demeter. I can't do such a thing, and if I could, I wouldn't!"

Androgeos did not stir. "I tell you that not only mother but father is set on the idea of confirming the Bull God as a deity." His tone was threatening.

Ariadne laughed. "King Minos intends to attack the high priestess of Dionysus? He'll put me in prison? He'll torture me? What will he do when the grapes rot on the vine and the wine is bitter as gall? What will he do if Dionysus—despite the fact that he hasn't come to the ritual—runs through Crete as he ran though Thebes?" She shrugged. "There's nothing with which you can bribe me or threaten me. I'll always be kind to Asterion because he's my little brother, because he loves me and needs me. I *will not* encourage the belief that he is a god."

"*You* will bring upon Knossos the destruction you Mouthed."

Ariadne again shrugged her indifference. "Perhaps. Perhaps if Queen Pasiphae hadn't chosen me to be Dionysus' priestess, the god wouldn't have answered the Call; Pasiphae wouldn't have become envious and coupled with Poseidon; Asterion would never have been born. So perhaps I am responsible. But nothing I do or don't do now will have any effect. If you want magical trickery and much finer than I can do, go to Daidalos. He will create much more convincing and spectacular miracles."

"You don't understand. Father hasn't spoken one word to Daidalos since . . . since the Bull God was conceived and has taken away many of his stipends and privileges—"

"Then this is a good time for them to be reconciled. King Minos shouldn't blame a servant for yielding to Pasiphae, to whom he, himself, yielded." She looked away for a moment and then looked back. "And I fear that Daidalos' arts will be urgently needed if the king and queen continue to tread the path they are now walking."

Ariadne laughed. "King Minos intends to attack the high priestess of Dionysus? He'll put me in prison? He'll torture me? What will he do when the grapes rot on the vine and the wine is bitter as gall? What will he do if Dionysus—despite the fact that he hasn't come to the island—[illegible] through Crete—or [illegible]?" She shrugged. "There's nothing with which you can bribe me [illegible]. I'll always be kind to Androgeos because he's my little brother, because he [illegible] and needs me. I will not [illegible] the belief that he is a god."

"[illegible] will come upon Knossos the destruction [illegible]."

Ariadne again shrugged her indifference. "Perhaps. Perhaps if Queen Pasiphae hadn't chosen me to be Dionysus' priestess the god would have answered [illegible]. Pasiphae wouldn't have [illegible] and coupled with Poseidon; Asterion would never have been born. So perhaps I am responsible. But nothing I do [illegible] will [illegible]. If you [illegible] and much [illegible] that I can do [illegible] go to Daidalos. He will [illegible] more [illegible]."

"You don't understand. Father hasn't spoken one word of Daidalos since [illegible] since the Bull Dance was [illegible] and had taken away many of the [illegible]."

[illegible]

CHAPTER 12

Ariadne wasn't surprised when Androgeos' visit was followed by one from her father. She had always understood her mother's purpose—to diminish her and Dionysus, who had rejected her—but her father, older and wiser, might have seen something she had missed. Fortunately Androgeos had given away the real reason for Minos' attempts to wheedle and bludgeon her into supporting the cult of the Bull God. All he was trying to protect was his pride. He didn't wish to humble himself to Daidalos. So, although Minos was far more skillful than Androgeos in his pleading and attacks, he was unable to waken either sympathy or fear in her.

Despite the wonder Daidalos had created for her to dance on, Ariadne was by no means fond of him. He was always sour and complaining, acting put-upon because he was required to give service for his keep. But fair is fair; ungracious as he was, it was Minos himself who had ordered Daidalos to give Pasiphae the seeming of a cow. He had no right to punish Daidalos for doing so.

Ariadne held to her absolute refusal to appear in *any* capacity, even as a simple visitor, in the temple of the Bull God. And not a ten-day later, she had cause to be passionately grateful that Androgeos had armored her against her father's wiles.

"Where is he?" the voice she had longed for, wept for, bellowed simultaneously in her head and in her ear. "Where is he?"

Ariadne shot bolt upright and fastened her hands to those that were grinding flesh into bone in her shoulders. She was mute with terror, fearing in her sleep-dazed state that Dionysus was accusing her of defection to the Bull God.

"She'll kill him! I must go there. Where is he?"

The exclamation that "she would kill him" cured that fear and the blind eyes that stared at her and didn't see, the beads of clammy sweat that glittered faintly in the dim light of the night-lamp, told her that Dionysus was in the throes of a Vision or the aftermath of one.

"Tell me! My lord, you must tell me! I only see your Visions though your voice."

He swallowed hard, struggling to explain. "A dark room but faintly lit with moonlight? A night-lamp? I'm not sure of that, but I could see a bed only . . . only near half of it was gone, swallowed up by a—a blackness."

He drew a gasping breath and Ariadne used the grip she had on his hands, which had eased their bruising hold on her, to pull him around somewhat so he could sit on the bed.

"An evil blackness?" she asked, not because she thought so—her heartflower was fully open and the silvery mist of strands from it was telling her that the blackness wasn't what brought beads of fear-sweat to Dionysus' face.

"No! No, there's no evil in the blackness. It's a disguise only—but I don't understand . . ."

"Understanding is my part, my lord. You need only speak your Vision."

His eyes grew even more unfocussed, and Ariadne knew he was literally replaying the Vision in his mind. "I See a glimmer of light approaching the door to the chamber," he began. "It grows brighter and a woman appears in the door way, holding a lamp in one hand; the other is closed over what I think is a small scrap of cloth."

Ariadne gasped and shivered as Dionysus' Vision suddenly became manifest to her. She not only heard him; a picture of his Seeing flowed back to her through the mist of silver tendrils, a picture filled with a terrible sense of fear and desolation. But she wasn't certain whether that emotion was coming from the Vision itself or whether it was Dionysus' fear and sorrow that she was feeling.

"She's beautiful, more beautiful than any Olympian woman, except perhaps Aphrodite," Dionysus continued, almost chanting, "but she's a native."

Ariadne heard him, but she was far more caught by the expression on the woman's face than by her beauty.

"She comes close to the bed and begins to whisper, gesturing with the hand that holds the piece of cloth. She's casting a spell. I can see it spin out from her hand and fall, like tiny beads of light, on the blackness. The beads sink into the blackness. I can see them drifting, marking out the figure of a man, marking out the threads of another spell, that one which creates the blackness. He stirs. The beads burst into flame. He screams and screams again. The blackness disappears. It's Eros—my friend Eros, writhing in pain."

Ariadne drew in a deep breath. She had glanced only briefly at the tortured man. Her attention had been all on the woman, who had staggered back when Eros became visible, crying out with a terrible dismay.

Dionysus grasped her shoulders tight again and shook her. "Mouth," he demanded, "tell me where they are! That's not Eros' chamber in Aphrodite's house. I know that room well. Tell me where they are so I can stop her before she kills Eros."

"She won't kill Eros," Ariadne said. The Vision was gone, but she could still see it.

"Where are they?" Dionysus roared. "I Saw her killing Eros. I'll tear her in pieces, and Aphrodite will help."

"No!" Ariadne cried, seizing his arms; through her hands pulse after pulse of soothing silver flowed. "The woman meant no harm to Eros and has done him no lasting harm." She spoke slowly and clearly, willing calm to him. "Didn't you hear what she said when the blackness drained away? She didn't know Eros was concealed in the dark cloud."

He blinked and his eyes focused on her. In the dim light, they looked as if the silver mist that was flowing out of her had colored them silver instead of bright blue.

"If she meant no harm," he asked, "why did she cast that spell, which caused him so much pain?"

He was still angry, but not frantic now. Ariadne

shrugged, but didn't loosen her grip on him. "Your Vision didn't tell me that. I can only Speak what I saw in the woman's face before she cast the spell—that was love, great love, and a desire to help whoever was hidden by the darkness."

"So much pain?" Dionysus whispered. "Are you telling me that I should do nothing?" His face creased with anxiety. "Eros was in agony. I could feel it."

Ariadne had felt it too, and her certainty in her interpretation was shaken. Seeking reassurance, she looked past Dionysus, to the blacker shadow in the opposite wall. Did it move? Gesture? Perhaps not, but she knew. Eros' pain wouldn't torment him long and wasn't important; however, there *was* something Dionysus must do.

"Yes," she said, her voice deeper, smoother than was natural to her, "there's something you must do. This time your Vision was sent to save your friend—but not from the spellcaster so it doesn't matter where they are. You must stop Aphrodite from harming the woman. If the woman dies, Eros will also die."

"He mustn't die," Dionysus said. "Eros is my friend. He doesn't say, 'Dionysus what do you want?' and give it to me immediately so that I'll go away. He offers me wine and cakes and talks to me. He mustn't die."

Ariadne was a trifle amused by Dionysus' simple self-centered reason for protecting Eros, but the need in his voice laid bare his terrible loneliness and the vicious circle of the hurt that led to anger, the anger that lashed out and woke fear, which led to withdrawal or avoidance and bred more hurt. There was nothing amusing in that. She reached out and touched Dionysus' face tenderly.

"Eros won't die," she said, and then impelled by some inner certainty, she added, "He's greatly beloved of the Mother and She has sent you this Seeing to save him. Go, Dionysus. Explain to Aphrodite."

Dionysus caught Aphrodite just in time, just as she was about to leap to where the woman lived and, he feared, kill her. He seized her, holding her fast, ignoring her outraged shriek, and shook her. Small fists pounded his legs and back; small nails scratched his hips; baby teeth fastened in one calf. He was too accustomed to the pain of bites and scratches to be distracted.

"Does Eros live?" he roared, shaking Aphrodite again. The attacks on him redoubled; there were shrill cries of rage; more small hands gripped him.

"Yes," she cried. "Let me go. Let me revenge myself on Psyche for the pain she caused him."

"No," he said. "Or at least your revenge must be such that it does her no real harm. My Mouth looked into my Vision and told me that if you harm the woman, Eros *will* die."

Aphrodite sagged in his grip and sighed. "I know it. I never meant to hurt her, only to make her suffer, to make her pay for what she did." Then she blinked at him. "You *Saw* Psyche bespell Eros? Why didn't you try to stop her?"

"I had no idea where she and Eros were! I was almost crazy with fear. I leapt to Knossos. The priestess there is a true Mouth. It was she who told me that Eros would suffer no permanent harm from the spell, but that if the woman who cast it was harmed—Psyche, you said she was called—Eros would die."

"He is deeply bound to her," Aphrodite said with an angry grimace and a sigh. "He calls her 'his soul.' What did she do? Why did she do it?"

Dionysus tried to help Aphrodite to a chair, but found himself unable to move. Each thigh was encircled; there were arms about his waist and hands on his ankles. He looked down and around at six or seven small faces. They were no more than eight years old for the eldest, but all were grimly determined to protect their goddess. He couldn't help laughing, which made Aphrodite look down too. He saw her mouth quiver, but she clicked her tongue against her teeth and gravely shook her head.

"Children. Children. Let Dionysus go. Look what you have done! He's all scratched, and bitten too. Oh, how wicked you all are!"

"He grabbed you."

"You screamed."

"He shook you."

Three shrill voices and wordless protests from the others.

"And you wished to save me," Aphrodite said gently. "Well, I'll forgive you, but Dionysus is a friend. You know that. You know he wouldn't hurt me unless it was very important. He was trying to stop me from doing something that would have caused great harm to Eros—who is also his friend. Now, say you are sorry."

There was a reluctant chorus, and Dionysus smiled at the downcast faces. "I understand," he said. "You're forgiven. Indeed, you're commended. Aphrodite is very precious and should be protected."

Her silvery laugh tinkled and she smiled, although her head was still half turned toward Eros' rooms. Then she sighed. "It's very late, children. Off to bed with you all."

They trooped off, two of the youngest looking back at him somewhat doubtfully. Aphrodite smiled at them but said nothing until the sound of their passing was cut off by the snick of a door. Then she listened for a moment more, but the house was silent. She beckoned and went into the central room. A gesture lit concealed mage lights; the walls were painted to resemble a garden, a small fountain tinkled, and night-blooming flowers shone. She took a chair and gestured toward another. Dionysus stood before it for a moment, looking in the direction of Eros' apartment.

"Would I do harm if I went to him?"

"He's asleep. Asclepias is with him."

Dionysus nodded with relief and sat down. Asclepias, it was said, could heal anything—sometimes even death. "My Mouth says Eros is beloved of the Mother and that She sent my Vision to protect him."

"Little as I like it, your Mouth might have spoken the truth. He could barely speak, but all he said was 'Don't harm Psyche. Don't.' Well, I won't, but she'll suffer for what she did. Why, Dionysus? You didn't answer me. What did Psyche do and why did she do it?"

"As to why, I don't know. I asked the same question of my Mouth and she said my Vision didn't explain why. Ask Psyche. What she did is easy to describe. On the bed was a blackness. Psyche cast a spell and the blackness disappeared. Although my Mouth didn't interpret that, it's easy enough to understand. Psyche sought to remove the blackness. Why, I don't know. What my Mouth *did* say was that she did it out of great love and a desire to help."

"Stupid bitch!" Aphrodite's delicate features were not made for rage, but reflected it nonetheless. "Likely she nearly killed Eros out of idiot curiosity, just to see what was under the cloud of darkness." She snorted delicately. "Natives! Your Mouth is native too. Do you believe what she tells you?"

"Yes. She's never been wrong." He frowned. "There's more. When I'm with her, I feel a touch within me. She can quicken the grapes alone as well as I. Like Eros, she's greatly beloved of the Mother. I have felt the power flow into her, both in the vineyards and when she performs the praise-dances. There's more to her than a simple native."

Aphrodite cocked her head. Although half her

attention was plainly on catching any sound from Eros' apartment, that statement had caught her attention. "As there was in Semele?" she asked.

"More than in Semele. I sought out Semele because she was my mother, because I believed Zeus had wronged her, because I thought . . . No, that doesn't matter. I was mistaken. Now I'm not. Ariadne isn't afraid of me and—and has no cause to be because she can contain my . . . my madness."

"Contain it?" Now Aphrodite fixed all her attention on him, concern in her expression. "Are you sure you aren't mistaken about this priestess?" she asked gently. "Silenos was here—he comes to tell stories to the children—he was all bruised and bitten. He didn't speak to me, but I could read his face and the marks told their own story of . . . violence."

"It's true enough." Dionysus' mouth was sullen. "I've been blessing the vineyards with blood and lust." Then he looked up at her and smiled, shamefaced. "More blood than lust. But that's not the fault of the priestess. I quarreled with her and have withdrawn from her for two years."

Aphrodite's eyes opened wide. "She quarreled with you bitterly enough that you withdrew from her for two years . . . and she is alive? She does then truly contain your rage."

"Calms it is a better description. It's not as if the rage were poured into a stoppered flask and would burst out again if the stopper were withdrawn." He grinned again. "It—it's as if she rained on my fire."

"You do not like to be quenched?" Aphrodite asked. "Is that why you left her?"

"No. She defied me." He shrugged. "She was right to do so. I even knew it, but . . . Do you remember when I was so troubled by the Vision of a white bull with a man's head?"

"Yes, I do." Aphrodite sounded surprised. "You

came to tell me about it and Hephaestus was here or came later. I'm not sure about that, but I do remember the Vision of the white bull."

"I couldn't rid myself of it, which is why I came to tell you. I hoped that would wash it from my mind. It didn't, but very soon after, Ariadne Called me and explained the Vision and it was gone. I had another on the same subject—" his mouth turned down with distaste "—and she told me it would mean that her mother, in the guise of a cow, would couple with Poseidon in the form of a bull."

"That's usually Zeus' ploy, isn't it? Was she confused between the two?"

"Oh, no. It was quite true. Out of that coupling a monster was born, a boy with the head of a bull."

"Oh, dear! Poseidon must have been very angry with your priestess's family."

"Yes. With cause. He'd answered King Minos' prayer for a sign he was the rightful king. Poseidon sent a white bull, which was then to be sacrificed, as the sign. But Minos liked the bull too much to kill it. He tried to breed it to his cows."

Aphrodite burst out laughing. "An exchange of cows? Natives! You should have withdrawn yourself as soon as the Vision was satisfied."

"I couldn't. I thought I could save Ariadne from much trouble so I told her I'd show her how to kill the babe with no pain or fear. Not only for her, but for the poor creature himself—to ward off the suffering he would endure and would inflict on the whole of her people. But she said *I* was the monster, not the poor malformed babe, and she would worship me no longer. So I left her. But she was right. It was a lesson from the Mother."

Aphrodite pressed her lips together uneasily at that avowal. There were many in Olympus who objected strenuously to worship of the Mother. Eros, on the other hand, acknowledged Her with devotion. Aphrodite herself cared little either way, only wishing not to be embroiled in the argument.

"So this Ariadne can quench your fire." Aphrodite grinned, avoiding approval or disapproval of his last remark. "And you have long needed a companion, aside from that mean-spirited Bacchus and no-spirited Silenos. Are you going to offer her the chance to come to Olympus?"

"You think that wrong?"

"Not if she is what you think she is and you can cozen Persephone into extending her life."

"I will speak to Persephone, of course, but I don't think her intervention will be necessary. I tell you the Mother gives to Ariadne without asking. No, I meant, would you be kind to her if I brought her here or would she be shunned as Semele was?"

"Dionysus—" Aphrodite leaned forward and touched his face gently "—Semele wasn't sensible. She wanted Zeus back." She laughed merrily. "Who can hold Zeus? And when we told her that and also that, strange as their relationship is, he truly loves Hera, Semele didn't take what we told her as well intentioned. She felt we were against her because she was of native stock. Ariadne will be treated . . . well, by most of us; I wouldn't swear to the behavior of Athena or Artemis or Apollo . . . as she invites."

"It is what—" Dionysus began, but a door latch snicked and Aphrodite was on her feet, running into the corridor.

Dionysus followed close behind, stopping a courteous distance away as Aphrodite accosted a tall, thin man with a gentle expression.

"There's no danger now," Asclepias said. "He'll live and without any harm done, but he must rest and do no magic, which would be very painful, for at least a moon. Another thing, he mustn't be worried or anxious about anything. He's fearful that someone will hurt a Psyche. I assured him she was safe and wouldn't be harmed a dozen times, but—"

"His lover. He's afraid I'll be angry with her. Well, I am! I'm furious!" She sighed. "But I'll do her no harm."

"Then the best way to reassure him is if you will stay with him yourself. Right now he's still fighting the drugs. By morning he should be sufficiently calm for you to leave him."

"I'll go to him—" She remembered Dionysus then and turned toward him.

"Go, go," Dionysus urged anxiously. "Since I'm not the only one warning you about Psyche, I'm no longer needed here." Then, looking at the physician, he said, "Thank you for saving Eros, Asclepias. I haven't so many friends that I can spare one."

"No one can spare a friend," the thin man said. Then his hand tightened nervously on his strange staff. "Eros should be as calm as possible," he added. "I don't think you should visit him. Any excitement will cause him pain, any strong emotion might do real harm."

He had only meant to thank the physician for his care, and this was how he was rewarded, Dionysus thought. Anger and resentment woke at the tacit hint he should go because he was so stupid or uncaring as to incite Eros to rage or lust. Before common sense could remind him that the physician would have said the same thing to any visitor, Dionysus' emotions flooded outward. Asclepias gripped his staff even harder. Aphrodite gasped. Before the fear of him could fuel still more intense flame and hurt a person of great value, Dionysus leapt for Knossos.

Two small arms caught him tight as his knees buckled, but these were loving, supporting, not angry.

Still they weren't much larger or much stronger than those of the children who had tried to defend Aphrodite. He had never hurt a child. The flames turned inward, but before they could sear him, they met a cool, soft barrier and died.

As the rage died, so did the remains of his strength. His weight became too much for both his knees and the arms that supported him. He began to slip toward the floor, but with a clever twist and push, he was turned so that he collapsed into a cushioned chair.

"You came back, my lord, you came back," Ariadne cried, sinking to her knees and kissing his hands.

Joy and peace filled the emptiness that his lost anger had left. Warmth from her grip soothed his cold hands. His body recognized the chair; he looked around and saw the gilded table, the golden bowl that had always rested on it, the cushion Ariadne had risen from. She had changed nothing in the years he had been away, and she had been waiting for him in "his" place.

The dimly lit room was as he remembered it from a time when rage didn't overcome him unbidden, when he could grip his fury and pain and use them as weapons he could control. A shudder ran through him. He was slipping away into real madness, he thought, but the rhythm and harmony of the groupings of the furnishings and the adequate open space around them let him breathe and kept panic at bay.

"Yes," he said. "I came back, and I never should have stayed away so long."

She looked up, eyes full of tears. "Will you forgive me for saying such dreadful things to you? For defying you? I'm sorry for that, very sorry, my lord, but . . . but I haven't really changed. I won't abandon poor Asterion nor allow hurt to come to him if I can save him."

Defiance again, but he felt only amusement and comfort because, even while she clung to his hands and her expression pleaded with him, she stubbornly maintained her position—and she wasn't afraid. He laughed.

"No, you won't, will you? Well, you needn't fear for the bull-head on my part. I'll do him no harm, nor ask you to harm him."

Ariadne sighed with relief and bent to kiss his hands again. When she looked up, she saw that his expression had changed to anxiety, the mouth downturned in self-loathing.

"In the end, you were quite right," he said when he saw her attention on him. "I *am* more of a monster than he—"

"No! No, you aren't. You are as much—no, more—a victim of those around you—"

He raised a shaking hand and stroked her hair. "If I don't force you to see me as I am, you will look aside from the evil I do, won't you, Chosen?"

"I love you," she whispered. "Perhaps I shouldn't look aside, but I love you. I can't help it."

"I believe you," he said, bending forward so that he could rest his head on hers and murmur into her hair, "I don't know of one other being anywhere in the upper- or underworld who loves me."

She put her arms around his neck. "That can't be true, my lord. You are—"

With her arms around him, Ariadne became aware that his skin was cold and clammy, that he was trembling. She raised her head carefully so that she didn't disturb his, shifting position gently until her cheek was against him.

"You're cold and wet and shivering," she whispered. "Are you ill, my lord?" As the words came out, she wondered how a god could be ill and whether he would be angry with her for noticing.

"No, not ill. Just tired. I've done too much leaping too quickly. Even my well of power can be drained."

Could the Mother's well of power be drained? Ariadne didn't think so, but she had no intention of asking questions to which she didn't really want the answers. Instead and before her curiosity could play traitor to her heart, she asked, "But you came in time to save the woman, didn't you?"

"Woman?" he repeated vaguely, then remembered why he was so exhausted, why he needed to be comforted by Ariadne. "The woman who cast that spell on Eros. Yes. Her name is Psyche. I was in time, but Aphrodite already knew she mustn't harm her. Eros—ill as he was—had already pleaded her cause. So a Vision that frightened me half to death was again useless."

"No, my lord, that's not true. You belittle yourself unjustly. That Eros pleaded for Psyche doubtless told Aphrodite how important Psyche was to him, but that is a two-edged sword. Intending to do no more than castigate Psyche for the harm she had done, jealousy might have lent just that sharp prod that could make Aphrodite forget herself. Your warning from the Mother will curb that likelihood."

That was very likely true, but it hadn't occurred to him. The hard bands that bound his neck and shoulders eased. He lifted his head, drawing back a little—but not so far that Ariadne's arms were pulled from his neck—stared down at her, then said, "Chosen, I have done much harm in the time we have been parted."

"Perhaps."

Ariadne smiled at him tenderly, feeling the mist of silver tendrils shift from a wall that held something confined into a comforting blanket that enveloped him completely. He must have felt it too, she thought, because he drew a deep breath and straightened a little more. She let her hands slip gently down his shoulders so she could grip his arms.

"But it will do you no good to sorrow over the past," she said, "nor, really, to try to think of how matters might be amended. You're too tired now. Come, my lord, my love. Come lie down in my bed and rest. In the morning, together we'll consider what has been done, what might be undone, and what can be restored."

As the words came from her mouth, she was appalled. She, a common native telling a god she would help him decide how to treat his worshipers? But he certainly wasn't angry. If his expression changed, it showed a lessening of tension and anxiety. She rose, pulling at him very gently, and he came to his feet also.

Their bodies were very close. Dionysus' arms tensed to pull her hard against him. He was tempted to do more than rest in her bed. But the arm that encircled his waist was as small and delicately rounded as a child's and the face she raised trustingly to his came barely to his shoulder. She was too young; he couldn't couple with a child.

He let her lead him to the bed and pull aside the covers so he could lie down. When she drew up the blankets they were scented by the perfume she wore. As his eyes closed, he recalled how her breasts had lifted her robe and how the curve of her hips filled it . . . but only for a moment before sleep took him.

He was aware several times during the night that the bed he was in was not his own, but that wasn't so unusual as to wake him completely. He merely bent his body into a more comfortable position. But when light beyond his eyelids and the cold metal of the foot of the bed pressing his ankle reminded him that native beds were much shorter than those of the taller Olympians, he did rouse.

The first thing he saw was the black statuette in the niche of the opposite wall. "You found Her!" he exclaimed, as the door opened and Ariadne came through.

He was not at all surprised that she knew he had wakened. That touch between them that was hers, which he now realized had been missing and by the emptiness it left behind had added to his misery, had warned her.

"Yes." Her face was troubled. "She was hidden away in an old chest, wrapped in torn rags. Why, my lord? Who would so treat this marvelous image of the Mother in such a way?"

"Likely the woman who took *my* priestess's place. She had no touch of the Mother in her. Perhaps the image raised some fear or some sense that she was lacking . . ." He smiled at her. "The things you ask me. How should I know?"

She acted as if she had not heard his last question, just smiled again and said, "Your bath is ready, my lord."

He climbed out of bed, stretching his cramped legs before he put his weight on them and becoming aware from the acrid aroma that he had slept in his tunic, sweat-drenched from his efforts and fears the previous night. As he pulled it off and dropped it on the floor, he was reminded of his desire for Ariadne and glanced at her.

Unlike some other peoples, the Cretans were not in the least disturbed by nudity. Ariadne was looking at him with frankness and admiration, still smiling faintly, but she was no larger than a child, and he could detect no desire in her expression. And then it changed to mild concern.

"Oh dear, you are scratched and bitten again. Shall I bring the salves . . ."

He laughed aloud. "The wounds aren't deep. It was Aphrodite's children. She and Eros are both so beautiful that adult servants invariably develop most unsuitable passions. Aphrodite has solved that problem by having small children, under the age when they know the difference between man and woman, serve her. They adore her, of course, as she's the kindest of mistresses and very fond of children—"

"Fond of children!" Ariadne exclaimed, laughing too. "I'm so glad to hear that. I was always terrified of her because little children are demanded by her priestesses and are never seen again."

"Believe me, they're happy and well cared for, much better than they could be in their parents' homes—" He stopped abruptly and smiled. "Why don't you come with me to Olympus? I'll take you to Aphrodite's house and you can see the little . . . ah—" he grinned, " . . . blessed ones."

Her eyes grew so large and round he thought they might fall out of her face. "Me?" she breathed. "Go to Olympus? I—oh, my lord, I'm afraid . . ."

He could see that; he could feel it in the dimming of the warmth of her touch inside him. He put out a hand, and although her face was gray with pallor, she came forward and laid her own in it. Fear usually sparked a terrible violence in him, but hers was so mixed with trust that he felt only tenderness. When nothing worse happened than a gentle squeeze of her fingers, she sighed deeply.

Dionysus drew her close and kissed her forehead. What had set off her fear, he wondered? Did she think he would whisk her away without any other preparation? He chuckled softly, realizing, with a touch of amusement, he might have done so if she hadn't reacted so violently. Then his amusement was gone. Had he done that to Semele? If so, he had made a mistake, yes, but at least she hadn't fled some loathsomeness in him. The pain of his mother's rejection was less sharp—and that, too, was a gift from Ariadne. He smiled again.

"Well, you've nothing to fear before I bathe and have breakfast," he said briskly. "Then we can talk about it. I think you would like Olympus. It's very beautiful, but doubtless I'll be more convincing when my mouth doesn't taste like a midden and I don't smell like a stable. That tunic must be washed, too, and will take time to dry."

"You left two tunics here, my lord, and I have cleaned them and made them ready for you."

"You expected me to come back then?"

She shook her head. "Expected? No. But I prayed. Oh, how I prayed. To the Mother, to you—"

Dionysus smiled and squeezed her hand again, then moved toward the bathing chamber. Were those prayers to the Mother what brought the Vision of Eros and Psyche to him, he wondered? Perhaps what Ariadne said was true, and his warning to Aphrodite was an additional protection to Psyche, but surely the Mother could have more than one purpose.

As he passed he glanced at the dark figure in its niche. A flood of warmth enveloped him and the last remnants of his exhaustion were gone. Did the shadow-mouth smile? Could the Vision, so terrifying to him, have also been designed to reunite him with Ariadne?

Bathed and clothed in a fresh tunic—clearly lovingly cared for and scented with a rich but not cloying perfume—Dionysus sat down in his chair and addressed a surprisingly massive breakfast. Not, he discovered a bit to his surprise, that it was more than he wanted. He was starving. If her "touch" had told Ariadne how hungry he was, he would have to be very careful when he brought her to Olympus. She would know far too much about him.

She nibbled this and that when he invited her to join him, but it was clear that she had no appetite.

"There is nothing to be afraid of in Olympus," he said somewhat mendaciously after a last swallow of a remarkably fine wine.

"Not for you, my lord," Ariadne said, smiling faintly. "You're a god and to live among gods is natural and right to you. For me—" she shuddered "—I don't want to die."

"Die?" he echoed, grabbing for her and gripping her shoulder. "What do you mean, die? What has dying to do with going to Olympus?"

"Doesn't one have to die before going to the blessed lands?"

He let go of her and breathed out explosively. "I wonder who put such weird ideas into your head. Olympus isn't the so-called 'blessed land.' It's the place where we, the Olympians, live. And we're all very much alive." His mouth twisted wryly. "Sometimes too much alive, I think."

"You mean you wish to take me, as I am, in my mortal flesh, to live among gods? Oh, Dionysus, that can't be right. How can it be possible for a common person like me to live among gods?"

"*You* are no common person, Ariadne. You're the Mother's beloved daughter and your strength, like mine, comes from Her. It wasn't I who blessed the vineyards, even when I went with you. The blessing came from Her, and it was through *you* that it flowed into the land."

"I acknowledge that. I praise Her with all my heart every day and I dance for Her on Her special festivals. But that doesn't make me fit to live with gods, my lord."

Dionysus sat silent, looking first into Ariadne's

upturned face and then out of the window well. He saw again the slight movement of shadow on the dark face of the image that could have been an approving smile. He recalled how careful Ariadne was to hide from everyone any sign of weakness about him—any sign that he could stink like any other man when he was overworked and overworn, that his flesh could be marred by wounds. She'd made it plain that she washed his tunics with her own hands and she had carried the salves in secretly and anointed his hurts privately.

"We aren't gods, Ariadne," he said.

CHAPTER 13

Ariadne felt the blood drain from her face and clapped her hands over her ears. Strong hands gripped them gently and pulled them away, and she heard Dionysus laughing.

"Silly child," he said. "Why do you try to close your ears? You've suspected for a long time that I wasn't a god."

Her eyes, which she had squeezed shut, snapped open. Her glance met his. The bright blue eyes were sparkling with amusement.

"How do you know that?" she asked sharply. "I

never told you or asked a question. Only a god can know what is in a person's mind without—"

His renewed laughter interrupted her. "Anyone not an idiot would've known what you suspected. I'm sometimes bemused, Chosen, but I'm not stupid. The very care you take to hide from your priests and priestesses that I can be sick and sad and tired, that when I am wounded, I bleed and don't heal instantly, that when I overwork it my body stinks like that of any peasant in the fields—that care betrays that you know and don't trust them to know."

Ariadne looked down. Dionysus put a finger under her chin and lifted her head. "You're only saying that because you want me to come to Olympus." She heard the shaken pleading note in her voice and tried to steady it. "How can you not be a god? You were here, as you are now, in my ancestress's time. You have lived as a young man for four or five lifetimes of my people. You *must* be a god."

"It's true that I want you to come and live with me in Olympus," he said, "but why don't you want to hear me confirm what you already know, Ariadne?"

Her lips thinned and although she tried to control her expression, she knew her eyes were bright with anger. "Who likes to know they've been dupes and fools, that they've been worshiping false gods? If you aren't gods, why should we bring sacrifices, why should we praise and pray?"

Dionysus raised his brows. "Why do the people of Crete bring your father tithes and taxes? Because he protects them from others, because he sometimes grants them what they petition for, because he is more powerful than they and would punish them if they didn't obey his laws. That's why you pray and sacrifice to the 'gods' of Olympus. I said we weren't gods. I didn't say we weren't different from the native people in this part of the world."

"Then you *are* gods."

Dionysus shivered slightly. "Many Olympians claim it. Perhaps by now they even believe it. But it isn't true. Our power comes from elsewhere—that's why it can be exhausted, as I was exhausted yesterday. I can feel that power come into me and leave me, and I believe the power comes from the Mother. Eros, who is one of the oldest among us, who remembers our coming into this land, prays to the Mother."

"The Mother is a true god?" Ariadne whispered.

"So I believe. Her power is inexhaustible. She needs no sacrifices to eat or drink, no offerings to furnish Her house. You can't see Her or touch Her; She can't be hurt, but She is *there*. And She can be felt here in Knossos, in Olympus, and in the East from where I come, all at the same time. She is never mean or petty, jealous of another's strength, and She knows, as we do not—everything."

"I believe that also," Ariadne said with a sigh. "That is how a god should be."

"Yes. And we Olympians aren't. Our faults stick out like black warts on a white face. Zeus the lecher, Aphrodite the whore, Apollo the unreasonable, Artemis the vicious, Athena who might as well be one of her statues for all she allows herself to feel, Poseidon the totally irresponsible, and last, but not least, Dionysus the mad. Oh, there are others who are nearly gods. Hades is kind and just; Persephone is . . . Persephone, a wellspring of power upon which others can feed—almost Motherlike. But they, too, are tainted with humanity because they love each other with the same foolish, unreasonable passion as any native."

Ariadne put a hand on his. "You are not mad, Dionysus. You are young and haven't yet learned to master your own will." Like Asterion, she thought, but she didn't say that. It wouldn't be safe to mention her half brother and less safe still to compare Dionysus to him. "I understand what you're trying to tell me," she continued, "but it makes me more afraid. I can't come to Olympus. To abase myself before a god—that I can do. I feel no shame to kneel before the Mother, to appeal to Her with lifted arms, but to do so to white faces with black warts . . . No, I couldn't. I would anger them, Dionysus. You say they are petty and mean and yet terribly powerful. They'll destroy me."

His lips drew back slowly, a show of teeth that was utterly vicious. "No. You need fear no Olympian. They know that if they anger me I can pull down their whole private world. I can make them all run mad and turn their power against each other. No. They'll do you no harm."

Ariadne gasped with horror, her hand tightening convulsively on his. "No. No. You mustn't. Not ever. Not for me. Not even for you. You can't destroy a whole people. You couldn't live with the memory."

His face had twisted in remembered pain. He had nearly done just that to Pentheus' people. The breath that he had drawn in eased out in a long sigh. He raised his free hand and stroked her cheek.

"Don't you see why I need you, Chosen?"

"Yes, I see. But if I should come to grief in Olympus, through my own weakness or stupidity, matters would be even worse. Can we find no other way except that I live in Olympus?"

He frowned. "Perhaps, but why shouldn't I have you always beside me?" The words, spoken in a kind of petulant resentment, reminded him of the woman who, out of love, had almost killed Eros. He bit his lip and got to his feet. "I must go. I'd almost forgot that Eros is very ill. I must find out if he's healing and whether Aphrodite has kept her word about not harming Psyche."

Ariadne had gotten to her feet too, still clutching his hand. "Will you return, my lord? I hope you aren't angry with me for being afraid to come with you."

He shrugged. "*I* cause you no awe and terror. I've told you no Olympian would dare harm you, so why should you fear them?"

"The difference is that I love you, my lord. Even if you make me run mad I will love you. I fear what I don't know."

"Perhaps if you learn more about us, you'll be less afraid. I brought a scroll here—unless you discarded my things when I was absent for so long?"

Ariadne laughed. "If I found a hair that you had shed, I would keep it carefully. The games and scrolls are all here in that chest." She nodded toward it.

"Very well. Among them you'll find one called *The History of the Olympians*. Read it. You'll see that the so-called gods are not very different from you and your people. They eat and drink, piss and shit, love and hate, can easily be managed by flattery and amusement, and can be just as silly as any native."

Except, Ariadne thought, that her people didn't throw thunderbolts when they were annoyed, or cause the sea to rise into mountains, or make sane men and women tear their families and friends into gobbets of raw flesh. But she didn't make that protest. She said, "But I won't understand everything. I know I won't. Won't you come back and answer my questions?"

He smiled and touched her cheek again. "I'll come, little wheedler, but I doubt that I'll be able to answer your questions." He shrugged, looking a bit shame-faced. "I've never read *The History of the Olympians* myself."

"But you *are* an Olympian. Don't you know the history?"

He shook his head. "I'm the youngest to breed true

from a mating of Olympian with native. You know I was born in the East and that to hide his infidelity from Hera, my father, Zeus, took my mother to the Underworld, leaving a shower of gold in her place. He left me in Ur with the Nymphai. I am not sure whether that was to protect me from Hera—who was terribly cruel to poor Heracles—or because he didn't want to be bothered with a babe. Anyway, I only came to Olympus when I was a man grown, long after these events." He grinned at her. "If you'd come with me to Olympus, Eros could explain—" The grin disappeared and he freed his hand from hers. "You seduce me, Ariadne. When I'm with you I'm at peace and I forget everything else. I must go now!"

On the word, he was gone. Ariadne sighed—a sigh of relief, this time. He'd return, he'd said so, so she hadn't lost him, and she had escaped, or delayed, being dragged away to Olympus. She shuddered at the thought and then wondered why, considering what he could do, what she'd more than once felt rising in him, she didn't fear Dionysus. But she knew why. He'd said it himself. She was his peace, his assurance that he wasn't mad, his hope that he could bring order to his life.

Ariadne sank down again onto the cushion beside Dionysus' chair. Her heartflower had closed, as it always did when he was beyond the reach of the silver mist, but not into a tight, hard knot. Her Call could reach him anywhere, she knew. Would the silver tendrils some day stretch that far? If so, she wouldn't need to leave Knossos and live in Olympus to bring him peace.

The thought was passing, but the "leave Knossos" echoed in her mind. Reconsidering the words, she suddenly began to wonder whether it was fear of the Olympians or fear of leaving Knossos . . . no, not fear, the *need* not to leave Knossos. Ariadne blinked slowly, then got to her feet and walked into her bedchamber to stand before the shrine of the Mother.

"You want me here," she said, and the shadows shifted slightly on the dark face. "Why?"

To that there was a response Ariadne at first didn't recognize and then perceived as a feeling of incompleteness, like a memory of a task left undone that wouldn't come clear. Although she didn't know what the task was, she was certain it must be accomplished before she could leave Knossos.

"May I tell Dionysus?" she asked—and felt a touch of warmth, and, more disconcerting, a kind of lightness, as if the Mother were amused, and then, almost as if she had been pushed, a need to look at *The History of the Olympians*.

Fortunately the book was in the trade tongue, which Ariadne could read, and she soon found herself lost in the epic, which began with Kronos' attempt to unseat his father, Uranous, from his throne. It was not clear where the land was, except that it was landlocked and surrounded by mountains that made those in Greece look like molehills. Ariadne read the descriptions of the land carefully, but it was clearly not a place to which any Cretan trader had ventured.

Kronos' rebellion was not without cause. Uranous, mistrusting those who might have a right to rule in his stead—for he was not loved by his subjects, who would be glad to replace him—had already buried one male child in the bowels of the earth and planned to be rid of all his children in the same horrible fashion

Despite his people's hatred of their ruler, the rebellion did not succeed. Although some of the younger men and women with power supported Kronos, many others said he was too much like his father, only a devil they didn't yet know well. Those felt they preferred the devil with whom they already knew how to deal. Still others would support neither and the realm erupted into chaos. Kronos couldn't overcome his father, but Uranous was weakened sufficiently to allow Kronos and those who supported him to flee before Uranous could catch them and cause the earth to open up and swallow them.

Had he followed, the writer of the history remarked, Uranous could have had an easy vengeance while Kronos and his people struggled through the mountains. There were enormous chasms that Uranous could have pulled shut over the refuges and cliffs he could have tumbled down atop them. Fortunately, the writer noted, Uranous must have been too busy trying to reestablish his authority over those who remained to pursue or too uncertain that he could defeat Kronos.

Even without Uranous' interference, the passage through the mountains was far more exciting and marvelous a story than any tale Ariadne had heard chanted for the pleasure of the court. It could never have been accomplished by mortals. When Dionysus returned in the evening, Ariadne questioned him eagerly about the Gifts of the Olympians, which the writer took so much for granted that he never described in detail.

"What does he mean when he says the rock was made brittle so that the strokes of the giants shattered them?"

Dionysus wrinkled his brow while he sought through a platter of sliced lamb for a piece done just to his taste. "I was not alive then, but it seems to me that I have heard Eros say it was Kronos' Gift to suck heat from any source. If you draw all warmth from anything, it grows brittle. Then Koios, who was a Titan and tremendously strong, could strike it with his hammer. I suppose the rock then fell to dust and gravel and opened a passage."

"But a whole *mountain*?" Ariadne cried. "And then another and another? I know how many hills pile about each other in the spine of Crete. How long would it have taken them?"

Having found the perfect slice, Dionysus folded it and stuffed it in his mouth. "If you do not eat, you will never grow," he said to her. "And you once promised me you would grow up as fast as you could."

"And you promised me you'd explain what I didn't understand in this book," she said, but she scooped up a stewed grape-leaf stuffed with savory chopped meat and vegetables.

"But you ask what I can't answer," Dionysus protested, laughing. "I wasn't born until Zeus had long been King-Mage in Kronos' stead. And Zeus was born in Olympus. Even he did not cross those mountains with Kronos. Koios would know." He grinned at her wolfishly. "Gather up your courage and come with me to the Underworld. Koios is there. He's Hades' steward. He's horrible to look at because he was badly mutilated in the war between Kronos' people and the Titans, but he's a kind and gentle person and I'm sure he will gladly answer any questions you have."

Ariadne stared at him reproachfully. "Well, I suppose it doesn't matter how long it took. Several native lifetimes, I'm sure."

Dionysus nodded and popped another stewed grape leaf in her mouth before she could go on. "Perhaps telling you to read that book wasn't such a good idea," he said.

Mention of Koios' mutilations had reminded him that what Ariadne would read in the later parts of the *History* was not at all flattering to the Olympians. What might have seemed at first a heroic effort on Kronos' part to protect his siblings and a truly epic struggle through terrible hardships degenerated as the challenges were overcome. Dionysus had intended that Ariadne see the Olympians as they were, rather than wrapped in an aureate cloud of godship, but what they were was sometimes very ugly and he was not at all certain she would not be so disgusted she would want nothing more to do with him or Olympus.

She made no protest but put the scroll away and began to tell him about an odd problem that was troubling the vines of a shrine near Mallia. He agreed to go with her to look at the vines and they finished their meal and leapt to the area. It was an insect—Dionysus showed her the small grubs that were pulling the leave all awry by wrapping themselves in silk. He knew no answer but for the farmers to pick them off.

"I can make the vines strong and the grapes sweet," he said with a shrug. "Bugs are no part of my Gift."

He was distracted enough, however, to forget that he'd intended to tell Ariadne to abandon *The History of the Olympians*, which had been her intention, so she was satisfied. She was far too fascinated by what she had read so far to abandon the tale, but at least Dionysus' discomfort had given her some warning. She was thus somewhat prepared for the descent from the heroic which the succeeding chapters disclosed.

The first sour notes were played when Kronos and his tribe came out of the mountains that ringed their homeland into more inviting country. Although the land was clearly fit for taming, a good mixture of forested and well-watered meadows, Kronos insisted they continue. The lands were empty of inhabitants, and Kronos had no intention of becoming a farmer or herder to keep food on his table.

Koios and the Titans felt differently. When they saw the specially fertile and well-protected valley of Olympus, they decided to go no farther. They were not afraid to swing their axes and hammers in a peaceful purpose, Koios said, and they would be content to found a city in that place. Kronos sneered a little at the notion of the noble Titans cutting trees and plowing the soil, but he made no real effort to force them to continue with him.

He and his remaining supporters continued south until they found primitive folk along the shores of the sea. Having seen that those people could raise no defense against his tribe, Kronos turned north again and attacked Koios and his folk, who had welcomed them back.

Ariadne shook her head over the treachery, but she was not nearly as horrified as Dionysus seemed to fear. Such acts were all too common among the nations with which her father had to deal. So, in a way Dionysus had gained his purpose. The *History* showed Kronos and his tribe to be not so different in their actions and desires from people Ariadne knew and understood. In another way their "humanness" made them more terrifying because their powers were so much greater.

A combination of surprise and lavish use of his and his supporters' Gifts defeated the Titans. Most of the men were killed outright without mercy; a few, like Koios himself, were held hostage for the passivity and good behavior of the womenfolk—tortured if the women resisted the demands of their conquerors. When Koios and the others had been reduced to helpless hulks and looked unlikely to survive more mistreatment, they were cast out of Olympus. The women and children, now habituated to obedience, Kronos kept to prevent the pitiful remnants of the Titans from seeking a suicidal revenge.

Kronos had married Rhea, Koios' sister, before they left their native land to bind the agreement between Mage-Lords and Titans. Leto, Koios' daughter, Kronos kept in his own household and put in the charge of his middle daughter, Hera.

When Olympus was secure Kronos took with him Thaumos, who could inspire terror, Phorkys, who could induce crippling cramps, and Phorkys' ferocious sons the Graiai. With them and a small troop of the unGifted, he winnowed through the helpless native people. He captured first hundreds, whom the Graiai drove over the mountains, and in raid after raid over the years, thousands. These, kept as slaves, tilled the soil in Olympus, which Demeter's Gift made bear triple and quadruple what normal fields produced, and built a city of surpassing beauty.

Ariadne read dispassionately. It was common enough for a conquering people to use the conquered as slaves. Kronos did seem harsher and more wasteful of lives than most, and he was even cruel and treacherous within his own tribe, which Ariadne was sure would lead to trouble, but she found nothing truly shocking except Kronos' behavior toward his children.

He ignored the females: Hestia, meek and seemingly only interested in the duties of householding, shielded the younger ones, and Kronos never heard of Hera's power as seer and manipulator of events. The eldest boy, Hades, was virtually imprisoned and totally isolated. Often, when other powerful mages came to deal with Kronos, Hades was actually kept in a dark cellar, apparently in an attempt to prevent any possibly dangerous dweller in Olympus from knowing that Kronos had an heir. Later, the history commented, it was said that Kronos had swallowed the boys. Ariadne shuddered. In a sense, that was true.

Rhea did what she could for her son but it was little enough. She tried to comfort him and warn him, explaining Kronos' fear of a powerful son by telling Hades of Kronos' revolt against Uranous. She brought

Hades light, made sure he was fed, taught him to read and write, brought him books to occupy his lonely hours. It was the books that exposed to Kronos the fact that Hades was Gifted. Having few other toys, Hades had always played with the rocks and stones of his cells. He found that he could heat them to warm himself and, even more fascinating, push his hands right through them. Thus, when Rhea warned Hades that Kronos intended a visit to the barren cells in which Hades lived, the boy became desperate to hide his books, his one pleasure, and having no other place, he willed the rock walls to open so he could hide the books within.

Kronos sensed the magic. He demanded to know what Hades had done; Hades had only the choice of silence or losing his books. He chose silence and was beaten, not for the first time; fortunately, the feel of Hades' magic was mostly within the rock and Kronos thought his son's Gift was a minor thing. Kronos wasn't yet ready to risk killing the boy. So far fear had kept Rhea silent, but Kronos suspected the death of her son would drive her to cry aloud of his unnatural act, and she was fractious now, big with her fifth child.

After Poseidon was born, matters grew worse, and when Rhea conceived a sixth time, she became desperate. She told Hades he must flee Olympus, that his father would kill him if he didn't. When he said he couldn't leave her to bear the brunt of Kronos' anger alone, she admitted that she too intended to escape. She offered to leave Hades' cell open, but he bade her lock the door so she wouldn't be blamed and he showed her his Gift, his power to walk right through the stone wall.

When Hades was gone, Rhea waited for Kronos to discover he was missing and set out to search for him. Then she took Poseidon and fled herself, driving herself unmercifully so she could be out of the valley of Olympus before Kronos returned. Beyond Olympus she found succor from Themis, one of the few Titan women who had escaped.

She was passed from one to another household, hidden, protected, but Kronos still searched and heavy with child as she now was, carrying with her a two-year-old boy, she was too easy a mark to find. On the island of Aegina, the childless king begged her to leave Poseidon, who already showed some mastery of water and its denizens. The island king promised to raise the boy as his own, to make Poseidon his heir. They would both be safer when they were separated, he pointed out to Rhea. Half mad with fear and only days from her delivery, Rhea left one son to go to Crete to deliver another.

Since Ariadne knew that Zeus was now the King-Mage of Olympus, she could easily guess that he'd grown to maturity and overthrown Kronos. She put down the scroll and stared out of the deep-set window toward the palace of Knossos.

In her society that a son should strike out against his father was almost unbelievable. How could such a son expect his sons to support *him*? Of course, Zeus had a bad example to start with. Even though Uranous was not blameless—hadn't he tried to imprison all his children in deep caves in the earth?—a family must hold its blood bond or be terribly vulnerable. Olympians seemed indifferent as if their own powers could protect them!

Ariadne suddenly sat up straighter. No wonder Dionysus had been able to suggest that she stop Asterion's heart when he was newborn. He meant no insult to her. He simply didn't understand that once her father and mother decided not to be rid of him, her half brother, no matter how useless and horrible, would have the protection of his family. Still the tale was fascinating. She propped up the scroll holder so she could read right through the midday meal and discover whether her assumptions had been right.

She discovered that the women were as bad as the men. Against their oaths and honor as wives, mothers encouraged and aided their children's rebellion. Not content with her escape—of which Ariadne heartily approved—Rhea implanted in her youngest son a hatred of his father, a need to be revenged against him, to bring him down to a powerless nothing. The lesson was indelibly imprinted when Kronos' tireless hounds began to close in and Rhea had to leave Zeus, who was nearly ten. The child was old enough to remember his mother well, old enough to resent violently the fear of Kronos that made her flee, and old enough to recognize in her passing him secretly to other guardians that Kronos was as great a threat to him as he was to her.

Ariadne shook her head and rerolled the scroll. What a tangled skein. Rhea, of course, had a terrible conflict. Her father's terrible mistreatment at Kronos' hands naturally warred against loyalty to a husband who also seemed to intend to murder her children. In addition, Kronos did seem unwilling to leave his sons in peace even when they didn't threaten him. But Ariadne couldn't see any end to the cycle. No one seemed to understand the concept of duty and blood bond.

In the afternoon she paid a brief visit to Asterion. He was, as usual, delighted to see her and she allowed him to show her how some toys worked. To her pleasure there were several new ones, given Asterion by two of the attendants and he called them to join him in his play, which they did. She praised them and Asterion and returned to the shrine thinking hard. Perhaps in the not-too-distant future, Asterion would no longer need her.

The thought was cheering and stimulated her interest in the Olympians. In the back of her mind was the knowledge that she'd either need to give up Dionysus or be deeply involved with them. If a new disaster was brewing . . . She returned with alacrity to *The History of the Olympians*, which, having described Zeus' new guardians and the devices they used to protect him, had now gone back to the doings of Kronos.

Here she found the first mention of Eros in the description of Kronos' hunt for Rhea, Poseidon, and her unborn child. Eros had played a despicable role of seducer and spy. He betrayed many, all of whom suffered and some of whom died at Kronos' hands, but Rhea had feared Kronos' use of such tools. She had confided in no one in Olympus, asked no one for help. No person, no matter how sympathetic to her and her children held any information; Poseidon and Zeus escaped their father's hunt and grew to manhood.

The revolt of the next generation seemed foreordained. The only surprise Ariadne felt was that it was the women who initiated it. Deprived of Rhea and suspicious of even his closest confederates, female as well as male, Kronos turned his eyes on the women of his household whom he believed to be helpless. Hestia was too meek and dull—Kronos liked a spirit to break—but there was Leto, his old enemy's daughter.

Kronos had underestimated the women. Hestia, from years of watching him, could often read his intentions before he had made them clear to himself, and Hera had some forevision and an ability to manipulate events. Between them, they convinced Demeter that she must arrange a need for the three daughters to travel the valley to ensure its fertility. They took Leto with them, and none returned.

Demeter gladly moved into the shrine that had been prepared for her, and Hera and Leto fled to Themis.

That Leto and Hera sought out Zeus rather than Poseidon, who was the older and more bitter, puzzled Ariadne. To Cretans, Poseidon seemed the more dominant god because it was he who shook the earth and raised up mountainous seas to drown them. Lightnings that leapt from sky to mountain top or even to house or tree seemed much less awesome.

Also Zeus was younger and rather frivolous; he intended some day to have his revenge, but he was in no hurry—until Leto seduced him and wakened both the hate and fear that Rhea had implanted in him. And once Leto was pregnant, Zeus knew there was no going back because Hera confessed that she had foreseen that Kronos wanted Leto in his bed. When Kronos heard that she had been taken by his son, the hunt for Zeus would start anew with greater ferocity.

Ariadne enjoyed the adventures of Zeus as he sought out his brothers and bargained for their help in destroying his father. She'd just reached the point in the story where Zeus had enlisted the aid of Hades, who agreed to open the earth so that those who supported Zeus could enter Olympus undetected, when Dionysus reappeared. His body blocked the light from the window well near which Ariadne had set a chair. She looked up and jumped up with a cry of mingled guilt and gladness, spilling the scroll from her lap as she stretched her hands to him.

Smiling, he took her hands in his, and when she babbled excuses for having continued to read the *History*, he kissed them, and let them go. For once he was not exhausted, physically or emotionally. His hair was combed, his tunic spotless, his eyes less overbright than usual. The mist of tendrils lifted toward him slowly, like an intimate caress rather than a protective barrier.

"You have been very diligent, I see," he remarked, bending to pick up the scroll and noting the thickness of rerolled parchment and the small amount still on its original spindle. "I should've known from the beginning that if I wanted you to read this, forbidding you would be more effective than urging you." He grinned at her. "If I forbid you to come to Olympus, will you begin to importune me to take you there?"

Ariadne took the scroll from him with a small sound of protest. Ignoring his final question, she said, "That's unfair. Usually I'm very obedient to you. But you made me interested . . . and you didn't *forbid* me, only said that maybe reading the book wasn't such a good idea. And you shouldn't be picking things up for me."

He touched her cheek. "Well, it's true that I didn't *forbid* you to read more." Then he laughed. "But haven't you learned anything from all that reading? Do you still believe we're such exalted beings that we can't pick up articles that fall to the floor?"

"I haven't got that far, if such matters are ever mentioned. All I've learned so far is that the Olympians don't understand what a family is. Father attacks son and son makes war on father. It's horrible! Even if they hate each other, my people know better than that. The family stands together against outsiders."

He looked at her soberly. "When you forswore your father and mother to become my priestess, that was a far greater sacrifice than I understood." He went and sat down; Ariadne followed him, sinking onto the pillow beside his chair. "I came and offered to take the place of your family, and you accepted that—" he grinned "—such innocence. But what if I hadn't come?"

She looked away. "My parents would still have considered me part of the family. In fact, they did even after you came. They expected me to continue to put the family first. My father was very shocked when I made plain that I would do your bidding rather than his . . . and I was very much alone when I angered you and you abandoned me." She shuddered and then, remembering what reunited them, asked, "How is Eros?"

"Safe but in considerable pain and will be for some time to come. Poor thing. He's in considerable agony of mind too, because he has no idea why Psyche hurt him."

"I wish I could tell you more," Ariadne said, frowning slightly. "All I know is that Psyche wanted to remove the blackness, and she wanted to remove it because she loved what was within it, but your Vision didn't tell me more than that." She cocked her head questioningly. "Is that Eros' Gift, to conceal himself?"

"No, Eros' Gift, in the beginning, was that all who saw him loved him."

"And he used it to spy and pry information, knowing that Kronos would kill or maim those he betrayed?" Ariadne sighed. "And this is the being for whom you are so concerned that you exhausted yourself to illness?"

"He's not like that now," Dionysus said. "What you read happened eons ago. Poor Eros was horribly punished. Aphrodite was forced to bespell him so that the full power of love that he had exerted was changed to revulsion."

"Aphrodite?" Ariadne echoed. "Is that the same Aphrodite who would have killed Psyche for hurting Eros? Why did she do it?"

"Because all the others demanded that she work the spell. She had no power to resist. And he *had* done ill. He deserved punishment."

"Yes, but why make *Aphrodite*, who was fond of him, pun ish him. Why didn't Zeus, or Hades, whom his actions might have destroyed, punish him?"

Dionysus looked very puzzled. "Well, I suppose because Eros's Gift was still functioning and Zeus and Hades couldn't bear to kill him. After all, all Zeus could do was fry him with a lightning bolt and Hades could have sunk him into the earth and closed that over him, but then he would have died, and they didn't really wish to lose him entirely by death or by draining him and casting him out of Olympus."

Now Ariadne looked even more puzzled than Dionysus. "But if Aphrodite could cover his Gift so that it repelled instead of seducing, why couldn't Zeus or Hades do it?"

"It's not their Gift to make or befoul love," Dionysus said, cocking his head to the side. "Oh, either one could have got the spell from Aphrodite and used his power to set it on Eros, but for one thing that wouldn't have been as strong as having Aphrodite do it herself and—" Dionysus chuckled "—for another, I'm sure neither trusted himself to cast the spell at all with Eros' Gift in his control. Aphrodite, whose Gift is also Love, is quite immune to Eros."

"But she seems utterly devoted to him."

"Yes, but as a friend. They've been together for thousands of years. As his Gift didn't touch her, so did her turning of that Gift touch her less than any other. She gave him a home when no one could endure to be near him and he gave her service and devotion. She doesn't couple with him nor he with her nor does either desire that. They are a safe haven for each other."

Ariadne glanced quickly at Dionysus. That might satisfy Eros and Aphrodite, but being a safe haven for Dionysus wasn't what *she* wanted. She spoke hastily to divert him from an idea that she felt was dangerous to her.

"I still don't understand," she said. "If Zeus had power enough to protect himself against Kronos—"

"But that was part of his Gift. Zeus can call lightning. Usually he uses that in the form of a thunderbolt, a strike to amaze, terrify, or destroy, but against Kronos he raised sheets of lightning and in trying to drain Zeus of heat, Kronos absorbed too much and was burnt. While he was weakened, Zeus drained him of power."

"Is that also Zeus' Gift?"

"Draining is not Zeus' Gift. I don't think anyone has so terrible a Gift, except the Mother, perhaps. That was a special spell, and it's rumored Zeus got it from a native—not easily. It was a one-time spell . . ."

"You mean the native is dead."

Dionysus shrugged. "I don't know. Zeus isn't often murderous and one would think he would wish to preserve so valuable a source. And Zeus didn't kill Kronos. I wasn't in Olympus then, but I was told that Kronos killed himself."

Considering what she knew of rulers in Crete and other places, Ariadne wasn't much surprised or horrified. She was more interested in discovering how the powers of the Olympians worked. "Are you telling me that *Zeus'* power is limited to one Gift?"

"Oh no. His great Gift is lightning and he has such enormous strength that he can use any spell bought, borrowed, or stolen. As a second Gift, he can create illusions." He smiled. "He made me look like a Cretan so I could come and watch you dance for the Mother."

"You stood just below the dancers on the step when I came for the turn of the year ritual!"

Dionysus smiled more broadly. "You knew me. I

knew you did, but I was still being stupid so I closed myself away." He touched her shoulder.

Ariadne put her hand over his and held it against her flesh. It moved a little, as if Dionysus was uneasy, and she said quickly, "But I've heard that Zeus appears here and there, as you appear. Can all Olympians leap from place to place as you do?"

"No. That's Hermes' Gift." Dionysus squeezed her shoulder, slipped his hand free, and laughed aloud. "And if it weren't so precious, that mischievous meddler would've been skinned and hung by his toes again and again. Hermes can make a spell of that Gift and give that spell to anyone else, as I gave the spell for stasis to you and the spell for lighting fire."

She sat blinking at him for a moment, then said in a very small voice, "Do you mean to tell me that if the Mother granted me enough power, I could leap from place to place, call lightning, move water . . ."

He laughed again. "Yes and no. No one, no matter what his power—or hers—will call lightning because Zeus doesn't release that spell. Of course, if he was overthrown as Kronos was and forced to disgorge the spell . . . But that's very unlikely. Although he has his faults, Zeus isn't a bad person and the other Olympians are satisfied with his management. He, in general, has treated his children well and they would support him. I would and Athena and Apollo and Artemis, even Hephaestus would."

Ariadne barely restrained a huge sigh of relief. It seemed as if the terrible cycle of son overthrowing father had somehow been broken. She looked forward now with considerable delight to reading the remainder of *The History of the Olympians*, but she didn't say anything and tried to catch up with what Dionysus was telling her.

"Illusions," he said, naming Zeus' second Gift, "he grants freely to whoever desires them—after proper payment, of course. Hermes will sell a spell to go from one particular place to another, but he has never—and I don't even know if it would be possible for him—transferred his whole Gift to another."

When the sense of what Dionysus had said penetrated past her original relief that no war among the gods was imminent, Ariadne shuddered and hid her face in her hands. "I couldn't bear it," she whispered. "Oh, I see what you're trying to teach me. I understand that if I came to Olympus and the Mother granted me power, I could have a little piece of all the Gifts that we common folk worship in the beings we call gods. Don't ask it of me, Dionysus."

"Why, Chosen?" He lifted her face.

Her eyes filled with tears and they hung in the lower lids for a moment before spilling over and running down her cheeks. "I know what I feel, but I don't know how to tell you so that you'll understand. In my own mind, I'm a small thing, my lord, my god—no matter what you say of yourself you are still my god. If I were suddenly made what to me is still godlike, I don't know how I could fit that into what I know I am. I think I would break apart inside myself and that my thoughts would become confused. I would be unable to recognize myself . . ."

Dionysus pulled her up and onto his lap, stroking her hair and holding her close. "It doesn't need to be today, Chosen. You're still very young. But you must promise me to think about this, to try to accustom yourself to the fact that you aren't a small thing. You're not only my Chosen but also Chosen of the Mother—and that's a very great thing." His eyes grew distant, but not fixed or fearful; they still saw her, and he added slowly, "As you grow into your power, you won't fit here in Knossos any more. Think about that."

"I will, but . . . but won't you help me, my lord? Won't you come often and stay long and talk to me of the people and doings of Olympus so that they become familiar to me and not a distant image one wishes for but can't really believe in, like the blessed lands?"

After a little silence, Dionysus lifted her chin so that she had to look at him. His lips were pursed with the effort not to smile. "You aren't a little thing but a great and terrible wheedler. *Perhaps* I'm a god in your mind, but that doesn't stop you from setting your will over mine, does it? You intend to have your way in all things. Ariadne wants Dionysus, but Ariadne won't come to Olympus so Dionysus must come to Knossos. Very well, minx. I'll come, but in the end a god must have his way."

PART THREE:

THE MINOTAUR

CHAPTER 14

In the five years after Dionysus again made the shrine on Gypsades Hill his second home, the wines of Crete had reclaimed all the fame they'd had during the years the ancient Ariadne had been high priestess of Dionysus. Crete was richer than it had ever been and many nations sent ambassadors to the court of Knossos. Most accredited the wealth and influence of King Minos to the Bull God, the Minotaur, who sat regularly on the golden throne in his temple for all to see and worship.

Some knew that the Bull God had nothing to do

with blessing the wine that brought wealth and power to Crete, that Dionysus often dwelt in his shrine in Knossos and walked the earth hand in hand with his priestess. Those brought gifts to the shrine, but even those came mostly in the dark of the night as when the Bull God was newly born and king and queen had demanded worship. Now, however, Minos and Pasiphae had no need to command attendance at the Bull God's temple. Almost everyone came without urging. Even knowledge of who truly blessed the vines and brought prosperity to Crete could not compete with the steadily growing awe of the Minotaur, the Bull God.

Over the years, his cult had spread throughout the island. Tales of the huge being that was visible to any who came to his shrine brought the curious—and then those became worshipers. It was true that no particular event, no supernatural act, could be attributed to the Minotaur's will, but the Bull God was no longer a restless little monster, horrible but not truly formidable. He now filled to overflowing the huge golden throne on which he sat, his pelt gleaming with brushing and jewels; his servitors came barely to his armpits and he was as wide as two men; his voice shook the thin trees growing in the courtyard and the sunlight glancing on his gilded horns dazzled the worshipers. To look at him made the throat close with fear and awe. Few noticed that his slightly wrinkled brow gave a look of permanent puzzlement to his beast's head and that the large eyes, still beautiful, were sad.

That sadness continued to bind Ariadne to Knossos, although she knew Dionysus was growing impatient with her reluctance to leave for Olympus. Her excuses were growing fewer also. She couldn't truly say that to leave her position as high priestess would damage Crete. The young acolyte Sappho's ability to scry had been refined; she could reach all the other shrines of Dionysus on Crete and could also reach Dionysus' house in Olympus. Through Sappho, Ariadne could be aware of what happened on Crete and if she were needed to deal with Asterion.

No, not Asterion, the Minotaur. Ariadne, who was still abed while Dionysus collected what he wanted to take back to Olympus from the offerings that had come in celebration of the turning of the year, shivered as her last meeting with her half brother came to mind. Immediately, her eyes sought out the dark figure of the Mother in Her niche, but She was all a mystery of shadows, unmoving, silent, adamant.

Ariadne shivered again and drew the covers more tightly around her. She'd begun this terrible cycle by binding Dionysus to her, by desiring him as maid desires man instead of merely worshiping him as priestess worships god. Dionysus' response had incited Pasiphae to couple with Poseidon. Out of that coupling, the Minotaur had been conceived—and Ariadne knew herself bound in some way to him, bound in some way to close the cycle she had opened.

She glanced again toward the dark Mother, but the form was implacable, the shadows impenetrable. She bit her lip, knowing but still struggling against the knowledge of how the cycle must be closed. Yet it was impossible for her to betray her half brother. He trusted her. He loved her. Tears filled her eyes again and this time ran out the far corners and into her hair.

Yesterday she'd been forced to give up her tenuous hold on her belief he could remain Asterion to her. Although the chain linking her to him had grown longer and sometimes as much as a week passed without his asking for her, yesterday Phaidra had come twice within a few hours.

The second time Phaidra had said, "Mother's been with the Minotaur." Her voice was quiet and steady, but there was a pallor to her skin that wasn't all the result of winter's lack of sunlight.

Ariadne remembered sighing impatiently. "You would think after all these years she'd know how to avoid making him angry. I really can't come again right now. I've just been there. It's only a few days to the dance for the Mother and I have to be sure the dancers know—"

"This wasn't all mother's fault," Phaidra interrupted. "Some fool must have mentioned your dance in the Minotaur's hearing and he told mother he wished to see you dance. And mother, of course, said he couldn't because he couldn't attend the Mother's ritual and you refused to dance for him in his temple."

"Oh, Mother bless me!"

"You'll need some blessing," Phaidra said sharply. "I don't see how you can explain this to him. He's not a two-year-old who can be distracted by toys any longer. He believes he's a god and can have anything he wants." Doubt and even fear showed in Phaidra's expression.

Phaidra's distress had stilled the further protest Ariadne had been about to make. Although she knew her sister had no affection for their half-brother, that his form was revolting to her, Phaidra hadn't been afraid of him since he was first born and she thought he was a supernatural monster. Thus, Ariadne said, "Very well, since it's my refusal that has set him off, I suppose I must try to quiet him," and went to get a heavy cloak.

She and Phaidra set off for the palace without further discussion. She heard Asterion bellowing as the doors of his apartment opened and as she entered with her hands over her ears, his attendants slipped out, placing lighted torches in holders to either side of the doors. Lighted torches in daylight? That was odd, but she had no time to think of it.

"When you yell like that, I can't hear what you're saying, Asterion," she said into a moment of silence while he was drawing breath.

He turned on her, horns lowered in threat, and shouted, "No more Asterion. Minotaur! Bull God! No baby Asterion. Grown up."

Ariadne was shocked by the implied aggression of the lowered horns. Aside from the time he'd come to her defense, she'd never seen Asterion threaten anyone. The jolt seemed to clear from her mind a lingering image of a horribly malformed babe that clung to her because no one else would touch him. At that moment, she saw the beast-man for what he was: huge, powerful, very dangerous—more dangerous than his size and natural weapons made him because he didn't have the control over himself that went with his mature body.

Moreover he had spoken the truth. He was no longer her Asterion. He was indeed the Minotaur. A prick of resentment stung Ariadne. A baby Asterion might need her protection, but the powerful Minotaur could fend for himself.

"Then Minotaur you will be to me," she said, her voice sharp, "no longer a little brother. You have no need to lower your horns at me as if you must drive me out. If the Minotaur is angry and doesn't wish to see me, I'll leave gladly."

"No go." The threatening horns were lifted, the Minotaur's hand was extended, palm up, in a pleading gesture. "Pu-puh-pease—" he struggled to form a word his mouth didn't find easy to shape "—want brother. Ridne no go."

Ariadne swallowed. One moment so dangerous her breath had caught, now abject. You fool, she thought, despite his looks, he's only eight years old, and he hasn't even an eight-year-old's common sense; he's ruled by a two-year-old's passions.

"Do you want to tell me why you're angry?" she asked more gently.

"I god!" he roared.

"Not *my* god," she said firmly. "You are my brother, and I love you, but you aren't my god."

"Siphe says Bull God 'portant. Ridne dance for Bull God."

"No." She said it calmly, quietly. "You may be a god, Minotaur, I don't contest that, but I don't dance for any god. I don't dance for Poseidon or Zeus. I don't even dance for Dionysus, who *is* my god because I was consecrated as his priestess. I dance only for the Mother."

His big eyes bulged. "You dance for Siphe?"

Ariadne smiled and touched his neck, stroked his shoulder. "No, of course not. There's a goddess, a great and powerful goddess for whom we know no name. From the time that men and women were created from the primordial slime, She's been worshiped simply as the Mother—not *our* mother, *the* Mother."

She didn't think he understood, but he shrugged off the explanation and returned to his own purpose. "Want to see Ridne dance," he said, his voice both pleading and petulant.

"You'll be bored," she responded, smiling again. "My dancing isn't nearly so interesting as that of your priests and priestesses. They jump and twirl and shine and glitter. I only step about and wave my arms a bit."

"You my Ridne. Want dance."

Ariadne stiffened and then suddenly relaxed, a broad smile curving her lips. "Why not?" she asked, having seen a way to satisfy the "little boy" who wanted to see his favorite sister dance and yet outmaneuver Pasiphae, who was still determined to bend Ariadne to her will. "If you'll help me pick up these toys from the floor and push these chairs aside, I'll dance for you right here and now."

"Now?" His mouth moved in what passed for a smile.

"Certainly, if you help me clear the floor."

He did so with a will, moving three and four heavy pieces of furniture at the same time without effort while Ariadne picked up a number of discarded toys. Some had dust on them, she noticed, and made a mental note that she would have to find something different that would interest him.

"Dance," he said, and moved back toward a chair near the wall.

Ariadne raised her arms, and began the dance of welcome. After a few moments, the Minotaur stirred restlessly. Ariadne continued, stepping east, then north, turning south, then west, swaying rhythmically. Actually she was finding the rehearsal useful, plotting the countermoves of the chorus in her mind, until the Minotaur spoke again.

"Dance tell story?" he asked.

"Yes, it does," Ariadne replied, stopping, turning to face him, and explaining what the moves meant.

To her surprise, the Minotaur listened attentively. "Like stories," he said.

Ariadne seized on that at once. It had been growing harder and harder to divert him with toys. His hands were so quick and sure, he made the simple ones work and tired of them in moments; the complex ones he couldn't understand well enough to operate and broke in a rage.

"I could bring you pictures and tell you the stories of what they mean," Ariadne offered. "Would you like that?"

He rose from his chair and came to her, bending almost double to rub his cheek against her shoulder. "Ridne always make Minotaur happy. Love Ridne."

For a moment her throat closed and tears stung her eyes. That gesture was all Asterion. "And I love you, dear," she said, stroking his fur. Nonetheless, she didn't wish to stay. He was tired of her dance and she had no other way to amuse him. Somewhere far back in her mind, cold and hard, was the glitter of the lowered, golden horns. "I'll go and look for pictures for you."

He'd let her go and she'd hurried back to the shrine, recalling some clay tablets on which scenes of wine making from pruning the vines to storing the pithoi were recorded. She could send those at once. Someone could make up a story about winemaking. However, she never had a chance to find the tablets or ask about them. Dionysus was standing before his picture, the priests, priestesses, and novices all in a half circle around him, looking terrified. Ariadne came to salute at once, left fist pressed to her forehead, right arm raised.

Dionysus' frown was replaced by raised eyebrows at the formal greeting and he asked, "Where were you?" in a milder voice than she expected from his expression.

"Pacifying the Minotaur," she said, her lips thinning. "May I dismiss your votaries, my lord?"

He caught her expression, and his brows went up again. Then he said, "Oh, yes," and waved a hand. The circle of attendants backed away and then fled through the priests' door. Ariadne dropped her arms. Dionysus' gaze followed the departing votaries, then came back to Ariadne. "I only asked where you were. Why are they so afraid? You're not afraid."

"You were angry at my absence and they felt your anger, my lord."

"And you don't?"

"I don't know how to answer that, Dionysus. I know when you're angry; I do feel your rage. But it's as if there's a gentle barrier between the heat and sharpness of that anger and myself."

"Is that why they call you when the bull-head rages? Does that mist preserve you from him also?"

"Never, my lord. My heartflower opens only for you. What preserves me from the Minotaur is his memory of my caring for him when he was a babe and a child." She hesitated, seeing again those lowered horns, but she went on, "Poor creature. No one cares for him, and he must feel it, so he still clings to me."

"And because he's pitiful, you put him before me. Even when I came to you in dirty rags, all torn and weary, you wouldn't leave him to care for me."

She laughed. "Because even dirty and torn you're a magnificent being—" the laughter checked and her eyes filled "—and he's . . . little more than a beast. Oh, Dionysus, he's not growing in understanding; he's not what a child of eight should be."

The bright blue eyes slid away from hers. Dionysus wasn't going to discuss the Minotaur, she thought. Somehow she'd have to disentangle herself from the problem without his help. However, she was wrong about his determination not to discuss her problem. It turned out that he was going to add to it.

After a glance around the open shrine, he started off without another word. Ariadne followed him into her chamber where they took their accustomed places. Still Dionysus said nothing, staring out the shaft window at the hillside, and Ariadne at last asked if he had examined the offerings that the household had set out for him and taken everything he wanted. He brought his head around.

"The bull-head is dangerous."

Ariadne drew a sharp breath. Had she been calling for help again and brought Dionysus to her? Had he seen those lowered horns? Icy fingers ran along her spine. Did the Minotaur have enough of a mind for Dionysus to affect? If not, could the Minotaur hurt Dionysus?

But Dionysus didn't seem angry, only troubled, and she didn't remember being really frightened for herself, only shocked at a ferocity she hadn't expected. She took a chance and asked, "What do you mean?"

"He—the bull-head—"

"He calls himself the Minotaur," Ariadne offered.

"He's been noticed in Olympus," Dionysus said as if she had not spoken.

A flush of hope that the Olympians would solve her problem for her was followed by a severe pang of guilt. But as Dionysus went on speaking it became apparent that it wasn't the Minotaur who was being threatened.

"Bacchus is a scryer—it's his only Gift—and he sometimes spies on the greater mages for juicy gossip." His bright glance flicked to her and away. "He always tells me anything that relates to you or Knossos." He hesitated again and then went on, "He hopes to make trouble between us."

"As long as you know that, he can do little to hurt me," Ariadne replied calmly.

"You can't like him living with me. I wouldn't like you to live with someone who spoke ill of me. But I don't know what to do. He's been with me for many more years than your whole life, since soon after the first Ariadne died. If I put him out, he would come near starving."

"No, I don't like it that he speaks ill of me. I don't wish him ill—"

He bent and pressed a kiss on her hair, but lifted himself away before Ariadne could turn her head and try to meet his lips. "You never wish anyone ill," he said.

Why wouldn't he respond to her desire for him?

Ariadne asked herself. But really, she knew. The women of Olympus were so much more beautiful than she. Still, if he didn't want her as a woman, it was cruel of him to urge her constantly to live with him. She curbed the bitter thought.

"My lord," she went on, "if you believe me a true Mouth, I have nothing to fear from Bacchus' venomous tongue. A true Mouth cannot lie. Was what he said about Knossos important?"

"About that, I'm not sure. Bacchus said he heard Athena tell Apollo that the people of her city are angry because the people of yours are putting the so-called Bull God before all the other gods."

"The people of Athena's city—Athens?" Ariadne echoed. "It's none of their affair. We don't tell them what gods to worship. Why should they tell us? And why should we care about what they think—unless they're appealing to Athena to destroy the Minotaur."

"No, I don't think so. It seems they wish to use the worship of false gods to prevent the signing of some treaty King Minos is offering Athens. But you might lose your monster another way."

Ariadne said nothing, and didn't lift her head. She was torn between the memory of her pathetic half brother struggling to say a word he couldn't form to beg her not to abandon him and the memory of his childish, unreasonable demands on her. She couldn't bear for the poor creature to be hurt, but she longed to be free of the burden of his need.

Dionysus must have understood her dilemma because he smiled. "I doubt this is something that need worry you. The Egyptian priests of Apis—the sacred bull—would like to have the bull-head for their own. But if they got him, they would do him no harm."

"They wish to *steal* the Minotaur?" Ariadne laughed as a hope flickered and then sighed as the hope died.

"My parents wouldn't part with him for any price, and taking him by guile or force . . . I would like to see them try. Likely if they asked him to come he wouldn't even understand them, and to abduct him—" she laughed again "—he isn't easy to manage. Still, it would do no good to antagonize Egypt or to have any ambassador from the pharaoh come to harm. I think I must tell this to my father."

Dionysus shrugged. "It's just what Bacchus has learned while scrying, not a Vision. If you wish to speak of it, you may; if you don't, you can hold your tongue. It's nothing to me."

Something in his voice made Ariadne cock her head even though the silvery mist that linked them was untroubled. "But something is making you uneasy, my lord?"

He shook his head. "No . . . Yes . . . I'm dreaming, but I can't remember, so the dreams aren't a real Seeing. They don't echo in my mind so that I'm bemused by them. Still, I *am* uneasy. Something lurks within the dreams." He turned his head toward the doorway to her bedchamber. "Has She spoken to you?"

"No. No hint. No feeling. Yet She's there. She hasn't withdrawn Herself. It's as if She's waiting for something. I know there's something I must do, but I don't know what."

Dionysus continued to look at the wall behind which, in Her niche, the dark statue stood. "It's something to do with the bull-head," he said at last. "Perhaps the scryings aren't as harmless as they seem. Perhaps the Egyptians or the Athenians plan war. Won't you come with me to Olympus and be safe?"

To watch you give to other women what I desire? But even while she was thinking that bitter thought, Ariadne's head lifted and turned so she was also looking at where the goddess's image stood behind the wall.

"In the end, I shall," she said, "but not now."

Both looked away from the wall toward each other. Ariadne shivered slightly, and laid her head on Dionysus' knee again. He played idly with the curled locks of consecration. After a time, she sat upright and began to speak of the celebration of the year's turning and he said that he hoped to come and watch her dance this year. They talked about the offerings that people made, and she asked as she had before whether she should try to reclaim the honor of the richness of the wines for him. And as he had before, he told her to forget the honor. Then, after a brief pause, he said it would return to him soon enough on its own.

Startled by the assurance in the casual statement, which implied the end of the worship of the Bull God, Ariadne asked what he meant. Dionysus looked puzzled by the question, then thoughtful, but finally he shook his head.

"I have no idea," he admitted. "But I'm sure it's so."

Later they ate and played a game Dionysus had brought, giving kisses as forfeits. At first the little pecks on cheeks and nose were delivered with laughter, but then Ariadne suffered a major defeat—perhaps not entirely by chance—and paid her forfeit at Dionysus' lips. He was still at first, almost as if he was startled, and then began to respond, rising from his seat and pulling her tight against him. She felt the readiness of his body, the heat of his lips hungrily responding to hers—and suddenly he pulled free and was gone.

For some time Ariadne simply stood where she was. Had he known she lost the game apurpose? Was he showing his disgust, his displeasure because she deliberately tempted him? But he must have known she had played stupidly before she began to pay her forfeit. Then was it something in her kiss that disgusted him and drove him away? Was that why he had never fulfilled the god-priestess ritual, even though he said it was for modesty not to couple before witnesses? Was he gone for good this time?

Slowly Ariadne gathered up the game pieces and put them away. That done, she couldn't imagine what to do with herself. The events of the day replayed themselves in her mind—the Minotaur's ferocity, finding Dionysus waiting, his telling her that Athens called the Minotaur a false god and that the Egyptian priests of Apis wished to have him in their own temple, the pleasure of the game . . . She refused to think beyond that, refused to face the pain of knowing she was repulsive to her god. She seized instead on the fact that her father should know about Athens and the Egyptians.

Dionysus arrived in the forest-glade atrium of his home still breathing hard. He had almost forgotten that Ariadne was only a child until he was embracing her so hard that her fragility had reminded him. Child? She was very small, but there had been nothing childlike in the kiss she gave him. And she had lost that game so badly . . . He suspected now that hadn't been by chance. She'd lost it so she could kiss him. And if that was her intention, she was no longer a child.

His lips parted to say the spell words that would take him back to the shrine on Gypsades Hill, but he didn't speak them. Why, suddenly, had she maneuvered him into a lustful embrace? Because she'd learned the joys of the body with some local man? So what would she do, now that he had responded to her lust but left her unfulfilled? Find her lover, of course, and satisfy her desire.

Dionysus stepped out into the corridor that linked his wing of the house with that of Silenos, Bacchus, and the servants and bellowed for Bacchus to bring his scrying bowl.

"Find Ariadne," he ordered briefly.

The picture formed as soon as Bacchus had set the bowl on one of the small tables that surrounded the fountain and filled it with wine. Ariadne appeared, gathering up and storing the game pieces, which had been scattered. She stood for some moments then, perfectly still, looked out of the window, and hurriedly picked up a warm cloak. A few moments later it was clear that she was going to the palace.

"Going to fondle that monster," Bacchus said. "Shall I look elsewhere, Dionysus?"

"No."

The sound was quick and hard. Bacchus glanced up at his master's face and then bent with more attention over the scrying bowl. To his surprise, Ariadne didn't walk past her parents' apartments to get to the Minotaur's rooms. She stopped and spoke to the guard outside her father's antechamber. He nodded, bowed, and waved her in. Dionysus' hand closed over the back of the chair Bacchus was using and the wood creaked under the pressure he put on it. Bacchus breathed very softly. That hand could also close on his neck and snap it like a twig—he had seen Dionysus do that. Sweat broke out on his face and trickled down his back.

In the scrying bowl, Ariadne walked past everyone in the chamber with no more than a nod of acknowledgment for those who greeted her. She spoke to the guard at the door of King Minos' private chamber and he nodded and said a few words that didn't come across clearly.

"I want to hear what they say," Dionysus snapped.

Bacchus fixed his attention more sharply on the

scene in the bowl and poured power into the image. A richly dressed man, face set in an angry frown, came out of King Minos' door. The guard bowed slightly to Ariadne and went in. In a moment he stepped out again.

"He'll see you now," he said to Ariadne, and held the door open for her to pass.

The image followed her through the door into a medium sized chamber with a floor of pale green polished tiles in a wave pattern. The doors to the bedchamber beyond were open and a window from a light-well on the other side admitted a golden glow. Between the light sources, King Minos sat at a mottled marble table on a dais. He was alone, no guards, no scribes. The walls of the room were covered with a magnificent fresco of a lush garden in which birds and butterflies played, creating an image of joy.

Dionysus released a sigh and relaxed his grip on the back of the chair, but he still watched the image in the bowl. Bacchus bit his lip. He was tiring and didn't know how long he could keep the voices coming clearly.

"Ariadne," King Minos said gravely.

She bowed her head slightly. "King Minos. Thank you for receiving me so promptly. I have news I think you should hear."

Minos nodded. "I will listen with attention. I promised to honor the Mouth of Dionysus, and I keep my word. I also have long wished to thank you for your efforts to make the Minotaur happy. It's not easy to keep a god on earth satisfied. Whatever his powers, they're still new to him; he's very young, too. He's growing restless and can't understand why he can't go where he likes when he likes."

Dionysus tapped Bacchus' shoulder. "Enough," he said.

So she wasn't unfaithful, not even burning with lust. She hadn't gone to assuage her need with a lover but, as she had said she would, to tell her father about the threat from the Egyptians and Athenians. He turned away from Bacchus and walked across the atrium, whispering the spell word that opened the door to his apartment. When he'd closed it behind him, he stared across the sitting room toward his bedchamber. In his mind's eye he saw the big bed, saw Ariadne's black hair spread over the white pillow. He swallowed.

When he had satisfied his body's need and hers, what would be left? There was nothing between him and his other priestesses except the heat of coupling and the bitter exhaustion when sufficient power had been leached out of him to bring fecundity to the vines. Or if the priestess could not even take and transmit power, the putrid excitement of wild couplings spurred by the impulses of lust he used to spawn fertility in the earth. He shuddered slightly. At least he was no longer driving his worshipers to spill blood to empower fruitfulness. But if he lost the peace and delight Ariadne gave him, would that need grow in him again?

It was to have the joy of her presence more constantly that he urged Ariadne to come and live with him in Olympus. Now he wasn't sure that was wise. If she desired him—and he desired her; he could feel his body stir just with the thought—it would be impossible to lie separately in two bedchambers separated only by a narrow corridor. They would be together on the second night, if not on the first, and if coupling destroyed their easy companionship . . . But would it?

He thought of Hades and Persephone, bound together by love well laced with lust, which only made their bond closer. They were as much one flesh, one blood, one bone as two beings could be. If he could have that . . . He drew a long, quavering breath. But would trying for it be worth losing what he had?

Ariadne was gratified when her father allowed her to precede the others waiting to see him, but she was puzzled when she saw that Minos was completely alone. Then she had to curb an impulse to grin. He was making sure there would be no witnesses if she delivered another unwelcome Foreseeing from Dionysus. Even as the thought came, however, she looked around uneasily, feeling eyes watching. The room was empty, except for themselves—and then her eyes flicked toward the open door of the bedchamber. Had the king sent his scribes and guards there? she wondered, as conventional greetings were exchanged. Why? The question became unimportant in the next moment when she heard the unwelcome news that the Minotaur was growing restless.

"The Minotaur wishes to be free?" Ariadne asked, shocked.

Discontent, even a flicker of rage, showed momentarily in her father's normally bland expression. "Your mother still has hopes of teaching him the responses for the year's turning ritual. She has held out the promise of his attending the ceremonies if he will learn, and that put the idea of going out into his mind."

Ariadne drew a sharp breath. "But the Minotaur *can't* give the responses—a son to a mother. The ritual is of mating and beginning life anew—"

Minos shrugged. "It isn't worth quarreling about. He'll never learn, but now if he can repeat two words he's demanding to be set loose."

Phaidra had not mentioned that to her. Ariadne saw again those lowered horns. The idea of her easily enraged half-brother wandering the palace or, worse, the town and farms struck cold to her soul, but she didn't mention his new aggressiveness. She doubted whether her parents would care if the Minotaur hurt anyone who annoyed him. Besides, she had another reason, one that might be more significant to her father, for keeping the Minotaur confined.

"I hope you'll be able to keep him from roaming free," she said. "What I've come to tell you is that the Egyptians—"

"How do you have news of the Egyptians?"

"From Lord Dionysus, who told me—"

"Dionysus? But he's gone. Your mother said he comes no more since the Bull God's worship was established."

Ariadne smiled. "The queen mistakes my lord's indifference to who is worshiped in Knossos, and even in all of Crete, for absence." She looked her father hard in the eyes. "You know as well as I that the Bull God has no power to bless vine, grape, and wine. That is my lord's Gift."

"As foreseeing is also Dionysus' Gift?"

"To his sorrow and discomfort, yes. But this matter of the Egyptians is not any Vision. This is only something he learned—that the priests of the sacred bull Apis desire to have the Minotaur in their temple."

Minos stirred in his seat. "I hope Lord Dionysus hasn't sent you to tell me to send him there?"

"No, not at all. I don't now speak as the Mouth of Dionysus, only as a bearer of news. I didn't know you'd heard of this already, but when you spoke of the Minotaur demanding freedom I could see a clear danger. If he were loose, he might be tempted away, or if he were unwilling to go with them and refused and force were attempted . . . I don't think they could succeed in abducting him, but I'm sure it would make trouble with the Pharaoh if any priest of Apis or any ambassador should come to harm."

Minos stared back hard. He hadn't challenged her about who brought the wine of Crete to such richness, but her knowledge about the priests of Apis seemed to have shaken him. "Little can be hidden from a god, I see," he said. "An offer has been made. I thought it was a jest. You say it's not. We'll take the problem under consideration."

"There's another reason why the Minotaur should be kept at a distance from his worshipers," she said. "The less contact strangers have with him, the better. His appearance is awesome, but his conduct and conversation aren't. Lord Dionysus also told me that the Athenians, or some Athenians, are protesting against the treaty you wish them to sign because, they say, you worship a false god."

That really disturbed King Minos. He half rose from his chair and snapped, "Who said 'false god'?"

"If you're asking me which Athenians are making a protest, I have no idea. If you're asking me who used the words 'false god,' Dionysus did—and he must know the truth."

Minos sank back into his seat. "That's not a rumor that should be spread from the lips of the priestess of Dionysus. Some might say—"

"King Minos," Ariadne said coldly, "no mention is ever made of the Bull God in my shrine. What I know—" she hesitated, glancing toward the bedchamber door, but the feeling of being watched was gone "—is mine and my god's. You surrendered me as a daughter to the Lord Dionysus, so I have no blood bond to honor, but I'm still a Cretan and desire the good of the people of this land. Not as Mouth, but as priestess and Cretan, I warn you. Keep your Bull God close and guard him carefully."

CHAPTER 15

Because Ariadne couldn't bear to consider the situation Dionysus' rejection had exposed, she thought about her father's revelations while she ate her evening meal and made ready for bed. She wasn't much troubled by the desire of priests of Apis for the Minotaur or the accusation of the Athenians. She was certain Minos would find all sorts of pious reasons for warding off the priests, and Athenians were always contentious, one group arguing against another. If the treaty was important, Minos would find a way to have it signed. On the other hand, Pasiphae's attempts to pervert the ritual of the Mother were frightening.

Pasiphae might be self-centered and selfish, but she had been a good queen and an even better priestess before the Minotaur had been born. She'd had a sure instinct for political possibilities and probabilities and a manner mixing arrogance and charm which, combined with her great beauty, enchanted ambassadors. As priestess, she had always known the meaning of every move of the bull dance and could interpret it faultlessly; moreover, when she sat between the sacral horns, she'd been a true avatar of the Mother.

Ariadne well knew the difference between her role and that of Pasiphae in the worship of the Mother. She was votary, representing all the people, offering prayer and sacrifice and hoping for favor; when her prayers and offering of dance were accepted, she was warmed and protected by the Mother as were all the people. Pasiphae, singing the warnings and promises in the ritual, responding to the male element, *was* the Mother, imbued for that time with Her Spirit to assure the regular turning of the seasons. But that had been before the Minotaur was born.

The queen seemed to have lost both abilities, even common sense, in her determination to prove the Minotaur a god—an utterly hopeless enterprise. Surely eight years of dealing with the poor creature should have taught her that, far from being a god, the Minotaur would never even be a man.

Ariadne didn't fault Pasiphae for continuing to encourage worship of the Bull God. The political advantages of a resident deity were obvious, and the Minotaur certainly looked godlike. To show him in his chair or even pacing the exposed areas of his temple could inspire awe. To try to bring him into the ritual for the Mother—aside from the blasphemy of implying that mother and son would couple to renew the year—would merely expose him for what he was: a pathetic and deformed creature, a weak-minded monster. If Pasiphae hadn't yet seen that, Ariadne feared for the queen's mind. Perhaps it was time for Minos to—

Before the thought was complete there was a chill Ariadne felt despite a burning brazier and warm covers. She lifted herself on an elbow and stared at the blackness in the shadow of the niche in the opposite wall. She could see nothing, but she knew that the shadows had formed an implacable face. For reasons she would never understand, Pasiphae was, indeed, sacred to the Mother, untouchable. Ariadne lay down again and closed her eyes. The Minotaur. Everything came back to the poor Minotaur.

As the Minotaur was the last idea in her mind before she slept, so he was the first when she woke. She remembered that she'd promised to find some pictures and tell him a story about them. She had little inclination to visit him again, but it was better than thinking about Dionysus, making herself accept the fact that he would *never* take her as full priestess, and deciding what she must do. She thought of sending for the chorus of dancers to fill her time, but it was too cold. Rehearsal must wait until the day grew warmer in the afternoon.

The pictures she remembered were in the storeroom, and she found them with little trouble after she had washed, dressed, and eaten. But when she held them in her hands, she realized how unsuitable they were in the light of what her father had told her. Showing such outdoor activities as pruning vines and collecting grapes might only stimulate the Minotaur's desire to be abroad.

She spent a little while longer looking through the stored items, but there was nothing she could use.

Carvings offered to the shrine were usually of nymphs and satyrs cavorting—and that was another idea Ariadne didn't want to put into the Minotaur's head. While she was moving stools and peering into long chests, however, she recalled that there had been pictures on thin sheets of wood on the walls of the children's room in the palace—more practical than frescoes because they could be removed and washed when smeared by sticky little fingers.

The pictures had become so familiar over the years that she hadn't "seen" them for a long time, but perhaps they were still hanging there or perhaps Phaidra would know where they had been stored. The walls, when she reached the children's room, were bare and the room—leaping from youth to age—was inhabited by a handful of old women folding linen. Ariadne went on down the corridor, glancing in through the door of her old room on her way to the Southeastern Hall where the royal family and household usually ate and sometimes lingered to talk. To her surprise, the bedchamber wasn't empty. Phaidra was there, sitting on a stool in front of the wall shelf that held her toilet articles and staring into a small, polished bronze mirror.

"Phaidra?" Ariadne said.

Her sister turned.

"Do you remember what happened to the pictures that used to hang against the wall of the old children's room?"

Phaidra stared at her, eyes widening, and then burst into tears. Ariadne hurried to her and took her into her arms. "What's wrong, my love?" she asked.

For a little while her sister's storm of weeping was so violent that she couldn't answer, but finally she sobbed, "You only think of me as a housekeeper."

Ariadne gave her a hard squeeze and then let her go. "I'm afraid I only think of you as my darling little sister," she said. "Nothing so august as a housekeeper. Oh, Phaidra, don't you remember how terrified we both were of that woman who was in charge of the laundry? She towered over us and boomed 'Dirty clothes again. Do you think I have nothing better to do than clean up little girls' messes?' "

"Well, it seems that I *have* nothing better to do," Phaidra said angrily. "And will have nothing better to do for the rest of my life than clean up the Minotaur's messes and attend to the household."

"Probably not," Ariadne said sympathetically. "It's what most women do. I may be priestess of a shrine, but attend to the household is what I mostly do."

"You have your shrine," Phaidra spat. "It's your place and you rule it. I have nothing that's mine. In this house I'm still the youngest child, the one who runs errands. But I'm *not* a child. I've passed nineteen summers. I should have been married three years ago. I should have a kingdom of my own, my own house, my own children. Instead I have been overseeing the Minotaur's clothing and meals, passing messages from mother to the servants and cooks—" she looked up at Ariadne, her eyes full of tears "—remembering where the paintings from the children's room are, where Androgeos left his sandals and Glaukos left his arrows, where the queen's rouge pot went and the king's favorite inkstick."

"Oh, dear." Ariadne sat down on the edge of the bed that had once been hers. "I know it doesn't sound like much when you say it in those terms, but you're really the most important person in the household, Phaidra. Everything would fall into disorder without you."

"Perhaps that's so, but it does *me* no good. Do I have a seat of honor at any feast? Am I presented to ambassadors and other visitors from foreign places?

Are cups of wine lifted to my name? Who even knows my name?"

"There are very few women whose names are known by any other than their own households—and mostly those whose are, are of ill repute," Ariadne said, smiling. "I doubt more than my priests and priestesses and this family know *my* name. Why is it important to you that your name be known?"

"Why? If Phaidra of Knossos, daughter of King Minos, were spoken of abroad, surely some prince would come as a suitor. Who would sue to marry an unknown least daughter?"

"Do you desire to marry and go so far? You remember when Euryale and her husband were so sadly at odds three or four years ago. If father hadn't been close by and of superior strength, she might have been set aside for some young slut."

"Oh, Euryale! Such a cold stick." Phaidra glanced at Ariadne under her eyelashes. "I'd know better how to hold a man and how to make him my willing servant. I don't fear going away. I fear rotting here, as if I were buried in a grave."

Ariadne sighed. "I suppose you have told your mother?"

Phaidra didn't bother to answer that, and Ariadne sighed again.

"Then go to your father." She hesitated, then went on. "I happen to know that King Minos is in the midst of negotiating a treaty with the Athenians. It's not impossible that the formation of a marriage bond to tie in the treaty would be a welcome idea to him."

"The Athenians?" Phaidra repeated. Her eyes brightened and she lifted the bronze mirror for a quick glance. Staring into it, she added thoughtfully, "There's a prince of whom the traders who come have spoken. Theseus is his name. Hero some have called him. I wonder . . ."

"I wouldn't fix my hopes too firmly on the Athenians," Ariadne warned. "I've also heard that not all are content with this treaty and some say it's wrong to make bonds to worshipers of false gods."

"What false gods?"

"The Minotaur."

Phaidra began to laugh. "Did you think I'd be offended by anyone saying so? Or that I would make enemies by defending the beast?"

"Phaidra, don't be foolish. You needn't defend the divinity of the Minotaur, but you mustn't support any contention that he's a false god. Don't you see that what diminishes Knossos will also diminish you? Even if your husband comes to love you, the daughter of a powerful king will be of more account than the daughter of a scorned or ruined one."

"You say that whose own god has been diminished by the accursed Minotaur?"

Ariadne shook her head. "No one can diminish my god. It's his blessing that brings half the wealth of this realm. That's real. His power abides, as does the strength of the Mother. But now, while Knossos makes a firm place in trade and builds its power, the Bull God is a visible symbol of divine favor. Don't tell tales of him. Let those who will, believe him a god."

Phaidra made a moue of distaste, but nodded agreement. "Oh, I know you're right. It just makes my gorge rise to see wise and powerful men bow and pray to him. For the Mother's sake, do you know that he can't always remember to raise his kilt when he pisses? I can't tell you . . . Oh, never mind. It won't matter if I can only convince father to use me for the treaty with Athens."

"If you go, I'll miss you," Ariadne said.

"And I you."

The sisters embraced, but Ariadne felt sad. Phaidra didn't sound grief-stricken at the notion of leaving her sister behind and her embrace was perfunctory. A moment later, she felt ashamed because Phaidra said "Aha!" and told her where the paintings from the children's room were stored. Clearly her sister's mind had been attending to her needs even though she seemed absent.

Fortunately there were three scenes that Ariadne felt she could use. Two she had carried up to Phaidra's chamber and stored there where she would be able to get them easily. She took the third with her. That showed a procession toward an altar: first came a youth carrying a rhyton, and in succession behind him, a fisherman with an octopus in one hand and a fish on a line in the other, several women with unidentifiable bundles in their arms, a man carrying a dead deer over his shoulder, and last another man leading a goat to be sacrificed. The painting was done in lively colors and there were pillars behind the procession, hinting that it moved along an indoor corridor. Ariadne felt she would be able to spin out a tale for each of those in the procession, such as where the youth got the rhyton of wine and why he was bringing it as an offering and so forth for each figure.

She didn't go so far along the corridor as the Southeastern Hall but went down the stairway that connected the children's wing with the queen's apartment below. No guards stood at Pasiphae's closed door, so Ariadne assumed the queen was elsewhere in the palace. Beyond were the rooms the Minotaur occupied. The guards saw her; both smiled, and one began to open the door. Through that, she heard an attendant say the second line from the Mother's ritual slowly and carefully, making each syllable clear. Immediately the words were repeated in the deep, rumbling bass of the Minotaur . . . but mangled, consonants lost, vowels blurred. The words were recognizable—barely. Though his voice was deep and strong, it carried none of the assurance, of the restrained power that could woo and fulfill the Mother.

Ariadne drew a sharp breath, caught her lip between her teeth, and shook her head at the guard, indicating that he shouldn't yet open the door further.

"Said it!" the Minotaur exclaimed as soon as the last word of the ritual sentence was complete. "Now go out."

"My lord, you've only begun," the attendant's voice was somewhat tremulous. "Those are only the first and second lines, only the beginning of the ritual. The queen insists that you learn it all."

"Not begun. Finished. You finished. I finished. Want bull court. See bull dancing."

"My lord, my lord, please! You can't! There's no bull dancing now. That's a different ceremony at a different time. Please!" And then, in a shrill shriek of terror. "Use the torch! Stop him!"

There was a bellow of rage, another shriek, either of pain or fear. Ariadne slipped between the guards and opened the door just enough for her to enter. She pushed it closed behind her. One attendant had backed against the wall, clutching a scroll of parchment to his chest. Another was waving a burning torch in the Minotaur's face. Her half brother's lips were drawn back exposing his tearing fangs in a terrifying way and he let out another bellow. The attendant thrust the flaming torch at his muzzle, close enough for him to feel the heat. He bellowed again but backed up.

"Minotaur!" Ariadne called. "I've brought the picture I promised. There's a whole procession on it, and I'll tell you all about the offerings and the people who bring them."

The attendant jumped aside so the Minotaur could see Ariadne but kept himself and his flaming torch between the other attendant and the angry beast-man.

"Ridne."

Most of the rage was instantly gone from the deep voice. The Minotaur turned his head to look at her. His mouth relaxed, the bovine lips covering the predator's teeth. Ariadne held up the picture and walked forward slowly. The Minotaur came toward her, the attendants shrinking against the wall as he passed, but all his attention was on the brightly colored panel she held for him to see.

"Come and sit down with me and I'll tell you the story I promised," she said, and the Minotaur followed her docilely to the chairs he and the attendant had probably been using.

"Outside?" the Minotaur asked, cocking his head to bring one eye into focus on the painting.

"No, no," Ariadne said, pointing to the pillars. "You see the columns. That's a corridor or a very large chamber where a religious rite is held. You've seen the chamber of the pillars below these rooms. You've passed through it on your way to your temple."

He nodded. "Other room. Not out. Only long dark to temple."

Long dark? It sounded as if a tunnel or covered passage had been built to convey the Minotaur from his chambers to the temple. Ariadne was relieved. She had wondered how he could be kept from escaping now that his mind seemed fixed on being free if they walked him, as they had in the past, down the long stairway to the temple. Someone, it seemed, had enough sense to take precautions.

He'd been looking at the painting, turning his head from side to side to bring each eye to bear on it. "Now bring offerings to big room?" he asked. His brow wrinkled in doubt. "Like temple. Look out. See things. People." The frown grew deeper. "Like temple!"

"Yes, of course you do. And offerings to you will always be brought to your temple. Minotaur, this is a story. A story isn't true. It doesn't really happen. It's only told to pass the time. Sometimes the story did happen, but very, very long ago. See this youth? See his clothing? Such clothing hasn't been worn for many years. If this procession took place, it was when the palace was new, hundreds of years ago."

"Why story long ago?"

"When we tell stories from long ago, we remind ourselves of both good things and bad things that happened. Then we can do the good things and avoid the bad ones. This is the story of a good thing, of a procession to make offerings to a god."

"Like me?"

Ariadne didn't answer that directly, only stroked the silky fur on his shoulder. He seemed to accept that and in return bent his head to rub his cheek against her hand. So she told him about the rhyton of wine, about what was in the bundles the women carried, about the fisherman and the hunter. And when she was done, she suggested that he should keep the painting.

Suddenly the large, beautiful eyes were very sad. "Won't 'member," he said, looking away from her. "Used to 'member."

Ariadne's throat closed and she swallowed hard to clear the lump in it. "It doesn't matter, love," she said. "I'll come and tell you the stories again. The picture is bright and pretty, so keep it."

He nodded happily and went off carrying the panel into his bedchamber. Ariadne went over to the attendants, still backed against the wall.

"I wouldn't trouble him with the ritual any more," she said. Tears stood in her eyes.

"The queen . . ." the man with the torch faltered.

"Will he remember any of it when she comes?" she asked. "How can she know whether you tried to teach him or not?"

The men looked at each other, but Ariadne didn't wait to hear any answer. She had another ugly decision to make now, which she considered while walking back to Dionysus' shrine and waiting for the dancers' chorus to come for rehearsal.

She knew she wouldn't dance the welcome for the Mother if the Minotaur sang the male role instead of Minos. On his own, of course, it was impossible that the Minotaur could learn the ritual, but in her madness Pasiphae might try to find a device to let it seem he was taking that role. What Ariadne had to decide was whether she should confront the queen at once and tell her she wouldn't dance before the Minotaur—to save him from being tormented to learn the responses—or just wait and see what would happen. This year, she believed, it was too late for the queen to arrange anything and she suspected the attendants would take her suggestion for the few days remaining before the ceremony. For next year . . . She put that thought away, concentrating on changing her gown for her practice dancing skirt.

The grief that Ariadne had been warding off with her concentration on problems surrounding the Minotaur didn't fall upon her on the Mother's holy day as she had feared. The eve of the turning of the year was mild and clear, a good omen, and she knew as soon as she approached the dancing floor that Dionysus had come. Her heartflower opened, the silver strands streamed out to touch in joy and welcome the tall, broad-shouldered Cretan who waited just two steps down from the entrance. Nor was her welcome rebuffed. He saluted her as she came up the steps to take her place at the head of the dancers, and there was a wave of fists going to foreheads and right arms rising through the whole crowd. There were also nervous looks toward the dais, but Minos and Pasiphae hadn't yet come.

No cloud of ill feeling between king and queen marred the ritual either. Ariadne was aware that the full concord that had once united them was missing—each had a walled-in place inside that excluded the other—but they weren't angry or hateful. They sang with good will, and each was looking forward to some satisfaction—even if those might be mutually exclusive. For Ariadne there was no doubt that the Mother accepted her worship; she grew lighter and lighter throughout the dance, feeling the lifting of her hair, the tiny tweaks on the locks of consecration that denoted affection, and the warmth of the golden ribbons of blessing about her. And when she walked back to the shrine, Dionysus was there.

That wasn't an unmixed joy. He greeted her, spoke to her, as if that lingering kiss had never been offered, taken, and then rejected. Ariadne could almost have believed that some god had wiped the incident from his mind . . . if he hadn't been a god himself (or something like) and if he hadn't so assiduously avoided touching her. He did take her hand when they blessed the vineyards, but at the full stretch of his arm, as if to touch her body was unbearable to him.

He didn't, however, simply disappear this night as he usually did. He returned with her to her chamber, reappearing suddenly in the middle of the room with a worried frown on his face. But he didn't speak until he had walked across to his chair and seated himself.

"Will you eat, my lord?" Ariadne asked.

He nodded, but not smiling and eagerly as he did when he was hungry, more as if he wanted the food to put off some other action. Ariadne swallowed fear and put it away as she ordered that the priestesses bring a meal—the best they had—for Dionysus. She no longer needed to bother with ringing her bell; now she simply projected her will into Hagne's mind.

"The food will come soon, my lord," she said

Dionysus didn't seem to hear her. He looked at nothing in the middle of the room and said, "Chosen, you know, don't you, that the blessing of the vineyards in Crete is different from the blessing elsewhere?"

To Ariadne's surprise, his white skin was flushed with pink, so darkly flushed that the color was visible even in the soft light of the lamps. And what he said was so far from anything Ariadne had been fearing that she just blinked like a witless owl. He cleared his throat uneasily.

"Mostly," he went on, "the blessing is accomplished by . . . ah . . . coupling, by which act power is drawn from me into the priestess and from her spread into the land. I know you are very young—"

"I'm not so young as not to know about coupling," Ariadne said, fighting a losing battle with her impulse to giggle and coughing instead.

"Yes, well—"

A scratch at the door made him close his mouth. Ariadne glanced sidelong at him as she went to take the tray from Hagne and saw that his face was even redder. When she brought it back and set it on the table, the color had mostly faded, but he didn't even look at the food, only went on as if there had been no interruption.

"—that's not the point. What I wished to say to you was that there's nothing between those priestesses and me except the act to make the vineyards fertile. They aren't Mouths. They bring me no peace. I like most of them well enough before . . . before we . . . But afterward I'm sick of them."

"Because they drain you, my lord," Ariadne said. "But I know the Mother doesn't frown on the mating of man or beast. My whole dance for Her is of the renewal of life through the union of male and female. Nor is it needful that I be virgin to dance the welcome. My mother, already married to my father and having born children, danced for Her when my grandmother was queen. I'm sure She wouldn't withhold Her blessing from me if—"

"It's nothing to do with the Mother's blessing," Dionysos interrupted sharply, red again. "It's to do with . . . with . . . Men and women united in that way are . . . If they liked each other once, they do so no more."

"My lord, that can't be true," Ariadne cried, relief and horror warring inside her. Perhaps, she thought, he didn't find her personally repulsive, just anyone associated with the sexual act. But before she could pursue the thought he jumped to his feet and began to pace the room.

"It *is* true," he said. "All over Olympus I see it. When Hephaestus and Aphrodite were married, they hated each other. Zeus and Hera do nothing but fight. I could go on forever telling you of couples who can't bear the sight of each other. Now that they are parted, Aphrodite and Hephaestus are good friends. They talk and laugh. Eros and Aphrodite, too, have never coupled and love each other deeply, whereas Psyche nearly killed Eros—"

"That was a mistake," Ariadne protested. "And haven't you told me about Hades and Persephone, whose love is so much stronger because it is well mixed with lust. My lord, it's the people, not the act. Are Zeus and Hera really changed from what they were before they joined? My two sisters both welcomed their marriages, but Prokris couldn't be happier while Euryale is sometimes content and sometimes miserable. But I swear to you that my sisters were so before their marriages. Union with their husbands didn't change them."

"I didn't say it changed a person's nature. It's the way that nature interacts with his or her partner's. When . . . when two people . . . Everything is changed." He stopped and turned on her. "What I have with you is precious to me, Chosen."

And he was gone. Ariadne stood gaping at the spot where he had been as she had not done since the first time he had leapt elsewhere. "What I have with you is precious to me" was sweet to hear, but in the context of the preceding conversation there was the knell of doom about it. Dionysus was willing to be her friend, to come to Knossos and bless the vineyards, to laugh and talk and tell tales of Olympus and other lands. He even wanted her to come to Olympus and live with him . . . as Eros and Aphrodite lived. She bit her lips. Could she endure that? To see him take other women to his bed and never herself kiss his sweet lips, caress his beautiful milk-white body, feel his strong shaft fill her?

Why should she endure it? What he feared was nonsense. He was confusing the sickness of draining and the revulsion he felt for the women who drained him with the act of coupling itself. Surely he was. Ariadne gnawed on her lower lip again. What if he weren't simply remembering how he felt when he was sucked dry? What if his past experiences had so scarred him that he did feel revulsion for the women with whom he coupled even when they didn't drain him? Was she willing to lose his companionship entirely in an attempt to satisfy her craving for his body?

Ariadne's decision about whether to try again for a sexual relationship hung suspended over her head, like the fabled sword of Damocles. It was made no easier by the fact that she wasn't at all sure it was her decision to make because Dionysus, who returned the next evening to look over the offerings made after the blessing of the vineyards, was now acting as if the conversation between them had never taken place.

The Mother's dark image was no help at all. It was blank and unresponding when she wept before it of her desire for Dionysus—except once, when she was sure she heard a woman's indulgent laughter. But when she ceased to speak of her god, she was afflicted by a constant feeling of incompleteness, of a task unfinished. By now Ariadne was sure that feeling pertained to the Minotaur, but it wasn't strong enough to drive her into any action.

For a time after the blessing of the vines, she was able to ignore the mild prodding because she was too busy—there had been many offerings—to think about the Minotaur. And she didn't wish to think about him, poor beast. However, when she had settled with Dionysus what he wanted of the offerings, placed the fruit and meat in stasis, written the accounts, and done all the other special tasks the coming of the new year brought, Ariadne found that she couldn't keep her half brother out of her mind.

Again and again images flashed before her—images of the Minotaur's exposed fangs, the burning torch guttering in the trembling hand of one terrified attendant, images she hadn't seen, of the Minotaur trying to force the doors that guards had barred and braced. She told herself such thoughts were ridiculous; that Phaidra would have come to summon her if there were any trouble, but she was frightened. The images were like those she caught from Dionysus when he described a Vision.

Ariadne fought her apprehensions, tried to ignore a growing unease that brought her nightmares every night until, after the spring quickening of the vines, Dionysus told her to hold all offerings. He would be leaving Olympus before the ten-day was out, he said, and be away for several ten-days. Hekate, who had done him many favors, had asked him to go with her back to her homeland to settle a long-neglected problem.

Over the years since their reconciliation, Dionysus had been away other times. Ariadne had always sensed his regret in parting from her; this time, although he said he would miss her, there was as much relief as dissatisfaction in his voice. She kept her face calm with an effort, refusing to allow the tears that stung the bridge of her nose and the back of her eyes to fill her lids. The time for her decision was coming nearer.

That night she couldn't sleep. She lay in her bed as tense as a drawn wire, her eyes wandering again and again to the dark image in Her niche. Ariadne saw nothing there, but she knew that she must go to visit the Minotaur the next day.

Even so, she delayed as long as she could, lingering over her breakfast and calling Sappho to her to scry the other shrines to judge the worth of the offerings. When she had seen what was available and decided to allow the subsidiary shrines to keep what they had, she dressed in a formal gown and told the oldest priest, Kadmos, to summon the merchants who customarily bought the offerings Dionysus did not choose.

She felt a small rise of hope while doing that business during the early part of the day because the draw—a sense almost of someone tugging on her locks of consecration—of the palace seemed less. Then, just before she was about to call for her midday meal, her hair was seized and pulled with such force that she cried out in pain. And before the pang had passed, she saw the Minotaur, fangs bared, charging at Pasiphae.

"No!" Ariadne shrieked and ran.

Again the Mother lent wings to her feet. She flew down the side of Gypsades Hill, across the empty front of the Bull God's temple, and up the stairs to the palace. Barely checking her speed for the guards to let her pass, gasping for breath, knuckles digging into her side where pain stabbed through her, she passed her father's chambers. The doors were closed. It was the time of day when he received petitions in the audience chamber below. But there was noise ahead, past Pasiphae's apartment, a babble of voices and Phaidra's high-pitched shrieks refusing to do something.

A crowd of servants and guards milled in the corridor beyond the Minotaur's shut door. Ariadne stopped short, seeing in fact what her Vision had shown—the new massive bars that had been set in huge bronze slots fastened to the wall on each side of the doorway. The shock of knowing her Vision was true prolonged her hesitation. Those moments gave the servants a chance to see her and some drew back. Through the aisle they opened, she saw Pasiphae dragging Phaidra, who was screaming and struggling to be free, toward the door. The queen's face was gray-green with fear and horror, but she was trying to speak calmly.

"He's quiet now," she said, shaking Phaidra. "Just divert him long enough for Isadore to slip out. He won't harm you. He knows you bring him food."

"No!" Phaidra shrieked. "No. He's killed Isadore and you know it. He's mad with blood lust. He'll kill me, too. He must be destroyed before he breaks free and—"

"I'll go," Ariadne said, stepping forward into the aisle left by the servants.

"Ariadne!" Phaidra cried. "No, don't! He must be starved until he is weak and then killed. I tell you, he killed Isadore. He's changing. He no longer fears the fire."

"A fierce and vengeful god," Pasiphae intoned. Her eyes stared, but apparently without seeing either of her daughters. "He must be pacified."

"He's only eight years old," Ariadne said. "You provoked him and he struck out, like a child. I hope Isadore isn't dead, but even if he is, I don't believe the Minotaur will hurt me. Still—" she looked away from Pasiphae and her sister to speak directly to the guards. "Don't bar the door when I go in and open it quickly if I call to come out. If two of you hold each door, he won't be able to open it."

There was a silence while more guards were summoned. Two came forward to help with the doors and two others stood ready with pikes advanced to repel the Minotaur if he tried to rush out. One of those at the door, whose face looked familiar to Ariadne, said, "Lady, you didn't hear the scream Isadore gave. It sounded—"

"Silence!" Pasiphae commanded. "Open the door and let the priestess of Dionysus in. She has her god to protect her." A smile that held no mirth or good will curved the queen's lips, but her eyes were still unfocussed. "We'll see which god is the stronger then, won't we?"

Ariadne stared at the queen, wondering how she could hold to so silly a fixed purpose as proving the Minotaur superior to Dionysus in the face of this disaster. Still, what she said had calmed the terror that had dried Ariadne's mouth and chilled her through and through at the thought of entering the Minotaur's chamber. Dionysus wouldn't—likely couldn't—fight the Minotaur, but he could catch her in his arms and "leap" them both to safety.

The guards had been listening, ears pressed against

the door, and the one who had spoken before said softly, "He's not near the door, lady."

Ariadne nodded. "Then open softly, just enough for me to slip in."

She was intent at first on sliding through as small an opening as possible and making no sound for the Minotaur's keen ears to pick up. Then she looked around for him and froze in place, just inside the door, rigid with horror. The area near her brother and the limp body of the attendant seemed to have been painted red, and the Minotaur seemed to be nuzzling at the corpse.

"Minotaur!" she shrieked.

He lifted his head and she put a hand on the doorframe to support her. For a moment her gorge rose and bile filled her throat and mouth so that she couldn't speak. The Minotaur's face was coated with blood, and a long sliver of skin and flesh hung from his mouth. She forced herself to swallow the bitterness.

"Stop!" Ariadne cried. "Men don't kill and eat other men. Stop! Stop at once!"

He heaved upright, glaring. "God!" he bellowed. "Bull God!"

He put a foot on the body, seized an arm, and without apparent effort, wrenched it off. Ariadne screamed. The Minotaur laughed.

"Sacrifice!" he said. "Gods eat men."

Shouting at him was useless. Ariadne licked her lips and swallowed. "No," she said, striving now to keep her voice steady and speak calmly. "No. Gods are kind. They help men."

She forced herself forward, shaking with horror but reminding herself that huge as he was—and he had apparently grown almost a foot taller in the ten-days she hadn't seen him—he was only eight years old. Children did strike each other and bite each other when enraged. Doubtless Pasiphae had enraged him and the attendant had intervened to save the queen. She tried to grasp his arm to pull him away from the grisly remains, but he pushed her with such strength that she flew backward and fell. The Minotaur dropped the arm he had pulled off and advanced on her. Ariadne gasped and tried to push herself backward. She tried to call out to the guards to open the door, but her throat was shut tight with terror.

"No hurt," he said in his usual bass rumble. "Sorry. Love Ridne. No hurt." He stopped, looked over his shoulder at the mangled corpse, then turned back, blinking his beautiful eyes. "Don't like? Go away. Minotaur like man flesh."

He bent and lifted her, not ungently, but his hands stained her flesh and her gown with blood. She choked and gagged. He shook his head, almost sadly, and carried her to the doors, one of which he pushed open easily against the weight of the two guards. Ariadne heard them crying out warnings, but the Minotaur didn't seem to notice. Nor did he try to get out. He merely thrust her through the opening he had made, and let the door slam shut behind her.

CHAPTER 16

In the corridor Ariadne was dimly aware of gasps and muted cries. She tried to speak to assure Phaidra who had screamed, "You are bleeding!" that she wasn't hurt, but she had no voice and all her strength was concentrated on a struggle to keep from fainting. Then much louder screams and shouts threatened that the Minotaur had decided to follow her. She tried to turn to beg him to go back, but a pair of powerful hands seized her. That was too much. The final horror sent her whirling away into a blackness of unknowing.

She wasn't spared memory, however. Before her eyes opened she recalled the blood, the torn flesh. She stiffened and pushed at the arms that held her, crying, "Let me go."

"You'll fall."

Her eyes snapped open to meet the blue of Dionysus' gaze. And they were in her own chamber at the shrine. "My lord," she breathed. "I thought you were the Minotaur." And she bowed her head onto his breast, weeping, gasping and rocking in her grief.

For a time Dionysus held her without speaking, stroking her hair and warming her with his body as she had warmed him, countless times, when he had arrived icy cold with Seeing. At last her sobs diminished and he led her, not to their usual place but to a couch where he could sit beside her.

"I'm so sorry, my love," he murmured. "Poseidon never cares whom he hurts. If he was angry at your father, he should have stricken him. . . . "

Ariadne threw up her head. "What? And perhaps have a king of Knossos who would be less devoted, less generous in sacrifice? Only once did my father defy Poseidon, and even then he gave three bulls for the one he kept." Her voice broke and she began to sob again. Dionysus pulled her against him and held her tight.

"What can I do, love?" he asked. "I haven't the power to change the Minotaur into a man. Even Hekate knew no way to undo Poseidon's will and she knows magic far beyond Olympian Gifts. I did ask. I even asked Zeus." He hesitated, lifted her face and kissed her tear-drenched eyes. "It would have been better if you had listened to me eight years ago," he said sadly. "It would have saved much grief, the poor bull-head's as well as yours and others, if he hadn't lived."

"Perhaps," she sighed. "But he was so little and

helpless, so horribly ugly. To kill him . . . No, I couldn't."

"You have too soft a heart. He wasn't little and helpless for very long. And now he's killed some innocent servant. What will you do about that?"

"You're a fine one to talk," Ariadne said, pushing him away. "You speak as if you've never killed, as if you're not also a cruel god who can't be bothered to try to help those who worship him. I've excused you for so many horrors. I told myself they were caused by lack of understanding. Now I see I lied to myself. You never cared. Likely you took joy in seeing Pentheus torn apart by his own mother and her women. You—"

"No!" Dionysus cried, paling. "I never meant that. I've killed and permitted killing to fructify the vines, mostly evildoers and willing sacrifices, but Pentheus was oppressing the women who came to my shrines. I only wanted them to be free, at least for a little while, of the bonds men had laid on them. I thought they would beat him, frighten him, teach him that he must allow women to worship me. I didn't know how deep went the hate . . . " His voice faded and he stared at Ariadne. "Do you hate me?" he asked faintly.

She looked at his face, turned, and took him in her arms. His eyes were staring, not with Vision, not blind, but wide with fear. "Not for being a man," she said, almost finding a smile. "Not even for being a god. Only when you're cruel and uncaring."

He shook his head mutely, too bound up in the painful acknowledgment that he'd fallen into the trap he'd been warned against countless times. He had fallen in love with a native, so deep in love that he couldn't contemplate living without her.

"You must come with me to Olympus," he burst out. "It's not enough for me to come here. I need you to be one with me, woven into my life. You blame me for being cruel and uncaring. You'd better blame me for being ignorant. How can I know about what to care? You desire me different? Come, live with me and teach me."

A lump of ice formed in Ariadne's breast, freezing the mist of silver threads so that they shrank back from Dionysus. "I can't live among gods," she whispered, but she knew that wasn't the reason.

"They aren't gods," Dionysus snapped. "We've talked about that and you've read *The History of the Olympians*. We're people like any other, except longer lived, and we didn't sacrifice our Gifted, so the Gifts grew stronger."

Ariadne shivered. "How can you not be gods when Uranous could bring forth monsters from the earth and bury alive in it those who were his enemies, when Kronos could leach all warmth from flesh, plant, and rock—"

"And could himself be drained so completely that he was no more than a common native man. Can you imagine draining the Mother that way?"

"No, I can't."

Ariadne frowned because Dionysus' words had made clear to her why her heart had frozen. The Mother was threatening to withdraw her Gift if Ariadne began to believe herself equal to the Olympians. No, there was something false in that idea, but she couldn't pursue it because Dionysus was saying that she was favored of the Mother, that power flowed from her into him in the blessing of the vines, that she need fear no Olympian if the Mother loved her.

She shivered again. "The Mother favors me here in Knossos. She doesn't promise equal favor elsewhere." Ariadne glanced at the wall behind which the dark image stood in its shrine. "And how can you take me to Olympus now when you must leave it? Will you set me in your house to be at the mercy of Bacchus and Silenos?"

Dionysus remembered his reasons for not urging her to live with him over the past months, but they were reduced to near nothing by the need that his fear of losing her had inspired. "Silenos won't do you any harm," he said. "Neither will Bacchus—" He hesitated and then went on quickly. "At least come for a few days, until I must leave. Let me make you known to Aphrodite and Eros and Psyche, and to that mischievous devil Hermes. When he knows *they* are watching over you, Bacchus will be as sweet as honeycomb."

Once she saw the beauty and enjoyed the luxury of Olympus, he thought, she might well be willing to stay. As to Bacchus—he could rid the house of him. No, he couldn't. Doubtless Bacchus would go to every Olympian who deplored too close association with the native folk and complain that Ariadne had caused him to be driven out of his home. That would set Athena and Artemis against Ariadne and those powerful women might poison the minds of many others so that poor Ariadne would be treated with dislike and contempt. But if she already had friends—specially that totally seductive trio of Aphrodite, Eros, and Psyche, and if he and Ariadne were together . . .

Mentally Dionysus groaned. They wouldn't be together. At least not in the immediate future. He was committed to go to the East with Hekate within this ten-day. He closed his eyes and pulled Ariadne closer against him. He couldn't even be rid of Bacchus that quickly, so leaving her alone in Olympus was impossible. Nor could he take her with him; there would be danger in what Hekate planned to do and, with all her power, Ariadne was not skilled enough in magic to use the power to protect herself.

Thoughts are swift, but even so there had been a

noticeable pause after his request, which meant that Ariadne had not burst into instant rejection. He released her, except for a grip on her hands, so he could look into her face.

"You will come, won't you? You'll give me a chance to prove all Olympians aren't monsters?"

To Ariadne the word brought an instant image of the Minotaur's bloodstained face, of the strings of flesh hanging from his jaws. "Yes," she said, clinging to Dionysus' hands, "I will go. Only let me—"

The caveat was too late. He swept her up into his arms and leapt. A moment of bitter cold, another of sick dizziness, which made her close her eyes, and then the musical sound of trickling water. Ariadne opened her eyes in a forest glade.

"Are you all right, Chosen?" Dionysus asked anxiously. "It's a long leap for one who has never traveled that way before."

"Yes," she said, "but why didn't you give me a chance to change my clothes. I'm all bedraggled and bloodstained." Then she looked around and her eyes widened. "This can't be Olympus. Where are we?"

"In Olympus indeed. This is my house." His voice was quick and eager with pleasure as he set her on her feet.

"House?" Ariadne echoed, looking at the massive tree trunks that surrounded the little open glade where a tiny fountain spilled from a rock into a small pool.

Then she saw that the floor beneath her feet was polished stone—green malachite, it looked like; she blinked at the thought of the cost—and it wasn't open sky above her head between what seemed like overarching branches but a strange clear substance that let in the light.

"Yes, my house," Dionysus answered eagerly. "Hades worked the stone to look like trees and made the roof of that clear stuff he calls glass. He and Persephone are very kind to me. She laughs at me. The Mother is so strong in her—as She is in you—that my madness can't touch her. And Hades takes me hunting in the caves of the Underworld. The King of the Dead is beyond fear of me. Besides, the peace and majesty, the silence of the caves calms me—" he grinned briefly "—and the beasts therein are such that they take all of a hunter's attention. And the beauty of the stone world! No one can think of self in such a place. There are crystal flowers that grow from the walls and the ceilings. Hades can light them so that they glow every color of the rainbow, and in some places the caves glitter with more points of light than there are stars in the sky—"

"I don't think I'm quite ready to go to the Underworld," Ariadne said hastily, half afraid that Dionysus would whisk her off to Plutos in his enthusiasm.

"No." He smiled at her. "Olympus first." The smile faded. "When I first went to the Underworld I was so lonely that I didn't care if I were trapped there. I told you, I went to fetch my mother and Persephone pitied me so much she asked Hades to let Semele go." His smile returned in a brief flicker as he added, "Hades is besotted on his wife; he denies her nothing." Then the flicker of lightness was gone, and he turned his head aside. "But it was all in vain. Semele wanted no part of me, so I was still alone."

His voice trembled slightly and Ariadne took his hand. "While you are my god and I live, you are not alone."

He looked back at her sidelong. "I will remind you of that promise some day." Then he tugged lightly on her hand. "One good thing came of my desire to have my mother with me. I have a fine apartment all ready for you. Come and see."

Because she had hoped to share his chamber, that

fact didn't give Ariadne much pleasure. However, the apartment was truly magnificent, the sitting room briliantly lit by three large windows of Hades' glass, the bedchamber so large Ariadne could have practiced her welcome dance in it, and Dionysus pointed out a handsome bathing chamber and toilet beyond. But the furnishings were horrid, dark and somber.

Still concerned with their closeness, Ariadne smiled rather mechanically and asked, "But will I be all alone here? Where is your apartment?"

He turned pointed across the short corridor off the main one leading from the glade-like reception room. "That's the door to my bedchamber. I wouldn't want you to come in thinking it was a sitting room and be shocked."

Ariadne glanced up at him but said nothing. Her first impulse had been to grin and say, "I wouldn't be shocked," but then she thought he might have been giving her a warning. If he customarily took a woman to bed with him and she walked in on their love play, she wouldn't only have been shocked but hurt and angry.

"Is there something I could wear?" she asked, wondering if a supply of women's garments were kept for his whores. "This gown is beyond cleaning, I think."

"What would I do with women's clothes?" he asked, laughing. "I'll send Silenos out to get clothing for you—he's infallible in judging sizes and what would best suit a woman—and combs and hairbrushes and . . . and . . ." He grinned. "And I haven't the faintest idea of what else you might need, but just tell Silenos."

"You don't think he might deck me out in purple silk with green and red decorations or some other totally unsuitable style or color? He can't feel very welcoming."

Dionysus shook his head. "Bacchus might try to spite you, although I doubt he would dare since I'm here with you, but not Silenos. He's really very kind, although he's not very brave or strong or very clever."

While they spoke he'd led her out though the short corridor into the wide one and back to the chamber of the forest glade where he rang a bell. A few moments later, a frightened looking servant edged into the room. In another moment, the man had straightened up from the hunched crouch in which he had entered and come forward. Ariadne watched with interest. She guessed that the man was afraid to come into Dionysus' presence—probably because he feared the backlash of Dionysus' emotions—but sensing his master was calm, he was not afraid of ill treatment.

"I want Silenos," Dionysus said.

The servant bowed.

"And this is the Lady Ariadne, my Chosen," he continued. "Any command she gives or request she makes is to be obeyed and satisfied without question or any need of further approval from anyone."

"Dionysus!" Ariadne exclaimed, laughing. "What if I suddenly went mad and told the man to set the house afire? At least say 'Any sensible command or request.' "

Dionysus laughed also and waved the servant out. He went at once, but not before Ariadne caught an expression of astonishment on his face. For a moment she was puzzled and then she guessed, remembering what Dionysus had said about everyone giving him what he wanted at once without question or argument, that the servant had not expected her to correct the god. Her attention came back to Dionysus when a bitter note entered his laughter.

"Not that the servants in this house would know a sensible command from a mad one," he said, and then added, "Poor things, they are accustomed to madness."

Ariadne could sense the rising hurt and wrath in him. The tendrils of her heartflower stirred and flowed outward, sluggishly at first and then more freely, but the heartflower itself was strangely still. It didn't pulse with warmth in time with the beating of her heart and give her a sense of strength and power. It was cold and heavy. I mustn't stay here long, Ariadne thought. The Mother hasn't yet taken away my power over Dionysus, but She's warning me.

Meanwhile Dionysus' resentful words had died away. Ariadne smiled at him. "They're afraid of the lash of your rage and pain, my dear lord," she said softly, "but they don't fear *you*. Didn't you see how gladly the man came forward to serve you as soon as he felt your calmness—"

She got no further. Around the corner of the door came the slightly sneering blond who had told her never to Call Dionysus again. Her mouth dried with nervousness. She had never discovered how much influence Bacchus had on his master.

"My lord," the blond said, bowing, "I met Myron in the corridor and he said you wanted Silenos, but he's asleep. He was, perhaps, a bit too merry last night, and he's not as quick to recover as he used to be. May I serve you?"

"I think I need Silenos," Dionysus said, frowning, but Ariadne put a hand on his arm.

An idea had occurred to her. She could test how far Bacchus would dare go. Dionysus looked down at her and she said, "Oh, don't wake the old man. Since he's so eager to serve, I'm sure Bacchus is well enough acquainted with women to find one or two gowns in the right style and color for me and such toilet articles as I'll need while I'm here."

Bacchus started slightly as if he hadn't noticed her or hadn't expected her to speak.

"This is the Lady Ariadne, my Chosen," Dionysus repeated, a tiny twitching of his lips showing that he knew the introduction wasn't really necessary. Then, when he had mastered that evidence of his desire to laugh, he added, "I am *very* sure you will do everything in your power to welcome Lady Ariadne, make her comfortable here, and please her. Since she's willing to entrust to you the task of outfitting her, I need only add the task I meant for you. I'd like you to invite Eros, Psyche, and Aphrodite to take their evening meal with us."

Bacchus bowed again, but his bent head didn't completely hide his expression from Ariadne, who didn't know whether to be pleased or annoyed at the flash of rage and frustration exposed. Whatever he had planned—if he had planned to discredit her in some way—had been ruined by the invitation to Aphrodite and her housemates. Bacchus' choice of clothing would be perfectly suitable, although he might choose unflattering colors. That wasn't important. Compared with the two greatest beauties in Olympus, Ariadne knew she would be like a peahen among peacocks even if she looked her best.

She should have been more nervous about meeting Aphrodite, Eros, and Psyche than about Bacchus, but she wasn't. It was Dionysus who suddenly looked alarmed.

"Maybe I shouldn't have invited them to eat here."

"Why not?" Ariadne asked, beginning now to worry.

But Dionysus' anxiety had nothing to do with her. He was concerned about his servants' ability to serve a suitable meal. Ariadne was about to say it didn't matter, but she realized he wanted to please and impress Aphrodite and her friends. Unfortunately she knew nothing about cookery, but then she remembered what she had read in *The History of the Olympians*.

"Hestia," she said.

Dionysus looked at her in blank befuddlement.

"I read that Hestia managed Kronos' house and that when Zeus became Mage-King he offered her great honor for protecting Hera, Demeter, and Leto and for helping Hera and Leto escape into his keeping but that Hestia said she preferred to remain as she had been."

"And so she has. Zeus likes his comforts and Hera is too often out of patience with him. If the housekeeping were in Hera's hands, eight days out of ten Zeus would eat thistles and sleep in an unmade bed. I will say that Zeus repays Hestia's care. He has arranged that Hestia has shrines everywhere, and she is greatly honored among women. But what has Hestia to do—"

"My lord, wouldn't Hestia be the one to help you either buy food from someone or borrow servants who could prepare what was needed?"

"Of course," Dionysus said, sighing with relief, "and I don't think I've ever spoken to Hestia before, so I doubt she'll be frightened before I begin to ask for help." He clutched Ariadne to him for a moment. "Always a true Mouth."

"Not if Hestia is as ignorant of householding as some great ladies I know," she warned him, laughing. "But let's hope for the best. And I beg you to be gentle, my lord. She doesn't sound like a very brave lady."

He nodded and went out at once, not disappearing but walking through the front door of his house and down a paved path toward the wide street in a most ordinary way. After wondering for a moment whether there were laws against "leaping" in Olympus, Ariadne gave herself a shake and went back to the apartment Dionysus had said was hers. She relieved her bladder and bowels and then feeling the stiff sensation on her skin, discovered how to let water into the hand bowl in the bathing room and washed off the smears of Isadore's blood. She was looking for a drying cloth when she heard Bacchus call her name.

Her heart leapt into her mouth, but then she reminded herself of Dionysus' not too subtle statement that he was *very* sure Bacchus would do everything he could to make Ariadne happy. Unless he planned to silence her by killing her, Bacchus wouldn't dare do anything to hurt her. She drew a deep breath and went into the sitting room to face him.

"You have guests, Lady Ariadne," Bacchus said, his eyes glittering with malice. "Will you come and greet them?"

Guests! So she had been wrong about his being unable to hurt her. He had brought some of the great mages, likely those who least favored natives, to see and disapprove of her. But how had Bacchus known that Dionysus would not blast them all? Even as the question formed she knew the answer. Bacchus was a scryer and he needed no ritual to form an image—well, neither did she now. Any smooth bright surface would have permitted Bacchus to watch her and Dionysus even after the spiteful devil had left the house.

Ariadne's immediate impulse was to flee back to the bathing chamber, bar the door, and somehow hide herself, but she knew that show of fear was just what Bacchus wanted. And a barred door would be no impediment to a great mage who wanted to enter. She reminded herself of how she had outfaced the merchants who intended to cheat her, outfaced her mother, whom she had always feared. She moved her gaze slowly from the top of Bacchus' head down to his well-shod feet.

"I will go and make *Dionysus'* guests welcome," she said. "This is my lord's house, not mine—and I do not forget it." Her statement made clear that the house was not Bacchus' either and that she knew he had taken an unauthorized liberty. "Now perhaps you will at last do your lord's bidding and bring me more suitable clothing. I am sorry it will be necessary to greet Dionysus' guests all bedraggled, but I will explain that no insult was intended by my lord and it was his servant's mistake that summoned them too soon."

For a long moment Bacchus stood staring at her, mouth dropped open with surprise. "Who do you think you are," he spat when he recovered, "one of the great ones?"

"Certainly not," Ariadne replied, forcing herself not to swallow hard or tremble. "I know exactly who I am, a native votary of the god Dionysus. *He* has named me high priestess, Mouth and Chosen, and I am his devoted servant. What are you?"

Bacchus' face flamed. "You won't rule here! You won't!" he snarled and flung himself out of the room.

For a long moment Ariadne shook so hard she couldn't move, but then she forced herself out of the door, along the wide corridor, and into the reception room. There, the knees she had locked in anticipation of facing angry gods, unlocked themselves and almost gave way. Sitting on the luxuriously cushioned seats that were made to look like rustic benches were the two most beautiful women in the world and a man who was probably more beautiful.

She grasped one of the treelike columns to support herself and uttered a squeak of relief. Bacchus hadn't dared summon anyone Dionysus hadn't named, no doubt hoping that he could claim Eros, Psyche, and Aphrodite had misunderstood him or been too eager to look at the queer thing Dionysus had dragged with him from native lands that they had come early.

All three looked immediately in the direction of the squeak, and Aphrodite jumped to her feet and ran lightly toward Ariadne, holding out her hand. She stopped abruptly when she was close enough to see Ariadne clearly.

"Child," she cried, "your gown is all over blood. What has that mad Dionysus done to you?"

"Nothing. Nothing," Ariadne gasped. "It's not my blood, Lady Aphrodite. And it's nothing to do with poor Dionysus. It was a—" she had to pause and take a deep breath "—a terrible accident caused by my half brother, the Minotaur."

Instantly Aphrodite, who had no interest at all in the Minotaur, was all smiles again. "As long as you aren't hurt. I was afraid Dionysus was out tearing another nation apart because you had been injured. He's so . . . impulsive."

"He's very young, Lady Aphrodite," Ariadne said, not thinking how ridiculous that might sound coming from her when Dionysus was probably ten or twenty times her age. "And he wasn't raised to understand that he must think before he lashes out with his Gift. When he's hurt, no matter how innocent or unintentional the cause, he grows angry. Then he sees the fear and withdrawal in those about him, which makes him angrier still—and afraid of what he is doing, too."

The second woman, as tall as Eros who walked beside her, had reached them. She nodded at Ariadne's words and took her hand. "Mouth and Chosen," she said. "You *are* why Dionysus has been so much at peace these past years. We didn't know whether to believe what he said of you, but it's true." She looked down at the hand she was holding and turned her head to speak directly to Aphrodite. "She is Mother-touched, too."

"You will make Dionysus what he was meant to be," Eros said.

"Men are too stubborn to let a woman make anything of them or they would all be perfect," Psyche remarked, but the solemn look had left her face and mischief lit her violet eyes. "But where *is* Dionysus? How did he come to abandon you to confront us all alone?"

"That was Bacchus' doing," Ariadne said. "He invited you to come at once and Dionysus had specified the evening meal. Poor Bacchus. He isn't very happy about my being here and he hoped, I think, that I would make a bad impression or refuse to meet you at all. Dionysus has gone to see about a suitable meal to serve. I suspect he doesn't have many guests and he felt what his servants knew how to prepare would be too coarse. He said Lady Aphrodite was accustomed to a plethora of small delicacies—"

"No, that was me," Eros said. "I used to have a very poor appetite and Aphrodite tried to tempt me with variety." He glanced sidelong at Psyche. "My appetite has improved. These days I could eat a baked horse without garnish."

Ariadne knew that was a joke and smiled dutifully, but she was mostly aware that Aphrodite's eyes were fixed on her gown. "I'm sorry I'm so inappropriately dressed," she said hastily. "It's no insult to you. Bacchus was supposed to bring me proper clothes, but—"

"It's a *beautiful* dress," Aphrodite said, eyes wide. Her fascinated glance fixed first on Ariadne's exposed breasts and then on the huge bell skirt that gave her a minuscule waist and broad hips, last flickered to the beaded apron that came to a point into which a large amethyst was fixed, which drew the eyes unerringly to the crotch between the legs. Cocking her head inquisitively, she added, "Well, it would be beautiful if it weren't all bloodstained. It certainly emphasizes a woman's best features." She turned on Eros. "How come I've never seen this style before?"

"Because you have no temples on Crete," he said. "They worship the Mother directly on Crete, although they acknowledge several avatars, like Potnia."

Aphrodite looked thoughtful. "Worship only as an avatar? I wouldn't mind, but—"

"Aphrodite, please!" Eros exploded. "Zeus and Athena would have fits, and I don't wish to be fried by a thunderbolt or skewered by one of Athena's spears while I try to explain that you wanted a new style dress."

The girlish mage shrugged. Power and offerings meant less to her than to most of the great mages since she was easily able to get anything she wanted without worshipers. She continued to examine Ariadne's gown, cocking her head this way and that, her smile growing more brilliant by the moment. Eros and Psyche glanced at each other.

"Oh, very well, I won't ask for a temple," Aphrodite said. "I don't have to be worshiped on Crete to wear the costume, do I? It just *speaks* to my very soul."

Ariadne's eyes widened in horror. She knew, because Dionysus had told her, that Aphrodite was totally and irredeemably promiscuous, that hardly a night passed when there was not one mage or another—or some favored native—in bed with her or she in his bed. Nonetheless, she looked and dressed like a barely nubile girl, not only exquisitely beautiful but of infinite sweetness and perfect innocence. It was the face of love everyone desired to see and know.

"Oh, my lady," Ariadne breathed, her arms coming across her previously proudly uplifted breasts.

There was something terribly obscene about the idea of Aphrodite in Cretan dress, a kind of exposure of the violence and voluptuousness that could lie under a seemingly perfect thing—something no one wanted uncovered; it was abominable.

"No, Aphrodite," Psyche gasped. "Not here. I don't think that style would befit you."

"Why not?" Aphrodite looked from one to another, her lips twisted. "It's a gown for a woman who knows every face of love and desires each." She looked toward Ariadne, now covering her breasts and half turned away from them in shame, and she laughed, a cascade of bell tones. "It's nothing to do with you, child. You wear the gown in innocence and all the simple pride of being female, without lust."

Eros groaned, but before he could speak, Dionysus stepped through the door. The subject of Aphrodite's desire for a Cretan gown was shelved in greetings and explanations. Then Bacchus returned with a handsome enough peplos—although it was too long so that Ariadne had to fasten the girdle about her waist and pull the garment over it, which made her body appear thick. Aphrodite protested, but Dionysus seemed almost pleased and relieved, although he promised that Silenos should find better fitting clothing.

Unfortunately the talk about clothes brought Aphrodite's mind right back to Cretan dress. The argument had to be explained to Dionysus, who innocently suggested that Aphrodite try it. Psyche jumped up, crying, "No," but Aphrodite was already gone, laughing mischievously. Dionysus asked what was wrong and Eros tried to explain that Psyche didn't think the style would suit Aphrodite. Before he finished, Aphrodite reappeared dressed in Ariadne's discarded gown.

There was a dead silence until Dionysus got slowly to his feet and backed away, shaking his head. "Take it off!" His voice trembled. "Take it off. I can't bear it!"

Ariadne jumped up and took his hand, silver mist pouring out of her to wrap him around. Tears ran down her cheeks.

Eros bowed his head into his hands, huddled in upon himself as if shrinking away from an unimaginable horror.

Only Psyche seemed unmoved, if pale. She looked at them and sighed, shaking her head. "She is as truly Cybele as she is Aphrodite," she said gently.

Ariadne jumped up and took his hand, [illegible] growing out of her to wrap him around. Tears ran down her cheeks.

Thus bowed his head into his hands, huddling in upon himself as if shrinking away from an unimaginable horror.

Only Psyche seemed unmoved, if pale. She looked at them and sighed, shaking her head. "She is as truly Cybele as she is Aphrodite," she said gently.

CHAPTER 17

Aphrodite laughed loud and long, peal upon peal, looking from one to the other as if, Ariadne thought, she were saying "There are none so blind as those who *will* not see. Beneath love lie many layers, and not all of them are beautiful." But then she went away, and she returned in her diaphanous pale blue gown, modestly high at the neck and with flowing sleeves, out of which her rounded, white arms peeped shyly now and again when she gestured.

"Come, come," Aphrodite said in her light voice, looking around at her shattered audience. "Here I am again, just as I ever was." She sighed heavily and pouted. "But it *is* a beautiful dress."

"Not for you!" came a loud chorus.

Fortunately before she could reply a servant came to announce the meal, and they all moved into the dining chamber. There the whole back wall was made of Hades' glass, and beyond it was a forested glade in which satyrs and fauns chased each other and played silly games of tag and leapfrog. Although Ariadne was still shaking inside, the others were immediately distracted by the charming creatures' antics and wanted to know how Dionysus contrived to keep them just where they were wanted.

His simple explanation—he fed them well and often played with them—smoothed the way into general talk, and after the meal, Psyche drew Ariadne aside to ask many questions about the Cretan worship of the Mother. She was deeply interested in Ariadne's description of the golden ribbons that gave her strength, of the way her hair was lifted when she danced and her locks of consecration were tweaked when the Mother was pleased. But Ariadne said nothing of how she had been pulled by the hair to see the Minotaur eat a man.

By the time Eros, Psyche, and Aphrodite left, Ariadne was sure that Dionysus' friends had accepted her, and she was far less frightened by the prospect of some day living in Olympus. Partly that was because the shock of what Aphrodite had revealed lingered. Just now Ariadne didn't care if Dionysus was sharing his bed or with whom. She was happy to go alone to her own bedchamber when it was time to retire. She no longer had any desire to tempt Dionysus.

The next day Dionysus took her around Olympus, showing her the great houses, the beautiful statuary, and outside the city a very old shrine to the Mother.

Ariadne froze before the entrance, drawing back and shuddering.

"She isn't here," she told Dionysus in a whisper. "She isn't wanted and has withdrawn. I can't stay here."

"She's among us still," Dionysus assured her. "The greatest shrine of all is Persephone's, in the Underworld, but there is one in the hunting lodge where Eros and Psyche sometimes live. And when you come to live with me, there will be a shrine in the garden where the fauns play."

"I can't stay," Ariadne pleaded.

"Yes, I know. I must go with Hekate and you would be unhappy here. But for a few more days . . ."

Later in the afternoon Dionysus took her to visit Hermes, and despite her best intentions to be respectful and awed, she found herself laughing out loud at the naughty stories he told. And when Dionysus tried to hush him over a particularly juicy tale about Apollo, he wrinkled his nose.

"He's mean," Hermes said, grinning crookedly. "I gave him the lute I had invented so he would forgive me for stealing his cattle, and I taught him to sing. Why did he have to take my voice so that I now sound like a crow?"

"To whom do you want to sing?" Dionysus asked.

Hermes laughed and looked aside. "No one, but I might some day."

On the third day Ariadne met Hekate. She had no trouble at all being awed and respectful, although she didn't feel afraid. Actually Hekate was rather kind, even though her silver-blue eyes seemed to be looking right through Ariadne into some strange and distant place. She asked whether Ariadne would be deprived in some way if Dionysus' went East with her. For the answer to that question Ariadne found a small smile.

"Only by my missing his company, my lady. I'm in

no need or danger. And he's said it's not only his duty but his pleasure to go with you. I think he's looking forward to the adventure."

"Looking forward," Hekate said, and closed her eyes. Then she shook her head. "I'll send him back safe, I promise." And after a pause she went on, "Call if you need him. It's far, but I'll make a spell that will carry your Call."

"Oh, please don't," Ariadne whispered. "I'm so foolish that I sometimes Call when I don't mean to at all, just if I'm startled or . . . or lonely. Don't let me Call him from what might be more important . . . or dangerous."

"You're a brave little lady," Hekate said, and Ariadne felt herself flush with pleasure because Hekate had not called her "child."

By the fourth day, Ariadne was on very good terms with Silenos, who'd taken her to several shops in the agora from which she'd come away with half a dozen really beautiful gowns. And whatever Bacchus thought, he'd done no worse than beat a servant on the second day for hurrying to fulfil an order from Ariadne. He thought the servant would be afraid to complain to Dionysus—and that was true, but he wasn't afraid to tell Ariadne. What Dionysus did, Ariadne didn't ask but everyone seemed happy to attend to her lightest wish.

On the fifth day, however, Dionysus found Ariadne in tears at the table when he came to break his fast. "What is it?" he asked. But the flatness of his voice said he knew.

"I must go back to Knossos," she sobbed. "I can't stay any longer. She's pulling my hair, pulling my heartstrings. My heartflower is cold and dead. I must go back."

Dionysus shrugged. He'd wanted to keep Ariadne with him until the day he had to leave with Hekate.

When he was with her, Olympus was a different place. Storekeepers served him without flinching and told him the price of anything if he asked. He'd been offered refreshments and had civil inquires made about Ariadne in several houses, Hephaestus' and Ares', and he and Ariadne had met Hestia in the street and she'd invited them to return to Zeus' house with her.

Nonetheless, he couldn't argue against her need to go. Truth was he'd felt it himself. The Goddess didn't pull his hair, but his heart knew it was time to return Ariadne to Knossos. Unfortunately, he also knew that likely as not she'd plunge into trouble trying to defend the bull-head. Nor was he sure he'd be able to rescue her. He had no idea whether Ariadne's Call could reach to the Tigris or whether Hermes' spell could carry him back so far—and Hekate refused to tell him anything except that she would not permit any harm to come to Ariadne. He shifted restlessly in his seat and Ariadne wiped away tears and looked at him.

"You are troubled, my lord?" she asked.

"I must go with Hekate," he said. "I promised. And, besides, she's done so many things for me."

"Of course you must," Ariadne agreed, smiling now. "You've been away before. I miss you, but so long as I know you're coming back, I can endure." She put her hand across the table to take his. "Some day I'll come back to Olympus, I promise you, but She wants me in Knossos now. And I'll be waiting there with open arms when you come back."

"If you haven't been killed by that half brother of yours. Won't you promise me to stay away from him while I can't come quickly to you?"

Ariadne's smile disappeared as she remembered her last sight of the Minotaur and she shuddered, but she couldn't promise what Dionysus wanted. "He didn't try to harm me," she assured her worried "god," trying to soothe him.

"I heard you scream."

"He pushed me away and I fell. But that was an accident. He didn't mean to hurt me."

"But your mind was black and red with fear. I've never felt such terror in you."

"It was because of what he'd done. It was horrible. Horrible beyond the words, which are dreadful enough. The Minotaur killed an attendant very bloodily. He doesn't even understand that it was wrong. The poor creature's been taught he's a god who can do anything and at the same time he's been denied anything he desires. I don't know what Pasiphae wanted of him, unless she was still insisting that he learn the king's responses in the ritual for the Mother for next year, but he must have been driven too far and attacked her. I imagine the attendant, Isadore, tried to drive him back with a torch—I saw that happen—but this time the Minotaur was so angry he didn't fear the fire."

She began to shiver in earnest, and Dionysus got up and pulled her into his arms. "There's nothing more you can do for the bull-head," he said. "And if he kills you, my love, that will kill me, too."

Ariadne smiled a little against his shoulder. "It's nice to hear, but one doesn't die of love lost, Dionysus."

"I will," he said softly. "You make 'being' real for me. If I lose that, now that I know it exists, I'll lose altogether my footing in this world, which has never been too firm. The other Ariadne was an anchor for me, but you've added to that love and friendship. Be careful of yourself, my Ariadne, for I *will* die of lost love."

How strange, she thought, that he speaks of love, that he says he'll die without my love, that he'll hold me, comfort me, caress me, but won't join our bodies in the natural fulfillment of love. But as she thought of trying once more to entice him, she remembered Aphrodite in the Cretan gown and the horrible laughter. He must either come to bed her because he could no longer resist or because they had talked the matter out and he understood she would still be his friend, Ariadne unchanged, after coupling.

"There's nothing to fear for me from the Minotaur," she assured him, reverting to the subject that had inspired the talk of love.

"The bull-head attacked his own mother," Dionysus protested.

"He's never been given any reason to love Pasiphae. Actually, he's been given good reason to hate her. He associates her with unpleasantness. He loves me, Dionysus."

"Why was there blood on your dress, on your arms?"

She swallowed hard. "I told you before, it wasn't my blood, my lord. The Minotaur not only killed Isadore, he was eating the body. He said he was the Bull God, that gods eat the offerings made to them, that Isadore was a sacrifice, and that he liked man flesh. But even when I tried to pull him away, he didn't hurt me. He said—" A little half-hysterical giggle forced itself from her. "He said that if I didn't like it I should go away. And then he picked me up, but quite gently—that's when I got blood all over me—and put me outside the door. He said he was sorry, that he loved me and hadn't meant to hurt me."

"I'm a little easier in my mind," Dionysus said, but he still looked dissatisfied. "Still you shouldn't go to him if it can be avoided. I'm not sure how long he'll be able to recognize you."

"How long he will recognize me?" Ariadne barely breathed the words.

"Hekate thinks that the spell Poseidon wove to set the bull's head on the body and to give that body strength to bear it wasn't perfect. She believes he'll grow, at least to the natural size and weight of a bull, and that as his body grows he'll be less and less a man and more a bull."

"I feared it," Ariadne said, tears filling her eyes. "He knows it, too." The tears ran over. "He said he didn't remember things anymore the way he used to remember them." Her voice broke into sobs as the memories came clear again, unblurred by the glories of Olympus. "I can't bear it. He's only a little boy, and now he'll be all alone. So lonely. So frightened inside that monstrous body."

Dionysus held her close. After a few moments he said, "Shall I tell Hekate I can't go with her and why?"

She clung to him, kissed his lips with a tear-wet mouth. "No." She sighed. "He still knows me now and that won't change in the few ten-days you're gone. I feel—" she remembered the empty, hollow shrine and felt a reluctance to name the Mother despite the evidence she had of the Goddess' power, "that there's something I must still do." The cold that had clung to her heartflower, even though the silver strands were free, warmed. She sighed again. "Have patience, my lord. My time of caring for the Minotaur *is* ending. Poor Minotaur. Poor creature. Poor, lost little boy."

She broke into weeping again, recalling her sense of a bewildered child dimly aware that he has done wrong but driven by an urge for which he had no name to tear at the specially sweet and soft flesh of what had been a man.

"You'll be happier here when you're free," Dionysus murmured, stroking her hair.

Then he rose, lifting her as he did, and again she

was cold and dizzy but safe in his arms. When her eyes opened, he was carrying her into her bedchamber. He unlaced her sandals and slipped her under the coverlet, then gestured at a stool, which moved through the air to settle itself by the bed, and he sat beside her and took her hand.

The image of a cowering child overlaid by the huge body and brutish head of the Minotaur, blood smeared and with shreds of flesh in the jaws, faded as Ariadne became absorbed in a more personal puzzle. There was nothing of withdrawal in Dionysus now. He hadn't leapt away from her kiss; he had carried her into her bedchamber and set her into her bed without balking. What was different? Her grief? His imminent departure? Had he forgotten the visualization of his own fears in what Aphrodite had exposed? Could she forget it? She was too exhausted to decide among the questions; a warm and enveloping darkness overtook her before she found an answer, and she slept.

Dionysus was gone when Ariadne awakened, but that last memory of him sitting patiently beside the bed, holding her hand, reinforced by the stool still in place, soothed her. The pleasant feeling was replaced by a sharp sense of loss, which surprised her. She was accustomed to living her own life while Dionysus lived his quite separately. Surely four days in Olympus could not have changed that.

Then the reason for the sense of loss came to her. Dionysus' presence protected her from demands by anyone else. Even Minos and Pasiphae did not dare intrude while Dionysus was with her. Now she would be without that protection for several ten-days. And just when the Minotaur had broken past the restraints placed on him . . . killing . . . devouring . . . Not today, she told herself—and touched Hagne's mind to tell the priestess that she was at home again—only to learn that her hope of one day's respite was in vain.

Hagne greeted her with a burst of welcome—and relief. Phaidra had been to the shrine every day growing more and more insistent that the priestesses send a message to her sister to demand that she return.

Ariadne sighed, pulled off the Olympian peplos and drew on a Cretan robe. She asked Hagne to make ready a bath and bring a meal, and then went out to the sitting room. As she passed the dark goddess, she thought a light tug of satisfaction twitched the lock of consecration closest to the image and when she looked at it, she could swear that lips, which were not truly carven into the face, were curved upward.

As she entered the room, Phaidra leapt to her feet. "Where have you been? Do you realize that until this afternoon your women wouldn't tell me where you were or agree to scry for you and tell you you were needed?"

"And quite right they were," Ariadne said rather coldly. "I've been away with Dionysus. Gods don't like to be disturbed by little mortal troubles."

Phaidra's lips parted, then closed. In a far less aggressive voice she said, "Is he gone now? Mother and father want you to come to the palace. Father wants to know what really happened in the Minotaur's apartment." She hesitated and then said quickly, in a lower voice, "He does not trust what mother told him."

Ariadne sighed. "You may tell them I will come when I have bathed and eaten."

"They want you now," Phaidra insisted.

"They know the answers I will give them." Ariadne shrugged. "I have nothing to say that either will want to hear, so whenever I come will be soon enough."

After several protests Phaidra reluctantly left to

carry Ariadne's message. By then the bath was ready. At another time, Ariadne might have lingered, relaxing in warm scented water while she tried to decide whether Dionysus' new loving warmth should encourage her to try again to tempt him into her bed. She did think about it briefly. Like the bloodstained image of the Minotaur, the vision of Aphrodite as Lust personified was fading and Ariadne's hunger for his body was renewed.

Sighing she put the thought aside. She suspected that her "soon enough" wouldn't suit the king's and queen's impatience after five days' waiting, and she cleaned herself briskly, considering dressing in full formal attire. That seemed excessive and she ended up calling for one of her most elegant long, straight gowns. Her suspicion was actually a good prognostication. Before she'd more than tasted the meal Hagne had brought for her, she heard voices in the corridor, and as the door to her chamber was opened, Pasiphae's speaking with angry intensity.

"I don't see why you've insisted that I come here or what Isadore's death has to do with Ariadne. The Minotaur has always been my concern."

Ariadne saw Minos and Pasiphae framed in the doorway, heads turned to each other, and she said sharply, "Not yours alone any longer, Queen Pasiphae."

Both queen and king stopped abruptly. Both stared at her and then around the room. It was the first time either one had been inside her apartment since she had rid it of its clutter. Brief expressions of surprise touched each face, but were immediately supplanted by a kind of anxious eagerness. Ariadne could guess that both hoped she would say that she could and would control the Minotaur. Nonetheless, Pasiphae couldn't easily yield her authority, especially to her rather despised third daughter.

"Why?" Pasiphae asked, drawing herself up.

"Because you can no longer control him, madam. Nor—before you ask it of me—can I."

"Why is there such a need to control the Minotaur?" Minos asked. "He killed an attendant because he was angry. You yourself have said over and over, Ariadne, that he's only a child despite his size. He's enormously strong. He may not even have realized—"

Ariadne put aside the little table holding her food. What time and Olympus had blurred, Minos' words had brought back all too vividly. She would eat no more now.

"He not only killed Isadore, King Minos," she said, "he *ate* him. And when I told him that men don't eat each other, he answered that he was a god, that Isadore was a sacrifice to him, and that he *liked* human flesh. Is this a creature you want loose among the people?"

"He must have gored Isadore and got blood on his face," Pasiphae said.

Ariadne swallowed. "There were strings of flesh hanging out of his mouth." She swallowed again. "Madam, you are sacred to the Mother—"

The queen jerked on the words, as if she'd been slapped, but then a kind of mad determination hardened her expression. "The Mother," she repeated. "But I *am* the Mother, and I have borne a god as my son. He is an angry and vengeful god—" she cast a sidelong glance at Minos "—because of the bull from the sea. If he demands human sacrifice, who are we to stand against a god's will?"

That broke Ariadne's control and she stood up abruptly. "The Minotaur is no god!" she cried. "He's a poor, deformed creature of weak mind who's been changed into a monster by one moment being told he's an all-powerful god and can do and have anything and the next moment being thwarted in the most innocent desire."

Pasiphae seemed to swell with rage and was about to step forward, but Minos—whose expression Ariadne noted was more thoughtful than horrified—put a hand on her arm. "We certainly wouldn't wish to have the wrong persons end up as sacrifices," he said. "Nor do we desire that the priestess of Dionysus speak her mind abroad when the Minotaur doesn't appear in his temple."

This time Pasiphae didn't make any remark about Dionysus having been driven from Crete by the more powerful Bull God or the lack of importance of a minor godling. Ariadne wondered briefly what, if anything, Dionysus had said to the queen or whether he'd merely flicked her with the lash of his rage. Whatever it was, Pasiphae was subdued.

Having seen his wife silenced, Minos turned to Ariadne. "For a day or two, only a short time, do you think you could bring the Minotaur to his temple—"

"I don't go to the temple of the Bull God," Ariadne replied quickly. "I have my own shrine and my own god."

"We aren't asking you to appear in the temple," Minos said. "Only to bring the Minotaur to the back entrance. He likes going to the temple, but no one has dared enter his apartment—"

"You mean you haven't fed him or given him water for five days?"

"If what you say about his victim is true, he's had food enough," Minos said stiffly.

"I couldn't ask any of the attendants to enter after what happened," Pasiphae added, with a glance at Minos that told Ariadne she might have done otherwise if the attendants hadn't been well born. "And Phaidra screamed so when I brought her to the door that the Minotaur began to roar." She shrugged. "Should I go in to feed and water him?"

He's your god, Ariadne thought, you brought him upon us. But she felt a stab of coldness inside her replacing the Mother's usual warmth, and what she said was, "No, that would only enrage him for he hates you bitterly, Queen Pasiphae."

"Even a god should love his mother," Pasiphae snapped.

"Gods are notoriously ungrateful," Minos said with a wry twist to his mouth. "Men—and women—also. You were once my daughter, Ariadne. You have your god now, but I hope you haven't forgotten it was I who sent you to his shrine. There is a debt, if not a bond of blood, between us. Right or wrong, the Minotaur has become important to my hopes for the future of Crete. I have the treaty with Athens almost in my hand. I expect to receive tokens from their king within the month, and Androgeos will go to Athens to bring our tokens to them by midsummer."

"Wasn't there resistance to the treaty in Athens?" Ariadne asked.

"Yes, which is why I want the Minotaur to appear just as usual until all is confirmed. I'm having a stair built that will go from his bedchamber down to the underground passage to the temple. Until that's finished, won't you take him through the room of the pillars to that passage and tell him to take his seat in the temple so his priests and priestesses can dance for him?"

Ariadne thought of the frightened, lost child inside the Minotaur growing hungrier and, if he couldn't remember how to get water from the bathroom where the cisterns on the roof had outlets, thirstier. "He doesn't like the dark passage," she said, not quite agreeing but not refusing either, hoping she could bargain for good treatment for the poor creature.

"The passage can be lighted."

"Not with torches!" Ariadne exclaimed. "His attendants threatened him, perhaps even burnt him, with torches."

Minos grimaced. "I'll tell Daidalos to provide mage lights for the passage."

He didn't like to appeal to the artificer, but so far so good, Ariadne thought. One thing more and she would agree to shepherd the Minotaur to his temple. "And do you think it safe to have all those tasty priestesses and priests dancing before him with no protection? Think of the reaction of those who come to see him if he should seize one of them."

"What if he does?" Pasiphae put in sharply. "They're his consecrated votaries; he may do what he likes with them."

Minos glanced at his wife and Ariadne bit her lip. His look betrayed sorrow and puzzlement, a terrible sense of loss, but it was quickly overlaid with calculation, followed by decision and distaste, and his eyes came back to Ariadne.

"I'll have his chair moved back into the passage and ask Daidalos to set a magical wall across the doorway. That should keep him in until we can decide whether a more permanent restraint is needed."

"Then for a few days I will walk him through the chamber of pillars. Don't forget to have the passage to his temple lighted. Remember that I can't force him to do anything. I don't fear he'll hurt me, but he'll simply put me aside and do what he likes."

"Could Dionysus—"

"No!"

The denial came simultaneously from both Ariadne and Pasiphae, but Ariadne's indignation seemed insignificant even to her, compared with the shame, fear, and startled recognition that appeared briefly on Pasiphae's face. For the first time the queen must have contrasted the Dionysus who had appeared before her to carry Ariadne away and the beast-man behind the barred doors.

Minos had shrugged again in the face of the unity of denial. "Will you come soon?" he asked Ariadne. "The guards say he is beginning to shout for you."

"I'll come now," Ariadne replied, "before he becomes so hungry he can't think of anything else. I must have prepared for me a large bowl of raw meat, the most tender and succulent, and haunches of kid and lamb skinned but uncarved. I'll come as soon as I have changed my gown."

The meat was ready and should distract the Minotaur, Ariadne thought, but she was a little frightened as she approached the door and heard him bellowing. She did her best to suppress it and resolutely thought only of her brother and not of Dionysus. She hoped Dionysus had gone with Hekate already. He would be furious to find that she had rushed to help the Minotaur after he begged her to stay away. Fortunately, there was no need for her to have been frightened. Her thrown voice produced instant silence within the room and then a meek promise to go sit in his chair while "Ridne" came in with nice fresh food for him.

She had a little difficulty controlling her stomach once inside the room because blood and dried scraps of flesh and odd bones were scattered about, but the odor of putrefaction was not yet very strong, and she had eaten very little. The Minotaur was doing what he thought was smiling at her, holding out his hand and saying her name with obvious delight.

"It's very dirty in here," she said, pretending to look about disapprovingly while her eyes were actually closed. "Let's go into your bedchamber so you can eat this delicious dinner I've brought for you. And will you let me call in some servants to clean this room? We can keep the door to your bedchamber closed so the noise will not trouble you."

He seized a gobbet from the bowl she carried and chewed. "Dirty," he mumbled around the chunk of meat. "Clean."

To Ariadne's relief, he hadn't carried any of Isadore into the bedchamber although the sheets of the bed were tumbled and stained with old blood. Setting down the meat, Ariadne found a bowl in which to get water and, between chunks of flesh, handed that to him. He drank eagerly, but refused more, reaching for the meat again. When he was busily engaged in gnawing on the lamb's haunch, Ariadne said she wished to oversee the cleaning. The Minotaur only nodded.

She found that the cleaning crew, three men and two women, was made up of criminals condemned to death, their executions commuted while they served the Minotaur. There were no weapons in the room; the torches had been replaced by mage lights; the poor devils had no way to protect themselves or to hurt the Minotaur.

Their faces, though seamed and hardened with old sin, were now pale, and hands and voices trembled. Gathering up and scrubbing away the remains of Isadore had showed them all too clearly what might befall them—not a clean death by the stroke of the double axe but being torn apart. They looked on Ariadne, who'd come unscathed from the Minotaur's inner chamber, with awe.

She pointed out some places that needed better cleansing and they hurried to obey. Then she told them that the Minotaur probably wouldn't harm them if they didn't anger him and that the easiest way to anger him was to oppose him. Let him do what he liked and mend matters afterward, if they could, she advised. If he asked for something, and they could obtain it, they should do so as quickly as possible. If he asked them to do something, they were to do it at once. Likely he would ask to go out, she said finally; then all they could do was show him they couldn't go out either.

"When I've taken him to the temple, change the linens on his bed and familiarize yourselves with everything in his apartment so you can bring him anything he asks for and groom him, which he likes done."

"Where do we go to sleep?" one man asked.

"Nowhere," Ariadne replied. "You sleep here. I don't think you'll ever go anywhere again," she added sadly. "I imagine food and bedding will be passed in to you—"

A woman gasped and they all drew back. Ariadne turned to see the Minotaur standing in the doorway.

"Go out now?" he asked, barely glancing at the cowering servants.

"It will soon be time to go to the temple," Ariadne agreed, "but your fur is all sticky. Sit here and let me and these other folk groom you. Then we'll go."

He sat down at once and Ariadne ran back to the bedchamber to fetch his combs and brushes and the cloths used to dampen his fur.

"Bath?" he asked, when she arrived.

"I don't think there's time to heat the water," she suggested. "When you come back from the temple, ask for a bath and these people will arrange it for you." And then she sent a man to get water from the bathroom and summoned a woman to her to wet the cloths and begin to rub down the Minotaur's fur. She thought the two might faint, but they tottered through their tasks and the Minotaur did nothing to alarm them further.

Nor did he give her any trouble when she walked with him along the corridor to the stairwell that led down to the room of the pillars. She was certain that guards watched through barely opened doors along the way, but nothing disturbed them until the Minotaur slowed his pace as they neared the end of the pillared room.

"Long dark," he said.

"No more dark," Ariadne replied. "I've arranged that the passage be lit. You'll like that."

Touchingly, he took her hand as if for reassurance, but he went forward, trusting her as he always had, and when he saw that the passage was, indeed, lit, he rubbed his cheek against her head in his sign of happy affection. Ariadne gave him a little hug although her eyes were filled with tears. Likely they had forced him into the black passage and chivvied him along it with torches. If they'd had the common sense to put the torches on the wall to light the place, he would have gone along without any resistance. A child afraid of the dark, he couldn't understand that they would come into light again.

At the back entrance to the temple, Ariadne stopped. "You know the way from here," she said. "Go and sit in your chair, love, and the priests and priestesses will come and dance for you."

"Long pro-pro- Many people?"

She stroked his cheek. "When you're tired of them, just get up and leave. No one will stop you. Come back through the passage that is now light, and I'll be waiting for you in the chamber of the pillars. You can have a bath, if you want one, when you get back to your bedchamber, and I'll tell you a story."

"Picture?"

"Yes. I'll find a picture for the story."

An uneasy peace descended for a while, except that in addition to building the stairway, Minos seemed to have decreed a major extension of the palace. Rumor had it that the king was building a whole secondary palace to house the Minotaur. Ariadne, who could see the work from the front gate of Dionysus' shrine thought that might be true, except she thought it more likely he was building a prison than a palace. Certainly Daidalos and a large crew of workmen were very busy measuring and digging foundations for walls from the base of the palace to the back entrance of the temple of the Bull God.

CHAPTER 18

The stair was finished first, within a ten-day, the entrance into the Minotaur's bedchamber closed with a heavy iron gate. This locked and unlocked with a magic key when the mage lights that lit the stair as well as the passage were turned off and on. Phaidra controlled them with a word of command.

At first she refused to enter the Minotaur's room without Ariadne, so Ariadne was also bound into the spell, but a ten-day in which no one had been hurt had reassured Phaidra. In addition, her father's flat statement that he wouldn't propose her as a wife to

Theseus, prince of Athens, to seal the treaty if she wouldn't perform that task and bring the Minotaur's meals had bought her obedience.

But three ten-days later another incident occurred. One of the men under death sentence tried to find a way to freedom down the stairway, which Phaidra left open until the Minotaur returned. The Minotaur heard him coming into the back of the temple and then saw him trying to sneak past the invisible barrier. He watched, mouth open in laughter, as the increasingly frantic man pushed and clawed at the solid nothing blocking off the doorway. Then he rose and came forward to grasp the man, who shrieked with pain and terror.

"Priest?" he bellowed.

The crowd of worshipers who had come to gaze on the Bull God sighed and stirred uncertainly. It was rare for the Minotaur to move until he tired of the procession of those with offerings and simply went away. He looked out at the priests, who had stilled at the sound of his voice but now, hearing the man's cries as the Minotaur's fingers dug into his shoulder, desperately resumed their leaping and gyrating in their glittering costumes. He turned his head to look at the priestesses, also garbed in sparkling splendor, who were frantically rattling sistra and blowing pipes, whirling in place.

"No priest!" he roared, stuck his fingers under the man's chin, and ripped off his face.

The crowd heaved, some screaming and shrinking back, others shouting with excitement and trying to force their way forward. The priests and priestesses redoubled their efforts, past experience telling them that their motions and the hypnotic shimmer of their garments usually quieted their god when he was restless. The Minotaur looked out at them for a moment and then carried the body of his victim, unable to cry out but still pumping blood, into the back of the temple. What the priests heard drove them to even more frenzied dancing and the priestesses added their voices to the music of sistra and pipes to drown out the sounds.

To the worshipers and the priests and priestesses, the Bull God's personal defense of the sanctity of his temple left no doubt of his power and awareness. Their worship, half curiosity in the past, gained conviction. News of what had happened spread over Crete like wildfire in a dry summer, met mariners at the docks, and drifted over the seas to foreign lands.

The Egyptians abandoned any notion of adopting the Bull God; they liked their deities safely immured in a human pharaoh, frozen into statues, or in the more manageable living forms of their sacred beasts. In Athens, seething with internal factions, the news was unimportant, except to one group, bitterly opposed to King Aigeus and his son Theseus, who claimed that Cretans practiced human sacrifice and connected that abomination to the treaty with Knossos. Since the diplomatic mission to make the treaty had already departed they hoped to shake King Aigeus's rule.

Minos had news of the death within moments of the event, but did nothing. Within him was a mingling of triumph and terror. The Minotaur had placed his own populace more firmly in his hand than ever—but for how long? What would happen when he ran out of condemned criminals? Crete wasn't a violent place; there were few who merited the death penalty and he was known as a just judge. But the Minotaur couldn't care for himself. He needed servants, and only those condemned to death could now serve him. Minos knew that pronouncing death sentences to supply the Minotaur, would turn the people against him, the distant terror of a god's disapproval being less fearful than the near one of an unjust king.

Gnawing his lips, Minos considered his alternatives, and at last the frown smoothed from his brow. Yes, the Bull God, having confirmed the divine right of Minos and Pasiphae by being born in the flesh, had now matured into his full godhead. Like Zeus, Apollo, Dionysus, and others, who had been raised in infancy by mortals, the Minotaur would now go to his own place. He would disappear and show himself only at unexpected and infrequent intervals. Minos congratulated himself on his foresight in the arrangement made with Daidalos. He didn't speak to Pasiphae about his plans; she would have to bow to necessity.

Phaidra had hysterics when the Minotaur returned covered with clotted blood and with scraps of raw flesh caught in his fur, but he simply picked her up and thrust her out when the guards opened the door in response to her shrieks. That had one good effect. Phaidra was finally convinced that the Minotaur wouldn't hurt her, whatever he did to others. She returned to the chamber calmly and ordered the two women servants to groom the Minotaur's fur. The next day a new condemned criminal took the place of the dead man.

When Ariadne heard, she wept, but she didn't go to the palace. All her mind's eyes could see was the Minotaur's blood-clotted face, the strip of flesh hanging from his jaw. The Minotaur and his fate were far beyond her now. She would still do what she could for her poor, deformed brother, for the little boy more and more lost in the beast, but she was no longer concerned as a priestess. The Minotaur would never be brought to sit before the sacral horns when she danced for the Mother, not even by any artifice devised by Daidalos and Pasiphae.

There were, of course, no more attempts to escape

through the temple, and ten times the number of worshipers crowded the temple precincts. If they came in the expectation of new horrors, they were disappointed. The Minotaur seemed content to sit in his chair at his regular times of appearance quietly watching the dancing priests and listening to the music of the priestesses.

Then Ariadne forgot all about the Minotaur because Dionysus returned. He was in a strange mood, mingling exuberance with moments of thoughtful horror mixed with satisfaction. He would not tell her what he had done, other than to say that Hekate had been successful in her purpose, but he had remembered her taste for hearing about strange lands and really paid attention while he, Hekate, and Kabeiros had been traveling.

"We could not leap from place to place after we passed Troja because Hermes had not been to those lands. So we went by ship." His blue eyes were wide with remembered astonishment. "Mother, that was unsettling. It's very strange to have the floor under your feet move about. Unsettling to the stomach, too."

Ariadne laughed heartily. Most Cretans were accustomed to travel by ship, and she had been sailing many times. But the god Dionysus had been seasick. How very ungodlike. How very human. He frowned at her, probably having expected sympathy, but there was no change in the feeling of the tendrils that touched him. Ariadne was surprised and almost disappointed. He wasn't being precipitated into an unreasonable and ungovernable rage by a minor irritation. Did that mean she was less necessary to him?

"I couldn't eat for three days," Dionysus said indignantly. "You think that's funny?"

"Well . . ." she temporized, relieved that he had received no hint of her new anxiety. "I know it wasn't funny to you. It's happened to me, too. One does feel as if one were like to die, but island people grow accustomed to the sea. You did grow accustomed, didn't you?"

"Yes." He shrugged away her amusement. "And the ports were wonderful. There were goods I've never seen before. Look."

He thrust his hand into the bosom of his tunic and drew out a soft leather sack. Within was another, smaller cloth bag that spilled into his hand earrings and a necklet of glowing stones, green with a dark stripe. He leaned forward, thrust his hand into the best light, and turned his wrist. The dark stripe moved as the position of the setting changed.

"How beautiful," Ariadne said.

"Cat's eyes they're called. And these—" Another cloth bag opened to show misty red stones with a bright silver star imprisoned. "For you."

He held them out to her and Ariadne, forgetting her doubt and Aphrodite's revelation, leaned forward and kissed him. He drew back and turned his head. Ariadne didn't open her hand to take the gift. He dropped the stones on the table beside his chair.

"I have more," he said. "Beautiful cloth and two books I found written in the Trade Tongue that tell of lands beyond where Hekate took me. They're in Olympus. Will you come and look at them?"

"Not yet," Ariadne said, swallowing resentment despite the evidence that he had been thinking about her all the time he was away. He would give her anything—except what she really wanted. "When the Mother releases me, I will come."

He disappeared then and Ariadne was frightened. She took the jewels and alternately wore the cat's eyes and the star rubies, praying he would return and see that she did appreciate what he had given her. On the third day—she was wearing the cat's eyes—he did come back. He said nothing about her necklet and earrings, but he was cheerful and full of tales of what he had seen and done. Ariadne was careful not to touch him.

Three more ten-days passed and then a new problem arose, but this one wasn't of the Minotaur's making. Daidalos told King Minos that he could no longer maintain the mage lights in the stairway and passage and the magical seal on the Minotaur's temple. Minos was furious, but even he had to acknowledge that for once Daidalos was not crying before he was hurt. The man was gaunt and gray with the drain on his power.

Phaidra came running to Ariadne with the news, begging for help. She told Ariadne that the delegation from Athens had come a few days earlier and they had seemed pleased at the suggestion of a blood bond to seal the treaty and even more pleased when Minos presented her as a suitable wife for Theseus. One of them was even painting a portrait of her to take to the prince. If the Minotaur should either not appear or break loose and do something terrible, she wept, the treaty would be set aside and her life would be ruined!

Because she had achieved the independence and freedom that Phaidra craved, Ariadne couldn't help being sympathetic. She didn't like to trouble Dionysus with her family's problems, but concern for her sister drove Ariadne to mention Phaidra's fears and ask if he knew how to increase Daidalos' power.

At first he didn't answer, seeming to look out through the shaft window at the lengthening shadows. Ariadne suppressed a sigh, thinking he was ignoring her request, but then she saw his fixed expression, that his eyes were blind, and she realized Dionysus wasn't staring at shadows but into a private place of his own.

"She will," he said, "but not yet."

The statement as it stood made no sense, but Ariadne's silver mist brought her the awareness that it referred to Phaidra's marriage to Theseus. About to thank Dionysus for the assurance, she was struck dumb as his continuing Vision seized her and she hung above a crowd of battling men.

They didn't have the lissome form of Cretans, being bulky of body, light-haired, fair of skin. Achaeans then. And fighting each other. She knew at once with that understanding that came to the Mouth of a god, that the treaty was the cause of the strife. Then, with a feeling of time speeding past, several ten-days or even months, the image changed to a broad harbor rapidly filling with ships—and these were Cretan, long, slender, swift, black ships, warships, their sides hung with shields, their oars flashing as the ships drove forward. And behind the oarsmen, brighter pricks of light from the polished bronze blades of swords and javelins held ready in the hands of the soldiers the ships carried.

"No," Ariadne breathed.

Her protest had no effect on the images that filled her mind. She saw the ships drive to shore, the Athenians come down to resist the landing, but in no unified force. Some fought the invaders, others shouted and gestured at each other while they charged, delaying their defense. Nor were they any match for the Cretans in numbers, for most of their strong young men were out on the lands surrounding the city.

More and more Cretans poured ashore. They drove the armed men before them; they broke open the doors of the houses as they passed and herded out the women and the children, who were sent back to the ships under guard. They broke into well-organized groups, most going beyond the city to capture the men who were farming. Other groups entered the palace and raged through that also, dragging out an old man in rich robes, whom they brought to the wide porch and forced to bid his fighters to lay down their arms.

Something in the Vision struck Ariadne as false, although Dionysus *always* Saw the truth. This didn't fit with what she had heard about the Athenians, who were said to be ferocious fighters and most passionate in defense of their land. In this battle they seemed half-hearted, and King Aigeus, known for his pride, seemed ashamed, willing to yield. But she couldn't fully consider what was wrong. An overriding horror drove the images from her mind.

"Minos will go to war to force the treaty on them," she said, as sense came back into Dionysus' expression. "But why?" she cried. "Have he and Pasiphae gone mad?" Then, as if physically drawn, her eyes shifted to the wall behind which the Mother's image stood. "No," she breathed, "no. It was growing in them both from the moment the white bull from the sea answered my father's prayer. And then you came to your shrine for the first time in generations. They saw themselves as specially favored of the gods, singled out to rule. Crete was not large enough to satisfy them. Hubris. It is hubris." She looked into Dionysus's eyes. "But why? Why does the Mother continue to protect Pasiphae?"

He shook his head. "She hasn't Shown me that, and for myself . . . I'm only a man." Then he shook himself, like a dog casting water from his fur, ridding himself of the remnants of Seeing. "So the Vision was of King Minos going to war . . ."

His brow furrowed on the words and Ariadne became aware of a deep sadness drifting through the silver mist that joined them. "You don't like war," she said softly.

He looked puzzled. "I don't," he agreed. "Armies

trample the vines and use the wine for ugly purposes. But it's not the thought of war that makes me sad. Something else. Something I didn't See or don't remember that made the Athenians hesitate to defend themselves. . . ." He shrugged. "If it was withheld from me, it won't haunt my sleep. You are looking beyond what I Saw and fear the Minotaur broke free of Daidalos' binding and the Athenians refused to make the treaty. But my Vision says that nothing will deter King Minos from this war so I suppose it doesn't matter if Daidalos' gate fails—"

"Dionysus!" Ariadne exclaimed, forgetting in her exasperation the feeling that the Vision was somehow false. "It would certainly matter to the person the Minotaur attacked and tore apart."

"Oh." He had the grace to look a trifle shamefaced. "But there's nothing I can do to increase Daidalos' power. The ability to use power is born into a person and the Mother grants power as She wills." He pursed his lips. "You have power enough. What I can do is to teach you how to transfer power to a set spell and I think Daidalos must have used one or more set spells for the lights and to block that doorway. You'll find them in the walls for the mage lights, I think, and around the frame of the doorway for the invisible wall."

The technique was more difficult to learn than calling forth a spell from among the leaves of her heartflower, and Dionysus, not sure he approved of what she would be doing but not willing to refuse her request for help or set limits on her use of her own power (no Olympian interfered with another in that way), left her to struggle with the problem alone.

To Ariadne the power to use a spell was intangible and had always come with the spell itself, hidden within the bright silver bubble. Eventually she found it, a dull golden glow that supported the bright bubble, like a drab background against which the colors of a fresco or a ceramic piece sparkled. Having identified the power that drove the spells, Ariadne could get no further because she needed to rehearse the dancers for the ritual of the spring equinox.

Except for the fact that Dionysus couldn't come—he was promised to a special new ritual far to the East, one Ariadne suspected he and Hekate had substituted for some other worship of which they didn't approve—the celebration was pure pleasure. The weather was mild and dry, the dancing especially joyous, the king and queen seemed at peace with each other if remote, and Ariadne had the inner warmth of Dionysus' promise to join her in blessing the fields. She also had Phaidra's delighted blessing; most of the Athenian delegation attended the ritual and were openly approving.

The blessing of the fields was at once a joy and a disappointment. Dionysus was *there*, not only in body but in spirit. He behaved like a mischievous sprite, playing hide and seek among the vines, leaving silly tokens tangled in the leaves, and once he even kissed her—but it was not the kind of kiss after which one hurries home to bed. Despite this distraction, Ariadne forced herself to "look" for the power that came flooding into her and to try to manipulate it.

A ten-day later Ariadne had learned to pull power from her heartflower without touching any of the spells. When she was satisfied, she went to the palace and reinforced Daidalos' spells, working backward from the door of the temple to the metal gate on the stair. She told no one, in case her attempt failed, but what she had done could not remain secret from those who worked magic. The next day, Daidalos—who already looked less strained and gray—came to the shrine and asked to speak to her.

"Thank you," he said, and nodded brusquely when he was admitted to her chamber.

"For what?" Ariadne asked.

"For empowering the spells on the mage lights and locks. If you're trying to tell me you didn't do that, I can't believe you. Your touch is all through the magic. I've watched you dance many times. Do you think I can't recognize the feel and taste of your power? Let's not spar with each other. Why did you do it?"

"Because my sister was afraid the spells would fail and loose the Minotaur. She didn't want any untoward event to disturb the Athenian delegation."

"I owe you less, then, but I still owe you. Can you continue to support the spells?"

"For a time," Ariadne said.

She didn't wish to admit to Daidalos that the drain on her had been nothing and the power was fully replaced as soon as she went to stand before the dark image and ask for the Mother's blessing. Daidalos was said to be violently envious of those who might be rivals; it was hinted that the crime that had driven him from his original home was that he had thrown to his death off the walls of that city, an assistant, who equaled and might have surpassed him.

She didn't fool him on that score either. She saw the way his eyes assessed her own, the color in her cheeks, the steadiness of her hands. She had powered the spells the previous night; if she were drained, the marks should be on her. But this time he didn't challenge her. There was a hint of calculation in his expression; that was all.

"Good enough." He nodded again. "Your obligation to your sister should be over by the ides of April, as I have heard the Athenian delegation will depart then or a few days sooner. Nonetheless, I believe it will be necessary for you to hold the spells longer.

I have a project in hand that will remove the need for those safeguards, but I can't finish it soon and I'll be most grateful to you if you can help me that long."

"If Dionysus will support me that long, I'll help."

"Dionysus?" Daidalos smiled, but his eyes shifted away from hers.

Before she could reply, he quickly thanked her again for her help, repeated that he would be in her debt, and took his leave. Ariadne was mildly annoyed. Plainly Daidalos didn't believe her power came through her god; he thought Dionysus was concealing the true source from her to better hold her in thrall, but Daidalos was too envious to tell her the truth.

The irritation didn't last long because as she reviewed what the magic maker had said, curiosity took its place. A project that would eliminate the need for keeping the Minotaur locked in his apartment? But nothing could change the Minotaur's inability to control himself or increase his ability to think, so he couldn't be allowed freedom. Yet freedom was what he wanted.

Had Daidalos conceived of a compromise? Ariadne had a vision of a small house in a high-walled garden where the Minotaur could walk and see the sky and trees and flowers. He might be happy in such a place, even as the beast overtook the man. She sat up straighter. Was such a hope not reasonable? If the house were attached to his temple—and Ariadne had seen signs of work behind the temple—the king and queen could still arrange for the Minotaur's presence there. Awe of the god made flesh would still bring people and encourage the offerings. Minos and Pasiphae would lose nothing and the Bull God would be easier to manage.

She thought about the hopeful idea from time to

time, and even went one day to talk to Icarus and plead with him to suggest the notion, but she was diverted to another problem a few days later when Phaidra came to bewail the departure of the Athenian embassy. Phaidra was uneasy because they had left earlier than they planned but more bereft because with the Athenians gone she again dwindled back to the last and least daughter.

Phaidra had flourished in the sunlight of the Athenians' praise and admiration. She told Ariadne with a proud lift of her head that two of the men had been so complimentary to her about her courage in serving so fierce a god as the Minotaur that she had begun to hope they would ask to take her with them to marry their prince. But they'd been hurried away before they could make the suggestion to her father.

Whatever they desired, they couldn't take her, Ariadne had replied, automatically soothing Phaidra. There was a strict protocol for a treaty marriage. Only Ariadne didn't think the praise, which had blinded Phaidra to everything but the flattery, had anything to do with the marriage. She had a suspicion that what the Athenians wanted was to hear more of the Minotaur, and she was much afraid that Phaidra hadn't been as circumspect as she should have been in speaking of her half brother, perhaps making him worse than he was to enhance her own value.

All too soon, however, anything Phaidra had said faded into insignificance. Not four days after the departure of the Athenians, the Minotaur burst free of his confinement with an ease that made it plain no ordinary walls or doors, barred or not, could contain him.

The cause was ridiculous. As Ariadne had warned them, he asked his servant-criminals regularly when he could go out. Mostly they told him about the next time he was scheduled to visit the temple.

Occasionally he roared a protest and demanded to go now, usually to some totally unsuitable place. The only defense the servants had was to show him that they couldn't go out either.

Unfortunately one of the women who now served the Minotaur had been a courtesan; she'd been condemned for murdering several besotted clients to collect legacies they had promised her. Her first move when brought to serve the Minotaur had been to groom him, hoping he would be favorably impressed, but when she realized he regarded her no more than he regarded his combs and brushes, she transferred her attentions to the door guards, with whom she flirted each time the door was opened to admit Phaidra or a meal or for laundry to be delivered or returned.

The guards were less resistant than the Minotaur, and when she promised her experienced favors, two who were guarding the door weakened. They didn't promise her freedom, only the small change of coming out to couple with each of them. Neither expected a long lovemaking and both were sure when they let her out early one morning that no one had seen her leave and that they could get her back inside before anyone knew she had been out.

Those inside, however, all saw her depart. Her fellow prisoners made no protest; they knew she understood that they would betray her to Phaidra if she didn't provide some advantage for them, and they were content. No one thought about the Minotaur, who had eaten his usual bowl of raw meat and bread and was sitting in his chair and staring, with his head tilted to the side, at one of the pictures Ariadne had left. They knew how slow and simple his mind was; they knew he hardly remembered anything from one moment to the next. It didn't occur to any of them that the desire to go out of those rooms, to be free, went deep enough into his consciousness never to be forgotten.

The Minotaur saw the courtesan leave and stared at the door for a few moments. The servants couldn't go out. He couldn't. But the servant did go out. The Minotaur rose and went to the door.

He tapped on it lightly, as she had tapped, and said, "Out. Now out."

A manservant hurried forward. "My lord," he said, "you know we can't go out. In a little while your sister will come and open the gate to the temple."

"Saw go out," the Minotaur said. "Now go out."

The servant dared to grasp his arm. The Minotaur pushed him away. The man flew across the room and crashed into the wall, after which he lay stunned.

"Out," the Minotaur roared, and pounded on the door.

The single guard outside ran to the chamber across the corridor where his fellow had taken the courtesan. As he flung open the door, he heard behind him the sound of splintering wood. Turning, eyes and mouth wide with disbelief, he saw the bars bend and then burst apart, the lock rip out of the wood, the doors fly open. For one moment he saw the Minotaur—huge, his head less than a handspan below the lintel. By instinct he leveled his bronze-tipped spear.

The thrust the Minotaur had exerted on the doors to break the bars and the lock impelled him forward when the resistance gave way. He hardly saw the little man across the corridor, but he came up against the spear and felt a stab of pain as it slid along his side. He bellowed and swung his arm. Spear and man were swept away, but another man appeared in the doorway. The Minotaur didn't know it was a second man. To him the first had returned defiantly. He ripped away the weapon the man held, broke the shaft, and thrust the splintered wood right through the annoying creature's chest. It made a large hole from which blood poured. The Minotaur sniffed, but he wasn't hungry and cast the body away.

A shrill screech offended his keen hearing. He grasped at the sound, caught a falling body, and squeezed the thin, vibrating neck from which the noise was coming. That noise stopped but others began. In the corridor were more servant people, screaming, pushing, some striving toward him, most trying to run away. Going out?

"Out!" the Minotaur roared, and set out after those who were running, who screamed louder and retreated before him.

His stride was longer, quicker. He overtook a man, grasped him and shook him, bellowing, "Out." There was a small snapping noise and the man was limp in his hands. He threw him down, angry now, and ran to catch another.

Minos was still in his bedchamber when chaos broke out in the corridor. He looked up, frowning, to be confronted by a white-faced guard, who gasped, "The Minotaur is loose," and fled out the doors onto the portico. Minos followed him with only the slightest hesitation, but he wasn't fleeing mindlessly. He ran around the southeast house, down the slope of the hill toward the road that bridged the river. He ran easily, with the long strides and steady, deep breathing of a man who has kept up his training as a warrior. Nonetheless, Gypsades Hill tried his strength, and he was gasping as he ran through the always-open gate, past Dionysus' altar, and burst into Ariadne's chamber.

"The Minotaur is loose," he said.

CHAPTER 19

Beyond the corridor connecting Pasiphae's apartment with Minos', the living quarters of the palace were a shambles. Ariadne was aware that she should be sunk in a heap, screaming incoherently. Indeed, she was aware of a place deep inside her that was knotted tight around that screaming, that terror and horror, but for this moment she was able to command herself—and more than that, she could force closed her heartflower and seal that part of her mind that Called Dionysus.

Bodies littered the floors of the two chambers she

could see and the corridor was full of splinters from the burst bars of the door. King Minos had disappeared as soon as they entered the Minotaur's corridor and he saw the strewn bodies, but Ariadne never thought he had run off in fear. She was afraid he had gone to summon an armed troop.

She swallowed hard as the screaming rose, threatening to force its way up her throat. Would the attack rouse the Minotaur to greater fury? She wasn't certain he could be killed. There was, she feared, that much of a god in him. He'd occasionally hurt himself when he was a child, once cut himself badly when playing with a knife, and the wounds had healed miraculously, closing and sealing themselves. Dionysus said it was a result of the spell that made possible the mating of a bull's head and a man's body.

The thought of an attack made her shudder when she heard a distant noise, thinking at first it was the shouting of armed men readying to fight. Then she realized that she was hearing screams and shouts mingled with the bellowing of the Minotaur. The sound was coming toward her. Ariadne caught her breath, panicked herself until she made out that the bellows were not mindless roars of rage; the Minotaur was shouting, "Out. How out?"

She realized he must instinctively have turned away from Pasiphae's apartment, to which he had been taken as a child, followed the fleeing servants who cared for that part of the palace, and come to the dead end of the outer walls. There had been a door, but Pasiphae had had it sealed up when she moved the Minotaur there—not to keep him in, then, but to keep the curious out. At least the frustration hadn't driven him into incoherent rage. He could still speak.

"Minotaur—" she cast her voice at him. "Come to Ridne. You are lost. Minotaur, come to Ridne."

At first she thought what she said had been lost

in all the other cries, but the Minotaur was attuned to what he heard as her voice and he separated that from the terrified squawks and gasps of those who ran before him.

"Where?" he roared.

"Let those people go away," Ariadne projected. "Then I will come to you."

But even as she spoke she was walking in the direction of the diminishing noise. A weeping woman passed her and then a man staggered by, holding to the wall for support, then two more women blanched with terror but unhurt. Beyond them, Ariadne saw two men lying in the corridor, one of them in a pool of blood. They must have been struck down when the Minotaur started in that direction. And then she saw the Minotaur, saw that he carefully avoided stepping on the bodies—and his face was clean!

Relieved of the fear that the blood was from a torn-out throat, Ariadne glanced again at the fallen man and saw that he had struck his head. The Minotaur had not deliberately harmed him. She glanced behind her down the corridor with senses no longer paralyzed with horror and terror and realized that those she had at first thought were dead were mostly moving. A few were bruised and bleeding, whimpering with pain or fear, but many were unhurt, some trying to cower into the smallest space and others trying to crawl away along the walls. The carnage was mostly accidental. Ariadne put out her hand and the Minotaur took it eagerly and gently in his.

"What are you doing here, love?" she asked softly.

"Want out."

Ariadne shook her head slowly. "There's no way out from here," she said, and tears filled her eyes. Likely there was no way out anywhere now for the poor Minotaur.

He looked bewildered.

"Are you lost, love? Would you like to come with me to your chamber? It's nearly time to go to the temple, but I could tell you a story if you wish."

"Story!"

"Then come," Ariadne said, smiling as well as she could.

Minos found them in the Minotaur's apartment, the Bull God sitting meekly in his chair while Ariadne propped before him a picture of a chamber with two children playing with a ball. Ariadne caught a single glimpse of the king and behind him Daidalos, then both men ducked out of sight. She sent a brief fervent prayer of thanks to the Mother that the king had sought out the magician rather than his soldiers.

Now she glanced repeatedly at the doorway, but her voice didn't hesitate as she described what the children had done before they were allowed to play with the ball. The Minotaur liked simple stories, the simpler the better. Minos came into view again and gestured toward the iron gate that opened the stairway and passage to the temple. Ariadne found a place to put the word temple into her story. Minos put his head around the edge of the door and nodded violently.

"And when they had played with the ball for some time," Ariadne said, "a servant came—" she pointed to a vague figure in the background "—and told the children it was time to go to the temple."

"Temple?"

"Yes. Would you like to go to the temple now?"

"Where Feda?"

"Oh, Phaidra isn't coming today. She hurt her foot and must rest it. I'll open the gate for you."

He stood up at once. Ariadne spoke the command; the walls of the stair were suddenly lit with mage lights; she pushed open the gate. As soon as the Minotaur had gone through and started down the stairs, she heard Minos ordering someone behind him to run quickly to the temple and get the priests and priestesses to dance. Ariadne sat down limply and began to cry softly.

At first she paid no attention when Minos brought Daidalos into the room, but she looked up when a heated argument began and noticed Icarus, Daidalos' son, shrinking into the shadows. The king demanded that the door be replaced by a spell; the artificer, who did look pale and drawn, protested that the greatest magician in the world couldn't serve in so many ways.

Ariadne drew close and after a moment surreptitiously touched Daidalos' arm. He looked angry at the interruption, but then saw it was not Icarus, who often tried to soften his manner. Ariadne nodded infinitesimally; Daidalos caught the gesture and understood that she would empower the spell. He made some diminishing protests and then began to chant and gesture, touching the doorframe. Ariadne felt the hairs on her skin lift slightly and saw the air warp around Daidalos' hands and then appear to sink into the walls.

By the time the spell was done, those hands were trembling badly and Daidalos' mouth was set in a grim line. "I have set the spell as you demanded, King Minos, but I can't fulfill your last order. I could build what you first asked; it is mostly done, except for the roofing, but to move the whole thing underground is a work for the Lord Hades, not for a mere mortal."

"It must be so. He is too dangerous. Even the metal gates may not be strong enough. He could break free—"

"Underground?" Ariadne cried. "No. No. You can't mean to imprison the Minotaur underground. He's afraid of the dark."

"Where else can he be kept safely?" Minos asked bitterly. "Nine men and a woman are dead. My men are scouring the palace and grounds for the condemned prisoners he let free. This tale can't be kept from the people. Too many saw. Too many were hurt. I can only tell them that the queen and I were at fault for keeping him here in Crete when he wished to join his father Poseidon and the other gods. Now, I'll say, we've let him go and he won't be seen again, except when he himself pleases to come. But how else can he truly be confined, except underground?"

"In my maze," Daidalos said, and described it. "He won't break free because he'll never find a door to break, and the walls, if broken, will lead only into other passages. I tell you I can't build the underground prison you desire."

"And I'll not suffer it," Ariadne cried. "No! He didn't kill apurpose. Something drove him to burst the doors and after that what happened was accident. He pushed people out of his way. He tried to stop them and ask a question."

"Are you trying to say the Minotaur doesn't need confinement?" Minos shouted.

Ariadne closed her eyes and then opened them to look at what remained of the doors. One of the bronze hinges was bent with the force the Minotaur had applied.

"No," she sighed. "Oh no. But not underground, King Minos. What's wrong with Master Daidalos' plan to build a maze so the Minotaur can find no door to batter down? This would even be a kindness and a kind of assurance, he'll be quiet because he'll never feel caged like a beast. He won't constantly be driven to seek escape by terror of the dark nor roused to fury by being imprisoned."

Minos gnawed his lower lip, his brows knitted as he thought hard, but after a moment the expression of rage that had distorted his face began to return.

"Have mercy, King Minos," Ariadne pleaded. Tears came to her eyes and ran down her cheeks unchecked. She held her hands toward him, palms up, almost as if praying. "I beg you to remember that he's only a little boy. Don't command that his prison be built under the earth. Don't keep him in the dark." Sobs broke her voice. "Let there be little open places where the sun can come, where flowers grow. Put pictures on the walls so there's something to take his eye, to interest him. He likes pictures."

Minos turned away without replying, but his rigid stance had softened. His shoulders slumped.

"And who will change the pictures?" Daidalos muttered sourly.

"There will be no need," Ariadne whispered. "He doesn't remember. They'll be new to him each time he sees them and give him a little pleasure. He's only eight years old. . . ."

She began to cry so hard that her voice was suspended, and she covered her face, rocking a little in her grief for the child who would never grow up, who would be forever alone. A hand touched her shoulder gently.

"I'll see to the pictures myself, I promise you," Daidalos' son, Icarus, said softly.

"Eight years old . . ." Minos muttered. "I'd forgotten. It seems like eight thousand years since he was born."

"To me also," Ariadne sobbed, "and the fault is mostly the queen's. I beg you, don't punish the Minotaur because she can't be punished."

Minos stiffened. "You think she's not punished?" he asked harshly.

He loves her still, Ariadne thought, and her heart contracted with sympathy—and a little envy, too. "Perhaps she is," Ariadne said softly.

There was a sound from the corridor, which had been as silent as the tomb it had become. Two men, looking around fearfully, with guards, equally fearful, behind them, crept into the chamber across the corridor and came out carrying the limp body of the courtesan.

The king drew a deep breath and looked from Ariadne to Daidalos. "Very well," he said. "On your heads be it. You, artificer, finish your maze. You, priestess, get the beast into it and see he stays there." He walked quickly to the doorway and promptly slammed into the invisible wall.

There was a choked sound from Daidalos, but his eyes widened when he saw Minos' expression; he touched the wall and said hastily, "*Thialuo kleithron*." And then to Minos, "The door's open."

The king stalked out, and Daidalos stood staring after him, his face momentarily twisted with hatred and despair. "He thinks I'm lazy and unwilling," Daidalos said bitterly. "I'd see to it all if I had the power. I haven't. I have the art, but I haven't the power." He whipped around, turning on Ariadne. "Have you? Have you the power to seal off an open maze?"

Ariadne didn't answer, and Icarus came between them and laid his hand on his father's shoulder, steering him toward the doorway.

"One moment," Ariadne called. "To whom will the spell on the door respond? And what are the commands?"

"It's the same spell as on the temple doorway, except it has no tie with the mage lights. Do you think it so easy to invent new spells? It's not, so I'll use it again to seal off the maze. Because it was first designed that way, it will respond to Phaidra, to you, and, of course, to me. You heard the words to open. *Epikaloumai kleithron* will relock the doorway."

Daidalos and Icarus went out and Ariadne stood staring into nothing. She didn't believe she had power enough to seal the maze, but she knew where such power could be had. However, if she asked Dionysus to provide the power, he would know that the Minotaur was locked away behind it. Would he demand this time that she go to live in Olympus? And would the Mother, knowing the Minotaur was safe, release her from Knossos? Could she bear to go, to live in Dionysus' house as . . . as what?

Ariadne had never seen the Olympian reaction to Dionysus when she wasn't with him. She had no idea how isolated he was, how rejection tainted the very air around him, even with those who liked him. She told herself that in Olympus he didn't need a priestess or a Mouth. And her recurrent nightmare invaded her waking thoughts. Could she bear to see other women taken into his bed and not be allowed to touch him herself? And who would she be in Olympus? There was more of Pasiphae in Ariadne than she liked. Here in Knossos she was of importance; in Olympus—

She was happy enough to abandon those thoughts when a thump drew her attention to the invisibly blocked doorway. A guard with a stunned expression on his face was pushing his hands against nothing, and the nothing was not yielding a finger's width. Behind the guard was the surviving woman of the group that had been condemned to be the Minotaur's servants and one of the men. One new woman, an aged harridan, and two new men followed.

Ariadne walked forward and spelled the door open. In the time before the Minotaur returned, she learned from the old servants what had driven the Minotaur to burst the doors and made clear to the new what were their duties and what would befall them if they failed. They knew the terms already—service with the Minotaur or execution.

She saw the two new men eyeing the gate with scarcely concealed interest, and she laughed and continued, "I'm sure none of you will attempt to go into the temple, and I assure you the stair and passage go nowhere else. Clea," she said to the surviving female servant, "tell them what happened to the last man who thought he could escape that way."

The woman, who had abducted, tortured, and forced into prostitution many innocent girls, and who had slit the throats of her victims when they were no longer useful, paled. "The Minotaur tore off his head—and ate him," she whispered. She was known in the criminal world; the men didn't doubt her word and were infected by her fear.

Not long afterward, the Minotaur came up the stairs and into the room. Ariadne spoke the words of command; the lights went out; the gate snicked shut; no one looked toward it longingly. The new men and the woman shrank back, away from the huge figure, from the wide mouth with its unsuitable predator's fangs, but the Minotaur paid no attention to them.

"Ridne!" he exclaimed. "Where Feda?"

Ariadne sighed softly. He didn't remember that only a little time ago she had told him Phaidra had hurt her foot. She repeated the false explanation of her sister's absence.

"Ridne tell why only priests? No pro . . . pro . . . people with offerings."

For a moment Ariadne was struck mute. She could think of no way of explaining what he'd done. There was too much of a chance that he would enjoy hearing of the havoc he'd wrought. Then she realized she could use a part of the truth.

"You left your apartment," she said. "The people thought you wouldn't come to the temple, so they didn't come either."

He only shrugged, and Ariadne recalled that he'd never much liked the processions of people bringing offerings and had no awareness of their value. It was too bad that the lack of procession wouldn't combat his desire to go out, but at least she'd done no harm. Then she saw his eye fix on the open door, and he started toward it.

"Out," he said.

"No." Ariadne hurried along with him, caught his hand in hers and pressed it against the nothingness, which was smooth but hard as stone. "It's like the temple doorway. No one except Feda and Ridne can go in and out. But see, you can watch the servants and others go by in the corridor. That will be more interesting than a wooden door."

"Say something?"

Ariadne drew a breath and swallowed. "No, love, because you're a god, and they're all afraid to speak to a god."

Conversation between the Minotaur and any passers by wouldn't please Minos or Pasiphae, she thought. Anyone who spoke even a few words to him would soon realize that the poor creature was feeble-minded. Hastily, she distracted him by suggesting that it was time for a meal. Going to the doorway, she called aloud and a guard who was standing beside the wall, out of sight, responded. He went down the corridor to the room at the end where the meat was prepared.

When Ariadne had seen the Minotaur contentedly eating his dinner and the servants, silent and resigned, at their own end of the room, she rose from the stool she had been sitting on. "I must go and see how Phaidra's foot is," she said. "I told you before that she hurt her foot and could not come to you today."

The Minotaur looked up. "Love Ridne more," he said. "Ridne kiss, stroke. Ridne tell story. Story?" he asked. "Puh . . . puh-lease, story?"

She swallowed tears. It seemed all she did in his presence was cry, but soon he would be locked away.

Would she be able to tell him stories? "Bring me a picture," she said, sitting down again.

He came back with a panel showing a group of young women playing a game, and Ariadne told him that the girls had brought their washing to the water and laid it on the bushes to dry in the sun. While they waited, she said, some talked together—she pointed to three figures seated to one side—and the others played.

The Minotaur cocked his head to see the group clearly. Then he said, "Outside—" pointing to the open doorway. "Why run away? Why fall down?" He hesitated, then added, "Minotaur ugly."

"No," Ariadne cried, jumping up and silently cursing his erratic and faulty memory that always brought back the wrong thing. "No, you aren't ugly. You're different from other men, but in your own way you're very beautiful, Minotaur. You are also very large and your voice is very loud. People are afraid. If you stand still and talk softly, as you do to me . . ."

However, she couldn't promise him anyone would talk to him or that they wouldn't run away, even with the magic gate between them. Too many knew of the dead and injured. The terrible tragedy of his life rose up and almost overwhelmed her. But for his sake she swallowed down the lump in her throat and fought her tears, leaning forward and pressing her lips to his forehead between the horns, stroking his fur.

"I must go now, Minotaur," she managed to say, and for fear he would hear her, didn't permit herself to weep aloud until she was well up Gypsades Hill.

She was still weeping when Dionysus appeared as usual to share his evening meal with her. He stopped, shocked by her appearance. Her eyes were swollen nearly shut and her sobs were hoarse with exhaustion. He didn't ask her what was wrong, only hurried across the room to her, took her in his arms, and held her.

"The Minotaur broke loose this morning," she said, hiccuping a little and resting wearily against his shoulder.

The whole tale followed: the Minotaur's desire to be free of his apartment, the courtesan's seduction of the guards, his breaking open the doors.

"They were double barred with beams a handspan thick, and he burst them into splinters and bent the bronze hinges. He killed nine men and a woman, most by accident because he grasped them too hard to stop them from running away or because he pushed them so hard they broke against a wall. To still the cry of monster and false god, my father is putting out the tale that the Bull God resented the oaths that bound him to Knossos and wreaked this havoc as a punishment for being held here against his will."

"So he's to be imprisoned more securely," Dionysus said, with a flash of the uncanny perception that came to him even when he had no Vision. He shivered. He needed to run free himself and understood. "Poor creature."

"I should have done what you bade me! I should have stopped his heart when he was first born," she cried, and began to weep again.

He shook his head, stroked her hair. "I think now it wouldn't have worked. I think She—" he gestured with his head to the wall behind which the dark image stood "—wouldn't have let him die." Her sobs eased and he smiled at her. "So what's decided? I won't have you weeping forever. You get me all damp. If I can make his fate easier, I will."

Ariadne sat up straighter, hope rising. If Dionysus would power Daidalos' spells, the open maze would be possible. The silver mist had brought her knowledge of his own horror of confinement, so she told him of her father's plan to make the prison underground and how Daidalos offered instead a maze.

Because Dionysus' horror only increased at the thought of being trapped in a maze, Ariadne said gently, "For the Minotaur, that would be wonderful. He hardly can remember anything, so each time he goes 'outside' it will be new to him and he can wander about until he finds a garden. But Daidalos hasn't the power to seal it, so it will have to be roofed and it will be dark and no flowers will grow . . ."

"Seal it?"

She explained what Daidalos had described and begun building: at the center, two chambers, exactly like the ones the Minotaur had now. Likely he would never know he'd been moved. These would have, as they had now, two exits, but instead of being closed to imprison him, the doorways would open into passages that would loop and intersect. A few of these would be real, but most would be illusions. The illusions would lead either back to his apartment or to one of the small gardens to the right and left of his rooms.

"He'll be happy there," Ariadne insisted. She sighed. "His mind is failing more and more. A few places would be enlarged into rough chambers and roofed as shelter from the rain, but all the rest would be open to the sky. He'll never know he's bound to a maze. And while he can still remember anything, he'll be able to go to the temple. There will be a passage, looking like the one he now uses, only much shorter, that will be hidden by an illusion which can be dispelled. To him there will be infinite variety."

Dionysus nodded slowly. "A beast wouldn't realize he was imprisoned in such a place. Even the little fauns I keep in my garden—they aren't very clever—would probably be content."

"Daidalos says that the illusions don't use much

power. They can be renewed at intervals, perhaps once a month. The problem is that the Minotaur is still growing. The Mother alone knows whether he'll some day top the walls. There must be a seal over them, but such seals take more power than Daidalos can provide. I can do the doors and the lights now, but I don't think I have enough strength to seal the maze."

"Not if you must support Daidalos' spell. That's a poor, clumsy thing." He fell silent, frowning slightly, then said slowly, "Hekate could weave a spell and bind it to the very earth . . ." He fell silent, his brow furrowed.

"Oh, I know you don't want to ask her because she's done so much for you already," Ariadne said. "And it would seem coarse and ugly to ask a favor right after going so far to help her. But would she listen to me if I prayed to her? Sacrificed to her? Would she pity my poor brother?"

"I have no idea," Dionysus said. "Hekate is *very* strange. I've known her since I was a young boy, but I *don't* know her. She kept me sane when I was tormented by Visions, so many and so close together that I lost touch with what was real and what was Seeing. And she came all the way back to fetch me after she had arrived at Olympus and discovered I was Zeus's son. But I have no idea why."

Ariadne smiled although a bitter pang pierced her chest. "Because she loves you, Dionysus."

"Oh no," he said. "She loves only the black dog Kabeiros. More likely she brought me here to torment Zeus. But I don't know why she would wish to do that; she's not one to torment others, although sometimes she laughs at things that make my blood run cold. Still, Hekate knows a magic that's beyond Olympian Gifts. I don't mind asking her to help us. That's not why I hesitated. I was just trying to think of a way to catch her interest."

By then the hope that Dionysus had given her and her own conviction that the Minotaur would be better off in the maze than imprisoned in his two rooms had restored Ariadne. She went and washed her face, ordered a meal to be brought, and combed her hair. As she smoothed the locks of consecration around her finger, she felt someone pat her back as if encouraging her. She spun about, thinking Dionysus had come into the bedchamber and hoping that pity had at last spurred him to comfort her with love—but there was no one there.

Ariadne put down the comb and went to stand before the statue. "I try to obey," she whispered, "but it's very hard not to grieve for my poor brother's pain."

The dark face had no features now, bare shadows for eyes and nose that provided no hint of expression. Ariadne bowed her head and turned away. One might importune an Olympian, but the Mother already knew what Her votary wanted and what was truly needed—not always the same. Ariadne knew she could only wait and accept.

CHAPTER 20

What Dionysus said to Hekate, or, indeed, if he said anything, Ariadne never knew. She had shared her evening meal with him, but had scarcely been able to eat because she was so exhausted by emotion. Then she had fallen asleep on the sofa right in the middle of a discussion of whether it would be best for her to find a crossroad and pray—there were no temples to Hekate—or best for Dionysus to approach her directly and simply ask for her help.

She woke with her skin tingling and the hairs trying to rise on her nape, aware that someone had "leapt" into her room. Eyes wide, she sat up. She was still on the couch, covered now with a large shawl against the chill air of the night. Directly before her stood a tall woman illuminated by a mage light that hung between them. Beside her was a huge, a man-sized, black dog with white eyes.

"Hekate," Ariadne breathed, for they had met briefly before. Then she bit her lip, stung suddenly by jealousy.

Hekate might not love Dionysus, but it wasn't at all impossible that Dionysus loved Hekate. She was a beautiful creature, almost as tall as he, with skin as milk-white, and eyes of a strange silver-blue, all framed in dark hair that showed reddish glints where the mage light struck it. And she could never be called a child, which he called Ariadne; Hekate's face and body were those of a woman in the full prime of life, old enough to be well experienced but young enough to enjoy living fully. Must she owe the Minotaur's comfort to this woman who doubtless had what she wanted from Dionysus?

"Yes, Hekate. And this is my black dog, Kabeiros."

Unwilling to look into Hekate's beautiful face, Ariadne looked down at the dog. The white eyes were dead and could show nothing, but there was something strange about the dog's face, some shading in the fur or wrinkling of the skin that shadowed beneath it the face of a man. If the Minotaur was dropping back into a beast, this beast was surely growing into a human. Was it worse to be a beast trapped in a human body and expected to behave as a man or to be a man trapped in the body of a beast?

"Greetings, Kabeiros," she said, putting out her hand.

Then, at last, she lifted her eyes to Hekate's and took a sharp little breath of surprise. Before her was an ancient crone, skin wrinkled like a winter apple, nose hooked, mouth sunken, with thin, straggling white hair. Her bent body made a travesty of the elegant gown that had graced the woman's form. But the eyes were the same, the same bright silver-blue—and, Ariadne's breath again sucked in with surprise, the eyes were those of a child, young as morning, twinkling with mischief, expecting joy.

"So you've seen what Kabeiros is and know why I've come to help you," the crone said, smiling. "You're all that Dionysus said you were—" and became a blonde girl, barely nubile, laughing aloud "—except for being so foolish as to be jealous of me. He doesn't desire me and never has."

"Nor does he desire me," Ariadne said, sighing, and rose from the couch and bowed. The black dog came over and nudged her gently. She looked down. "I don't know which is more terrible, your state or my poor brother's. If only I could be sure that the child in him would fade totally into the beast and not know, he wouldn't wring my heart so much, but he has times of human knowing. He desires freedom and wants company, asks to hear stories . . ." She bit her lip. There was no purpose in beginning to weep again.

"I wish I could tell you," Hekate said, "but I can't. I don't know what Poseidon did. It only seemed to me that the stasis between the beast's head and the man's body couldn't be maintained forever without reinforcement."

Ariadne had looked up when Hekate spoke, and the beautiful woman was there. Ariadne, oddly, felt no surprise and her mind clung to the Minotaur's fate.

"What will happen to him?" she asked.

Hekate shook her head. "I don't know that either, but I believe if the spell fails the Minotaur will die."

"I don't know what to feel," Ariadne whispered.

Hekate raised curved black brows. "No matter what happens you're the kind to feel guilt over it. I can't help your nature." Then she smiled slightly. "And you are *very* young, even younger than that fool Dionysus. Still Dionysus is quite correct; you have too tender a heart. I can at least save you from feeling sorry for Kabeiros, who greatly enjoys the attention and sympathy he gets from such innocents as recognize what he is and don't know any more about him."

On the words, the black dog nudged Ariadne again and let his tongue loll out of his mouth so that she knew he was laughing. Faintly, Ariadne smiled.

"Likely you're right and I make most of my grief for myself, but you did say, didn't you, Lady Hekate, that you had come to help my poor brother?"

She laughed. "Adept at getting your own way, aren't you? But, yes. I said I would help." For a moment the bright silver eyes misted. "Poseidon shouldn't have done what he did. He is arrogant, and even more careless than Zeus. The Minotaur is innocent—as innocent as my black dog, who has also killed—and should live, as long as he does live, free of torment."

"And he's only a little boy, only eight years old," Ariadne said.

Hekate nodded. "Tell your magician to build his maze as best he can but to put no magic in it. When it's finished, I'll bespell it, add the illusions, and lock into it the earth-power that stirs your land. The illusions and the seal will hold until the earth shakes enough to bring down Knossos. You and your sister Phaidra will be bound into the spell, and I'll give or send you the words of command."

"Oh, thank—" Ariadne began, but before she could finish Hekate and the black dog were gone.

Ariadne breathed a tremendous sigh of relief and realized she was starving. She started forward to order food and almost overturned the table on which Dionysus' meal had been set. Most was still there but when she reached for the cheese, her fingers would not grip. Surprised, because Dionysus was not usually of a saving or particularly thoughtful nature, she realized he had put a stasis on the platter to keep it fresh. He was learning to care. She murmured *Thialuo stasis* and began to eat.

The Minotaur would have his maze, and Ariadne didn't doubt for a moment that if Hekate spun the illusions, they would not only be perfect but pleasant for him. She chewed slowly, thinking that Hekate wasn't so strange. Perhaps she was strange to the Olympians because they were prone to express anything they thought or felt and she didn't. She had a strong sense of what was just also, Ariadne decided; her lips twisted wryly—that would certainly be strange to the Olympians. And just possibly, Ariadne thought, Hekate spoke so sharply about the foolishness of having a tender heart because she was afflicted in the same way.

A pleasant idea but with nothing much to support it. Ariadne could only hope that Hekate wasn't as careless of her promises as many Olympians were and would, indeed, bespell the maze. But there was nothing she could do about that now; the construction had many ten-days to go before it was complete. She would have to watch that construction; Icarus couldn't always induce Daidalos to do as he had promised, but now that "she" was providing the power, Ariadne would have a right to an opinion. And she must go to Phaidra tomorrow, explain what had happened, make her understand that most of the deaths and injuries were accidents, and the Minotaur was no fiercer than he had been all along.

To Ariadne's surprise, Phaidra only nodded and shrugged over her explanations of the Minotaur's behavior—and that was, it seemed, an omen. After all the fear and horror, everything was so much easier than Ariadne had even hoped that she grew increasingly anxious, which made Dionysus laugh at her. Surely if something was going to go wrong, he teased, he would have been cursed with a Seeing.

Ariadne hoped he was right, but it made her uneasy that the Minotaur should be on his best behavior, Phaidra should have resumed her duties without any protest, and behind an outer wall that enclosed the precincts of the Bull God's temple and then stretched backward to the base of the palace, Daidalos should be building his maze without problems or interruptions.

One ten-day passed, a second, a third began. On the tenth day of the end of spring, King Minos made ready the tokens that would confirm his arrangements for the Athenian treaty. He also chose golden necklets and armbands for the king and the prince, ordered pithoi of wine and oil to be prepared, provided a beautifully carved and gilded box for the magnificent robe Phaidra had sewn for Theseus, and gathered an embassy of high-born courtiers to be led by his own eldest son and heir, Androgeos. The finest warship of the Cretan fleet took the embassy aboard and set sail.

Phaidra was full of the departure, full of hope that after the summer solstice the Athenians would return—perhaps Theseus himself would come—to perform the ritual of marriage and take her back with them to Athens. She fretted over whether her father had offered enough in the way of bride goods, although, of course, the treaty was the primary benefit of the marriage. Ariadne listened with half an ear. The good progress of the maze, the calmness of the Minotaur, and Phaidra's good spirits left her too much time to dwell on her private frustrations and dissatisfactions.

Although Phaidra's hopes and fears weren't enough to hold her mind—or perhaps too close to her own desires to distract her, she wasn't unwilling to bury her problems in concern about moving the Minotaur. Only there was no need for concern. On the day chosen he changed quarters easily. Daidalos concealed the usual passage with an illusion, and when the Minotaur came out of the back door of the temple, he simply walked into the passage that led to the maze. He did stop and stare ahead, though, when he saw the gate to what he thought was his bedchamber.

"Oh, there you are, Minotaur," Ariadne called, opening the gate, "I've come to visit you today."

He hurried toward her, but when he entered the room, his broad nostrils spread and fluttered with his breath and his eyes glanced around suspiciously. More beast than man, Ariadne thought; he smells the difference. Fortunately he asked the simplest question.

"Where stair?"

"King Minos changed the way to the temple," Ariadne replied with perfect truth. "Does it matter to you?"

The brow between the horns furrowed. Ariadne hurried to distract him from a question too complex for him and likely to make him angry. "Come through and see what else King Minos has arranged for you," she said. "Now you can go out."

"Out? Ridne take out?"

"You don't need Ridne to go out," she said, taking his hand. "You can go out all by yourself."

He hurried through the sitting room and to the open door, where he put his free hand out, expecting to meet resistance. The hand went through.

"Open!" he exclaimed. "Ridne make open?"

"No, it will always be open," Ariadne said gently, and then silently in her mind, *Anoikodomo apate*.

Unaware of the illusion closing around him, the Minotaur hurried out into the corridor with Ariadne following behind. After a time his steps slowed when he found nothing but more corridor, but before he could strike the wall or vent his disappointment in any other way, a cross corridor, much more brightly lit—by the open sky, in fact—appeared.

He turned toward the light, staring up at the sky open-mouthed when he entered the new corridor. After that he walked more slowly, with more patience, looking up every few steps and once even sitting down and just staring up at the clouds that moved over the blue vault. Eventually he came to one of the gardens.

Ariadne wondered what he would do, but for a time he just stared. Since the maze had been decided upon as his place of confinement, Ariadne had found pictures of gardens and told him about them, about how the flowers grew and could be killed and broken if they were torn up or trampled upon. She had no idea whether he would remember, but it seemed that something had stuck in his mind because he touched the plants quite gently, then sat down again and stared around.

He spent nearly the whole remainder of the day in the garden looking at it and the sky and going from one spot to another. As the light began to dim, however, he pulled off the head of a flower, put it in his mouth, and chewed. It was spat out more quickly than it went in, and he got to his feet and roared, "Food," then looked around for a servant with his bowl.

"Not in the garden," Ariadne said, walking into his line of sight. "Come with me. We'll go back to your room and your dinner will be brought to you there."

To Ariadne's surprise, he hesitated, looking intently at her. "Come out again?" he asked.

"Yes, of course," she said. "You can come out any time now. King Minos has arranged this new dwelling for you."

"Good. Eat soon. Love Ridne. Not hurt."

Metakino apate, Ariadne thought, and noticed that three of the five paths out of the garden disappeared. She put out her hand and the Minotaur took it. This time when he came close, she realized he had grown even larger. Her head barely rose above his waist now.

"Eat soon," he said.

The repetition bothered Ariadne, but the uncomfortable feeling was dissipated by arriving at the outer chamber of the apartment and finding Phaidra waiting there, her expression anxious. The Minotaur rushed to his bowl of meat and began to stuff pieces in his mouth.

"What in the world happened to you?" Phaidra asked. "I've been waiting since before sunset. I was afraid the maze wouldn't respond to your command and you were lost."

"No, no. I'm sure this maze will never fail in any way," Ariadne assured her sister. "The Minotaur was enchanted by the garden and the clouds in the sky. He watched and watched and I didn't want to spoil his pleasure."

"I heard him yell for food. You couldn't have been very far away, but when I set out to find you there were only endless corridors. Then suddenly I looked around to see if I should try to go back—and I was about fifty paces from the door of this chamber. Daidalos has outdone himself with this illusion. But let's leave quickly, before the Minotaur finishes eating and wants stories or me to comb him."

Ariadne nodded and the two women slipped out. She dismissed the illusion; that made no immediate change in the passageway, which turned sharply left, then right and left again, blocking any view of its continuation. Naked of illusion, the corridor, after those two turns, led directly to the bronze gate which yielded to Phaidra's touch and opened into the lowest floor of the palace.

Their ways parted at that point. Before they parted, however, Ariadne touched her sister's arm. "I think," she said, "that you'd better arrange for the Minotaur to have as much food in the morning as is provided for his afternoon meal. If he goes out into the maze soon after he wakes and loses himself there or in one of the gardens, he might get very hungry before he can find his way back."

"If he's hungry he'll come back sooner," Phaidra said impatiently.

"Not if he can't find his way," Ariadne pointed out. "That's one thing we forgot about. He wouldn't harm you or me—and, of course, if you were carrying his food you could just hand it to him—but if he should be very hungry and meet one of his servants wandering in the maze . . ."

Phaidra shuddered. "I'll make sure plenty of meat is provided. And we can leave bowls of bread in the gardens. And I'll warn the servants not to go into the maze."

The precautions were taken, but in vain. For one thing, the warning Phaidra gave the servants was ignored. They believed themselves clever, having evaded the normal rules of society for some time, and were convinced that they could defeat the maze even if the feeble-minded Minotaur couldn't.

Four days later, one of the new men was gone. The others didn't report him missing; they were sure that he'd found a way out and escaped. Thus on the Mother's day, when she danced her thanks for the richness of the summer growth and her hope that the Mother's favor would be continued to a fine harvest, Ariadne didn't know the Minotaur had killed again.

Her own offering of dance and music was accepted, she knew that; her hair floated around her, supporting body and spirit, the golden ribbons wrapped her warmly and strengthened her. Nonetheless, Ariadne felt peculiar, as if—chief votary as she was and representative of all the people of Crete—a good part of the Mother's attention was directed elsewhere. If so, she thought, resting after a particularly lively interchange with the chorus, the Mother's attention should be directed to the avatar, Pasiphae, but that hardly seemed possible. In fact, to Ariadne's eyes and perceptions, the Mother had withdrawn herself completely from the queen. Although Pasiphae had sung the part of the goddess faultlessly, as she had for many years, there was no life in her voice and no sense in her eyes.

Ariadne was frightened at first, thinking that Minos had for some reason confined his wife and set a simulacrum created by Daidalos in her place. Very shortly, however, she realized that whatever had happened, Minos was guiltless. He was as troubled as she, and several times touched Pasiphae surreptitiously, as if trying to recall her to herself.

All through the dance Ariadne watched the queen and slowly made out that Pasiphae's expression was a sullen rebellious denial of pain. It wasn't the Mother who was withholding Herself, but Pasiphae who wouldn't accept what was offered, seeking within herself for the power, the god-force that she didn't have. Ariadne watched her growing greyer and more frozen, thinking that if she didn't soon open herself, she would die.

Oddly, the spectators didn't appear to have noticed the gray pallor and frozen expression or that Pasiphae had sung her part in a voice that might have come from the grave. They left the dancing court in the best of spirits, talking lightly of the ceremony, of Ariadne's grace as a dancer, of Sappho's leadership of the chorus, of the favor of the Mother to Crete.

In another group that passed her, one man said that life had been very good since the coming of the Bull God, another nodded, but a third muttered something about the heavy demand for offerings, and a fourth, who didn't speak, shuddered. She wished at that moment she had Dionysus' ability to make herself invisible. She would have liked to follow the men and hear what they thought, expressed freely in trusted company, but she didn't know the spell, she was tired, and, thinking again, wondered if she really did want to know.

Was this a deliberate blindness visited on the people to hide from them their impending fate? Had the Mother withdrawn her favor from Crete? Not from herself, she didn't fear that for she recognized that she hadn't been scanted in the Mother's giving of help or power, but Pasiphae hadn't drawn the goddess's being into herself. Would some great evil befall them? Reaching the shrine, Ariadne passed right by the food set out for her and went to huddle in her bed.

The day after the ritual, although Ariadne didn't hear about it for another five days, the Minotaur killed again. That evening the old woman, who had replaced the courtesan and because she was cleverer than the others had escaped retribution longer, noted that when he did return, the Minotaur only picked idly at the meat in his bowl. The next day, he wasn't hungry either, and the day after that Phaidra asked pointed questions about the leftover meat and the two missing men.

The old woman caught her breath. Two and two had just come together in her mind. Clea and the remaining man made glib excuses. The man she hadn't seen for five days spent most of his time in the gardens; the other had gone out to look for the Minotaur to tell him it was time to eat. Phaidra didn't believe them, but she said nothing. When the Minotaur wasn't there to protect her, she had a fear that the criminals might attack her and try to hold her hostage.

Neither of the missing men was in the Minotaur's apartment when Phaidra again brought food. She didn't ask for them, but went out at once, reinvoking the illusion as soon as she stepped out of the door and only removing it after she had made the left and right turns that she knew were real. Even so, she found herself in a cross corridor and had to retrace her steps before she could get onto the direct path.

Angry and frightened enough to forget for a little while the expected return of Androgeos with the confirmation of the treaty and her marriage, Phaidra didn't return directly to her room to work on her Athenian gowns. Instead she went up Gypsades Hill to the shrine and told Ariadne that two of the prisoners had escaped.

"Don't be silly, Phaidra," Ariadne said. "No one can thread that maze, and even if one of the men came by chance upon the gate to the palace or to the temple, those are magic locked and he couldn't open them."

"Who says he couldn't? You and I can unlock those gates with a touch of a finger, why shouldn't one of those criminals know magic?"

"Magic wasn't a crime listed against any of them."

Ariadne's voice was now uncertain. Although she didn't believe any ordinary human magic could break Hekate's illusions, a man might have come upon a gate by accident. The gate locks weren't Hekate's spells but Daidalos', and those another magician could undo. And then she thought that one man might reach a gate by chance, but two? Could Hekate have overlooked something?

She raised the question to Dionysus that evening

and he didn't reject her doubt out of hand. "Not overlooked in an ordinary way," he said. "But sometimes with such a complex spell, or maybe two or three spells working together, an added bit of magic of a different kind could disrupt the illusion. Still, two men? Both able to do magic that would negate a spell of Hekate's?" He hesitated and sighed. "There's another explanation, a simpler one."

Ariadne remembered how the Minotaur had looked at her and repeated, "Eat soon," and her back went cold. She whispered, "I'll have to go and look tomorrow."

"No. I think we should both go tonight. When they're all asleep, you can release the illusion. Then we'll have time to look for the lost men, and I think with most of the power gone from Hekate's spell that I'll be able to tell if anyone has meddled with the locking spells on the gate."

Dionysus found the lock to the back of the temple unchanged; no one but Ariadne had ever touched it. They never bothered to check the lock that led to the palace because they found the bodies of the missing men in one of the roofed shelters. Both had been dismembered and partly eaten, but Dionysus assured Ariadne, who was so sick and weak that he had to support her, that both had been killed quickly and mercifully. One had been strangled and the other dispatched with a blow to the head that had smashed his skull.

"They were condemned to die for horrible crimes," he said, "and caught trying to escape. You weren't troubled by the fact that the soldiers killed the others that tried to escape. These men's deaths were no worse than if they'd been executed by the double axe. Those driven out onto the hills for the maenads to sacrifice don't die so easily."

"But I've seen these men," Ariadne breathed,

burying her face in Dionysus' tunic. "And he *ate* them."

"He's a beast . . . mostly," Dionysus said indifferently. "He was hungry and man's flesh is soft and sweet."

Ariadne shuddered in his arms but didn't withdraw from them. "You too?"

Dionysus laughed. "Not by custom, but Hekate's father began a cult . . . Never mind that. It's ended now." He gave Ariadne a rough hug. "You stay here. I'll take the remains of these and leave them just outside the door of the Minotaur's rooms. The servants will know the men didn't escape and they won't go into the maze again. Since they'll have food to offer the Minotaur whenever he returns to his chambers, he isn't likely to attack them there."

The words were very comforting—especially after the mangled bodies were gone, and Ariadne found her horror diminishing as she waited. When Dionysus returned, they left the maze the way they had entered it, Ariadne reinvoking the spell from outside the gate. By the time they reached the shrine, she had recovered completely, and she wondered wryly whether she would soon grow accustomed and not care at all.

Still, the memory was not pleasant, and she said, "Thank you, my love. I've no idea what I would've done if I had been alone. Stood and screamed like an idiot, I suppose."

The moon was out and silvered her black hair, carved dark shadows into her face. She laid her hand on Dionysus' arm and stroked the fine, gold hair. He drew in his breath and pulled her tight against him.

"Say 'enough' then, and come with me to Olympus. I'll arrange for someone else to hold the key to the illusions of the maze and see that the bull-head is fed. He's as happy as he ever will be. There's no more you can do. Sooner or later the spell Poseidon wove will come apart and he'll die."

"Yes," Ariadne sighed, pressing herself against him, aware of his warmth, of the thrust of his shaft against her belly. "Let me see my sister Phaidra married to Theseus and safe in her own home and I will come . . . But Dionysus—"

Before she could finish, he had thrust her away and disappeared.

Her plaintive, "Why won't you love me?" remained a thin whisper in the air.

Ariadne slept very little that night but, struggling to find something, anything, besides Dionysus' rejection to think about, she discovered the need to tell King Minos that two more servants had been killed. In the morning, she sent one of the boys, grown from novice to acolyte, to request a private audience and was received promptly. The news she brought evoked very little reaction.

Minos, whose mind was plainly elsewhere, was only mildly annoyed when she described how she and Dionysus had found the missing men. "So long as this news does not get out," he said. "I will arrange for two more servants to be delivered to him. But he cannot go on killing them at this rate. I doubt there are more than two or three more condemned criminals being held for execution."

"There's nothing *I* can do to stop him," Ariadne pointed out sharply, then sighed. "I doubt there will be any more deaths soon," she added, and explained that the servants had thought they were clever enough to defeat the maze and escape. Instead the Minotaur had caught them. "Either he was hungry at the moment, or he simply felt they were intruders—as he did with the man who tried to escape through his temple—and got hungry later."

Minos swallowed. "Hungry . . ." he repeated barely above a whisper. "You don't seem to care."

"He's only a beast, poor creature," Ariadne replied. "You called him a god and taught him he could do what he liked. You didn't train him to respect humans. I've done what I could, but it wasn't enough. Why should I blame him now for being what he is?"

The king made a dismissive gesture. "Is he so far gone that he can't be shown in the temple in the next day or two? I expect the return of the Athenian delegation very soon now, and it would be well if they heard that the god has gone to his own place, but did once manifest himself in his temple." Then he looked at Ariadne's face and added hastily, "It's for Phaidra's sake, too. I don't want anything to cast a shadow that will interfere with her marriage to Theseus."

Ariadne doubted that Phaidra's marriage actually counted for much with her father—he was interested only in binding the Athenians—but the marriage was important to Ariadne. "Possibly I could get him to the temple," she said, "but he won't stay if there's nothing to amuse him."

"That's no problem. Since the god departed, I've arranged for many more priests and priestesses to be inducted. There's no time, day or night, when a group isn't dancing before the empty throne chair."

"Very well," she agreed.

She fulfilled that promise later in the morning, when she escorted two guards and two men with their hands bound through the maze. Before she left the men with the living servants, she showed them the gnawed bones not far from the entrance and told them what had happened to those who thought they could escape.

Having seen the guards out the gate, she sought the Minotaur. He wasn't in either of the gardens, which troubled her. Wondering sickly whether he was looking for what he had left there, she started toward the shelter where she and Dionysus had found the bodies, but was spared that horror only to be confronted by another. When she came across the Minotaur, looking at a picture, he heard her footsteps and was upon her with a leap, his fist raised to strike.

"Minotaur!" she cried. "I am Ridne!"

The hand fell to his side then reached for her, slowly, tentatively. "Ridne?" he said.

Ariadne gulped air and pressed a hand against her chest where her heart was beating as if it would break through the flesh. The passage seemed to grow darker and she grasped the hand that barely touched her, afraid if she didn't hold onto something for support, she would fall.

"Yes, Ridne," she insisted, then asked, "Are you hungry?"

"No eat Ridne," he said. "Love Ridne."

"And Ridne loves you." Had he almost killed her, she wondered? Was Phaidra, coming each day with food, in danger? "Why did you want to strike me, Minotaur?" she asked.

He tilted his head to see her more clearly. "Mine," he said and gestured.

"The maze is yours, and no one else must walk in it?" she asked.

"Mine," he repeated nodding.

He dropped her hand and turned away then, as if he would leave her. Ariadne's blood ran cold. Asterion as a child, the Minotaur later, had always clung to her. She tried to find her voice to bid him wait, but fortunately his eye fell on the picture he had been looking at when Ariadne found him. He turned back.

"Picture," he said.

Minos wanted the Minotaur in the temple once

more before the Athenians came. If that would influence them to confirm the marriage to Phaidra and free her from this duty, Ariadne thought, it had better be this very day. The Minotaur was changing too fast to waste any time.

"Oh, yes, I know that picture," she said, moving to stand before it. "You see how well dressed the people are. They have jeweled headdresses and are wearing their best gowns. They are going to the temple to bring offerings to the Bull God. Would you like to go to the temple, Minotaur?

"Temple?" The word was more question than recognition, but after another moment, he said, "Temple. Priests dance."

"Yes. The priests dance for you. Would you like to see them?"

"Temple," he said. "Where?"

"I know the way," Ariadne said, holding out the hand he had dropped, and he took it and went with her.

From the shadows behind the back entrance, Ariadne watched the Minotaur take his place on the massive throne that had been built for him. When he appeared, a loud shout went up from the priests and priestesses and runners came out of the buildings that had been erected to either side of the temple to house those that served. The dancing and singing went on with renewed fervor and soon Ariadne saw that worshipers were gathering and entering the shrine. Good enough, she thought, word of the Bull God's reappearance will spread.

It was not good enough, however. On the last day of the month Ariadne learned that nothing would have been good enough. Phaidra came, tear smeared and with disheveled hair, to tell her that a ten-day before then, on the very day of the Mother's ritual when Ariadne had sensed that something was wrong, a band of Athenians had fallen upon and killed Androgeos.

It was pure treachery, Phaidra wept, all the talk of how King Aigeus welcomed the treaty and that Theseus was eager to marry her, all treachery even to the last moment. Androgeos had been all unarmed and suspected nothing, having been warmly received by the king and his son. The attackers had cried aloud that he was a worshiper of a false god, an eater of man's flesh, and that all Cretans were cannibal monsters.

Stricken, for Androgeos had been her favorite brother, Ariadne accompanied Phaidra back to the palace to mourn with her family. She found little comfort there. Minos was in a towering rage, in which his grief for his son was totally submerged. He had withdrawn, as was proper, from the public rooms to his private chamber, but instead of sitting with his other sons and daughters and speaking of Androgeos to those who came to offer condolences, he had called in the master of his armies and the chief of the ships' captains and was giving orders to make ready for war.

Beside him Pasiphae sat silent, offering nothing. Looking at her, Ariadne wondered again if the queen was fully alive, until turning to look for a clerk, Minos noticed her.

"You fool!" he snarled. "You brought this on us. Even after the whole world saw the Minotaur for what he was, Poseidon's curse, you had to challenge the *Mother*."

Then Pasiphae came alive and turned on her husband, crying. "You were at fault, greedy for that accursed bull. If you'd sacrificed it as you promised, I wouldn't have been driven mad by Poseidon. And why accuse me now of challenging the Mother? You hoped I'd win, didn't you? And thought at worst *I* would be the one to suffer her wrath if I failed."

"My fault?" Minos bellowed. "It's yours and yours alone! You agreed about keeping the bull. You said you had no sign from the Mother against it. All this had nothing to do with the bull from the sea. It was all you and your pride! You were too proud to be priestess of one you called a little godling, but when Dionysus answered Ariadne's Call, you had to Call a greater god. Poseidon was satisfied with my three bulls until you troubled him with your lust."

"And what of me?" Phaidra wailed. "Who's suffered most from that accursed Minotaur? Who's fed him and cleaned him—and now my last chance for a marriage is gone. Who will have me, tainted with attendance on a false god?"

"Selfish little beast," Pasiphae shrieked. "You've lost a nothing marriage. I've lost the chance to be a goddess."

As the words left her lips, Pasiphae seemed to hear them and understand what she'd said. Under the paint that subtly enhanced her beauty, she turned gray-white.

"Lost . . . Lost . . ." the queen whimpered, crumpling in on herself and sliding from her seat.

Choking on sobs of mingled grief and horror, Ariadne fled.

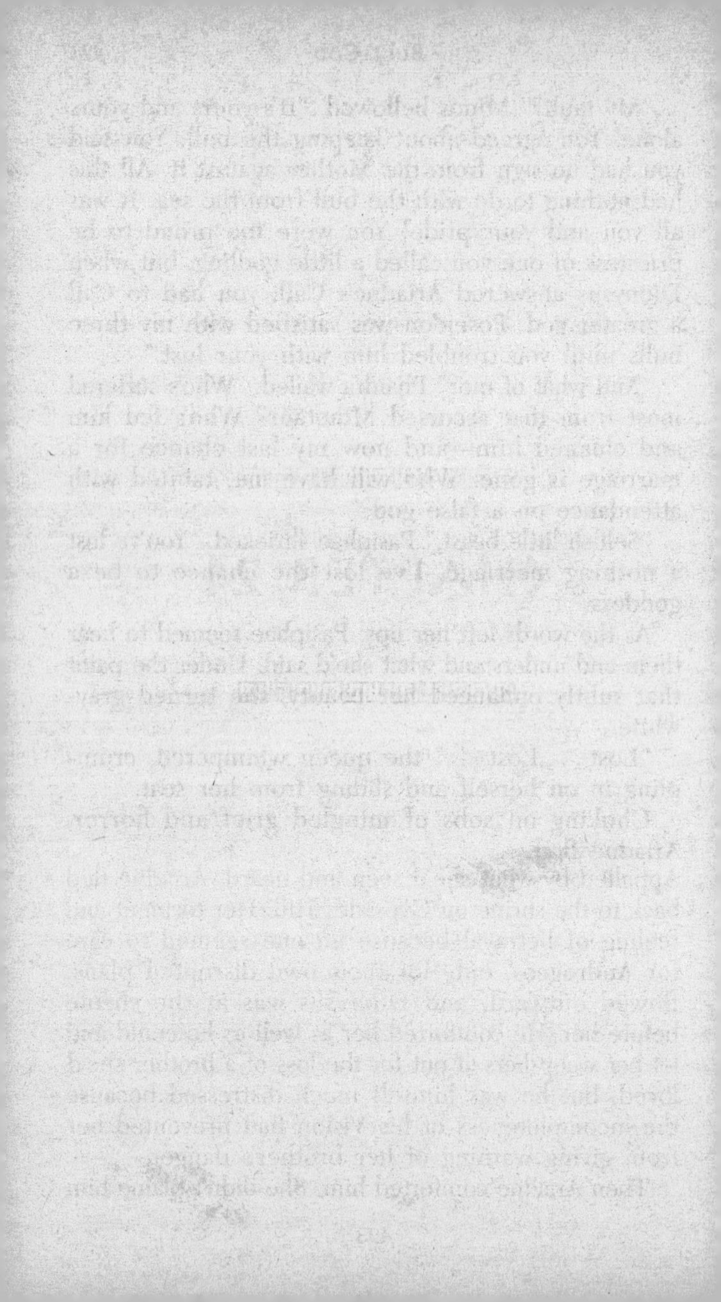

"My fault?" Minos bellowed. [illegible]

[illegible]

"And pride of me?" Pasiphae wailed. [illegible] [illegible] and now my last chance for a [illegible] is gone. Who will have me, tainted with [illegible] on a false god."

[illegible] little beast," Pasiphae [illegible]. [illegible] I've lost the chance to be a goddess."

As the words left her lips Pasiphae seemed to hear them and understand what each said. Under the paint that subtly enhanced her beauty, she turned grey-white.

"Lost . . . Lost," the queen whimpered, crumpling in on herself and sliding from her seat.

Choking on sobs of mingled grief and terror, [illegible]

[illegible]

CHAPTER 21

Appalled by what she'd seen and heard, Ariadne fled back to the shrine on Gypsades Hill. Her torment and feeling of betrayal because no one seemed to care for Androgeos, only for their own disrupted plans, flowed outward, and Dionysus was at the shrine before her. He comforted her as well as he could and let her weep herself out for the loss of a brother she'd loved, but he was himself much distressed because the incompleteness of his Vision had prevented her from giving warning of her brother's danger.

Then Ariadne comforted him. She didn't blame him

or herself. She reminded him that at the time they had Seen together men fighting in Athens, Dionysus had been saddened by something he didn't understand. Now both knew the Vision had been sent incomplete, and Ariadne was sorely tempted to take the black image of the Mother down from its niche and toss it into the river that flowed between the shrine and the palace.

Ariadne told herself that the disgusting scene she had witnessed in the palace was owing to shock. She returned there the next day, thinking that grief might well flow in when rage was exhausted, but she found little change except that Pasiphae had withdrawn to the secret shrine deep in the bowels of Knossos. That place was all that remained of a stronghold erected by the distant ancestors of the current Minoans. The stronghold itself had been shaken to rubble by Poseidon's rage over some past sin, but the deep room in which a stone phallus stood before a strange obese goddess, both incredibly ancient, remained untouched. The queen had gone alone, her maids said, and Ariadne nodded without comment. She was not wanted or needed.

Minos needed what Ariadne had to offer no more than his wife. He barely spared her a few moments for civil thanks before returning to his plans for wreaking vengeance on Athens. Had he seemed driven by the loss of his son but fearful of the outcome of a war against so strong an adversary as Athens, Ariadne might have spoken of Dionysus' Vision. There was, however, no doubt in Minos' mind of his victory; it was as if he had partaken of Dionysus' Seeing himself. But the worst of all was that under the appearance of grief that he presented, was a hard satisfaction.

"It is as if he were glad Androgeos had been killed so that he could wring from Athens whatever terms he desires without needing to offer them anything in return," she said to Phaidra.

In her sister's chamber she had found red eyes and sad features—but not, she discovered, for the loss of Androgeos.

"What will become of me?" Phaidra wailed. "I'll never find a husband or freedom from this place."

Ariadne shook her head, and left. She passed Glaukos on her way back to the shrine. His face was set and there was grief in it; he and Androgeos, so close in age, had shared many things. But Ariadne saw, beneath the surface grief, a sense of gratification. Androgeos, the elder son, had always been first; unless he was shown to be unfit, he would have inherited his father's throne. And Androgeos hadn't been unfit. Now Glaukos would inherit.

Sick at heart from seeing too much and too clearly, Ariadne hurried back to the sanctuary of Dionysus' shrine. None here had known Androgeos and their formal expressions of grief and sympathy didn't trouble her. They were sincerely sorry for *her*, and beneath the formality was nothing but a reasonable indifference about someone they didn't know.

Ariadne sighed and dropped onto the cushion beside Dionysus' chair, although they seldom sat that way now. Mostly they shared a sofa or chairs opposite each other across a small table to play some game. As the thoughts passed her mind she sighed again. Even her own grief was muted. Androgeos had been the best and kindest of her brothers, but they'd grown apart. She remembered him mostly as a boy, though to her he had seemed like a god then. He'd protected her from Glaukos, fixed her toys; once—when no one was there to see—had carried a heavy bucket for her. The man had been harder, more fixed in purpose, like his father, Minos.

Well, he'd be avenged. Dionysus always Saw true,

and his Vision had showed Minos victorious. Oddly the thought gave Ariadne little satisfaction. She remembered how feeble the defense of Athens had been, how beaten and broken King Aigeus had seemed—and he hadn't even led his fighting men. That was strange. He was old, but not that old.

Ariadne sat up straighter, recalling the Vision, and looked reproachfully across the room at the wall toward the hidden image of the Mother. She understood now why so many Athenians had seemed reluctant to defend themselves and their city. It was a great impiety to kill an invited envoy, and they felt the attack and conquest by Minos was a direct punishment of their sin. Tears pricked her eyes. Likely Androgeos' death had nothing to do with Crete and was designed to humble the Athenians. Perhaps it was Athena's doing? Or Poseidon's? Should she ask Dionysus?

In the end she didn't ask. What could Dionysus do? Punish one of his fellow gods for the death of a common native? Ridiculous. Spite and hatred might follow or outright retaliation, pitting god against god . . . or all the gods against Dionysus. And Androgeos would still be dead.

Later, when Dionysus had come and simply taken her in his arms to hug, then sat down beside her, she realized she didn't want to know. If she went to Olympus as Dionysus wished, the last thing she needed was the knowledge that one of the Olympians had condemned her brother to death, carelessly, without even knowing him or anything about him, for a purpose that had nothing to do with him.

It was a silent evening. Once Dionysus said, "Do you still want a person who can lock and unlock the maze, now that your sister won't be leaving?"

Ariadne nodded. "I think Phaidra will refuse to serve the Minotaur any longer. It was the price she paid to be proposed as a treaty bride. She expected the service to end when she left Knossos. Now, I think, she'll simply refuse and Minos will be too busy with his war to care."

"A woman—a girl, really—will come in a ten-day or so. She's a priestess from the Bull God's temple at Zakro. My priestess there said she has a strong Gift, which will make the binding of the spell to her possible, and that she's a true believer in the Bull God. You can tell her that bringing the food—call it an offering—is a ritual practiced where the Bull God actually appeared."

Although she had some reservations and begged Phaidra to continue attending to their half brother—which Phaidra absolutely refused to do—Ariadne also looked forward to training the new priestess. It was a task that would divert her mind from the comings and goings at the palace, which too clearly spoke of preparations for war. And when Hesper arrived, Ariadne was amused by her fanaticism. Hesper truly believed the Minotaur was a god who had shaken free of the dross flesh with which he had been burdened by his birth and become a pure spirit.

Ariadne had to hide a grin. She couldn't help thinking of that "pure spirit" Dionysus' solid flesh and hearty appetite for bread and cheese and olives. Then her smile twisted wryly. There was nothing dross about his flesh—it was all too attractive. But Ariadne had no intention of arguing with Hesper. She simply used the girl's fanaticism by warning her that the Bull God, like her own god, Dionysus, did from time to time visit his childhood home and appear in his temple.

"However, he doesn't like to be spied on," Ariadne said, "so if you should catch a glimpse of him, immediately invoke the maze and take a few steps away. That way he'll know you respect his privacy. Don't speak to those within the chambers. They are condemned criminals selected to be scapegoat sacrifices if the Bull God should be offended. Hand them the meat. Invoke the maze immediately, and go your way lest one try to follow you and escape. When you're sure you're alone—don't look; listen for footsteps following you—dissolve the maze and leave."

She went with Hesper for the next ten-day, sometimes accompanying her openly, sometimes following quietly behind, making sure that the girl was able to lock and unlock the gates, clear and invoke the maze—Hekate had given Dionysus a spell, which he had given to Ariadne, to make this possible—and would do so at the correct times. It also made clear to the criminal servants, of whom only three remained, that Hesper was being guarded. Now, Ariadne thought, if only she could arrange a sighting of the Minotaur, she would be sure that Hesper would believe that he did appear and remain alert.

In the end, it was easy enough to do. Ariadne had no objection to Hesper thinking her more powerful than she was so she told the girl it was time for her to see her god and that she, Ariadne, would summon him. Then Ariadne called the Minotaur aloud, removed the maze, and continued to call until he came to her.

"Ridne!" he bellowed.

Hesper dropped silently to the floor in a dead faint. Ariadne didn't feel too steady herself. The Minotaur had grown even larger and the bull's head was somehow coarser and more bestial. Worse, he was no longer the clean, shining creature he had been, with gilded horns, attired in a beautifully embroidered kilt and a jeweled collar. The collar was gone, the gilding mostly scraped away from the horns. His fur was matted, his kilt tattered and stained with urine and feces. His nails had grown into long, curved claws—and he stank.

"'Member Ridne," he said raising an arm to reach out to her.

He was looking down at her, and the arm crossed his sight. The dull, tangled fur held his gaze, and then, as if awakening, he slowly looked down at himself.

"Minotaur," Ariadne breathed.

"No god!" he roared. "Siphae lie. Minotaur no god. Beast! Beast! Ridne. Ridne. Help Minotaur!"

"I will, love, I will," she sobbed. "Come to your room and I'll comb you and bathe you."

She reached toward his hand and started to take a step in his direction, when suddenly he bellowed, "Mine! Maze mine!" and struck at her. Starting back, she tripped over Hesper's prone body so that she fell, escaping his blow and crying as she went down, "Ridne. I am Ridne."

He stepped back, then back again. "No hurt Ridne. Love Ridne . . ." It was a whimper. "Not 'member. Beast not 'member." He stood staring down at her, eyes glazing, lips pulling back from his tearing fangs, then suddenly turned and ran away, crying as he ran, "No eat Ridne. Love Ridne."

"Anoikodomo apate," Ariadne breathed through her sobs and knew that the Minotaur wouldn't find them again.

She was afraid that Hesper, having seen the beast, would no longer believe in the god and be unwilling to serve, so she concealed her own revulsion and terror, but the girl hadn't really seen anything beyond the huge looming figure. Fear and fervor had felled her before she could be disenchanted. When they were safe in the temple grounds, she told Ariadne that it had been wrong of her to summon the Bull God.

"Mortals are too weak. They aren't fit to see a god. You're too proud and presume too much. I'll be a better priestess and never offend him."

Ariadne didn't say she was not the Bull God's priestess or that she saw a being much nearer a god than the Minotaur every evening and presumed to tease him and laugh with him. She simply nodded and agreed. And aside from making sure that the priests and priestesses of the Bull God's temple would report to her if Hesper didn't return to her quarters each day and occasionally questioning Hesper herself, she did her best not to think about the Minotaur.

She was not entirely successful. "Help Minotaur," he had cried. Slow tears trickled down Ariadne's face. There was nothing she could do to help him. As always, Dionysus had Seen true when he told her it was for the misshapen creature's own sake as much as for that of others that the poor monster should die. She wiped away the tears. The Minotaur was past weeping for; she could only pray that Hekate was right, that the spell would unravel and her poor half brother would be released from his torment.

Meanwhile, the fervor of preparations for war reached a peak and then stopped. On the last day of the month of high summer, Minos led his fleet out into the ocean toward Athens. Ariadne didn't forbid those of the shrine to go, and the young acolytes, as filled with martial fervor as any other, went down to mingle with the people of Knossos who stood on the docks and on the hills that looked over the harbor. The men cheered; some of the women wept and prayed for good fortune for those who sailed.

Ariadne wasn't among them. She had no fears, no doubts of Minos' safe arrival or of his victory. Dionysus always Saw true—if he could understand what he Saw, and if no greater power than his meddled. Pasiphae was not among the watchers and well-wishers either. She was still, Phaidra told her sister, down in the ancient shrine. Food was brought to her, soil carried out, but no one had seen the queen since she had whimpered, "Lost . . . Lost . . ."

The tasks of summer filled the days, hoeing and weeding, gathering early fruit. Slowly over the weeks, Ariadne healed from Androgeos' death and the horror of the Minotaur's decay. With the absence of the Bull God from his great throne, even the gyrations of the priestesses and priests of his cult couldn't draw the number of worshipers that had once come. Nor did any pressure from the rulers of Knossos urge the people to worship and sacrifice. Minos was gone to war; Pasiphae seemed to have disappeared from the life of Knossos. However, the grapes swelled on the vines, their skins growing richer and darker as the hot sun kissed them, promising a bountiful harvest and a precious vintage.

More offerings came to Dionysus' shrine more openly. Ariadne was occupied with spelling the perishable stuffs to stasis, with displaying and setting aside what Dionysus chose and selling what he didn't want. For a while she pretended to be puzzled by his choices; much of the cloth was more delicate and feminine than he ever wore, and the little tables and other items of statuary and furniture seemed smaller and more fragile than he would find comfortable.

Eventually, however, Ariadne could be blind no longer and had to admit to herself that he was choosing items to give to a woman. Restraint broke its bounds, and she accused him bitterly, but she got no satisfaction, not even an argument or an order to hold her tongue. Dionysus laughed immoderately but he wouldn't deny her accusation nor would he explain beyond suggesting that she come to Olympus and see for herself.

"Besides seeing what happened to the offerings,

there are lots of things I had no time to show you," he said, glancing at her sidelong. "Wouldn't you like to see how Hades works metal? It's really wonderful to see him take a double handful of earth and rock and squeeze it until gold and silver dribble out between his fingers."

"Dribble out between his fingers?" Ariadne echoed. "He is a god, indeed. His hands don't burn?"

"No, he doesn't burn when the rock heats by his will, but that doesn't make him a god. I've seen him burn his tongue on a hot dish of food or a drink. On the other hand, he can't heat food or burn a person by his will. Only stone and metal—anything that takes part of the earth—respond to his Gift."

"I know Hades helped build your house in Olympus and you said you went hunting with him, but isn't the Underworld . . . strange?"

"Strange, yes." Dionysus smiled at the widening of her eyes. "But Hades is a friend. He wouldn't trap me there—not that it would be so terrible. It's a beautiful place, parts of it so beautiful they take away your breath."

"I shouldn't imagine you'd have any breath to be taken away if you were dead," Ariadne said tartly.

Dionysus laughed. "Hades isn't dead. Neither is Persephone. And I'm not either, although I've been there many times. They wouldn't mind if I brought you. And before you cry out and refuse, I swear that you won't be dead either before you go or after you return." He sat silent for ten or twelve heartbeats and then said slowly, "And you'd like Persephone, I think. She's a true daughter of the Mother, although the power granted her is of a different kind than that granted you when you dance."

"Persephone." Ariadne again echoed his word. "But she's the most awesome avatar . . ."

"She can be. I wouldn't care to cross her, I admit.

But mostly she's full of fun and teasing and very loving to Hades."

"But didn't he carry her off to the dark Underworld against her will, steal her from her mother's care?"

"I suppose he did." Dionysus grinned. "But she was a bit beyond the care of a mother when he took her—she was all of nineteen summers—and had been trying to escape Demeter's overprotection for some time. Do you know her mother had never named her and called her always Kore, which means girl, because she wanted Persephone to take her place and thus give her immortality."

"But the great mages are immortal already!"

"Only almost." Dionysus shrugged but then went on without hesitation, "Which meant, that Persephone would never have had a name and life of her own. I think Persephone didn't mind much when Hades carried her away from Olympus—although she still teases him when anything goes wrong that it wouldn't have happened if he hadn't abducted her."

Ariadne shook her head. "I'm still not ready for the Underworld."

"Then perhaps you'd like to go to Egypt with Hermes? He likes company and I try to go with him as often as I can. He's such a devil that I fear for him sometimes. The Egyptians call him Anubis, and stick the head of a jackal on his shoulders. He doesn't seem to mind. Well, he loves bright things as much as a jackdaw and since he's most often called in Egypt to lead the dead spirit, and Egyptian funeral goods are very rich, he finds good pickings."

"The god Hermes is a *thief*? He steals from the *dead*?"

"Oh yes, he's a thief." Dionysus laughed. "A very good one. And the dead are safer to steal from than the living. They don't complain. Moreover, since the tombs are sealed after the body is disposed within, there's little chance that anyone living would notice."

Ariadne rolled her eyes. "Hades and Persephone are surrounded by the dead; Aphrodite, Psyche, and Eros are one long bedtime story. Are any of your friends respectable?"

Dionysus thought for a moment. "No," he said finally. "All the serious, sober gods are too uncomfortable in my presence to count me a friend."

There was an undertone of hurt in Dionysus' voice, and Ariadne shrugged. "I have a feeling that's just as well. Just think how dreadful it would be if they were friendly and you found that you were bored to death in their company. That happened to my poor sister Prokris after she was married. She had always resented being left out of the gossip and talk of the older ladies of the court. Once she was a wife, all the stuffy matrons of the noblest families, whom she didn't dare offend, insisted on visiting her for hours and giving her advice."

"Are you comparing Apollo, Artemis, and Athena to a bunch of stuffy matrons?" He burst out laughing, and the hand with which Ariadne had covered her lips dropped to show her answering grin. "Giving hours of advice. That's all too possible. But it means I have very few friends."

"Do you miss your homeland?"

He frowned over that. "I don't know how to answer that. In one way, not really. I didn't have friends in Ur either and Olympus is much more beautiful. My house is mine and my life is my own, as it was not in Ur—but then I remember that I was much younger when I was in Ur; perhaps if I'd been older . . . But there are things I miss: the fields of barley and wheat; the flocks of sheep and goats. The lambs and kids are endlessly amusing in the spring. In Olympus such ordinary sights are kept well away from the city, which is why I have my garden of fauns. On the other hand, the rulers of Ur held a tighter grip on their people and were very cruel."

"That's sometimes true here also," Ariadne said soberly. "My own grandfather replaced a very cruel tyrant. And my grandmother—she who was priestess after the first Ariadne—was that tyrant's daughter. I've heard my father say she wasn't an easy person."

"Perhaps I should've killed her when I found her in my priestess's place."

Ariadne giggled. "No, because then the succession of priestesses would've been different and likely I wouldn't be your priestess now."

He laughed too. "You're right. That would've been quite dreadful." And then he added, quickly as if on an impulse he couldn't resist, "Come to Olympus. I have something special to show you also."

Her amusement was suddenly gone. He didn't sound as if he really thought it would be dreadful if she hadn't become his priestess. And what did he want to show her? The woman for whom he had taken all the feminine offerings? Ariadne shook her head as a new fear engulfed her. What if what he wanted to show her was the woman he had chosen as life companion?

"Not yet," she got out between stiff lips.

To her horror, Dionysus seemed more relieved than disappointed. He nodded acceptance cheerfully, said he must go and that he would see her the next day. Ordinarily that would have given Ariadne all the comfort she needed. Now she stared at the spot from which he had leapt with a sinking heart. Doubtless he would come the next day, as he said, but for how long would he continue to come, if he had a new woman to assuage his loneliness?

Time didn't stop for Ariadne's fears and they were never realized. Ten-day followed ten-day peacefully, the time of growth and ripening winding down into the time of harvest. And eight days after the ides of the month of ripening, Minos and his fleet returned home. Not one ship had been lost and very few lives. The king was greeted with huge celebrations and announced in person and by proclamation that Crete's dominance over Athens and Athens' acceptance of the Bull God was complete. Athenians would pay tribute to Crete and acknowledge the Minotaur as a true god. Each year a group of seven youths and seven maidens would bring the tribute and remain to serve the Bull God. In expiation of the murder of Androgeos, prince of Crete, this first year Aigeus' own son, Theseus, prince of Athens, would bring the tribute.

Phaidra carried that news to Ariadne as soon as she heard it. She was bursting with it, and had no one else to tell, no one else who would listen to *her* private hopes and fears. Others thought of victory and tribute; Phaidra only cared about the fact that the treaty Minos had desired had been confirmed with several additional clauses that favored Crete. To her, that meant that her marriage to Theseus might still be possible.

"They *will* come with the tribute," she insisted to Ariadne, who hadn't denied it. "Father's no fool. He hasn't dismissed the fleet and army. He allowed the Athenians a grace period of a ten-day to permit Theseus and Aigeus to settle their affairs and stabilize their realm. However, if the Athenian tribute, gold and human, doesn't arrive in another ten-day, father and his fleet will set out again, and this time they'll kill the men, take every woman and child into slavery, and burn Athens to the ground."

"They'll come," Ariadne agreed, but before she could add that they would come out of honor, not out of fear, Phaidra was speaking again.

"Yes, I think so too. They're too afraid of father to disobey. And that means the treaty will be enforced—and part of the treaty was that I should marry Theseus and some day be queen of Athens. Oh, Ariadne, it will be *wonderful*." She laughed. "Sometimes a foreign queen is scorned, but with father all but ruling Athens, I don't need to fear that."

Ariadne bit her lip, realizing it would be fruitless to try to explain to Phaidra that what defeated the Athenians in the first place wasn't the Cretan fleet and army but their horror of the dishonor and impiety of the murder of Androgeos. To double that impiety and dishonor by refusing to fulfill the terms of their surrender—no matter what the cost—wouldn't be possible for them. But she had to say something; she couldn't let Phaidra force a marriage with Theseus and then act as if she were the ruler of a defeated enemy. She wanted Phaidra to be happy.

"There are other reasons for them to fulfill their agreement," she said, "but even if Theseus does come because of fear of King Minos' retribution, you must remember the retribution can't arrive quickly. When you go to Athens, you'll be surrounded by Athenians and Minos' fleet and army will be nearly two ten-days away. If you should be ill-treated, you would have to find a messenger willing to go to Crete, and then you would still have to wait until the message could be delivered and Minos could sail to Athens. Think what could befall you in that time."

"Are you trying to convince me to withdraw from the marriage?" Phaidra's eyes narrowed with suspicion. "Why? I will never again attend that monster in the maze! Not if I must rot here in Knossos forever."

"No, of course I wasn't urging you to repudiate the marriage agreement. From what I've heard, Theseus is a worthy person. I think he would make you a good husband—but only if you make him a good wife. Consider how bitter it would be for a husband to have thrown into his face that he married out of cowardice and to have his wife look down upon his friends and family. Wouldn't it be better if you made him care for you so much that *he* would defend you against any scorn or dishonor?"

Phaidra blinked. "Yes. Yes, of course. Father never permitted anyone to missay or scant honor to mother. But what if Theseus doesn't care for me?"

"Why shouldn't he, silly girl? You're beautiful. You're clever. You can make a man lust after you and also be merry. You'll be able to manage his household to his benefit. You desire to be his wife. What more could a man want?"

Ariadne saw Phaidra go back to the palace buoyed up with hope, and she knew that hope rose to even greater heights when the Athenian ship came into harbor and the Athenians, escorted by a strong detachment of Minos' troops, made their way to Knossos. As a result of her sympathy and support, Ariadne heard, as soon as Phaidra's feet could carry her up Gypsades Hill, that Phaidra had seen Theseus on the day the tribute was delivered and had even been introduced to him.

It was apparent to Ariadne that all thought of being a conqueror's daughter had flown out of Phaidra's head with that first meeting. Phaidra's eyes almost glowed as she announced that Theseus was such a man as she had never seen before, taller and stronger than any Cretan. Beyond that, he had said openly that she was lovely and a wife he was eager to take; he was the husband she had dreamed about all her life. There would be other meetings, she told Ariadne, because a second audience with King Minos to define their service to the Bull God had been set for a sevenday later.

The first tiny shadow of a doubt touched Phaidra the next day when she learned that the Athenians were now housed in the Minotaur's old apartment. "Why?" she asked Ariadne. "There are separate quarters for embassies from other nations. Why did father put the Athenians in those rooms, sealed by magic, as if he needed a prison for them?"

"They're not exactly an embassy," Ariadne pointed out. "They're part of the tribute King Minos exacted from Athens. They are guilty of the death of Androgeos."

"No, they aren't!" Phaidra cried. "It wasn't Theseus and his father who conspired to kill Androgeos. It was their enemies, and they used that stupid false god excuse." Her lips pursed with distaste. "Not that the Minotaur *isn't* a false god. I've never seen a falser."

"Well, part of the atonement for all Athens—whether any particular person was guilty or not—is for the tribute youths and maidens to serve the Bull God."

"Then why not house them in the temple with the priests and priestesses?"

Although Ariadne said what she thought might be soothing to Phaidra, a horror was growing in the back of her mind. She had, after the tribute was safely delivered and the king was giving his attention to domestic matters, asked for audience and mentioned that all but one of the servants were gone from the maze. She felt he had a right to know, but hadn't asked that the servants be replaced. Minos had smiled. Smiled, and told her she needn't worry about the supply of servants. He had already arranged the matter.

Now what Phaidra said about the Athenians being imprisoned in the Minotaur's old apartment and separated from the priests and priestesses that served the Bull God took on a sinister aura. A connection between that apartment and the palace-side entrance to the maze could easily be established. Did King Minos intend that the service of the Athenians to the Bull God should be to feed him?

Even if they had been guilty of Androgeos' death, that seemed too harsh a fate; Athens had paid and would continue to pay blood money. And if they were *not* guilty—as Phaidra insisted, and, as seemed likely to Ariadne, who couldn't imagine any reason for them to invite an embassy and then kill its leader—they mustn't be sacrificed so horribly. Ariadne went to the palace; the magic-sealed door opened to her command, and she spoke to Theseus herself.

She came away convinced that if the Athenians weren't to be trained for bull dancing or for ceremonial duties in the Bull God's temple, she must do something to save them. Theseus irritated her; she didn't like his attitude of male superiority or the too-interested glances he had given her and the practiced way he had tried to flatter her. Despite her irritation, she really didn't doubt the distress he felt about Androgeos' death or the truth of the actions he had taken to avenge it and to cleanse the Athenians of impiety. Too late, however. Minos had been upon them before they could send him the few traitors still alive or explain what had happened. To fight back would only have compounded the impiety, so they had yielded.

Ariadne considered whether she dared raise the question of the Athenians' fate with Minos. Would her pleas for leniency help? Surely her father knew she had loved Androgeos and wouldn't wish to belittle his death. Or would her interference only harden Minos' decision? Worse, would it put into his mind a horror he had never intended?

Ariadne waited, hoping that Dionysus would See and forbid what she feared, but he had no Visions.

He remained amused and cheerful as he had been for weeks—which sometimes drove her near to despair by implying he no longer cared enough to be aware of her feelings and often made her want to kick him. Worst of all, he no longer urged her to come to Olympus. Ariadne began to fear that that last haven would be closed to her.

Then, at the end of seven days, the fate of the Athenians drove Dionysus' intentions out of Ariadne's mind. Phaidra came flying to the shrine after the morning court weeping so hard that she could hardly explain what caused her anguish. The king, Ariadne finally made out, had passed sentence. The Athenians, in an order he would later decide, would enter the earthly home of the Bull God—a maze only the god could safely decipher.

If each Athenian could pass through the maze and reach the back gate of the temple, that youth or maiden would have proved his or her acceptance by the Bull God. When all the Athenians had passed through the maze, they would be free to return to Athens or to remain in Crete. And the first to enter the maze would be Prince Theseus, who must be the most worthy and could intercede with the Bull God for his lesser companions.

"Oh, it's horrible," Phaidra wept. "Father has become a monster. The whole court cheered him. The tale of Theseus's capturing and destroying the faction that caused Androgeos's death has spread about and now there's much sympathy for the Athenians. Now the court believes that father is being merciful and has chosen a fine way for the Athenians to acknowledge the Bull God and to set them free afterward. And if they die, of course it wouldn't be *father's* fault. It would be the Bull God's judgement."

Ariadne shook her head and sighed. "I think you must free them," she said. "I understand that their ship is still in the harbor, waiting to bring back news of the fate King Minos chose. If you set them free as soon as it is dark, likely they could get to the port and sail away before their escape was noticed."

"But the guards—"

"Drug their wine."

"Can't you—" But before she finished speaking, Phaidra's eyes shifted and she rose.

Ariadne didn't try to keep her nor ask her to finish the sentence. She guessed easily enough that Phaidra had been about to ask her help and was glad that, for whatever reason, she hadn't. Theseus didn't appeal to her; she wished him no ill, but preferred to have as little to do with him as possible. But Ariadne was not to escape from further involvement so easily. Before the shadows had shortened by a thumbnail, Phaidra was back, almost incoherent between fury and terror.

"He won't go," she got out. "I took him aside and told him the truth, that father's sentence was not an honor-saving device to set him free but a condemnation to death. I told him about the maze. I even told him what the Minotaur was. Do you know what that idiot said? He said, 'Your brother is dead. I should have guarded him more carefully.' "

"He's an honorable man," Ariadne remarked a bit absently, her brows knitted in thought.

"Honorable!" Phaidra spat. "He's ruining my life as well as losing his, and he doesn't care. I begged and I pleaded. He caressed me and said he was sorry I wouldn't be his wife, but that King Aigeus had given his word that he and the others would abide by King Minos' decision, whatever it was. I pointed out that it's our father who has been dishonorable, that he has always known the Minotaur wasn't a true god and had no right—"

"But I'm sure Theseus believes dishonor on

another's part doesn't justify further dishonor on his. Never mind—"

"Never mind!" Phaidra shrieked. "Are you satisfied that he should die? Are all my hopes to be blasted?"

"No, I'm not satisfied that Prince Theseus should die," Ariadne said calmly. "But I accept that for his honor and Athens' honor, Theseus must go into the maze. I said never mind because there's another way to solve this problem that won't offend his honor."

"How?" Phaidra wailed.

Ariadne's lips thinned but she kept her impatience out of her voice. "He must enter the maze, but there's no reason for him to be trapped in it for long. It's a very simple maze. I'll give him a large ball of fine yarn. With that as a guide, he won't be fooled by illusions into tracing and retracing his own steps. Before the Minotaur can discover him, he'll find the gate to the back of the temple. You can wait there for him and open it. He will have honorably completed the sentence King Minos pronounced, and be free. And the king won't dare harm him or forbid the marriage because he knows the court believes that was his intention from the beginning."

Phaidra had been so distraught when she rushed into Ariadne's chamber that she hadn't sat down, and Ariadne had risen, intending to embrace her. Now Phaidra backed away, eyes wide, face intent.

"I can't," she said. "I can't wait by the back gate. I must be with Theseus when he enters the maze. Who else can unlock the palace gate?"

Daidalos could, but Ariadne didn't think of him because she was so horrified at Minos' cruelty in making Phaidra open the gate for the destruction of her hoped-for husband. She wondered how he had prevailed on Phaidra to do it, but that wasn't important; Phaidra had many weaknesses. As for why Phaidra couldn't run from the palace-side entrance to the maze to the back of the temple and be there in time, Ariadne didn't even wonder about it. It was entirely normal for Phaidra to ask Ariadne to save her trouble.

Later she realized she should have known Phaidra would not leave to her sister the greeting of the hero when he emerged safe, but that realization came far too late. At the moment she thought only of the plans for Theseus' escape. First she pressed on Phaidra a very strong, brightly colored, but thin yarn used for stringing looms to train girls in weaving. There were stadia of it in the ball and it would easily cover the maze. Then she reminded Phaidra to describe to Theseus the turns of the real maze. She was a little surprised at how indifferent Phaidra seemed to the plans, nodding and agreeing but as if her mind were elsewhere, but she was also accustomed to her sister being easily cast into despair. Hoping Phaidra wouldn't forget anything essential, Ariadne merely assured her again and again that Theseus *would* escape if she followed the suggestions.

She told Dionysus nothing, partly because she was so ashamed of her father's behavior and partly because she was very angry at him for taking another woman and lying about it. She was doing her best to wean herself away from her need and desire for him and that evening, distracted by her concern over Phaidra and Theseus, she tried too hard. They parted on less than totally amicable terms, Dionysus having finally been pricked into reaction by her absence of mind. If she weren't interested enough in him to talk to him, he had said, he could find livelier company in his own house—and disappeared.

Misery makes an uncomfortable bedfellow, so Ariadne was awake very early, which was just as well because once she arrived at the Bull God's temple, it took her longer than she expected to avoid the notice of the dancing votaries. Conscious of her steadfast refusal to appear as a worshiper of the Bull God, she had enveloped herself in a long hooded cloak, but she still had to wait until one group retired to make way for another before she could sneak up to the magic-sealed doorway and spell herself through.

After a moment's thought, sheltered behind a wall, she left the doorway open. It would be very impressive if Theseus walked through what had been an impenetrable barrier for so long. In the excitement of that event, she could slip through also and then reinvoke the spell.

Even with that delay, she was at the back gate of the temple long before she expected Theseus to arrive there. She wasn't impatient. A new set of votaries were performing, and this was the first time she had ever been able to see what Pasiphae had devised to keep her feeble-minded son willing to sit on his throne for long periods. Ariadne was impressed with the effect the priests and priestesses produced, and felt saddened that the poor Minotaur could no longer be trusted to enjoy the spectacle.

Ariadne was so fascinated herself, and the clashing cymbals, rattling sistra, and twittering pipes filled her ears with sound so that she became aware only very slowly of a growing din behind her. When she turned to look, she could see nothing at first but a short passage that bent sharply to the right—and then she caught her breath with horror. She was seeing the true passage. The illusions of the maze had been dissolved.

Without thinking, Ariadne touched the gate to open it and ran through. In that first moment, she felt that in his insane desire to punish the Athenians, Minos had found a way to break Hekate's illusions. In the next moment, she knew that was impossible, and almost simultaneously realized it was Phaidra who had broken the illusions. Minos hadn't demanded Phaidra open the gate for Theseus; Phaidra had decided to cover herself with glory by saving him herself.

Sobbing with fear but unable to decide whether to wait where she was or try to find them in the maze, Ariadne stood still and listened. Stupid, stupid girl, she thought. Hadn't Phaidra realized that without the illusions the Minotaur would be able to track them by scent and sound and surely catch them before they could get through? No, of course not. The idiot girl had only thought of the quickest way to get out of the maze, and probably told herself that Ariadne had selfishly withheld the idea of removing the spells out of jealousy.

The noise from within the maze was growing louder, the Minotaur's roars mingling with a man's shouts and a woman's screams. Unable simply to stand still, Ariadne started forward again only to jump back as Theseus, with a bared sword in one hand and half carrying a fainting Phaidra in his other arm, burst around the corner of the corridor.

"Here!" Ariadne called. "Come this way, quickly!"

She hoped they could all run out the back gate before the Minotaur appeared and that she could lock him in—but he was too close. Theseus turned his head, saw her, virtually threw Phaidra at her, and whipped back to face the corridor around the curve. From that a huge bellow echoed. Ariadne ran forward to grab Phaidra and haul her to her feet. She wasn't quite a dead weight, but as she came upright the Minotaur erupted into the straight section of the corridor. Phaidra froze in place making it impossible for Ariadne to drag her to the safety of the gate. Phaidra shrieked wordlessly as the huge body, arms extended, rushed at Theseus.

"Stop, Minotaur!" Ariadne screamed. "Ridne says stop."

Whether he responded to the words or was startled by the piercing quality of Phaidra's shriek, the Minotaur did stop—or, at least, hesitate—for a moment. In that moment, Theseus leapt forward, right under the long-clawed, reaching hands, and plunged his sword, which had a strange, blue-gray hue, deeply into the bull-head's body. The Minotaur roared and reared back, both arms raised to strike down at Theseus.

"No!" Ariadne cried, pushing Phaidra away from her and running forward, but whether to prevent the Minotaur from striking Theseus or Theseus from striking the Minotaur she didn't know herself.

Whatever she intended, it was too late. The Minotaur's arms dropped, but without force or intention and he didn't touch Theseus. Theseus had already driven his gray-metal sword into the Minotaur's chest again. This time, as he pulled the weapon free, the huge body toppled, struck the wall, twisted, and slid down on its side. Ariadne flung herself down beside it, caught and cradled the bull's head in her lap.

"Oh love, love," she sobbed. "I never meant you to be hurt."

"No hurt. Love Ridne."

She could hardly make out the words; they were more like the broken lowing of a beast than the moaning of a man. She couldn't speak for weeping, but it didn't matter because the Minotaur could no longer hear or understand. The big eyes with their beautiful thick lashes were dimming. Ariadne stroked the now-ragged fur on his forehead.

"Love Ridne," he sighed, and his breathing stopped.

Ariadne bent above him sobbing bitterly, only to be seized by powerful hands and pulled away. She cried out in protest, trying to cling to the Minotaur's head, but a horn came off in her hand and the features seemed to be melting. She screamed and, senselessly, struggled against the hands that pulled at her. And then there was a sharp pain in her head, and nothing, nothing at all.

CHAPTER 22

Ariadne slowly became aware of the regular movement of the bed under her. She was frightened at first, thinking the heaving was owing to an earthquake, but the terrible roaring and grinding was missing, there were no crashes of falling objects, and the motion continued constantly without slowing or increasing.

In the first moment of alarm, Ariadne had opened her eyes, but a pain shot from them right through to the back of her head, and she shut them again. She thought muzzily that if she had been struck by something because of the earthquake, nothing was falling now and she must be safe.

By the time she realized the motion was not caused by an earthquake, she had been attracted by the sound of low but angry voices. One was her sister Phaidra's; the other she was less sure of, but as she listened she decided it must be Theseus'. He was explaining—sounding a little weary, as if he had said it all before, more than once—that he was sorry he had hit Ariadne harder than he intended.

"The mob was almost upon us. She was sitting there with that rotting *thing* in her lap and she wouldn't let it go. Could I leave her to the mob's mercy?"

"I told you not to worry about her. Dionysus would have come to protect her."

"Dionysus!" There was a hint of scorn in the voice. Ariadne stirred, but her body was heavy and reluctant; it was too hard to protest. "Another god made flesh," Theseus continued. "I know she spoke of him as if he were real; you've said so more than once, but did you ever see him?"

"Once . . . I think. It was the day the Minotaur killed Isadore and my mother wanted to push me into his chamber. Ariadne went in instead, but the Minotaur thrust her out. Then Dionysus came and took her away. I was frightened . . ."

"You saw a big man who carried your sister away. I believe that. A god . . ." He snorted. "Even if I believed that tale, I wasn't going to take the chance that she would be injured by the crowd—after all, she saved us both by ordering the Minotaur to stop. I couldn't leave her there."

"Then why not take her to her shrine? Why bring her on this ship with us?" Phaidra's voice was sharp, accusatory. "What will she do in Athens?"

Theseus murmured a reply, but Ariadne didn't pay

attention. She was on a ship. That was the reason for the heaving motion. She felt a sense of satisfaction at solving that problem and then the rest of Phaidra's speech struck her. Athens. Theseus was taking her to Athens? Dionysus would go mad when he discovered she had gone off with a man! Kind as he had always been to her, she knew how jealous he was. She opened her eyes again and struggled upright, this time fighting the pain in her head and the nausea it aroused.

"Take me back," she cried. "Take me back to Knossos at once."

Theseus turned and came to the padded shelf on which she sat almost upright. "Thank all the gods that you've recovered your senses. I'm sorry I struck you so hard. I had forgot that the sword hilt was in my hand."

Ariadne's hand wavered to her head and she tried to swing her legs over the side of the shelf to face him, but there was an upright edge that caught her feet. Theseus leaned forward and lifted her out, standing her upright but solicitously holding her steady with an arm around her. Phaidra came to her and pulled her free of Theseus' arm. Ariadne swayed and almost fell. Theseus caught at her and Phaidra pushed him away. Grasping at an upright that supported the deck above, Ariadne pulled free of both. Her headache and the sickness generated by it were beginning to diminish.

Ignoring Theseus' apology, she said, "Take me back to Knossos at once. Dionysus isn't a god who can be scorned or robbed. He's very real and very powerful."

"I know you believe that," Theseus said in a patient, superior voice. "But we can't go back to Knossos. I killed your Bull God, unfortunately in the sight of a whole crowd of his priests and priestesses, one of whom screamed for the others to attack and destroy us. Worse, a crowd of your people, some from the court, who had come to see whether I would pass safely through the maze, cried 'blasphemy'—although how it can be blasphemous to kill a man-eating monster, I have no idea. But they joined the priests and priestesses. We had to flee back through the maze and out through the palace to save ourselves."

"He was only a little boy," Ariadne said softly, "only eight years old. He liked stories. . . ." But she didn't continue, only shook her head sadly. "Mother, be kind to him," she prayed, "take him to yourself and love him, for he was innocent." And a breeze, warmer than the air around her, caressed her cheeks and stirred the locks of consecration.

Theseus was looking at her as if she were mad and he went on as if she hadn't spoken. "I have no way of knowing how King Minos will react. With that thing dead and rotting on the floor, I can't see how he can continue to claim it was a true god and that we Athenians must serve it. And we of Athens fulfilled the sentence he pronounced. I brought the tribute and I and the other youths and maidens passed through the maze. Still, if he wishes to claim that we didn't fulfill our agreement and attack Athens again . . . You must see that I must warn my people."

"I tell you Athens is in worse danger from Dionysus than from Minos, and Dionysus can reach it more quickly," Ariadne said. "Take me back."

"Theseus," Phaidra said, laying a hand on his arm. "I'm sure with the Bull God so publicly dead that my father will have more to do than set out for Athens at once. There will be time enough. If you don't wish to sail back to the port near Knossos, leave her at Khania. That's at the very western end of Crete."

"Yes, yes, I'll gladly go to Khania. I'll go anywhere, so long as it's off this ship."

However, Theseus wouldn't listen, claiming that to

sail against the wind to Khania and then turn and retrace their path toward the coast of Greece would take almost two days. Still with an aching head and sick stomach and terrified of Dionysus' response to his perception that she had abandoned him and her duties, Ariadne simply sank down onto a bale of some goods and tried to think of reasons Theseus would accept for setting her ashore.

The one device she wouldn't use was to Call to Dionysus. He had told her that he could come to wherever she was, and to Call him would probably save her from his wrath. It wouldn't save anyone else aboard the ship. Within her Ariadne could feel the lash of his rage, the rising lust to inflict pain, to draw blood, to kill. Ariadne couldn't bear that those on the ship should be driven to killing each other. Phaidra was her sister and she was doing her best to convince Theseus to return her. Theseus himself had done wrong, but for a good reason. Ariadne's heartflower was folded so tightly around her heart that each beat was painful.

She and Phaidra argued with Theseus on and off all day, with no more result than that sometimes he turned his back on them and sometimes he laughed at them. However, being caught leaning over Ariadne's bed that night, which made her cast a spell of stasis on him, solved the problem. He fell like a log atop Phaidra, who lay between them on the deck. She clutched him happily in her arms and began to kiss him, until she realized he seemed lifeless.

Phaidra's screams convinced Ariadne to release the spell, whereupon Theseus' arms finished the gesture they had begun before the stasis froze him and reached over Phaidra to Ariadne. Both women recoiled in horror, and Phaidra broke into loud weeping. Theseus denied the implication vigorously, explaining that he had heard Ariadne weeping and just leaned across to waken her.

Since her cheeks were wet, Ariadne was inclined to accept the excuse, although she was coming to believe Theseus was the kind to bed any pretty woman he saw. In this case it was ridiculous. Her sister was between her and Theseus and any hope of a quick coupling, even with an accomplice far more willing than herself, seemed out of the question.

Phaidra was less reasonable. She accused them both of behavior that was totally impossible, considering the short length of time Theseus had been in Crete and that Ariadne did not live in the palace. She wept and she cursed and then withdrew into offended silence. Theseus was, in Ariadne's opinion, amazingly patient—although she realized later that he was flattered by Phaidra's jealousy—but for her own reasons Ariadne aided and abetted her sister.

Soon, Ariadne saw, Theseus bitterly regretted whatever attraction he had felt for her, whatever notion that he could have both sisters—one as wife and the other as a priestess who must remain unwed. By midafternoon he made it quite clear that he didn't relish a woman who could paralyze him with a word and a gesture and, moreover, he was already contracted to marry Phaidra. Ariadne would have to go. She was more than willing, but he wouldn't return her to Crete.

On that subject, he was immovable. The most he was willing to concede was to sail somewhat eastward to leave her on the island of Naxos. There, he told her, was a temple of Dionysus where she could find shelter, and he promised that he would find a neutral ship that traded with Crete and send a message to King Minos to say where she was. It was plain enough that he didn't believe Dionysus was more than an illusion she had created in her own mind.

Almost, as she trudged up the hill to where the temple had been built, Ariadne wished it were so.

Dionysus would be furious. They had parted in anger and he would believe that she had willingly gone away with Theseus. If she Called him, wouldn't he also believe that she had been put aside in favor of her sister and only Called because she had been abandoned? But if she didn't Call at all, would he believe she didn't want him? Perhaps he didn't care. Perhaps he would even be glad.

The high priestess of Dionysus' temple was Achaean, tall and blonde, full-breasted, wide-hipped. She was plainly suspicious of Ariadne, not too willing to believe the tale that the suppliant was the Mouth of Dionysus in Knossos and had been abducted by mistake. Still, Ariadne guessed, the woman could see Ariadne was Cretan and was too cautious to turn her away. The news of Minos' conquest of Athens was still fresh; even a priestess wouldn't wish to offer insult. Moreover, her hesitation to offend told Ariadne that Cretan ships must frequently put in to the port.

Having asked what she could do for Ariadne, the priestess' lips pulled down when she heard that Ariadne had come for shelter and couldn't say for how long. Clearly she was sorry she had given even so cold a welcome. How, Ariadne wondered, could I say for how long I will need shelter? What if Dionysus doesn't come for me? What if King Minos blames me for the Minotaur's death and the escape of his Athenian hostages and won't accept me back in Crete?

Ariadne was fed thin soup and hard bread and shown a small cell with a hard pallet on the floor. Aside from thinking once that she must make sure her own household didn't treat guests quite so frugally, she hardly noticed. She ate what she was given, rested sleeplessly on the hard pallet, and rose obediently when a novice tapped on the doorframe to call her to the evening sacrifice.

Knossos had no such service, but Ariadne rose obediently and followed the novice to an inner shrine, roofed to provide protection from wind and rain. Priests and priestesses were arranged before the altar, behind them a small crowd with various offerings in their hands. Ariadne barely glanced at those. Feeling the high priestess watching her jealously, she took a humble place behind the Naxos votaries, just barely ahead of the common folk.

Not knowing where to look to avoid increasing the priestess's suspicion, Ariadne fixed her eyes forward and saw that this shrine had a statue of Dionysus rather than a painting. The image was amazingly like him. Ariadne nearly turned green with jealousy as her eyes flashed from the image to the voluptuous priestess. Doubtless for that heavy-uddered cow he had come in person so that the artist could see him.

The fine marble of which the image was carved was very white, like his skin, and had been carefully tinted to reproduce his overlarge blue eyes and smiling, rosy lips. It wore a wig of gold-colored hair. Tears filled Ariadne's eyes as she gazed on it. The hair was not brushed smoothly back, but lay in curls on the figure's forehead as it did when they had been running wildly through the vineyards. Ariadne was tempted to push it back. Insensibly the leaves of her heartflower opened.

The air in the chamber seemed suddenly too thick, and it rippled as if a large stone had been dropped into a small pond. On the altar, where the disturbance centered, another image appeared.

"What are you doing here?" the god bellowed, leaping off the altar and bowling over the priest and priestess who held the central positions to reach Ariadne who was behind them. "Where have you come from? Why are you here?" And even louder, so that she was tempted to put her hands over her ears, "How have you hidden yourself from me for three whole days?"

He seized her by the shoulders and shook her so hard she thought her neck would snap. Ariadne grabbed his arms to steady herself.

"These people hid you!" His eyes bulged with rage and Ariadne felt the lash of his fury, felt the stirring of those nearby, heard the low, animal growls.

"Don't you dare!" she shrieked, letting go of one arm and slapping his face. "Don't you dare punish these folk for taking me in and feeding me when I begged for shelter. You have less sense than the Minotaur. He, at least, was hungry when he killed. If you are angry at me, punish me!"

"Punish *you*?" His hands dropped from her shoulders. "I can never punish you, no matter what you do. You are the core of my life. My Mouth. The one firm place in my universe. So long as I have you, I'm not mad."

The imprint of her hand was red on his pale cheek. Around them Ariadne could hear cries and groans and whimpers, soft scraping on the stone floor as those in the shrine tried to retreat. Ariadne put a hand gently over his lips.

"We don't need the whole of Naxos to be witness to what is between us," she said. "Let's go to where we can be private."

His arms went around her and there was a familiar moment of coldness and dizziness. Then they were in her own chamber. She still held tight in his arms.

"Did you hide yourself from me to teach me that I can't live without you? You didn't need to be so cruel. I knew it already. What do you want of me?" he asked.

The tone, despondent of defense, said he would grant whatever she asked. What did she want? She had a sudden vision of the full-bodied Achaean high priestess and was furiously jealous again.

To add to that, as her fear disappeared, Dionysus having come and she having ridden out the worst of the storm, her body began to react to his nearness, to their touching, and, she realized, to the feeling flooding back to her through the tendrils of her heartflower. Her nipples were hard; her nether lips full and wet. Dionysus' question had cut the cord holding up the sword of Damocles. Her moment of decision was upon her.

"What do I want of you?" she echoed. "I want you to take me fully as your priestess, which you have never done. How have I failed you, Dionysus? Why do you reject me?"

"Reject you? I never have." He reached for her again. "Never. You are my Chosen, my dearest. My Mouth and my safe haven in a mad world I don't understand . . ."

"Dionysus!" She pulled away and seized his upper arms, shaking him slightly. "I've offered myself to you, I don't know how many times, and you pushed me away. Each time I caress you, you flee me as if I carried the plague. Most of the time you won't touch me. For a time you made me think that there was something repulsive about me, but my heartflower doesn't lie. I know you desire me. Why are you willing to lie with every priestess from west to east but not with me?"

He drew his arms across his chest. "Lie with you? But you're a little girl, a child! I may be a killer but I've never harmed a child."

"Child? Are you mad? Just because I don't look like that heavy-uddered cow who is your priestess in Naxos? I am more than twenty-one summers old. Look at me! Dionysus, look at me!"

She stepped back suddenly, unclasped her belt, and

tore off her travel-stained gown. She stood before him naked, except for the loin cloth that covered her genitals.

"Look at me," she insisted. "I may be small. All Cretans are small compared with Olympians, even compared with Achaeans, but these aren't the breasts of a child. These aren't the hips of a child. I'm a woman, as full grown as I'll ever be. Haven't you looked at me in all the nine years that I've served you?"

In truth he'd done his best not to see her. He was afraid if he acknowledged her a woman, if he inflicted on her the violent lust that was all he knew—the face of sex that Aphrodite in the Cretan dress had exposed—he would lose the comfort and friendship, the peace and stability she brought him. He'd refused to see what she was now forcing on him. What had been barely swelling buds when he first saw her naked before the altar were now fine, upstanding breasts, round and smooth, the nipples protuberant with excitement; the waist was narrow, the hips broad, the buttocks full. Dionysus drew a deep breath. She was no child. They were not touching, but he felt her heat.

He stepped forward abruptly, lust rising. Knowing no other way, he was about to seize her, throw her down and himself atop her, but she reached out a hand and took his. Her other hand moved, not to grope for his rod or pull up his clothes, but to smooth back the hair that had tumbled over his forehead. Something flowed from her in the cool, silver mist that always enveloped him when she was near, an eagerness that was also innocent, and when she smiled at him, he saw Aphrodite in her guise of love as pure sweetness.

"It will be the first time for me," she said. "Will you be gentle with me, my lord?"

His eyes widened and filled with tears. "I don't know gentleness," he whispered. "Can you teach me?"

Her smile broadened. "We'll learn together." And she tugged at his hand and led him toward the bedchamber.

Dionysus would not have believed so many lessons could be crammed into so short a space of time or be so utterly indelible. He knew he would never forget a single moment of the playful loving that roused without maddening him. He would not forget that coupling, slow, careful, to ease the hurt of a virgin's broaching. Nor would he forget the caresses and explanations that had followed their mutual joy.

What had happened to him—not the satisfaction of his body, which he could obtain anywhere, but the knowledge about himself, the confidence in himself, that he had gained—was of ultimate importance. In the back of his mind he knew that later what Ariadne had given him would bring him balance, the ability to laugh at his self-dramatization. But now, still breathing hard, still feeling the faint tremors in his thighs and groin that echoed his release, he thought that he would have ended his life if he hadn't known he could renew the peace and joy he had found in his union with Ariadne whenever he liked and as often as he liked. But could he?

"Ariadne," he whispered, "why did you run away and hide yourself from me?"

"I never did," she said, cuddling close and resting her head on his shoulder. "Oh, I know I was gone, but it was none of my doing. It was a mistake." She paused and then asked, "Did you know the Minotaur was dead?"

"Yes. Sappho was so frightened because there were riots and you were missing, that she scryed Olympus to beg for help. I came, but I couldn't 'feel' you at all. I . . . I thought you blamed me, but the bull-head's death was none of my doing."

"I know that. I was there. And you couldn't feel me because I had been deprived of my senses." She felt him tense and she stroked his cheek. "No, now. There's no need to murder anyone. It was a mistake and meant for the best."

Whereupon she told him the whole tale, weeping quietly when she repeated the Minotaur's last words and shuddering again with horror as she described how his body had virtually fallen apart in moments.

"The spell was undone," Dionysus said, tightening his arm around her, "and as Hekate said, only the spell was keeping that body together. I suspect that gray-bladed sword that Theseus used was one of Hephaestus' iron weapons. Athena has a fondness for Athens and for that family. She might have given that sword to Aigeus and Aigeus gave it to Theseus when he thought his son might be going into magical danger. Iron and magic don't mix well. Hades can manage both, but Hephaestus hasn't Hades' power or art. So, when Theseus stabbed the Minotaur, the spell was broken. But I don't see—unless you lost your wits from horror—why you lost your senses or why I couldn't find you for three days."

So she had to tell him about Theseus striking her to save her from the mob and intending to take her to Athens. Dionysus released her and sat up. Ariadne grabbed him.

"No! Theseus will be my sister's husband. I think she is making a mistake. Athenians seem to believe that women are lesser beings—"

"It's a problem with nearly all the Achaeans. Pentheus wouldn't let the women worship me." His eyes were dark. "Perhaps Theseus also needs a lesson."

"Not that kind!" Ariadne said sharply. "It's too

permanent, and Phaidra wouldn't like to be a widow—at least not so soon."

He looked at her. She shrugged. "I didn't take to Theseus. I suspect Phaidra will find him less appealing as time goes on, but after it became known she went into the maze with him and he killed the Minotaur so publicly, it was best for her to be out of Crete. He was better than King Minos' wrath."

"True enough. I was here, seeking you, and I took the form of the Cretan so that I could mix among the courtiers to hear if you had been hurt or . . ." his voice shook " . . . killed. I heard Minos railing against the Athenians, saying that they had broken the terms of their surrender because only Theseus had been through the maze."

"No, they'd all been through the maze," Ariadne put in. "I can speak for them if needful. Theseus explained that when Phaidra removed the illusion, the Minotaur must have sensed them and he began to roar. Theseus' companions then forced Daidalos to open the gate and rushed after their leader to help him. But they didn't know the true path, so they didn't catch up until the Minotaur was dead and I was unconscious."

"It doesn't matter. Minos never set out for Athens. That day his army had enough to do to keep down the rioting. There was considerable fury over the false god." Dionysus' face went stiff and gray. "I thought you were dead. I was afraid that was why I couldn't feel you."

Ariadne sat up, too, and embraced him. "I'm sorry I made you suffer, love. I never intended that. I was only so frightened that you would slay all aboard the ship for carrying me away that I closed my heartflower." Then she put both arms around his neck and smiled at him. "It won't happen again, beloved."

"No," he said, also smiling but with twisted lips.

"I doubt I'll have the courage to cross you for any reason."

"But I didn't do it apurpose, not at first." And then she drew a sharp breath. "Oh. If my father is planning to fight Athens again, I'd better tell him that he'll have no easy victory this time. The reason Theseus wouldn't turn and bring me back to Knossos was that he didn't want to waste any time before warning his people and telling them the Minotaur *was* a false god and that it would be no blasphemy to defend their city with all their strength and skill."

"It won't be necessary. Pasiphae came forth just as Minos was about to judge as traitors those who'd led the riots against him—"

"Pasiphae!" Ariadne exclaimed.

Dionysus shrugged. "She came as avatar. She sat between the horns on the dancing court. The Mother was so strong in her, that she even drew me there."

"Pasiphae," Ariadne repeated wonderingly. "But she was like one with near no mind, a dead thing walking, the last time I saw her."

"No more," Dionysus assured her. "The queen was reborn, stronger than when I first saw you dance for the Mother. But she has paid a price—a great price. She rivals you in beauty no longer. Her body is worn away to bones and wrinkled skin, her face no more than a skull. And it is not her face; it is . . . there was something in it of the face of the Mother in Persephone's shrine."

Ariadne sighed softly. "I don't know why Androgeos died. Perhaps it was Her doing because she desired Pasiphae as avatar or because she desired to curb my father's lust to hold more power. It's not so difficult to know the purposes of the Olympian 'gods,' but She is beyond understanding. Or perhaps Androgeos' dying was nothing to do with Her and She simply used another 'god's' ploy to punish Athens. Poseidon, I have heard, hates Athens. Perhaps She used that to cure my mother's madness."

"It's certainly cured," Dionysus said. "First Pasiphae made Minos pardon the leaders of the uprising, saying it was just to be offended when a false god was forced upon the people. Then she took them and all Cretans to task for failing their duty. The time to have rebelled with the blessing of the gods was when the Minotaur was first brought before them. She acknowledged her guilt and Minos' for incurring the curse, but blamed all Cretans for grasping at what she and Minos had offered because of pride and greed."

"It's a wonder they didn't leap on her and kill her."

"Not her!" Dionysus shook his head and hunched his shoulders as if he feared a blow. "She shone with power. But then she softened her tone, admitting the Minotaur had been a punishment, but that the evil she and Minos had done had been expiated, that Athens had also been punished for civil unrest and evildoing and had expiated its sin. I have never seen the Mother's will so clearly stated and so . . . so firmly enforced. Every man who had rebelled then saluted Minos as king and renewed his vows of fealty."

"Poor Minotaur," Ariadne murmured. "Poor innocent tool." Then she remembered the momentary warmth of the breeze on the ship and the caress on her locks of consecration. "He is at last at peace and in the Mother's care, I believe."

Suddenly Dionysus got out of bed. "I wonder what excuse you'll find now to refuse to come to Olympus."

Ariadne laughed. "None. Would you like me to come now? I am ready."

He blinked. "Now you are ready? Without even putting on a gown? Why did you fight me for so long?"

"Sometimes it's easy to tell that you are only a man and not a god." She giggled. "You're also an idiot! I fought you because you wouldn't take me to your bed. I had visions of watching a procession of cow-uddered nothings enjoy your favor while I was left alone to the scorn and snickerings of your friends and household."

Dionysus' mouth hung open. He closed it and swallowed. "But I don't bring women to my house. I have enough coupling out in the fields. I—"

"Liar," Ariadne said succinctly. "I saw a woman in your bed when I Called you one morning." His mouth opened and closed again. "And you won't make me believe you're innocent by pretending to be a fish," she continued tartly. "Nor will lying help you in the future. *I* intend to be in your bed, so there will be no room for other women, and *I* intend to accompany you when you bless the vineyards and the vines so if coupling is necessary, I'll be there."

"Yes," he said simply, his eyes lighting. "It's better to couple your way. But Ariadne, I'm not a liar. The woman you saw in my bed was Aphrodite. One doesn't . . . One doesn't refuse Aphrodite. And she had come to thank me for a gift I'd given her."

"I forgive you," Ariadne said loftily. "At that time I still was a child and wouldn't have enjoyed you so much."

"You're laughing at me," he said, laughing suddenly himself.

"Of course. I'm not such an idiot as not to know that men will be men. Likely I will have to forgive you many times, but—"

He shook his head and color rose to dye his cheeks. "I won't. . . . It's ugly!" he burst out. "Mostly when I'm finished I feel sick. Those priestesses would have coupled with a dog as quickly as with me."

She came to him and took him in her arms. "Perhaps the coupling and the killing won't be needed if we're together. Here in Crete we only run and dance among the vines. If we are together I hope your divine madness will be turned to other expressions. . . . I See a dais, like that where the sacral horns are displayed, but on it men declaiming and around it in serried rows watchers weeping and groaning and laughing too . . . and learning lessons of the heart. Perhaps your Gift of moving the emotions will go into the telling of tales in a manner so real that hundreds will be cleansed without injury or bloodshed."

"Mouth, I have Seen that also, and never understood it, but I never asked to have it explained, for the Vision has been with me all my life and it always made me happy. Now I know—and I am even happier."

Then he took her, just as she was—as she had jestingly said he could—to Olympus. They didn't arrive in his apartment, however, neither in the sitting chamber or the bedroom she had glimpsed when Calling him. They came into the chamber that had been hers on her visit, but now it was all changed, filled with light from huge windows that were somehow shielded by Hades' glass.

She would have exclaimed with amazement, but she laughed instead. All the fine furniture, the dainty statuary, the elegant carpets that she had accused him of collecting for a woman were here. And when she shivered slightly, more with excitement than cold, he hurried her into an equally lavish bedchamber where the chests yielded up all the fabrics he had taken, all made up into Olympian-style gowns in her size.

Nor, before the day was done, did she need to wonder what she would do with her time. The servants came to her cringing and weeping with joy, begging that she would give them orders as she had during the wonderful five days she had been with them. Or if she didn't wish to be troubled so much that she at least make some rules that they could follow for they were often punished for not knowing what to do.

Ariadne reassured them. She would see that they did their work, she warned them, but she would also protect them from the erratic demands of Dionysus and his guests. So she would have the household in her hands and, very likely, knowing Dionysus and suspecting what Bacchus and Silenos were, the management of the offerings Dionysus chose to keep for himself.

Silenos came and joined them for the breaking of their fast, almost bouncing with joy and planning all sorts of expeditions into the shops and slave markets. They would get a decent cook first and then see about other matters Dionysus would never attend to. Bacchus didn't appear, but later he made an excuse to run into Ariadne in the forestlike antechamber and told her with sly glances that there were lands he would travel alone, serving as Dionysus' surrogate.

Ariadne didn't permit herself to laugh until he was gone. So Dionysus had thrown him a bone and the hungry cur had snapped it up. She suspected the vineyards Bacchus would "bless" produced such bad wine that even Dionysus could not improve it.

Still, later that night she was quiet after they had made love in her rich, new bed, and Dionysus said, "You are not happy. What have I done wrong?"

"Nothing, love." She kissed him tenderly. "I am not unhappy. I was just wondering who would dance for the Mother in Knossos. The time is very near and—"

"*You* will dance for the Mother," he said. "Do you think I wish to have Her hand fall upon us? I'll carry you to Knossos as often as needed to prepare the dancers, and you can bring the black image here. I'll build Her a golden shrine where the fauns play. Or

I'll stay with you in Knossos. I don't care, so long as we're together. I won't be parted from you again, Ariadne."

She turned to him and kissed him. "We'll always be together," she said and, after a pause, went on with strong assurance. "I *am* a true Mouth and I have Spoken because I have Seen what is in your heart and mine."

PRAISE FOR
LOIS MCMASTER BUJOLD

What the critics say:

The Warrior's Apprentice: "Now here's a fun romp through the spaceways—not so much a space opera as space ballet.... it has all the 'right stuff.' A lot of thought and thoughtfulness stand behind the all-too-human characters. Enjoy this one, and look forward to the next." —Dean Lambe, *SF Reviews*

"The pace is breathless, the characterization thoughtful and emotionally powerful, and the author's narrative technique and command of language compelling. Highly recommended."
—*Booklist*

Brothers in Arms: "... she gives it a genuine depth of character, while reveling in the wild turnings of her tale.... Bujold is as audacious as her favorite hero, and as brilliantly (if sneakily) successful." —*Locus*

"Miles Vorkosigan is such a great character that I'll read anything Lois wants to write about him.... a book to re-read on cold rainy days." —Robert Coulson, *Comic Buyer's Guide*

Borders of Infinity: "Bujold's series hero Miles Vorkosigan may be a lord by birth and an admiral by rank, but a bone disease that has left him hobbled and in frequent pain has sensitized him to the suffering of outcasts in his very hierarchical era.... Playing off Miles's reserve and cleverness, Bujold draws outrageous and outlandish foils to color her high-minded adventures." —*Publishers Weekly*

Falling Free: "In *Falling Free* Lois McMaster Bujold has written her fourth straight superb novel.... How to break down a talent like Bujold's into analyzable components? Best not to try. Best to say: 'Read, or you will be missing something extraordinary.'" —Roland Green, *Chicago Sun-Times*

The Vor Game: "The chronicles of Miles Vorkosigan are far too witty to be literary junk food, but they rouse the kind of craving that makes popcorn magically vanish during a double feature." —Faren Miller, *Locus*